SORAYA

The Other Princess

SORAYA

The Other Princess

Inspired by the Life of a Bright and Tireless Woman

In Recognition of Millions of Afghan Women
Who Struggle Silently for Their Dignity
and That of Their Motherland

Saber AZAM

To order additional copies of this book, contact:
Xlibris
1-888-795-4274
www.Xlibris.com
Orders@Xlibris.com
766156

In memory of two great women of our family!

I hardly embraced the arms of my biological mother, Niazbibi. Like many Afghan women, she fell victim to maternal mortality in her very prime. However, my cherished stepmother, Nazoko, reared me as her own. Believing in the importance of education and showering us with love and affection, she was adamant that all her children succeed. As a very young widow, she inculcated the values of learning in our minds and souls. Though illiterate, she had a way of supervising our homework and ensuring that we were provided the appropriate environment. Nozoko too passed away at a very young age. She drew her last breath at the age of thirty-three. Her honesty, energy, commitment, and fairness live on in each and every one of us in the family.

May their souls rest in eternal peace!

Contents

Introduction.. ix

Chapter 1: Birth and Childhood.......................................1
Chapter 2: Teenage and University Years 54
Chapter 3: Marriage and Early Days of Real Politics 145
Chapter 4: Political Maturity and Life under Communist Rule... 191
Chapter 5: In a Free and Challenging World—The Fight for
       Afghanistan's Liberation 282
Chapter 6: Disappointing Free Afghanistan and the Dark
       Years of the Taliban Rule 364
Chapter 7: The Chagrins of Post-2001 Liberation.......................419

Epilogue 491
Final Words..497
List of Abbreviations and Names Used.....................................499
Important Quotes 515

Introduction

Edison failed 10,000 times before he made the electric light. Do not be discouraged if you fail a few times. Victory is always possible for the person who refuses to stop fighting.

—Napoleon Hill

This fictional story is inspired by the life of a wonderful individual, Soraya Ludin, daughter of Kabir Ludin, a renowned and much admired politician. A distinguished personality, he became an outstanding diplomat of Afghanistan, whose service to his nation was exceptional. I have had the honor to know Soraya for over four decades. My respect and admiration for her has sprouted over the flow of years of friendship, collaboration, and collegiality. Every day I ascertained more about her inner contemplations, devotion to humankind in general but women in particular, vivid spirit, and magnificent mind. Like all Afghan women and despite her exceptional academic background for her epoch and outstanding professional achievements, she opted for a reserved role in the society, a *backbencher* as she herself called the status. Such has been the destiny of the overwhelming majority of bright women in this country. It is my earnest anticipation that the volume at hand will render homage and pay tribute to all of them. Most have suffered from prejudice and violence for centuries. However, their incomparable resilience and striving must be lauded.

This book is in no manner Soraya's biography, nor does it recount the recent seven-decade history of Afghanistan or present an in-depth analysis of women's conditions in the country. It synopsizes partly what I believe most educated women of Afghanistan have endured in their endeavors in support of their motherland. But its content could certainly depict the perception of the majority of Afghans, inside or outside their country, about unfairness of cultural barriers, systematic ineptness of their leaders, and existence of discrimination in their society, as well as ravages of war that left indelible scars in the hearts and minds of peoples. This book also underlines the mischiefs of invaders. Some intervened by force to subjugate this land; others pretended to be friends and bearers of good governance and democracy.

Occasional and rare recognition aside, Afghan women have constantly been neglected and suppressed by their male-dominated society. It is awkward to pinpoint one or another rationale solely. Their intolerable plight could have multifaceted causes. Culture, lack of adequate understanding of religious principles, historic context, poverty, family burdens, and more are certainly important grounds. But education in general and, more specifically, its deficiency, scarcity, dearth, and pitiable quality in all corners of the country have undeniably been the mother of all concerns. The percentage of learned population in Afghanistan was already dwindling before the major crisis in 1978 that put the country on the path to an abyss. Religious misperception about women and their role in the society has also aggravated their plight. Finally, forty years of war, destruction, killing, discrimination, and ideological rivalries produced devastating effects and drain on them very specifically.

Rabia Balkhi, Nazo Ana, Aisha Durani, and Malala Maiwand were exceptional personalities, whose postmortem prominence in the society and history has been acknowledged. However, that does not mean that the country did not possess other talented and brilliant women, who by their sacrifice, intelligence, and dedication influenced the wild Afghan society to transform for the better. But their voices have often been silenced. Even Queens Gawharshad Begum and Soraya of the country, women in power and forerunners of advancement in science, literature, arts, and equal rights, could not escape an unfortunate destiny. While the first was cowardly executed at an age well beyond eighty years in 1457, the second was forcibly exiled in 1929, when she was only thirty years of age. Their paths were trailed by numerous other publicly unknown figures who stood for fairness, social justice, gender equity, and evolution in the country at the cost of being misjudged, ignored, tormented, ill-treated, or assassinated.

The history of the country can be traced back to around 3000 before the common era as part of Persian, Greco-Bactrian, Maurya, Kushan, and numerous other illustrious recent empires such as Samanid or Timurid. But the modern Afghanistan was founded initially by Mirwais Hotak of the Ghilji Pashtun tribe. It was formalized and expanded by Ahmad Shah of the Durani Pashtun tribe. However, the country has other stout ethnic groups too, such as the Tajik, Uzbek, Hazara, Baloch, Turkmen, and some others. Alas, in the course of history, little endeavor has been undertaken to bring together these components of the society around delineation, preservation, and defense of common values where women's rights would represent a vital cornerstone. So far rulers have reigned above all for the gain of their families and ethnic groups. The ill-fated trend endures yet today. Under such circumstances, it has been hard to say whether a solid and undisputed Afghan nation does in fact exist. This being said, none of the social groups solemnly consented for their women to flourish and through their dedication, competence, and ability play their role in shaping the society openly, freely, and innovatively. Oftentimes, religious principles and ancestral customs were exploited as instruments of manipulation and alibis. Women were subjugated to obey the yearnings and commands of the "*master*" squires.

Some consider the 1960s and 1970s as the golden era of modern Afghanistan. A parliamentarian democracy between 1963 and 1973 allowed many women to come out of their reserved and hidden status to claim equity with their male counterparts in politics, sciences, literature, and diplomacy. Awkwardly and as in the past, their aspirations were short lived as the country, once again, became the center of the new "great game" between the West and the then Soviet Union, facing tensions, crises, and conflicts of all natures for more than four decades now. Nobody grasped for what real purpose superpowers engaged once more in proxy wars in this country. The peoples of Afghanistan and more specifically its women inherited tears, sorrow, death, and more segregation than ever before. Even the Communist regime, who claimed egalitarian rights for all, did not spare them. Naheed Shaheed, a young high school student, symbolized and represented all women of her era. She was brutally murdered in 1980 simply because she expressed her opinion and led a student demonstration in Kabul, the capital of Afghanistan, against the invading and occupying Soviet forces.

Since more than four decades ago, the country is again the center of internal and external rivalries, at the cost of hundreds of thousands killed, millions made handicapped or homeless, and a country crippled. From the brutality of the Communist regime to the carelessness of the mujahideen (holy warriors), the dark era of the Taliban, religious extremists, and tarnished post-2001 hopes of liberation and democracy, Afghan women have paid the heaviest of prices. When the populace of the country was ready to celebrate their New Year on March 21, 2015, once again tragedy struck women ferociously. Farkhunda Malikzada, a university student, was publicly beaten, tortured, burned, and killed because she had spoken her mind against the obscurantism of religious charlatanism and extremism. No one, even numerous policemen who were present at the scene, defended her, most probably because she was a woman. She too embodied the women of a "*free Afghanistan.*" The issue is not whether Naheed and Farkhunda were right or wrong, but the brutality of dozens of men who had no mercy and were enjoying the suffering of defenseless young girls. Despicable pugnacity against women in Afghanistan has not been curbed, even today. And a handful of parliamentarians or ministers do not reflect the reality of their plight. The history of the country has demonstrated that in each sensitive period, women have been sacrificed for the ambition and success of men.

The sharp knife of injustice has cut muscles, veins, and nerves and has now reached the bone of patience. It is time for Afghans to reply to the wake-up call and take effective and giant steps to constitute a meritorious nation and protect their women from oppression. They must curb and eradicate all forms of brutality against them so that they can take a meaningful part in the social, political, and economic development of their country without fear of persecution and death. They are their mothers, sisters, daughters, wives, or beloved ones. Harming and oppressing them is an unforgivable sin, severely punished by the divine laws since *"women too have rights over men similar to the rights of men over women."* For a long time, Afghanistan has been a doomed country. Men made it so! Women would have surely made different contributions.

The solution to this perpetual calamity lies in the commitment, dedication, and hard work of Afghans themselves. They should lay down the foundation of a strong and solid nation, free of nepotism and corruption and built upon equality of rights and opportunities for all, where competence would govern. No foreign power will provide real remedies for the wounds that have inflicted the souls and bodies of Afghan women. As Nelson Mandela said, *"The task at hand will not be easy …. to change [the country] from a land in which the majority lived with little hope, to one in which they can live and work with dignity, a sense of self-esteem and confidence in the future…. It always seems impossible until it is done."* To fulfill such a noble ambition, it is requisite to create the vital space and protection for the female population.

Like other Afghans, I have known remarkable women in the country who not only had extraordinary talent and intelligence but were extremely hardworking and diligent mothers too. Soraya Ludin herself has had an exceptional life journey. As other women, she became a silent fighter for justice, equity, and liberty. She is a remarkably quick thinker and hard worker. Her analysis of any given situation in the world is deep and profound, based on intensive investigative research. Outspoken, logical, spirited, assiduous, and courteous, she undoubtedly has a beautiful mind too.

Therefore, through Soraya, who has been inspirational, this book is dedicated to all Afghan women for their continued struggle to exist and to have a meaningful role in building their war-shattered country. It is hoped that all who are interested in Afghanistan, but citizens of Afghanistan, the United States of America, the United Kingdom, and the Russian Federation in particular, will find time to read it.

Versoix, Switzerland
September 2018

Chapter 1

Birth and Childhood

Only the children know what they are looking for.

—Antoine de Saint-Exupéry,
The Little Prince

Afghanistan is situated in the heart of the vast Asian continent. Landlocked, its geography is an ornament of lofty mountains, deep and profound valleys, coarse deserts, and quaint four-season paints. Its springs have inspired poets, writers, and philosophers to describe heaven. Its summers are a combination of tenderness in vales and torrid hell in arid and forgotten corners. Its autumns bestow joy and sense to life. Its winters inflict the unthinkable knock to the spine of empires. This country hosts a mosaic of communities and has embraced diverse beliefs and cultural values. Buddhism, Hinduism, Zoroastrianism, Judaism, paganism, and Islam have all been observed in this wild, squally wonderland. Pashtuns, Tajiks, Hazara, Uzbeks, Baloch, and Turkmen primarily comprise the morphology of its inhabitants, though countless minorities have strived to endure too in the course of its existence.

Afghanistan has a rugged history. Its antiquity has not been logged and explored properly. However, the postclassical era is marred with tragedies and sorrow for its populations. Afghanistan has been the battleground of empires and superpowers, and its renowned conquerors of both ancient times and the modern past have been intrigued by its stunning beauty, harsh geography, resources, and geostrategic position. They have invaded it with might, resolve, and brutality, but left shattered, broken, and defeated. Afghanistan also had its own conquerors who consistently did not spare anyone on their campaigns, which were fueled by a variety of motives—wealth, religious expansion, territorial gain, or simple punishment of adversaries. However, recent centuries of its history have been marked by weak and selfish rulers who served above all the interest of foreign powers as well as their own community and kinfolk at the expense of the welfare of the larger population.

While Afghanistan, and its earlier designations as Khorasan or Ariana, existed as a country with defined boundaries at any given moment of history, its inhabitants hardly constituted a nation. The rulers never desired to weld distinct communities around common values and interests. As a result and with the addition of foreign interference, domination, exploitation, discrimination, and violence, internal community bonds consisted of never-ending disputes over symbols rather than the essence for nationhood. This has been the cornerstone of the prime challenges that Afghanistan has encountered in its midmodern and contemporary periods. For nearly fifty years, not only have crises and war ravaged this land, but its devout populations seem to have been forgotten by their creator as the curse continued with unprecedented drought and climatic calamities. Most of the roaring rivers no longer irrigate the valleys, and crops die of thirst. Yet something is very special about this country that has always left no one indifferent.

Afghanistan is surrounded on its eastern and southern borders by Pakistan, in the west by Iran, and in the north by the immortally enthralling Central Asia. The whole region has been part and parcel of territories conquered by the Greats of this World with shared culture and historic values. While the first, a country with only seven decades of existence, appears to suffer from an existential and identity syndrome, the second still licks the wounds of a glorious past, and the third confronts the joys and snags of a postcommunist liberty. Thousands of miles farther in the west is Saudi Arabia, a regional power and the cradle of faith in this area of the globe and a strong confederate of Pakistan; both are often accused by experts of expanding extremism and terrorism around the world. Much to the south is India, a country that is historically and culturally linked with Afghanistan, like two components of the same braid. India's partition to permit creation of Pakistan in 1947 was the most laborious and sorrowful tragedy in the continent that ensued after the Second World War. Since then, the laceration and its lesions have never healed between the two countries. At its extreme northeast, Afghanistan edges the predominantly Muslim Xinjiang province of the People's Republic of China. Great Britain, the Soviet Union, the Russian Federation, and the United States of America have been vital chess players of social, economic, and political developments in this country too. They have indeed been the effective actors of the new "great game" in the region.

The social structure of most communities seems to be weirdly built on wealth and power. Accounts of brothers challenging each other before confronting the families of their sisters or cousins are common. The cycle of violence, revenge, and mistrust appears to continue at all levels. Since three centuries ago, only a few Afghan rulers have passed away in peace, surrounded by their families, though they have all been from the same ethnic group. Murdering, rendering blind, and even pulverizing with cannons pretenders of power, no matter their degree of belonging to the larger family, have been the trademark of men in power. They simply never thought of any other interest than their own. The fear of the *"enemy within"* has forced sovereigns to seek support and wealth from outsiders, paving the way for invaders to enter the country. The following proverb describes the traditional complexities and intricacies of human relationships in Afghanistan as well as the absolute requisite to address them before a strong and peaceful nation will effectively be reborn:

> *To a stranger may you not be without a kin, to a kin without a brother, to a brother without a son and to a son without gold.*

Within such a context, Soraya was born on a bright evening of August 1945 in the capital city of Kabul in Afghanistan, where King Zaher Shah and his uncles were supreme rulers. She was the only child of the family. Her father, Zamir Suri, was a renowned, educated, and handsome lawyer from the mountainous land of Logar. This province, situated south of the capital, hosts all ethnic groups, who have coexisted peacefully at all times. He was a graduate of the University of Bombay under the British Empire, now called the University of Mumbai. He then obtained a doctorate degree from the Dickinson School of Law in Pennsylvania.

In his youth, Zamir was impressed by King Amanullah Khan, who reigned over the hearts of millions of subjects between 1919 and 1929. Amanullah Khan was the leader who had forced the British out to assert the independence of his *"nation."* The king and his wife, Queen Soraya, had undertaken a vast modernization and reform project. Emancipation of women was one of the significant cornerstones of his vision for the future. Surrounded by refined individuals, he personally fostered the education of future generations, primarily girls, and visited schools. During one such inspection in a high school, the king encountered the young Zamir Suri, quizzed him on a variety of topics, and publicly praised the assiduous and clever boy. He even gave him his own watch as a reward. King Amanullah Khan's revolutionary vision for his country did not materialize, as he was ousted abruptly by a plot that many viewed as British instigated. A few *"religious leaders,"* who had been earlier brought to Afghanistan by the colonial power from essentially Middle Eastern countries, declared the royal couple inept. However, Soraya's father had kept fond memories of them.

Zamir Suri admired Mahatma Gandhi too. When in Bombay, he had carefully listened to the Indian leader and met him on two occasions. Bapu, as his close collaborators called him, had lectured in the university about his nonviolent actions against the British colonial power to gain independence of his country.

4

On the day of Soraya's birth, two facts struck Mr. Suri, who was then deputy chief justice of Afghanistan. When he took the newborn baby in his arms, he addressed his wife and said, "This little girl has bright green eyes and magnificently long limbs." He underlined his remarks with a gratified smile on his lips. Then he continued, "She will be brilliant and beautiful."

In her early childhood, Soraya was a skinny, sweet infant who was busy searching for wonders in the yard of their big house. She was less interested in what other children of her age looked for, such as toys, candy, or playgrounds. She wanted to discover the world in their garden by looking at every stone or colorful object, flower, tree, bird, and butterfly. In the spring she admired the miracle of the rain, the flip-flop of its contact with the ground, as well as the streams of water generated by the tiny drops. Her fascination was incredible with the sight of a rainbow. She wondered how in a gray sky arches of different colors appeared in a marvelous manner. She gazed for hours at the coming of blossoms in fruit trees or the making of a leaf, pondering how an ugly branch of wood could give birth to such admirable artifacts. In the winter, she stared for long periods at the snowflakes falling on her face and giving her a fresh and icy sensation that compelled her to rush under the private alcove's *sandali*, a sort of covered Afghan furnace. The hot summer days gave her a lethargic feeling, and cold water was her remedy. Autumn induced reflection in her mind. She marveled at the colorful foliage and was terribly saddened to see bare trees and fallen flora. She asked too many questions of her interlocutors and rarely changed her mind until convinced of the contrary.

She quickly comprehended that only her father had enough time and patience for her. By nature, she was curious and often compared objects. One day, she sprinted to her father and probed him about why there were too many animals on earth.

5

He candidly replied that it was the wish of God to diversify nature. Some flew with their wings, others galloped with their feet, certain ones dwelled in holes, and a number rejoiced at their existence in water.

She instantly declared that she did not wish to be in a chasm or in the sea but to fly like a bird and watch everything on earth. She recalled her father advising, "My little darling! Watching is not enough. You must also understand and learn how everything functions."

Her mother was a talented woman and made beautiful dresses for her daughter, but as soon as she was out in the yard, running after wonders on earth and upside-downing every piece of dirt to find what she thought was worthy, her clothes quickly needed to be changed since they were collecting the pollen of every flower and the grime of each plot in the garden.

Her curiosity often led her to the kitchen of the family, outside the residential area. And there, Abai—the family's cook, an old Hazara lady—received her with much love and attention. She was her nanny and an integral part of their family for years. Abai had a say on issues when she desired, and Mr. Suri heeded her. Abai called Soraya *Emerald*, not only because of her green-colored eyes but also as a gentle way of recognizing her priceless beauty at a prime age. As usual, Soraya asked thousands of questions about cookery. What is this? Why do you put it in this pot and not in the other? And if you do it otherwise, would my father get annoyed? Abai always calmly responded, devoted time to clarify, and even experimented in her presence with new blends of spices and ingredients. Oftentimes she was the first to taste the variety of delicacies that Abai prepared with utmost care for *Merza Jaan*, the family nickname of the deputy chief justice. For Soraya, she became a second mother. The little skinny, curious, inquisitive, remarkably intelligent, and honest child loved munching at the kitchen to the extent that at the family table, she was hardly hungry. Her mother was irritated and occasionally reminded her that she should not eat too much with Abai—to no avail as the day after, Soraya was again in the scullery asking why the wood was burning, what was the flame made of, and who was pushing the smoke upward.

Her father was indulgent with his daughter. Every evening and after dinner, she was next to him asking questions, giving her opinion, and debating about what was right or wrong. Zamir Suri loved talking to her and was impressed by the intellectual curiosity of this cute child and her honesty. He always responded to the questions posed and often told her stories and what had happened in the office. The more she heard, the more additional interests were created in her mind. Even at that age, she disagreed with him, and he gently took time to explain the rationale of everything he said. Like a healthy sapling, she was raised in a most convenient environment. While her mother often became impatient, Mr. Suri was enchanted by his daughter's perseverance and bright mind. One day, he urged his wife and said, "Do not get angry at Soraya all the time; treat her carefully. She has a beautiful mind, no fear of expressing her opinion, and tries to see what is behind appearances. She is a gift of Almighty God!"

Her mother retorted, "She drives me crazy with her questions! Every now and then, I have to change her clothes because she walks around the yard so much, runs after every animal that flies, and befriends Abai in her kitchen."

Soraya's father extended his hypnotic smile with a gaze full of meaning to his wife without pronouncing a word. He was always giving tender kisses on the forehead of his daughter.

Among all the meals in Abai's kitchen, Soraya loved the watery rice best; it was spiced with turmeric, some salt, and other perfumed ingredients that only Mr. Suri knew where to find in the market. She always consumed two big cups at once. On other occasions, she desired a simple soup, some meat, and warm bread. She then mixed it all up and employed her fingers to devour it. Even if Abai tried to impose the use of cutlery, she declined. Already at such a young age, Soraya had a perfect sense of spices and adored witnessing her nanny's trials. Mr. Zamir Suri candidly called the kitchen Abai's laboratory.

Mr. Suri was the most refined gentleman, lawyer, and politician of his time, one of those rare intellectuals that Afghanistan has never seen since. He was intertwined with all the communities of his country. Hazara, Pashtuns, Turkmen, Tajiks, Baloch, and Uzbeks all saluted him with veneration. Mr. Suri was among the brightest in the University of Bombay, where he had encountered many young proponents of Mahatma Gandhi's nonviolent resistance to the British domination; they were Hindu, Muslim, Sikh, Christian, and Parsi. At Dickinson School of Law, he was praised for his legal expertise on international affairs; and as a government official, his dedication, vision of the future, and work ethics were exceptional. He comprehended the cravings of his people for quality health and education, appropriate infrastructures, good governance, fair justice, and equal opportunity for all. As a young student, he trotted on the back of his horse every day back and forth from Logar to Kabul, some twenty-five kilometers, to attend his lessons. His colleagues and friends were aware that he did not appreciate nonsense, laziness, and dishonesty. In his function, he reached all remote corners of the country to monitor courts, get wind of customary laws of each region, and establish closer ties with diverse ethnic groups. He devoted time to the commoners, or *"opra"* as the royal family disdainfully denominated others than their own kinfolk. He was admired and genuinely respected by all groups.

Every night he read books or perused documents in the modest library of his house before going to bed. Soraya was at his flank when he was grazing through a favorite quid or searching pieces of paper. He voiced to his daughter how important it was to read, as learning was the source of knowledge and wisdom. And if she wanted to know about butterflies, blossoms of apple or apricot trees, or bees making honey, then she needed to peruse and study. Already at the age of four and while she was reluctantly keeping an eye on the dolls that her mother had woven, Soraya asked her father to buy her books of her own choice, a request that he could never honor as Afghanistan and the Afghan society were unfamiliar with children's paperbacks. She was fortunate, though. Her father had all the fortitude and patience of the world to listen to her for long hours, elucidate subjects she raised, and respond to queries. His only concern was that she strolled late at night to the library. Often when he solicited her to leave and sleep as he had other matters to look after, Soraya was distraught and even pained. She always wanted to acquire more from her father and never seemed content. She obliged with a plea to resume the evening after. But, her green eyes imparted her innocent grief.

One morning, Mr. Suri asked her to dress and come with him.

She was excited and queried, "We go to your office, Father?"

"No, darling," he replied.

"Why not? I would love to see your office."

"No, my child. I take you to school! That is where you can learn about everything!" he assured her.

"But I want to see your office too."

"I promise to take you there one day!"

The principal of Malalai Girls School was warned by Soraya's father that his daughter was very inquisitive and curious and asked many questions. Mr. Suri urged her to inform the instructors of the preschool class where she was admitted. The school was near their house, located in the New City section of Kabul. Its pupils were comprised essentially of daughters of the aristocracy and high dignitaries of the government. The school was named after Malala Maiwand, the famous young Afghan legendary female poet and warrior, the equivalent of the French Joan of Arc, who fought the British army in the battle of her hometown and was martyred in July 1880. Indeed, as a result of their conquest of the Indian subcontinent, the British colonial troops invaded Afghanistan on numerous occasions without colonizing it. They were successful in influencing the rulers and chieftains but hardly gained the consideration of the population.

Soraya was bright and interpellant in the class, often receiving no convincing replies from educators for her questions. She brought them home for disclosure and debate with her father, who was her upright and most trusted guide. She worshipped him at this tender age. In class, she lent her opinion and faced disciplinary measures. Oftentimes, she asked herself why the class was not like home, where she could ask any question and receive an answer. Apart from encountering and playing with her fellow classmates, she barely enjoyed anything else there.

One day, Soraya did not return home. The wife of a close family friend, whose daughter was her classmate, had taken her from the school. Mr. Zamir Suri was immediately alerted. He left the office, and the search began to no avail. When around four o'clock in the afternoon, she appeared at the gate of the house, her father was fuming with anger. "Where were you for the sake of God?" he crossly asked.

She retorted, "I was at a friend's birthday party, Father! Her mother picked me up from school and dropped me off just now!"

That day, she received her first and last punishment from Mr. Suri, who later on explained to his weeping daughter how people can be cruel and she could have been kidnapped by ill-intended individuals. He, however, assured her that he would have had no objection if her mate's mother had the courtesy to inform the teacher or her parents. This was her first bitter comprehension of the society she lived in.

For several days, she seemed puzzled why children were snatched from the embrace of their families. Finally, she resolved to hate the culprits and anyone else who harmed others.

Mr. Zamir Suri had meanwhile become chief justice in an extremely sensitive moment of post-World War II history of his country. The youngest uncle of King Zaher Shah was the prime minister. His endeavors to strengthen relationships more specifically with the United States as a strategic ally and procure American military equipment were leading nowhere. The newly created Pakistan was deemed more useful; only limited development aid was offered to Afghanistan. This infuriated some within the palace who, in spite of the formal recognition of the new neighbor, began articulating their disdain of the manner in which the British Empire had defined borders before its demise. At the same time, they proposed other alternatives to King Zaher Shah.

The famous Darulaman Palace was the Chief Justice Bureau, and Soraya's father occupied the oval office in the center of the edifice. She loved his workplace and occasionally spent her afternoons using a small desk that Mr. Suri had specially ordered for her.

As advised by one of his most esteemed childhood teachers, Mr. Suri wanted to do *"big things"* for his country. He wished to support the legal framework for construction of highways, hydroelectric dams, bridges, and so on and ensure that fair justice for all was effectively practiced. He had witnessed significant regression since King Amanullah Khan was ousted and replaced by Amir Habibullah Kalakani, particularly in the field of women's rights. The society at large did not adhere to the official account of the history books and were of the opinion that the British manipulated the innocent Kalakani to revolt against the reformist king. They then armed and supported Nader Shah, the man of their choice and father of Zaher Shah, to take over less than a year later. He murdered Kalakani as well as many others and opted to put aside the reform process. He imposed veils and restricted women's freedom of movement. At the same time, he colluded with the so-called clergy leadership to fortify his family's power base and purge his rivals. He was a brutal and merciless individual who, in turn, was assassinated three years later by an adoptive son of one of his victims

When outside the country, Mr. Suri had nurtured a special ambition to advocate for robust reforms in Afghanistan. His logic was simple. The world was changing quickly, and development programs needed the earnest contribution of both Afghan women and men. He was an adherent of gigantic enterprises as they would provide services to the communities at large and employment for significant numbers of people. He was a sharp-witted lawyer and instantly embarked to negotiate with Americans on the establishment of law and political sciences faculties at least in the other four main cities of the country. Washington seemed in agreement and required forthright approval of the aid budget from the Congress. In addition, Mr. Suri was tasked to supervise elaboration of a framework for Morrison-Knudson, an American construction company, to undertake hefty hydroelectric dam and irrigation projects in the southwestern valleys of the country in compliance with the Helmand River Water Sharing Agreement between Iran and Afghanistan, though it had not yet been ratified. Numerous barrages and gigantic agrarian canals were either overhauled or built anew, promising a prosperous future for the whole region of the country.

Rumors quickly spread about the Soviet Union attempt to infiltrate the palace and invest in the person of Prince Daoud Khan, eldest cousin of the king, who had been utterly dismayed by the attitude of the United States toward his country. In addition and in order to counter the religious approach to politics, numerous underground communist leaders received support from the Soviet Embassy. Soon the communist giant judged Zamir Suri's endeavors as contrary to their interests. Morrison-Knudson embodied the *American imperialism that had been substituted for the British colonial power* in a country that they considered within the sphere of their influence. They commenced to annihilate the projects. Iranians in the west were not pleased with this venture as it would have ultimately prevented water of the Helmand River from discharging into their territory. The Soviet scouts barked foul and deemed the projects stinking.

The calamity against this much needed and useful undertaking endured over two years. Neither King Zaher Shah nor his uncle the prime minister rushed to defend the promoters of the initiative that they had fully endorsed. While all senior officials who belonged to the royal family remained as usual impervious and untouchable for their obvious misdeeds, the *commoners* were held accountable. Mr. Suri and several others were informally notified of an eventual investigation and put under house arrest. Some believed that after the institution of modern Afghanistan in the eighteenth century, the country quickly turned into a British-wrought territory. Learning fast from their protectors, rulers demeaned valorous sons and daughters of the country who inspired to blow fresh winds of hope.

As a noble man and liable government civil servant, Mr. Suri tendered his resignation and pleaded for a trial to defend himself in the court of law. This had never happened before. Those blamed had never defied the palace! The king and his entourage were stunned and worried. Zamir Suri was an internationally recognized lawyer. His gesture would certainly make jurisprudence history. The palace was fearful of the political ramifications of such groundless charges against the most refined and ethics-bound chief justice of the country. He opted to be his own attorney and began to collect evidence of his claims.

Soraya did not comprehend why the black limousine was not coming anymore to pick up her father in the morning. "Father, where is your car? Why are you not going to work?" she inquired.

"My little angel," he countered, "there are times I have to work from home."

"I understand, Father, and I am happy," she replied. "You will have more time to talk to me."

"Indeed, darling. But I have to work also," he stressed.

The library of the house became Mr. Suri's new office. However, contrary to judiciary norms, the government denied giving him access to the project files. Zamir Suri was revered as a man of honor; this was one of the essential principles of life he had communicated to those around him. But he had also defied the palace and comprehended that the retribution would be merciless. He did not want his family to face the fate of others who had ended in prisons or exile. Therefore, he resolved to prove his innocence and clean his name of all allegations. The now former chief justice was desperate to retrieve the records, and some friends and colleagues had even stopped visiting him.

The mood at home was not as it was before. Soraya was around him a lot in the library. Growing up, she was asking pertinent questions; perhaps she was reading her father's troubled mind. One evening, the doorbell of the inner court reverberated, and she sprinted to open the small flap of the enormous metallic gate. A wiry, medium-size, white-bearded man was standing there. Soraya glared at him and asked who he was.

The man smiled gently and touched her head affectionately, replying that he was her new uncle.

She ran to her father and screamed, "Father, Father, my new uncle has arrived."

"Who is your new uncle?" Mr. Suri queried. "Who told you that you have a new uncle?"

"He is at the gate, Father, and said that he was my new uncle," she replied.

Mr. Suri also used the flap. The white-bearded man leaned to kiss his hands. This is a customary ritual in Afghanistan. People embrace the hands of esteemed seniors and those who have higher governmental and religious functions. Her father withdrew his hands after shaking those of the *"new uncle"* to demonstrate his own respect to the guest and indicate that he appreciated the gesture but treated him equally. "Haji Saheb, welcome to my house. Please enter," Mr. Suri invited.

Haji Saheb was looking fretfully around while hastily coming in. The former chief justice guided him to the living room. Soraya was looking curiously at the man and, somehow, liked him. With her scintillating green eyes, she was staring at his beard as if she had never seen one before. She was contemplating the guest, who was regularly wiping drips of sweat on his face with a beautifully handwoven fabric while courteously addressing Soraya's father. In response to Zamir Suri's invitation, Haji Saheb asked for a glass of cold water. Soraya volunteered to bring a jug, full of icy homemade juice of pomegranate, the snifter she and her father used to have when talking to each other, but she was too small to be able to do so. As usual, her father gave a kiss on her forehead and went out. He informed his wife that Haji Saheb of *Khak-e-Paak* was in their home. The word *Khak-e-Paak*, which means Holy Land, was a denominative used by inhabitants of Logar Province to amicably describe their realm. Soraya's mother had heard of him as an honest, upright, self-made man working as head of the criminal department under her husband and swiftly ordered Abai to prepare the drink.

Haji Saheb was sipping the succulent juice while conducting light chitchat and speaking of ordinary topics. Soraya was leaning on her father's knees and listening carefully as if she understood every word spoken by the visitor, who described the intent of his visit.

Haji Saheb said fervently, "Sir, you know Khak-e-Paak is the land of our respective families. We are aggrieved by what happened to you and the way the palace is handling the southern valley's projects. We know there is a conspiracy against you and your good work. I have been working in the chief justice's office for two decades now and know well the actors in and outside the building."

Mr. Suri replied, "It is God's will to test my strength. I know too that all is politically orchestrated."

"They have ordered all files to be locked, and access is barred," Haji Saheb informed him.

"I know, and this is very malicious; in every country where the rule of law prevails, an accused or the defendant attorney has access to the files."

"You do not have to worry, sir. This is why I came to see you. I have uncovered avenues to access them."

"No, no, Haji Saheb!" Mr. Suri firmly replied. "I do not want any hindrance for you and your family; they are very cruel!"

"Sir, a man without dignity is nobody. Helping you to reveal the facts in this affair will be my pleasure, please!"

Mr. Suri was mystified and staggered by this expression of solidarity. Haji Saheb offered to fetch the required records in the evenings regularly for the former chief justice to review them at night and prepare his defense. They were to be recovered the day after at dawn and put in place before employees regained their posts.

Soraya was observing the confab and was dazzled without knowing what was at stake. She just loved the seriousness of the matter being discussed. After the retreat of Haji Saheb, Mr. Zamir Suri felt more relaxed, and his daughter comprehended at least this aspect of the matter. For her part, she cuddled her father too, with a warm kiss on his forehead before disappearing in the yard again to proceed to the kitchen quarters and have her favorite watery rice. Haji Saheb appeared regularly in the evenings and then after the morning prayers. Soraya never forgot that candid bearded face, the one who always blessed her by caressing her head and extending a fatherly, tender look.

After nearly three months, Zamir Suri's defense was finally ready. Solid, based on facts, documented, and visionary, it terrified those at the top rungs of power. He urged a public hearing! Within the palace, the prime minister was criticized for having tolerated the former chief justice having access to *classified documents*. But in reality, nobody discerned who had leaked them. To prevent shame on the palace, the king ordered an amicable solution. The case against Zamir Suri had to be shelved promptly. Mr. Suri stayed home enjoying his family life, a proud man who had triumphed over the mightiest. It was a David against Goliath fight, indeed! The matter was now public. Tribal leaders, politicians, and common people from all shires of the country were turning up to see and congratulate him. Even those who did not know him appeared to glimpse and greet the man who had confronted the heart of power successfully.

The entire population seemed anxious how they would deal with Zamir Suri, who had the people of all the valleys, mountains, and deserts behind him. The history of Afghanistan had mostly been shamefully colored by tragedies and betrayal of its rulers, who primarily sought protection of foreigners to keep themselves in power. Zaher Shah's father was notoriously guileful. He signed copies of the Holy Koran as insignia of amity and forgiveness and relayed them to his opponents through his brothers as invites. Once they were dragged into the palace, they were instantly murdered. His predecessor, Amir Habibullah Kalakani, the only Tajik king since 1709, and his lieutenants, the Haider Khan Charkhi sons, heroes of Afghanistan's independence under King Amanullah Khan, and the renowned mayor of Kabul, Abdur Rahman Ludin, all perished with the same ruse. It is the worst offense in Islam to ignore an oath by the Holy Book! The extensive list of politicians, intellectuals, tribal leaders, military officers, and ordinary people who were victims of his killing machinery reveals an actual period of terror. However, it seemed that Hashem Khan, King Zaher Shah's eldest uncle, who was regent from 1933 to 1946 and dubbed the Machiavelli of the country, was more astute in destroying adversaries.

Abai's kitchen had never been so busy. Those who were in search of a national hero had found one! The former chief justice was knowledgeable, western educated, handsome, spoke *farangi*— English—and above all had successfully challenged the palace and their moles. Soraya enjoyed staring at the mass of individuals pouring through their house. Those who arrived from distant provinces stayed overnight, increasing the already heavy workload on Abai and her daughters. Soraya roamed around her father's sofa till late at night, listening to conversations. Often she was slanted on Mr. Suri's left or right thigh, warily contemplating those who spoke, as if she was ascertaining their sincerity through their facial expressions and words pronounced. Everybody loved her for her innocence and intelligence.

One day, a short, handsome young man, with massive hair on his skull, knocked at the gate. Soraya was playing in the yard with Abai, and her hands were full of mud. Mr. Suri knew and admired the guest, who was the son of a prominent leader of the eastern province. He greeted him in the library to learn about the worry of provincial leaders regarding the political reform process in the country. Curious, Soraya quickly joined them, but for once she did not grasp any word of what they conversed about. She observed carefully the facial expressions of the guest as if she investigated his inner thoughts. From his posture, she appreciated his devotion to her father. This simple encounter proved significant years later when the young man became prime minister of the country and Soraya his assistant.

Mr. Suri's wife was fretful about the cohort of people coming to see her husband—and so was the palace! They had eliminated other opponents. But Zamir Suri was different; the entire country stood behind him, blessing his resilience and proud of his success. Not only annoyed, Daoud Khan, pretender to the throne and eldest cousin of the king, was stunned! The popularity he coveted so desperately belonged now to someone else. On a sunny summer evening, the prime minister called Ali Khan, the minister of justice, to his office.

The prime minister began, "Mr. Minister, we know you have a special relationship with Zamir Suri."

The minister of justice humbly replied, "Indeed, Your Highness! And I am glad the case was dropped against him."

The prime minister continued disappointedly, "We are also aware that too many people from across the country pour into his house."

"It is unfortunate, Your Highness. I am sure it is against his wishes," the minister replied.

The prime minister concluded, "We have secured him a senior international position in Washington, DC. He has to leave the country!"

A few days later, Soraya ran again to the library, where her father was consuming his days by reading newspapers, receiving tribal chieftains, summarizing his conversations' notes, and skimming his books when he could.

"Father! My uncle with the big car has come to see you," she screamed.

"My darling! You have introduced me so far to so many of your uncles!" Her father jokingly patted her on the head and went out to greet the uncle.

He was astonished to see his buddy Minister Ali Khan, with his huge, luxury, black Buick, and warmly invited him in. Like with Haji Saheb, Soraya liked the visitor and took hold of his right index finger, towing him toward the library. He graciously took her in his arms and gave her a fatherly kiss. He was impressed by the little, skinny girl with glossy green eyes, who was already acting as her father's assistant.

Mr. Suri instructed that the other guests be taken to the main reception room and ordered the delightful sheer chai, a special black tea with milk and cardamom, and bolani, a delicious, flat, warm Afghan vegetable ravioli.

Soraya sprinted to her mother, recognizing that the new uncle was a singular guest, and it was her mother's task to ensure that her father's wishes were fulfilled.

Alone in the library with Zamir Suri, Minister Ali Khan briefed him about cabinet parleys and stressed, "Zamir, you should think of your family. How long do you plan to stay home without a job?" Minister Ali Khan said with affection.

"God has given me enough land and property in my ancestral Logar to live with," Zamir Suri said. "I do not need to work now and would like to spend time getting to know better my country and its peoples."

"Precisely. This is the problem, and you should not do it. I know you may not need the derisory salary of the government. But you know very well that those opposed to the palace have had tragic destinies, even members of their own families."

"What do you mean?"

"They seek a senior international position for you in Washington that will also cover the United Nations affairs in New York. You will be based in the capital of the United States but frequently travel to the headquarters of the world body," Ali Khan advised.

"They want me out of my own country, you mean," Mr. Suri concluded.

"You said it," Minister Ali Khan confirmed.

Soraya's mother was anxious and nervous. She twigged the resolve of her husband and his unbreakable loyalty to his people. However, she did not want her child to be orphaned and was supplicating her husband to consent to the offer of the palace, pleading that if he was not pleased, Soraya would at least have suitable education outside Afghanistan. Soon after, the government announced publicly of his appointment to Washington. The atmosphere altered, and preparations for the long journey started. Soraya noticed the change and was probing her father about where, why, with whom, what to do, and so on. Mr. Suri knew that the time of adieus with his motherland had arrived and that he would never return to dwell long enough, serve, and heal the wounds of his people. He often looked at Soraya, and tears came to his eyes. She was lucky, but how many millions of other girls would perish with lack of education and forced marriage, as well as cultural and religious dogmatism?

The itinerary and date of the big journey were finally fixed. Minister Ali Khan received words of obligation from the prime minister. The first leg east and southward—Kabul, Peshawar, and Karachi—was to be by road. Peshawar was the biggest Pashtun city of the neighboring Pakistan, while Karachi was its then capital. Mr. Zamir Suri and his family were planned to travel to New York via Amsterdam and London using the Royal Dutch Airliner KLM. And for the final leg, New York to Washington, DC, the Suri family would use the train.

Leaving for new horizons was like a move to uncertainty for little Soraya. She was puzzled and could abide everything except losing the sight of flying butterflies in the garden and Abai's luscious watery rice, full of spices. She questioned where America was, and her father candidly opened the world atlas. She instantly thought it was next door and received at the age of seven her first lesson on relativity from the talented lawyer who cherished science. Mr. Suri elucidated to his daughter that what seemed tiny might not be so in reality and spent time clarifying the notion of scale.

Finally, the day of the departure arrived. Minister Ali Khan was there. He took Soraya in his arms and with a hoarse voice said, "Darling, I know you are going away for a long time, but I promise you that I will be your marriage godfather!"

"You will have to wait for a long time, uncle," Soraya said. "My mother told me that when I am as big as she is, I can then marry someone."

"Yes, darling! Your mother is right, and I will wait for that day."

A comfortable car was catered by the government, and Zamir Suri and his family proceeded by the Lataband path, a very difficult, sinuous, and mountainous route to Jalalabad, capital of the scenic eastern province of Afghanistan and a winter resort for rich families. At the *Lahori Gate*, crossroad to the south and east provinces, his heart was aching. His thoughts were with his larger family and what could happen to them in his absence.

Though Soraya had been to Logar on numerous occasions, the view of the majestic, rough, dry massifs along the road to the east fascinated her. She saw unusual birds flying and was stunned to see mountain goats jumping from one peak to another without falling. Above all, she was curious to grasp what slumbered underneath the rocks and many times queried her father. At her age, she did not have any idea what minerals represented, and her father expounded that treasures slept under the rocks of the mountains. She was content to conclude finally that her country was rich.

On top of the Lataband Pass, they stopped for a while. Mr. Suri took deep breaths of fresh air, and little Soraya felt cold but she still stared around to register the image of mountains full of snow. They had lunch in the city of Jalalabad and ordered *Chapli Kebab,* a browned, flat, mashed meat mixed with vegetables and spices. It did not taste as good as Soraya's father expected, but he loved the environment of the restaurant. For once, he felt free, not under the familiar scrutiny of the government in his movements.

Soraya took some pomegranates before they crossed the famous Khyber Pass, the border between Afghanistan and Pakistan, to reach Peshawar in the evening. The pomegranates were tiny and made her laugh, as the ones her family usually received from Kandahar were big and red.

At Khyber Pass, Mr. Suri paused again on the peak of the mountain and had a long gaze at the beautiful plains of the eastern province of his country. He had a strange feeling. Convinced that he would not be permitted to come back to and live in his motherland, he lingered as long as he could, viewing down toward the west. He loved Afghanistan more than anything else despite its unsurmountable challenges and had declined the loftiest personal and professional offers in British India and in the United States. He had opted to return home and serve his country. Today he felt very sad to leave it forcibly.

In Peshawar, they proceeded to the Deans Hotel, in the middle of the new residential quarter, the most luxurious lodge of the city, full of bungalows, gardens, and flowers of all breeds. The colorful garbs, discipline, and particularly fancy turbans of the guards captivated the little girl. Before dinner, Soraya retreated to her room to dress. She was captivated by the flowing water as well as the bath bubbles and stayed for a long time, playing with air pockets. She desired to remain longer in the *teeny swimming pool*. The weather was already too hot for her.

The day after, Mr. Suri went in person to *Quessa Khwani*, the bazaar of stories, where hundreds of bookstores offered classic volumes. This is where the fall of the British Empire had begun. On April 23, 1930, the colonial troops had massacred countless demonstrators.

That was the beginning of their end in the subcontinent. He wanted to take the most important books with him across the Atlantic. It was an amazing place that recalled in many ways organized chaos. Nothing was logical, but everything moved and functioned. Thousands of people seemed busy. Kebab shops were full of guests, including the unwanted cockroaches, which moved freely on the floor. Butcher stores were invaded with millions of flies kissing and consuming the dangling carcass of a sheep, goat, or cow. Surprisingly customers purchased meat and consumed at the restaurants without realizing the health hazards. The main road and its adjacent alleys looked like garbage. Debris of paper, broken glass, fruit wastes, and all genera of other discarded items imbued their surface. Some even piddled by turning their faces to the wall. The whole area reeked badly. However, nobody seemed to care, and business continued.

The move to Karachi was smooth. They stayed in the Pearl Intercontinental Hotel for one evening only. Upon arrival, Soraya's mother informed her that they would not have dinner together.

"What happened, Mother?" inquired Soraya. "Why will we not be together as usual?"

"There is an official function, darling! Your father and I have to attend it without you," her mother replied gently.

"Will it be like this all the time where we go?" Soraya asked.

"Perhaps, my child! We do not know yet." This was another setback for the little Soraya. She left her preferred garden and Abai in Kabul; now she was bereaved for losing her father's enchanting discussions every night. This was the first time that the couple had revealed to their child that due to an *official function*, they would not be together for dinner. Soraya was curious to know what the *official function* was and decided to look out. She was stunned! Her mother had a striking, long white dress with her hair styled high, and her father was attired with a dark suit, white silk shirt, and bow tie. She was like a fragrant brittle angel, while he was towering, handsome, and protective. Soraya queried what was smelling so nice. Her mother disclosed the name of her perfume, *Shaame Paris* the famed Bourgois-created *Soir de Paris* and showed the impressive blue flask to her daughter. The image of the striking crown-shaped bottle remained forever in Soraya's mind. She was so proud to see her parents going down the majestic stairs of the hotel.

The day after, the Suri family was aboard a KLM flight for Amsterdam via the Arabian Peninsula. Soraya did not believe that such a titanic air vessel existed. She scaled the steep airstair on her own. At the plug door, everything appeared tiny down on the ground! She was impressed by the refined blue attire and convivial attitude of the flight attendants and mystified by the spotless seat display. Instantly, she was tendered cold orange juice. They gained the cruise altitude quickly. For her, flying in the sky was the apex of all dreams. She was always asking herself what the birds were looking at when they fluttered their wings up in the sky. And now she had her own opportunity! For a while, she thought of meeting angels if she scaled to the top of the airplane. She had a window seat and did not eat or drink any more. She was thrilled by looking down and memorizing different pictures and landscapes.

The ride in the air had its own quests for the little girl. She wanted to meet the *driver.* The pilot acceded to her request and came to meet her. She was taken for a tour around. In the cockpit, she was enthralled by the view as well as the buttons of all kinds and lights of all colors. She did not stop asking questions of the pilot, who candidly obliged. Then her father had to improvise responses to additional queries about the cockpit instruments she had seen.

They had a few hours stop in Doha before leaving for Amsterdam. It was in the morning that they were flying over the Alps. Gorgeous views of the majestic mountains were visible from both sides of the aircraft. The sun had enlightened the massifs and parts of the valleys, presenting stunning natural scenes below. The aircraft was passing between Mont Blanc and Mont Cervin, also called the Matterhorn. Both offered splendid pictures full of snow. The glaciers were visible and shining. For the seven-year-old Soraya, who was lodged again into her window seat, they were all miracles. She admired the iconic shapes of both massifs and, somehow, had a sentiment that she would visit them one day.

In Amsterdam, the family of Mr. Suri was guided into a hotel to rest and change before their night journey to New York. Everybody slept during the nocturne leg of their voyage. In the morning, Soraya had her usual orange juice, one sunny egg, and toast with marmalade. She was stunned by the service and asked the steward many times where the kitchen stood and whether there was enough food for everybody in the aircraft.

She kept an amazing description of the Empire State Building when landing at the New York International Airport known as Idlewild and now named after the late President John F. Kennedy. She was looking at this massive and beautifully tailored building that had become an iconic identity for New York City during the twentieth century. She asked her father what it was. As a graduate of Dickinson School of Law in the 1930s, Mr. Suri had enough knowledge about the building and delightfully explained to his daughter that it was the tallest monument of the world, inside which there were thousands of apartments and offices. Soraya was stupefied to see something so majestic, striking, and picturesque. From the airport, they were taken straight to Pennsylvania Station for their onward journey to the capital of the United States.

Numerous employees of Mr. Zamir Suri's new office were waiting at Union Station in Washington to receive the family. They were taken to their residence in Georgetown, where the young Soraya did not waste time before discovering every corner of the house and its vast garden, accompanied by Mama, their new cook, and her caretaker, who was expounding every detail of the mansion that had a magnificent view of the Potomac River and Roosevelt Island. Soraya did not apprehend her lingo and was scanning in her mind every word pronounced and gesture accomplished. But she liked her and befriended her instantly. In some way, she prompted Abai's image in her mind. There was no need to build trust between the two.

"You do not understand me, darling!" Mama recognized. "But Mr. Suri will sort this out soon," she murmured.

Mama was a gorgeous African American, with a tender heart. She conversed gently and softly. Soraya took her index finger in her right hand for the rest of the visit, ran after every flying creature, amassed Margaret flowers, and even dashed to the Potomac shore. She could not believe that such a gigantic river could exit but was quickly frustrated when Mama did not comprehend any word of her questions. She had seen the ocean from the sky and felt practically nothing except for admiring the infinite blue color. But in Georgetown, she felt the breeze and heard the waves crashing on rocks and people jumping in and relishing the water.

The day after, an Iranian lady appeared. She was the English teacher. Mr. Suri put in place strict rules; the tutor was hired full-time for a period of six months. Five days a week, lessons lasted from eight to twelve noon and from three o'clock to six o'clock in the afternoon. Mr. Suri returned home at lunchtime to probe the progress achieved. Dinner was served between seven-thirty and eight o'clock. Any given homework should be completed between nine o'clock and ten o'clock before going to bed.

The former chief justice of Afghanistan loved to lunch and dine at home with his family. However and often, he was prevented by his heavy workload on Capitol Hill or journeys to New York, where he followed particularly matters related to the Security Council and

General Assembly, two of the United Nations main organs that he personally monitored. Soon, diplomatic and political circles spoke of this refined Afghan who mastered Islamic and international laws, grasped perfectly the essence of the history of humankind, and offered effortless answers to thorny political and diplomatic challenges. The circle of his colleagues and admirers in the Congress, Senate, Department of State, White House, and the United Nations amplified steadily.

Within two months, Soraya and her mother were English conversant. Mama was the happiest woman in the world, as she could finally communicate, particularly with the mistress of the household. Soraya loved chatting with her because she had time and patience to elucidate about the neighborhood, country, and school. Soraya's mother began again reprimanding her daughter for spending more time with Mama. In autumn of the same year, Soraya was enrolled in the Hyde-Addison Elementary School, situated in Pleasant Plains. She enjoyed being in the classroom, as no instructor ever reprimanded her for questions posed. The enchanting afterdinner debates resumed with her father, who as usual had time to listen, to argue, and to respond. She was no more the little skinny girl, but a wonderful and promising child. Mr. Suri had furnished the house exquisitely and reconstituted his library, where he was spending most of his leisure time.

Soraya loved gabbing with people but hated gossiping. Mama was a great source of inspiration, for she recounted to Soraya every day part of her challenging life and the brawl of her community for basic rights. Soraya quickly understood that African Americans were regarded as second-class citizens in the United States. More sophisticated public facilities served only white citizens. She was dreadfully saddened and distressed as Mama was a fabulous person and could not see why she or someone like her should be abused by white people. Eyes full of tears, she questioned her father in the evening.

The former chief justice had resolved to intensify the depth of discourse with his daughter, and the calm atmosphere of the library was propitious. He calmly explained that segregation was one of the ugliest sins, one that God would never forgive. There were always wicked and gentle among human beings, and the vicious attempted to abuse the kind ones. If mistreatment was not punished effectively by the law, then there would be unfortunate victims.

"You know, darling, we are better Americans than a lot of those who do not like us," Mama proudly said. "We have been in this country for centuries. But some of those ones came perhaps ten or twenty years ago. We have to persist and endure; one day we will win." She underlined her feelings with the smile of a conqueror.

Soraya was perplexed. What was Mama going to win?

In school, some of Soraya's new friends were Hispanic and African American; they were affable and approached her with affection and regard. She loved frolicking and conferring with them. They also fancied her, for she had a solution for every hitch. However, Soraya could not ignore that her group of friends was often mocked and ridiculed by others, ones with blond hair and blue eyes.

Among all her friends, Sara was special. An African American too, she was taller, smart, and sportive. Her father was a captain in the fire services of the city and deemed a well-off man by his community. Soraya was authorized to partake in Sara's birthday celebration in the afternoon of a sunny Friday. They toddled together for the event. Sara told her that even her father was maltreated on a daily basis by his hierarchy, and he spoke about it openly to his family, inviting the children to never give up the struggle for equal rights.

Back home after the party, Soraya seemed distraught. Her father knew that she had been hassled by something. After dinner, he invited her to accompany him to the library. Soraya was exhilarated; she adored being summoned to a place that she cherished so much.

"Tell me, my love, what is upsetting you?" Mr. Suri gently asked his daughter.

"Father, why do black Americans have to fight for their rights? In Kabul, we were all the same! This is not a good place here!" She argued and recounted what she had seen and heard in Sara's home.

"I know, darling, it is not just. But there are things that take time to change, Sara's father is right. They should persist," he replied.

"But, Father, being black is not a crime! Me too. I have tanned skin," she insisted.

"You are right, my child. All human beings are equal, and they should be treated so," Mr. Suri emphasized with a soft voice.

"Sara's father said that they must give their seats in the bus to white people, even if they are ill and need to be seated," Soraya continued, weeping.

"Yes, my love. As I told you the other day, there are a lot of bad practices and people. But there are also good individuals," the former chief justice assured his daughter.

He surprised her when he acknowledged that in Afghanistan, too, people were abused and discriminated against because of their ethnicity or religion. But nobody conversed about it. Soraya felt distressed for them. But she still seemed eager to know why black Americans did not have equal rights. Her father patiently described the conquest of America by Europeans centuries ago and the brutal killing of the native people, often called redskins. He also depicted the dark history of slavery, which was formalized some three hundred years earlier. When Soraya affirmed that all conquerors of America were bad people, her father contested it and lectured his daughter about Abraham Lincoln, who abolished slavery and fought for equal rights and opportunities for all Americans until his assassination. He assured his daughter that black Americans would soon get their full rights, as they had great past and present leaders. He gave the examples of Frederick Douglass, Percy Julien, Bayard Rustin, and Malcolm Little—who had just been liberated from prison—and many others.

After the outrage and grief, Soraya was now relieved for Sara, her family, and the group of girls who were her friends in the Hyde-Addison Elementary School. She quickly grasped that under the circumstances, ignoring was the best answer to harassment. She valued Sara and relished exchanging views with her. Often she impatiently waited for her father to return home and chat, strengthening further the bond between the renowned lawyer and his daughter. Soraya was settled in her school and learning fast. Mr. Zamir Suri discerned quickly that his daughter had a structured mind, was often appalled by social issues, and had the audacity to express her opinion, but at the same time, she sought seclusion when offended. At such a young age, she was already grown up, exchanging views and arguing as an adult. He enjoyed spending time with her. She soon comprehended what the United Nations was and what her father's job was. She liked the spirit of being together but was quickly disenchanted when her father explained that the existence of the United Nations did not mean the countries of the world acted in a unified manner and that each one defended its own interest.

The weather in the United States was getting cold, and autumn in the Georgetown area was colorful. As usual, Soraya was fascinated by the dance of falling leaves and felt sad to see trees losing their beauty. The fog was making the weather grayer than she had ever witnessed in her hometown of Kabul. Finally, the year-end break arrived. Pupils were animated, and everyone was nattering of their family's plans for Christmas and New Year's Eve. Soon the Zamir

Suri family draped their mansion with a big tree, colorful bulbs, and lights. They engaged in a family discussion about what to do during the festive period, which was getting colder every day.

Mr. Suri had other but more critical concerns to deal with in New York. The Norwegian politician and diplomat Trygve Halvdan Lie, who was secretary-general of the United Nations, had to resign due to massive pressure by the Soviet Union. He was indicted of prejudice in the Korean War. Among other mischiefs, he was also charged for passing secret military and diplomatic information to the state of Israel. Moreover, his legal adviser had just committed suicide. The first secretary-general of the United Nations had no choice against the fury of the member states but to quit. The diplomatic brouhaha led to the election of a new secretary-general swiftly. Prominent member states were lobbying for their candidates and ideas. Mr. Zamir Suri was towed into plentiful private meetings, lunches, dinners, briefings and many other United Nations proper events. He, however, always had time for his family back in Washington, though his preoccupation was apparent.

One evening of late November, Soraya lingered long to have her usual talk with her father and now friend.

"Father, what is the matter?" she asked while putting her hand on Mr. Suri's shoulder.

"Nothing, my darling." Mr. Suri responded gently. "Some minor issues in the United Nations."

"You need to work at night like in Kabul?" she fretfully argued, referring to his informal indictment and house arrest.

"No, no, my child!" he assured her. "The boss of the United Nations has to be replaced. There are lots of legal issues, and my view is solicited by many."

"Why? Is he a bad man, Father?" Soraya queried.

"I do not know precisely. He has renounced his job," her father affirmed.

"Then advise for a good one!" Soraya innocently uttered.

"I will, my love!"

She gave a warm kiss on the large brow of her father—that had by now become her trademark—before sprinting to her room. Soraya loved her father's hands and forehead the most. She could observe him for hours writing, as if she knew the association of brain and fingers. No one wrote better than Mr. Suri. Though a bright Afghan judge and lawyer, his command of the English language, sciences, philosophy, and history was startling. He always wrote his texts and speeches either with a black Montblanc or a golden Sheaffer fountain pen that he liked especially. They were always in his suit pockets.

Soraya once accompanied her father to New York and visited the United Nations building. She did not enjoy the outing as she was left with a staffer for hours. However, there was something special about New York. She liked the city and her father's office, located in the Empire State Building. She posed questions about each towering edifice, and Mr. Suri regaled her with accounts that she understood. Soraya was riveted by large and long lanes on which hundreds of cars were coursing. The flow of people and the beauty of shops and malls were astonishing. She had never seen so many human beings on the boulevards and items in the stores. She loved the evening excursion and was staggered by the glows and drive of people as well as the electric escalators that took countless up-and-down trips. She was convinced she would like living in New York forever.

For their first Christmas in the United States, the Zamir Suri family had invited Soraya's classmates and their families to his residence the evening of December 26. The decoration of the house looked gorgeous, and Mama had the personal support of the mistress of the abode to bake her turkey. Sara and her parents were in attendance. The buffet dinner was succulent. There were no leftovers. Everybody was extolling the welcoming environment and asking about decorations, the yummy stuffing, and the lip-smacking cranberry sauce. And Mama was enjoyably explaining that they were all the result of Afghan and American knowledge and savoir faire.

Mr. Suri talked with everybody, but he spent more time with Sara's father. Their discussion focused on the children first but turned quickly around the plight of African Americans in the United States. Sara's father was of the opinion that the legacy of Abraham Lincoln had been betrayed and his community continued to struggle for their rights. He acknowledged that a few white people, such as Edwin Stanton, had significant roles in the abolition of slavery, but he considered most of the political leaders as cowards and lamented their behavior. He spoke at length about the real history of foot soldiers and a young pastor, Martin Luther King Jr., who promoted nonviolent resistance. He called him the Mahatma Gandhi of America.

Meanwhile, Soraya was engaged with her associates. She took Sara's hand to show her the house.

In the big corridor, Sara pulled her friend aside. "Tell me," Sara inquired, "are you Christians?"

"No, we are Muslims," Soraya responded.

"But you celebrate Christmas better than most Christians," Sara continued.

"Oh!" Soraya countered. "My father says all religions are the same; only people make them different. Come on. Let me show you my room.

The winter season was stark. Soraya fancied walking with Mama on dry snow and enjoyed the sound of *"kreek"* with each stride. Mama's answers to her unsullied interrogations were reigniting the feeling of desolation and sorrow for African Americans. Those who battled alongside their white countrymen to defeat the horrible Nazi regime and liberate Europe, earning admiration of the old continent, were racially abused in their own country, the *"biggest democracy on earth."* Often, Soraya cried for Sara and Mama, as well as their families, and disclosed her distress to her father during their evening chats in front of the main fireplace.

Within a few months, Soraya had matured. She was not anymore the tiny girl who often put her two sweet arms on her father's lap to ask questions and argue. She sat in the green sofa next to Mr. Suri and carefully listened to the only man that she profoundly revered. During their discussions, Soraya enjoyed contemplating the flames; she was captivated by their dance and wondered how light could contain smoke. For her, the first represented virtue and the latter evil! Her father was pleased to recognize that his daughter explored consistently thoughtful paths to facts and truth.

During the rest of the winter season, Mr. Zamir Suri and his family were engaged in numerous political and social events in Washington. However, in New York, the campaign for electing a new secretary-general for the United Nations was at its highest intensity. Various countries were lobbying for their contenders. As an internationally known lawyer, Mr. Suri was lugged into manifold *friendly* congregations. Meanwhile, Soraya had learned enough about the history and geography of the United States and was chattier. She was planning for when the snow thawed in the spring. Visiting Niagara Falls was at the top of her list. Her parents often invited her peers home on Saturdays to savor famous Afghan winter dishes, such as *landi palaw*—dried lamb meat pilau, *kitchiree quroot*— Afghan risotto with yogurt and meatballs, and *shola goshti* and *ghorbandi*—two types of mashed rice with lamb meat prepared in the oven with or without sauce. Soraya's father was exceptionally bighearted. He had his own recipes and was occasionally in the kitchen to please his daughter. But the finest of all was his wife, who had now trained Mama to take the preparatory steps and act as her assistant. She was also a first-rate tailor and designer. Often she bought fashion magazines to inspire herself, but she always had her own creations, dressing her daughter with most refreshing and striking attires. Mr. Zamir Suri valued the talent of his wife and had transformed a room in the main building to serve as madame's atelier, with the most modern and beautifully painted Singer hand-crank and treadle sewing machines, electric irons, tables, and other tools. Soraya was the best dressed in her school and had a particular faculty of combining colors. She loved all colors, but her favorites were green, yellow, and blue.

In April 1953, Dag Hammarskjöld from Sweden was elected secretary-general by the General Assembly of the United Nations. Mr. Suri was happy and considered the new patron of the *"arduous house"* a man of high integrity.

The same evening, Soraya asked him, "Father, is he a good man?"

"Yes, he is, my child," her father replied.

However, the situation in Afghanistan had taken a new twist. The split in the palace was now known to some *commoners*. The prime minister and his nephew, Prince Daoud Khan, chief of the armed forces and former defense and interior minister who benefited from the sympathy of loyal military and internal security officers, diverged about the future of the country and its external ties. The prince was pushing his uncle out of the office. As a nationalist and known stubborn prince, Daoud Khan had fostered inexplicable indulgence toward the Soviet Union since the refusal of the United States to provide weapons to his country. He also seemed upset about the unconditional support of the West toward recognition of the new state of Pakistan, disputing the border demarcation. Indeed, in 1893, the then king of Afghanistan, Daoud Khan's own ancestor, and the British Empire envoy had signed a one-page memorandum of understanding, containing only seven short articles, through which Afghanistan temporarily ceded parts of its territory in the east and south of the country to the queen of Great Britain. A nearly two-thousand–three-hundred-kilometer-long border was defined and known as the Durand Line. However, since its success in the third Anglo-Afghan war and independence of the country in 1919, Afghanistan had not forcefully claimed return of its territory. The foundation of Pakistan in 1947, coinciding with the collapse of the British Empire, provided another opportunity to do so. But King Zaher Shah opted for silence, recognizing Pakistan and its boundaries. Many in the country comprehended Daoud Khan's position and supported his views. Afghanistan too needed weapons and political support to be secure and in peace.

Though Mr. Zamir Suri was de facto pushed out of his country by the palace, he had kept a close relationship with Prince Naim Khan, the younger brother of Daoud Khan, who was an astute, diplomatic, and clever person. He relied on the legal advice of the bright Bombay and Dickinson graduate for internal and external hot topics. Soon the intrigue at the palace was known to the public at large in Afghanistan, but more decisively in Kabul. Mr. Suri received numerous letters from his friends. Each was unique in revealing part of what the writer believed was the truth. Haji Saheb wrote most often. In April 1953, rumors spread that King Zaher Shah had summoned his two cousins, who were at the same time his brothers-in-law, to call for the respect of the authority of their uncle the prime minister. Daoud Khan had not obliged, leaving the king in despair. The arm wrestling between the two had taken a dramatic shape. The big question that experts examined was who would concede.

It looked like Daoud Khan, who hardly esteemed or even recognized the ruler, was winning the rivalry in the palace. His imminent appointment as the new prime minister of Afghanistan and the identities of the *new* ministers were subject of gossip in the bazaars of the capital. Most whispered that the trade and finance minister, Malik Khan, would be the first *fatality*. Daoud Khan had always deemed Mr. Zamir Suri and Minister Malik Khan "*too friendly with America.*" But still, his sudden animosity with the trade and finance minister was mysterious for many as they were known to be good friends.

Mr. Suri was extremely concerned that the country was slithering to the Soviet Union sphere of influence already. He demonstrated fretfulness for his people, and his angst was apparent. Mrs. Suri was even more anguished. She knew her husband was a man of honor and stood for the interest of his people. But she did not want him to get drawn into the *palace politics* and remembered the visit of Minister Ali Khan back in Kabul notifying her husband to leave the country. Mr. Suri was often invited not only by the Department of State and Capitol Hill, but also by social circles, universities, and business communities to lecture about Islam and Afghanistan. His intellectual repute was recognized in New York and Washington. He was practically a second ambassador of his country to the United Nations and to the United States.

Soraya always waited for teatime after dinner to share precious moments with her father. One evening, she stayed longer than usual, in spite of repeated calls by her mother to go to bed. In a quiet moment, she turned to Mr. Suri and asked, "Father, they want to harm you again?"

"Who, my darling?" her father queried.

"Those back home! You look anxious," she replied.

"Yes, my love! I am worried for our country, but no one wants to hurt me anymore," Mr. Suri calmly replied.

"I do not want you to go back! We are all happy here," she murmured.

"We will always be together, my child!" he assured her.

As usual, she gave a warm kiss to her father's forehead and went to bed. Mr. Suri chuckled and was enchanted with the extent of his daughter's care.

The embassy of Afghanistan was on Twenty-Fourth Street Northwest. Near Pennsylvania Avenue, the edifice was designed by the famous architect Nathan C. Wyeth, who was well known for his subtle and artful work, having created numerous classics such as the Oval Office, the west wing of the White House, and the Cannon, Russell, and Longworth Congressional buildings, as well as masterpiece embassy structures. Hashem Maiwandwal, who later on became prime minister of the country and faced a tragic destiny, was the ambassador. As a shrewd, intelligent man, he venerated Mr. Suri for his knowledge and stature. He never objected to his regular exchanges with high American officials.

The Suri family needed to hire a second residence staff member as Mama could not handle all the preparation for the myriad of bigwigs who frequented their table. Maggy, an enchanting American in her late fifties who spoke Spanish, was tasked to look after Soraya. She had landed from her native Peru in the United States with her family some thirty years earlier. Of Machu Picchu origin, she perfectly represented her ancient Inca background on the heights of the Andes mountains. Like Mama, she was a very refined lady. Her attitude portrayed an aristocratic upbringing. Soraya took to her from the first instant; they befriended each other quickly. Her smile and sincere face were unique. She recounted the beauty of her crags, full of trees, as well as her odyssey to Los Angeles due to life hardship, using a fishing vessel, and facing death. But she had ambitions for her children and moved to the East Coast. Though her son and daughter had comfortable jobs, she pursued her work; this was how she had earned money for their education. In the last fifteen years, she had assisted many foreign diplomats, but she had never seen such a warm and charming family.

The similarities between Mama and Maggy were startling. They had both been discriminated against in their own country yet demonstrated an extraordinary resilience. Soraya had become friends quickly with numerous offspring of ambassadors and would recount her school encounters to her father frequently. Every weekday, Maggy woke Soraya up, bathing and dressing her to be at the table for breakfast. Most often, she teased her to display amity and regard.

Mr. Suri enjoyed the interaction between the two. One day before breakfast, though, he did not seem content. He began, "Maggy!"

"Yes, sir," she softly answered.

"You assist Soraya to wake up, bathe and dress, and be on time for breakfast," he said.

"Yes, sir! I do everything because she should be impeccable," Maggy added.

"I know, Maggy. But she has to learn how to deal with her affairs and be self-reliant. I may not be in this position forever. Soraya has to learn quickly to face the odds of life," Mr. Suri advised.

That day, the unique child of the Suri family comprehended that she needed to stand on her own feet. And this is how she has lived ever since.

During his frequent trips to New York, Mr. Suri had established a remarkably friendly rapport with Dag Hammarskjöld, the most efficient and respected secretary-general of the United Nations so far, who later on lost his life in an apparent assassination plot. They often conversed about world affairs. But the international top diplomat and politician was eager to learn from him about Islam,

Afghanistan, and the Soviet bid to acquire access to the warm waters of the Indian Ocean. Mr. Zamir Suri gave brilliant lectures about the painful history of his country, as well as the occupation of other neighboring nations by the communist giant. He acknowledged that Afghanistan faced the looming danger of falling within the Soviet sphere of influence.

On September 6, 1953, Radio Kabul broadcast that the prime minister had resigned due to health concerns and His Majesty's cousin, Daoud Khan, had been tasked to form a new cabinet. It seemed that a bloodless coup had brought to light the fracture within the royal family. A day later, the new prime minister was in firm command of the country and picked his younger brother, Naim Khan, as foreign minister. Some members of the royal family did not lose their ministerial posts. Perhaps Daoud Khan did not want to further antagonize his kinfolk during a phase of history when he had in mind to alter its course. His stratagem entailed advocating for the legitimate restitution of Afghan territory ceded under the Durand Treaty. Radio Kabul began diffusing the slogan of *Daa Pashtunistan Zemouge— This Pashtunistan is ours,*" implicitly reproving the Durand Accord and Line. Foreign Minister Naim Khan was assiduous in traveling around the world.

Daoud Khan was disillusioned in September 1954 when key countries in Europe and Far East Asia, together with the United States, Australia, and New Zealand, congregated in Manila and decided to establish a military pact, SEATO, the South East Asia Treaty Organization, in which Pakistan was to be a pivotal member. The new prime minister was further devastated in February 1955 when, under the influence of the United States, the United Kingdom, Turkey, Iran, Iraq, and Pakistan effectively developed another functional pact called CENTO, the Central Treaty Organization. Afghanistan was deemed extraneous in both organizations. For obvious reasons, the Soviet Union leadership exploited the anger of the new Afghan prime minister to their maximum advantage.

Shortly after, it became apparent that the foreign policy of Afghanistan would be based on a strong tie, including military cooperation, with the Soviet Union, at the expense of the United States and its European allies. Nikolai Bulganin and Nikita Khrushchev, the two topmost leaders of the Soviet Union, journeyed together to Kabul and tendered a 100 million US-dollar package to Daoud Khan. As an upshot, not only scores of young military officers were sent to Moscow and other major cities of the empire for "instruction," but Soviet fighter jets, tanks, machine guns, and so on also commenced to arrive in Afghanistan. The West was undeniably losing their long and traditional friendship with this eternal buffer zone of history between the superpowers.

At the same time, the quarrel between Trade and Finance Minister Malik Khan and Daoud Khan about political, military, and economic strategies of the government became apparent. Their frequent fracases in cabinet meetings were publicly recognized; the old buddies had become foes. And Daoud Khan now had the upper hand. Malik Khan, the mighty minister, was despised, dismissed, and even detained. He then spent over two precious decades of his life in lockup. His "crime" was not divulged, and he was never tried. It was rumored that the ambitious prime minister had personally ordered torture of the former minister in prison. Some spoke of hundreds of kicks with heavy military boots into the chest, kidney, and head of the poor man. The vital question for common people in the marketplaces was why friends of the former trade and commerce minister abandoned him. Even the traditional international human rights entities and governments of the free world did not intercede in his favor.

In Washington, Mr. Zamir Suri was invited as a friend regularly by Secretary of State John Foster Dulles to elucidate the shift of policy of the new government in Afghanistan. He recurrently conveyed to his interlocutor that the unequivocal support provided to Pakistan by the West in general and the United States in particular was biased and jeopardized the neutrality of Afghanistan, leaving no choice for

Daoud Khan. Moreover, the methodical sneering at Afghan stands had been noticed by its leaders. A strong bond of respect had been established between Secretary Dulles and Mr. Suri. Even President Dwight Eisenhower esteemed the knowledge of the Afghan lawyer and former chief justice about the Islamic world and his vision of Southwest Asia.

While her father played his role on the world stage, Soraya assiduously attended to her studies. At the age of ten, she already exhibited outstanding aptitude for reading and writing. Her phrases flowed like poems, and her lucidity in conversation was rock solid. Above all, her father loved her honesty. She was particularly interested in the American Civil War (1861–1865), as well as one of its major upshots, the end to slavery and the starting of a struggle for civil and human rights of non-European Americans. Perhaps what she had ascertained from Mama, Sara, and now Maggy had affected her. She purchased books with her pocket money and spent long hours in her father's library reading to grasp the kernel of the topic and make sense of what she believed was the truth. She had developed a special reverence toward Abraham Lincoln, who had valiantly faced the reality and against all odds thrust to end slavery.

One day of summer 1955, she had a row with her teacher when the instructor asserted that slavery was abolished at the beginning of 1863 when President Lincoln issued his Emancipation Proclamation.

Soraya raised her hand. "Ma'am, I believe that is not true," she gently argued.

"Oh? You think so?" the instructor interjected. "Where are you coming from?"

"I am from Afghanistan, ma'am," Soraya countered.

"Then you know our history better than me," the teacher mocked.

"No, ma'am. I do not pretend to, but I read that slavery came to a close legally when at the end of 1865, the amendment to the Constitution of the United States was ratified."

"Maybe. Now you sit down!" the tutor ordered.

Soraya was distraught and felt demeaned. However, she had a rock-solid supporter. Her father consoled her, asserting that she was right.

Two days later, one of her classmates, the daughter of a top foreign diplomat, scoffed at and shoved Soraya, mocking her knowledge of American history. Soraya remained silent but was boiling with anger. She knew the teacher was wrong and her classmate a goon fool. The offspring of the top diplomat continued her mockery, and suddenly for no good reason, the poor girl tumbled on her face, rolled down a slope for several meters, and was bleeding all over. It looked like divine punishment!

In the evening as soon as he came home, Mr. Suri summoned Soraya to the library. The others were curious, and Maggy was anxious.

"Why did you hurt my friend's daughter?" Mr. Suri probed instantly.

"Father, she jeered me for the argument that I had with my teacher. You know about it," Soraya said.

"You have no right to attack people unless there is a compelling reason. And this is not one, you understand? Tomorrow you must apologize," Mr. Suri concluded.

"Yes, Father. I am sorry, Father," she retorted. "But it was not me, but God who punished her. I did not even touch her," she murmured.

"Now, my darling," Mr. Suri softly inquired, "what was the issue that irritated you so much?"

Soraya passionately explained the motives of her discord with the classmate and the latter's ignorance about American history. Mr. Suri was joyful and proud that at such a young age, his daughter had the slant of an intellectual. Once again, he explained that it took time for a society and its people to change. They engaged in an extended conversation about the iniquity of humankind. Soraya asked why more human beings were made miserable, wounded, and even exterminated by their fellow humans. Ferocious animals did not kill so much! And why could God, who is omnipotent and determines everything in the universe, not be fair and impede all types of nescience, misdeed, and prejudice?

Finally, after an hour and a half, the former chief justice and his daughter came out of the library, walking side by side and continuing their candid chat. Maggy and Mama were relieved and rushed to the kitchen. They both fancied Soraya in their own ways, devoting hours to enlighten her about the plight of native people and other minorities in the United States.

During this period, any claim of right was suffocated by McCarthyism as those who demanded respect of the First Amendment of the Constitution were quickly tagged as communists with subversive ideas. Special television programs were tailored for this purpose. One Thursday, American neighbors of the Afghan Embassy joined other protestors to throw stones at the building and chase employees to express their fury about closer Afghan-Soviet relationships. It was a paradoxical situation as the United States had systematically refuted the views and approaches of Afghanistan, leaving no other choice for the country. While Ambassador Maiwandwal protested formally, Mr. Suri did not hesitate to criticize in his interventions such an immature attitude.

At the same time, even legitimate petitions of Hispanic and African American communities were rebuffed and their leaders apprehended under the ploy that they acted against the United States of America.

However, the young pastor Martin Luther King Jr. had become extremely strident. At the end of the same year of 1955, he and his friend Ralph Abernathy led the Montgomery Bus Boycott, thus becoming the genuine leaders of civil rights. There was hope; King was handsome, eloquent, dauntless, and clever. Secretary Dulles had the grim task of responding to queries of diplomatic envoys about this new young star of American politics and calls for respect of his dignity and safety.

For Mr. Zamir Suri, it was time that Soraya crammed too about her own country. But there was barely literature available, and most authors were at their early stages of unearthing Afghanistan's mysteries. He decided to be the coach of his own kid. The time was opportune as he was called by the secretary of state recurrently to discuss matters related to Southwest Asia. The SEATO and CENTO military pacts were deemed critical components of US foreign and security policies, and Secretary Dulles had personally invested time and effort to make them effective realities. With the growing influence of the Soviet Union in Afghanistan, the rival power of the West perceived a major hindrance for the interest of the United States. President Eisenhower was worried about the establishment of a Soviet Union-Afghanistan-India axis. The prime minister of Pakistan had been summoned at various occasions to Washington and urged to promote democracy and rule of law in his country in order to be at least a credible ally, but to no avail. The directorate of the military Inter-Services Intelligence, known as the ISI, established in 1948 immediately following the foundation of Pakistan would decide who governed the country. They ran Pakistan, brutalized civil rights campaigners, and even murdered those considered "*Indian spies*." The United States had given up, and both Dulles and Eisenhower fumed.

Afterdinner tea was served in the library when Mr. Zamir Suri did not have formal commitments. It offered the opportunity to converse about his daily occupations. Though Soraya was still too young to comprehend everything, she was very attentive and posed questions that bestowed occasions for her father to explain historic, political, and economic realities of Afghanistan. He had a placid voice and fancied his offspring grasping facts of her country of origin, at least as of 1709, when Mirwais Hotak proclaimed self-rule from the Iranian Safavid Empire. Soraya was distressed to learn that for over two centuries, only four kings had ended their existence peacefully in their palaces. The others had been killed, banished, or blinded, mostly by their own kin. She felt sorry for Queen Soraya and King Amanullah Khan, who were pioneers of modernity, progress, and hope for Afghanistan but exiled because of religious fascism. By the winter of 1956, she had absorbed enough to debate with her father.

During the same year, she stood next to him at the Independence Day commemoration banquet that the ambassador of Afghanistan had organized. Numerous US high government dignitaries, other diplomats, and renowned personalities of Washington, DC, were in attendance. Suddenly the noise of sirens was discernible. Initially, Mr. Suri thought it was a guest that the security forces escorted. But, within a few minutes, from among a huge convoy of cars, Vice President Richard Nixon emerged.

Once the excitement of his presence was over, he approached Mr. Suri, whom he had encountered many times earlier. Mr. Nixon did not have fond memories of his trip to Afghanistan, considering the country of no interest for the United States. He, however, considered the former chief justice an outstanding international lawyer and "potential hope" for the future of Afghanistan. He surprisingly engaged in a rather lengthy chat with Mr. Suri's eleven-year-old daughter, who already presented the allure of a princess. The vice president was impressed by the yet-to-become young lady. She innocently asked him if he had met with Martin Luther King Jr., who was a good man, and was astonished to discover that he had not. Mr. Nixon was dressed in a white coat and bow tie. She thought the vice president would have looked better in dark-colored suits. She found him an impatient man, rushing on topics discussed! Soraya was already very composed and

47

addressed her interlocutors as an adult. Her father had taught her to listen, digest, and research about what people claimed before making her own opinion.

One evening, the deliberation was more candid; she had resolved to engage in more personal discussion. "Father, is it true that King Amanullah Khan rewarded you with gold coins and a golden watch?" Soraya softly asked.

"Who told you that, my child?" Mr. Suri replied.

"My mum!"

"If your mum disclosed the matter to you, then it is true." He smiled.

"Why did he do it, Father?" Soraya pursued.

"My darling, when he inspected our school, I was able to reply to all his queries, and he was pleased. Both the queen and the king were good people, though they had their own shortcomings," Mr. Suri responded.

"How did you name me, Father?" Soraya asked.

Mr. Suri explained to his daughter that her name was of Arabic origin. He further apprised her that she shared her name and gorgeous green eyes with two queens, Soraya Esfandiary of Iran and Soraya Tarzi of Afghanistan. She instantly replied that she did not wish to be a queen and preferred to remain her father's daughter. He took her in his arms and gave a warm kiss on her forehead. Then Mr. Suri related that when she was born, the sky was full of stars, and this was why he named her Soraya, the brightest of all celestial bodies. But he also acknowledged that he revered Queen Soraya of Afghanistan, who was an exceptional woman.

Back home, Daoud Khan was going nowhere. His pro-Soviet stratagem had enraged the Shah of Iran, another neighbor and chief ally of the West. His dogma on the Durand Line was flopping as the Pashtun leaders in Pakistan, affected by the Durand Line, favored autonomy rather than separation. Their most renowned chieftain even joined the Pakistani Socialist Party and, later on, the National Awami Party and proved, therefore, an integral figure of the country's political and social arena. The ISI had cornered all Pashtun and Baloch leaders. Fear of being labeled *Indian spies* and eradicated without a judicial process prevented them from expressing their opinion. No one seriously pondered Daoud Khan's once-publicized threat of war with Pakistan. He fathomed that he could not regain Pashtunistan, the eluded territory. As a stubborn and arrogant leader and in response to western blind support to Pakistan, he was forced to strengthen ties with the big communist neighbor. Soviet expansionism all around the world was a momentous threat. President Eisenhower was apprehensive. The Cold War was at its uppermost intensity, and the reinforced Afghan-Soviet bond was perceived as a serious threat to the most trusted allies of the United States in the region.

In spring 1957, Secretary Dulles extended Mr. Zamir Suri an invitation from President Eisenhower to meet with him, and he was once more in the Oval Office.

"Mr. Suri, I am glad to see you again!" President Eisenhower said. "Once more, I assure you that this meeting is considered as an exchange between two friends. We have briefed the Afghan ambassador, who has no objection. Let me tell you that we are gravely worried about the path that your country has taken."

"Mr. President, I do not represent the Afghan government, as you know! But as a friend, let me highlight that your unreserved patronage of Pakistan is partly to be blamed," Mr. Suri replied.

"I understand you," President Eisenhower acknowledged. "You are an internationally renowned lawyer, and I have fastidiously looked into the history of the region, as well as the dealings under British India. While there may be some legal ground for Prime Minister Daoud Khan's claims, he must realize that all has changed after the Second World War. We do not rely only on official channels, and we need your help," the president pursued, alluding to Mr. Suri's friendship with Foreign Minister Naim Khan.

The conversation lasted for an hour. President Eisenhower notified Mr. Suri that he was inviting Prime Minister Daoud Khan to the United States and had already tasked Vice President Nixon and Secretary Dulles to work the specifics out with the Afghan ambassador. Mr. Suri clearly realized that the United States was aware of mistrust between Maiwandwal and the prime minister of his country. He did not wish to get involved in bilateral issues but received a phone call the next day from the foreign minister and his friend Naim Khan, who sought advice and more information. Though the invite was greeted with skepticism, the trip was proposed to take place the summer of the year after.

Meanwhile, Soraya was trailing in the footsteps of her father what was occurring in the world. Indeed, her structured mind developed steadily. She spent long hours with Mr. Suri to flawlessly cognize an issue of concern and was interested in everything. She never concurred on something for the sake of pleasing the interlocutor. Her father was patient, taking time to persuade her or be convinced. The interaction between the two was special. Soraya loved Friday and Saturday nights as she could linger without being reminded of school the day after. On one such evening, she asked, "Father, is it bad back home?"

"Well, the country goes through difficult moments."

"Has Afghanistan become communist now?" Soraya inquired innocently, looking straight in her father's eyes.

"No, darling! But there are certainly people of such opinion."

"Why doesn't Daoud Khan listen to you?" she replied immediately.

"He is not obliged, my child," Mr. Suri responded. "I advise his brother when he asks me; to accept or not is his right. This is how the government system functions."

"He does not look like a good man," Soraya affirmed.

"No, you cannot say so. He is certainly stubborn, though," Mr. Suri countered.

"Does he listen to his brother?"

"Sometimes," her father stated. I get along better with his brother, who seems a more balanced person."

"Then I like his brother!" Soraya concluded.

In the summer of 1957, Mr. Zamir Suri was notified by the foreign minister that he was being recalled to Kabul for consultation and appointed special adviser to the prime minister, with the specific task of preparing his visit to the United States for the year after. Nobody was pleased with the news. Soraya's mother was the most distressed. She believed her husband would be jailed upon his return to Kabul and pleaded for him not to leave his international position. But Mr. Suri had no choice. The date of the departure for Kabul was scheduled, the itinerary was decided upon, and preparatory steps were taken. The Suri family were going to New York, cruise to Europe, visit Pompeii, Rome, and Geneva, and fly to Delhi and then to the south of Afghanistan before driving to Kabul.

Soraya entreated her parents to invite Sara and her family the day prior to their departure for New York for a private farewell dinner. Mr. Suri assented, and the event was candid, attended by Mama and Maggy too. Sara and Soraya had their own chat, while their fathers were, once again, addressing political developments in the United States. After a dramatic victory in the Montgomery Bus Boycott, Pastor Martin Luther King Jr. had helped form and presided over the Southern Christian Leadership Conference to push one step further American democracy and equal rights for all and fight more efficiently the racist White Citizen's Council and the Ku Klux Klan. Sara's father seemed optimistic and believed that a solid alliance between the African American and Hispanic leadership on the one hand and the Democratic Party on the other hand would be the best that could happen in his country.

The Suri family journeyed to New York for three days. Mr. Suri was required to attend farewell events organized by his United Nations colleagues and friends. The family stayed in the Pierre, on Sixty-First Street East near Central Park. This was Mr. Suri's favorite hotel. He had fond memories of the place and had stayed there in a suite on the top floor, overlooking Central Park, when in New York. Jean-Francois, the manager, esteemed the former chief justice and always reserved for him the same room.

While her father was fulfilling official duties, Soraya and her mother were tasked to go for vital shopping. The weather in New York was exquisite during the early summer of 1957. The priority for her mother was to visit Turnbull & Asser in order to preselect shirts and suits for her husband before he would make his final choice. Soraya recalled her father disclosing that he used to save money for months when studying at Dickinson Law School to buy suits and shirts from Turnbull & Asser. John, the manager, greeted them.

"John, this is my daughter, Soraya," Soraya's mother apprised him.

"Oh, my God! She is already a princess and beautiful like in a fairy tale!" John said.

"Thank you, sir," Soraya interjected. "I have come with my mother to choose shirts and suits for my father."

"Of course, my lady," John replied. "I know his taste, but your advice will be most precious."

The next day, they visited Bloomingdale and Saks Fifth Avenue, where Soraya was offered her first Hermès gift. It was a golden and greenish color scarf, decorated with horses and horseshoes, and matched her green eyes perfectly.

Chapter 2

Teenage and University Years

I have no special talent. I am only passionately curious.
Imagination is more important than knowledge.

—Albert Einstein, On Education

The Zamir Suri family departed New York aboard SS *Constitution* for a journey to Naples via Gibraltar and through the Atlantic Ocean. The gigantic vessel was a mind-blowing cruiser that could host up to four hundred guests. It was the most luxurious object that Soraya had ever seen. Everything was sophisticated and lavish. Men and women demonstrated exemplary discipline and were well dressed. The captain greeted Mr. Suri and his family. Instantly they were notified that during the weeklong journey, the captain would receive them at his table at their convenience. Over a year earlier, Grace Kelly had sailed with the same vessel, using the same route to reach Monaco and marry Prince Rainier III.

Soraya had her own room, next to the suite of her parents. She was eager to visit the moving city and more specifically the library and pool area on the lido deck. She had already concluded to regularly rush to the library, grab some books, and read them either in her own room or next to the swimming pool. From her window, she could see the beauty of the infinite ocean and, despite the unbelievable scope of the ocean liner, felt the power of the waves. She distinctly enjoyed the *shlap* clatter as well as the up-and-down movements of their contact with the water. From time to time, she could differentiate another moving object, but far away since the ocean was vast.

She received her first lessons of hydro and aerodynamics from her talented father and understood that air and water behaved in similar ways. Mr. Suri described the notion of density of materials as well as the thrust and drag forces that guided the drives of objects that sailed or flew. In response to his daughter's query, he described that not only the cruise of the vessel created waves, but there were three main reasons for their formation. Soraya was astounded to learn that friction of wind with water, the attraction force between the moon and the earth, as well as natural calamities like eruption of volcanoes and earthquakes or man-made disasters such as nuclear tests underwater could generate mammoth waves, and their intensity depended on the force of the cause. Some explanations were way above her head, but she nevertheless strove to comprehend.

Recalling the howling of sirens in Washington, television programs, and school instructions on how to seek protection in case of an attack, she then quizzed her father for hours about what a nuclear bomb was and how it was made. She felt very sad for the people of Hiroshima and Nagasaki. Not only was she determined to help people, but she felt relieved to comprehend that her father was not a nuclear engineer but a lawyer who defended legality. Sometimes she looked for hours at the unlimited sea.

At their dinner with the captain, she was smartly dressed. Though she already liked bouffant hairstyles, that evening her massive hair was tied up behind her head with a beautiful chignon, adorned by a small white rose. The captain was a refined gentleman and soon had to answer questions.

"Where is your cockpit, Captain?" Soraya inquired.

"My lady," he replied, "in a vessel, it is called the Great Cabin. It is on the top floor."

"Can I visit you there?" she pressed him.

"Of course! I will send an officer tomorrow morning to guide you," the captain offered.

"How do you see at night? It is very dark, the ocean," Soraya probed again.

"I do not see, my lady! My vessel watches all around."

She was puzzled! The captain gently elucidated that the eyes of the cruiser were called radar, and they sent piercing invisible waves at all times and recorded their contact with any object. This was how they determined what was going on around the ship and at what distance. And if there were any hazards at the horizon, the captain decided on measures to opt for. Soraya was mesmerized to recognize that there were waves that someone observed, others that were felt, and the rest were imperceptible. On sunny days during the journey, she invited her father to take her to the lido deck for a chat.

When they attained Gibraltar, she was surprised how time had elapsed so quickly. The rock that resembled the back of an elephant was discernible in the distance. She was fascinated to realize that the exact name of the mountain was *Jabal Tariq*, named after the famous Muslim commander Tariq Ibn Ziyad, who crossed the African continent from Ceuta to reach mainland Spain at the beginning of the eighth century. In response to her curiosity, Mr. Suri patiently and passionately lectured on the world's geopolitics and the resulting rivalries of empires and religions.

She was captivated and stupefied at the same time. Why did people who believed in the same God destroy each other? And why did each religion assert possessing the whole veracity at the expense of others? But then she recalled her father's statement that all faiths were the same, that only people made them different. She was, however, tormented when she learned about the crusades of Christian and Muslim rulers. Soraya did not stop perusing whatever she unearthed in the vessel's library or asking her father to expound on the madness of crusaders who massacred millions of Christians, Jews, and Muslims in the name of their own legitimacies. Her father had taught her that God was unique, all-powerful, and merciful, and that he belonged to all humanity on earth and other beings in the universes. Her best friends in school were Jewish, Christian, and Hindu. The unanswered question in her mind was why God permitted an angel to become Satan to inculcate misdeeds in the minds and hearts of some people, who then committed unpardonable crimes in the name of their religions or anything that suited them.

At their destination, Mr. Zamir Suri did not stay in Naples city but moved straight to the Bosco de Medici Resort in Pompeii, conceived by the Palomba family to combine tourism with the physical and emotional welfare of the guests. They visited the ruins of a majestic Roman city that was transformed into ashes in the year 79 by the sudden eruption of the Mount Vesuvius volcano, just weeks after the death of Emperor Vespasian and takeover by his son Titus in Rome. The entire population of Pompeii perished under extremely hot dust particles. Soraya was amazed to learn that the volcano was still active and the last eruption had taken place more than a decade earlier. Alfredo, the manager, was pleased to demonstrate the antiseismic structures of the resort that prevented the building from collapsing. She was informed that the city had meanwhile developed an impressive volcano eruption alert mechanism. Though it would not save the city from another massive eruption, at least it would warn people to escape and withdraw in time.

In the morning of their last day in Pompeii, Soraya added fruits to her breakfast. Among them all, she preferred pomegranate, watermelon, and mango. Her thoughts were with some sixteen thousand men, women, and children who became cinders within seconds, so abrupt was the ferocity of the volcano. What they might have gone through before perishing and whether they felt any pain were questions that anguished her. She felt their despair and shared her feelings with her father. He expounded that the passage from life to death was extremely short; however, the period leading to the instant determined the suffering of those who faced it. In his opinion, people who succumbed to the heat, dust, and lava of Mount Vesuvius might not have agonized a lot as the event was so sudden. She was somehow relieved, but still her heart had a strange palpitation. Her father noticed and wished to change the theme of the conversation.

Mr. Suri took a deep breath and announced that the former king and queen of Afghanistan expected them in Rome. Soraya leaped and ran to her father, encircling his wide shoulders with her tiny arms. She was going to meet the royal couple who had indelible significance in her family's life. She had basic knowledge about their efforts to propel the country to the sphere of respected states with clearly defined policies and reasonable economies. They had failed for lack of comprehension of their own society and due to foreign intervention. She began quizzing her father about the lifestyle of the former king and queen.

A car with a chauffeur waited outside the Bosco de Medici Resort. Mr. Zamir Suri had opted to voyage through coastal highways. They passed Naples, Pozzuoli, and Gaeta before having a relaxed lunch on the second floor of Terracina's Bottega Sarra restaurant. Soraya loved the modernized traditional Italian food. She was struck to realize that pasta was an integral part of each dish. The flavor of Italian food with the use of condiments and garlic was special for her, and the sparkling water was succulent. The chef was generous and offered his best lobster to the guests. Soraya and her father had a quick walk through the Roman Forum, ruins of the four-sided arch, and the front of the Capitol. The family arrived in Rome later in the evening and dwelled in Villa San Pio in the heart of the city, a few blocks from the Tiber River. The choice of the hotel was intentional to make the visit of the ancient sites of Roman glory and prestige easier. Soraya went to bed early, excited that she would meet the next day the famous

Queen Soraya of Afghanistan, her namesake who very long ago had the courage to be seen unveiled in public.

The former king and queen received them personally at the door of their villa. Both were most kind and gracious. Soraya was astounded to see an elegant lady with green eyes! She instantly felt closer to her and walked behind the two couples. She sensed that the king looked frail. Mr. Suri occupied a sofa next to the king. At the request of the queen, Soraya sat on her left side and gazed at the royal couple delicately. King Amanullah Khan had lost his hair but not his distinction and allure. His wife had distinguished features and was dressed in dark green attire. But Soraya intuited the sadness of their souls.

After the usual courtesies, debate turned quickly to political issues. The former king desired Mr. Suri's opinion about the country's evolution, as well as the East-West rivalries in his beloved land. As a seasoned lawyer and judge, Mr. Suri was cautious. But the former king seemed up-front and voiced his deep concern for the future of his country. He believed Zaher Shah was too soft and Daoud Khan dreadfully ambitious, fearing that the latter would commit the madness of forcibly implementing his views. He further underlined that Zaher Shah's father should not have instated an era of terror and massacred countless numbers of people, including Amir Habibullah Kalakani. He specifically referred to the assassination of valorous nationalists who had served under his command during the independence war against the British Empire. He lamented the duplicity of King Zaher Shah's father, who had created more division in the country. There was no doubt in the mind of the former king that his own downfall had been as a result of the rivalry between the Soviet Union, which was among the first countries to recognize the independent Afghanistan, and the British, who never absolved Afghans for their stern resistance to the deeds of their empire. He believed that boundaries between India and Pakistan were a reflection of the Durand Line, aimed at dividing people and families in order to germinate the seeds of eternal discord.

Queen Soraya proposed more social discussion as in her opinion, politics in Afghanistan had always led to tragedies. The life of an Afghan family in Washington was reviewed. She revealed that the king had missed his lunch when inspecting the school where he had noted the young Zamir Suri. He had later on professed to the queen that if his country had a few more similar talents, the future would have looked brighter. The former king was impressed by Mr. Suri, who at the age of only thirty-six had become the chief justice of his country, and stressed that he was right in his assessment when he first saw him in the high school. The moment was opportune for the little twelve-year-old Soraya to intervene.

"I liked the watch Your Majesty gave to my father," she said.

"I am glad, my child, the former king averred. "We had our reward too as he became one of the brightest sons of our country."

"I wanted so much to meet Your Majesties and thank God for having made it possible," Soraya said.

"Thank you, my darling," the former queen said. "What would you like to do when you grow up?" she inquired.

"I want to be like my father," Soraya innocently responded.

"We have learned that you play piano," the queen said.

Soraya was guided to the Steinway grand piano at the extreme corner of the living area, where she played her favorite, *Für Elise* by Beethoven.

In the ensuing conversation, Soraya asked the queen if she was indeed born in Syria. She confirmed it and elucidated that her grandfather was exiled from Afghanistan by the then king, the notorious Abdur Rahman Khan, whose brutality and disdain toward others than his own family was renowned. They were refugees in Damascus and lived in poverty for a long time before reaching Turkey. However, the queen's father gave high priority to their education, and she owed the crown to her father and his tutoring. The queen further advised that their second and current exile in Rome had been very painful. Little Soraya was proud of her own father and felt bereaved for the king and queen. She feared being a refugee one day. The former queen fancied this child, who inspired her with extreme innocence and intelligence. She held her hand all the way to the gate and gave two warm kisses on her checks. The former queen and king of Afghanistan left an indelible mark in Soraya's memory for the years to come for their kindness and humility. She liked their human qualities above all.

The Zamir Suri family toured Rome in the next two days and visited Palatino, the Circo Massimo, the Colosseum, the Roman Forum, and the Trevi Fountain. Soraya was fascinated by the history of the Roman Empire, the rise of Christianity, and the takeover by the Ottoman Empire. Her father, once again, was an excellent lecturer. She was most intrigued by the twelve Caesars and, among all, found Jules vicious, Augustus brave, and Nero extremely stupid. She felt sorry for Cleopatra and her Egyptian Empire and asked many times whether she loved Julius Caesar or Marks Antony. Her father seemed perplexed, underlining finally that she might not have cherished any but her own power. To save Egypt from the might of Romans, she might have pretended to fancy any Roman general or envoy. Soraya felt sad for such people and asked her father why Nero put ablaze half of Rome for a poetic inspiration that never occurred. Mr. Suri stated that deranged rulers were realities of history, not only in Europe but everywhere, and he gave additional examples of Emperor Caligula of Rome, Ivan IV of Russia, Adolf Hitler of Germany, Genghis Khan of Mongolia, and even the son of Mirwais Hotak, who in 1722 massacred about a hundred thousand individuals in his siege of Isfahan, the capital of the Iranian Safavid Empire. Their visit to Rome ended with the pilgrimage of Trevi Fountain. Not only did Soraya like the place as well as the adjacent tiny streets, cafés, and restaurants, but she liked the symbol of throwing pennies. She moved around the pond, repeatedly projecting to the water all the coins she possessed in her pockets and wishing good luck and health for her father.

A day later, Mr. Suri and his family landed in Geneva on a Swissair flight around midday. They proceeded to the Beau-Rivage Hotel, an establishment with rich history. This is where the famous Austrian empress Elisabeth of Wittelsbach, called Sisi, stayed and lost her life in September 1898. Soraya had been on the seashores in the United States, but the view of the calm, blue Lake Geneva, with mountains full of snow in the background, was unique. She just fell in love with the city.

In the evening, Mr. Suri took the family for a tour of the city in a carriage. They then sauntered on the Quai Mont Blanc along the lake and passed Quai Wilson to reach the Mon-Repos Park. In the middle of the nineteenth century, Philippe Plantamour had devised the site and constructed his mansion on it. One hundred years later, the park was wider, with a slope full of flowers, trees, plants, and wonderful alleys overlooking the lake. Soraya was dressed in a white summer robe, promenading next to her father. She was curious about everything and inquisitive about Switzerland's ability to remain neutral during the Second World War while all of Europe was overrun by German Nazi tyranny. Mr. Suri sat with her on a bench while his wife enjoyed a stunning summer afternoon ambling the park lanes.

History and logic were among Soraya's favorite topics, though her mother had always been keen to tutor her on haute cuisine and fashion. At home and outside, she inspired honesty and candor. Mr. Suri was never in haste when conversing with his daughter. He expounded that between 1940 and 1944, Switzerland had an untenable situation as the country was torn apart between the Axis Powers (Nazi Germany, Fascist Italy, and Japan) and the Allies (Britain, France, Australia, Canada, New Zealand, India, the Soviet Union, China, and the United States of America). Geographically, it was encircled and encased by Axis Powers territories. The country had few options and became a perfect base of espionage for all. Its policy of neutrality was threatened when some pro-Nazi high officials and officers such as Andre Beguin, Arthur Fanjallaz, and Eugene Bircher formed the Swiss Patriotic Federation and numerous Allied airmen were prevented from escaping to northern France, which had just been freed from the Nazi grip. The Allies and Nazi Germany were both exerting pressure on Switzerland; parts of the country were even bombed. The refugee protection policy of the country was one of the most controversial, though it had harbored more Jews fleeing extermination than any other country in Europe. But their self-sustainability during the harsh years of war had been a remarkable success. The federal foreign minister, Marcel Pilet-Golaz, with his Hitler-looking hairstyle and mustache was not trusted by the Allies and was incapable of defending his country's stance. The end of the war was a massive relief for Switzerland, leading to the departure of Pilet-Golaz and the arrival of the charismatic Max Petitpierre, who then ruled over Swiss diplomacy for the next seventeen years and reshaped it.

Soraya heeded charily and occasionally interrupted her father to better understand the context. Her brain was sharp and grasped all essentials instantly. She felt sorry for the tiny, mountainous Switzerland caught in the middle of Nazi, Fascist, or occupied territories but somehow admired the tenacity of its people to resist the German Nazi regime at all costs. The family had an early dinner at the *Perle du Lac* on the bank of the lake, a scenic establishment intimately linked with the creator of Rolex watches.

In the ensuing days, Mr. Suri and his family visited the *Palais des Nations* and numerous other historic spots on the left flank of the lake. The final day before departure was devoted to shopping. They entered the Patek Philippe on the Rue du Rhône. The manager was a delightful man who patiently responded to questions.

"Father, we choose for each other?" Soraya softly suggested.

"Let it be so!" Mr. Suri replied.

"I recommend this watch for you, but the wristlet must be of thin mahogany leather," she proudly said.

"Why so?" Mr. Suri teased his daughter.

"Well, you see, Father," she insisted, "the watch is a thin golden beauty. And this bracelet is too thick! I am sure the manager would agree."

"I concur with you, my darling." Mr. Suri smiled. "Now, I offer you this pearl necklace."

"Oh, no! That is too expensive, and I am only twelve years old," she argued.

"No, my child. Nothing is equal to the beauty of your eyes and mind. I insist and hope it will always remind you of our visit to this country, which is a paradise on earth," Mr. Suri explained while caressing her cheeks gently.

On their way back to Beau-Rivage, Soraya was weeping of joy. She twigged how much her father loved her and was the last to be ready for dinner as she was trying the exceptional set of pearls with various outfits. They were all perfectly spherical, of the same dimension and color. Mr. Suri, for his part, was stunned by the choice of his watch. It was a Calatrava 1956, the fine yellow golden object of rare simplicity and splendor.

The flight to New Delhi was smooth. The captain of SS *Constitution* had offered several books to Soraya, and she devoured them in her comfortable seat of the Swissair flight. In the aircraft, Soraya felt so at home because the beautifully red-dressed staff of the Boeing 727 were candid, warm, and professional. The Swiss perfection exercised in this long-distance flight left all the passengers rapt with wonder.

Mr. Suri was surprised to notice the Indian protocol officers welcoming the family at the airport. They were driven to the Claridge's Hotel, where he was informed that Prime Minister Jawaharlal Nehru, who also assumed the function of foreign minister, wished to meet him. While studying in Bombay, Mr. Suri had never met Nehru and did not know him. In fact, Vijaya Laxshmi Pandit, Nehru's sister who served in New York at the same time as Mr. Suri, had strongly recommended her brother have a private discussion with this exceptional Afghan. The encounter was set for the day after in the prime minister's office, located in the south block of the Secretariat Building.

Nehru was in his late sixties and had been in office for nearly a decade. His only child and daughter, Indira Gandhi, who was formally her father's personal assistant but in reality dealt with foreign affairs, was in attendance. She was ten years younger than Mr. Zamir Suri. Nehru received the guest in his private office. Kashmiri *kahwa chai* (black tea with milk and spices), green tea with cardamom, *charmaghzi sheerpera* (an Afghan soft candy with walnut), and numerous other Indian confections were on the delicately ornamented coffee table. Mr. Suri found Nehru and his daughter most alluring, gracious, and clever. They treated him as a genuine friend.

Nehru began. "Mr. Suri, we apologize for having disturbed you while you pay a private visit to our country. My sister, whose judgment I respect, has great admiration for you. We will make sure that your stay will be most enjoyable."

"Thank you, Mr. Prime Minister. My family's association with India goes back to the fifteenth and sixteenth centuries. Therefore, I have loved ones in your country, and my emotions are boundless."

"Indeed, Mr. Suri! We owe your family the glory of Agra, as well as the foundation of Ludhiana and so many other wonders, including the Lodhi Gardens here in Delhi," Prime Minister Nehru acknowledged. "We have been briefed about your new function in

Kabul. Our countries need to attend to common gauntlets caused by the formation of Pakistan and the longing of the western powers to dominate us using different stratagems."

"Mr. Prime Minister, I am not yet involved with politics or diplomacy in my country. But as an individual, let me point out that you endorsed the creation of Pakistan. They are recognized by the international community. Therefore, we all have to live with the consequences. The peoples of the region have not changed because new borders were designed. They need peace, security, and stability to prosper," Mr. Suri stressed.

"I agree! The British created Pakistan, not us. We consider it a punishment. And what you just stated are fundamentals of the Congress Party. Based on these doctrines, India is ready to back without reservation the new prime minister of Afghanistan, his team, and his government. The world must realize that India is an effective democracy, while Pakistan is ruled by ruthless military generals who are recyclers of the British Empire army."

"I am confident that Your Excellency has imparted the offer to the government of Afghanistan through diplomatic avenues."

"I comprehend you, Mr. Suri. Indira and I value you and your family. Please remember that you will always have a home in India."

The confab was friendly and forthright and lasted for nearly two hours. Nehru had full knowledge of Mr. Suri's bright studies at the University of Bombay. He acknowledged that most of his senior colleagues who had studied in the same institution spoke highly of him.

Indira Gandhi contributed keenly in the discussion. She was enchanting and appeared to be acting as her father's hostess. There were some parallels between her and Soraya. Both were unique children of their illustrious fathers. Their intelligence and courage were evidenced from the instant of their encounter. However, age and personal character separated them. Contrary to Soraya's warmth and friendly approach, Indira seemed of a cold and distant nature. Mr. Suri contemplated such a bright future for his daughter, but his mind was preoccupied as to whether the Afghan political and social misfits would permit educated women to thrive and serve their country. For the rest of Mr. Suri and his family's stay in India, the office of the prime minister had organized tours of Delhi, Agra, and Jaipur, the famous golden triangle.

In Delhi, the Suri family was taken to visit the Red Fort, Chandni Chowk, Old Fort, Qutab Munar, Humayun's Tomb, Gurudwara Bangla Sahib, and many other memorable places, including the Lodhi Gardens. Soraya was enthralled by the Red Fort or *Lal Qila*, a breathtaking monument constructed in 1648 by the fifth Mughal emperor, Shah Jehan, who founded Delhi. Lal Qila served as the royal residence for nearly two hundred years. It is where the last Mughal emperor, Bahadur Shah II, was captured in 1858 by the British invaders and exiled to Rangoon; he died in misery and despair, taking with him to the grave the secrets of his illustrious predecessors. Soraya was also captivated by the architecture of Shri Digambar Jain Lal Mandir, located just opposite of the Red Fort. This amazing red sandstone temple was originally built in 1656 under Shah Jehan by the Agrawal Jain merchants. Both monuments, representing the harmony of Hindu and Muslim cultures, were close to Chandni Chowk, Moonlight Square, the oldest and perhaps busiest business area in India, which had its roots back to the seventeenth century. The topography of the Jamuna River flow in this part of the country triggered Shah Jehan to establish his capital, Shahjahanabad, now called Delhi.

Agra, a city also located on the bank of the Jamuna River, was established some two hundred kilometers south of Delhi in 1475 by Raja Badal Singh, a brave Rajput king. Agra was very special for

Mr. Suri as one of his renowned ancestors, Sultan Sikandar Lodhi, who ruled India from 1488 to 1517, was the first emperor of Afghan origin to make it his capital in 1504. Mr. Suri was mesmerized to be there and was even serving as tourist guide for his family. He knew every historic, architectural, social, and political detail of the city. Soraya was entranced with the Taj Mahal and the love story between Emperor Shah Jehan and his favorite wife, Mumtaz Begum, the sudden death of whom led to the creation of this most cherished marvel of the world. The construction of the ivory white marble memorial and its unique gardens was finished in 1643 to host the tomb of Mumtaz and that of the emperor. Soraya was, however, saddened to learn that Soraya Banu Begum, one of the emperor's daughters, had died at the age of only seven years. The Zamir Suri family also visited the Agra Fort, a red sandstone citadel that had been home to illustrious makers and shakers of India, including Babur, the founder of the Mughal dynasty and more importantly, his son Emperor Humayun who was crowned in the fort in 1530. Soraya was staggered to see the unique role and importance of red sandstone in Indian culture. The visit to Fatehpur Sikri, an enormous palace built in 1659 by the famous Mughal Emperor Akbar, was also demonstrative of the positive cultural and historic values that rulers of Central Asian and Afghan genesis had brought to India. Her father disclosed that they had also committed atrocities and looted the wealth of local sovereigns, temples, and individuals.

In Jaipur or the Pink City, the capital of Rajasthan, founded in 1727 by Maharaja Jai Singh II, the Suri family visited Nahargarh Fort, Hawa Mahal, the Amber Palace, and many other wonders, gorgeous ancient palaces, and very colorful people. Jaipur was the heart of Rajputana, the land of the Rajputs, the brave, handsome, courageous princes who have glorious chapters in Indian history. Soraya could not believe when she visited the Hawa Mahal, the Palace of Breeze. It was constructed by Maharaja Sawai Pratap Singh for the women of his court to observe street festivals. Some 950 windows artfully designed on a five-story arch overlooked the marketplace. The architecture was most innovative, permitting natural airflow. In the lower two levels, behind each window, there was a private chamber, leading to a patio, while the upper three floors were conceived with only one rear room. The Nahargarh Fort offered the most spectacular view of the city. Soraya lingered on the roof terrace of the fort, listening to her father, who passionately elucidated the common traits of Indian Rajputs and Afghan Pashtuns. The place appeared so serene and the surroundings stunning. Soraya sat next to her father under the shade of a broken wall that certainly had a glorious past and inquired why all faiths were expanded by the force of swords and use of ruses. Their veracities should have been enough to magnetize disciples voluntarily. Mr. Suri described multiple reasons that had led to invasions of foreign territories in the past, but religious beliefs had often been invoked to justify them. As God did not speak to humankind to express his consent or disagreement, might and vigor dominated sanity and humanity.

A few days later, the Suri family landed in Kandahar, south of Afghanistan. They went straight to the clay house of Zamir Suri's sister, whose husband served as deputy governor of the province. It was situated next to the King Canal, the artificial waterway. It was a poignant reunion with Southwest Afghanistan, a spot that was the reason of his pride and suffering. The souvenirs of his time as chief justice and his undeniable support to the Helmand River projects were still fresh in his mind. He had not forgotten the so-called accusation and house detention initiated by communist politicians and endorsed by the palace.

Three days later, Mr. Suri had to leave. "It is time for me to depart for Kabul," he said. "However, I would like my family to remain here for a while."

"What is the matter, Zamir?" his brother-in-law queried.

"I want my wife and child to stay here under your good care till I give you the signal."

"I desire to grasp your motives," the brother-in-law insisted.

"The royal family has so far been notorious for breaking their own vows and oaths. I do not know what is going to happen next."

"What do you wish to convey, Zamir? Be explicit!"

"Look!" Mr. Suri resolutely addressed his brother-in-law. "Should anything happen to me, please take my family to safety, first to India and then to Geneva in Switzerland. This is the bottom line," he concluded.

"Enough! I understand," his brother-in-law acknowledged.

The next day, Mr. Suri asked to have tea with *quaimaq*, a special clotted cream favored for breakfast in Turkey, Caucasian countries, Central Asia, Iran, and Afghanistan. Soraya understood that she would not accompany her father. Though she was advised that he went to Kabul to arrange their house in New City before the family reunited, she discerned a heavy atmosphere. She sat anxiously just next to her father, asking questions to apprehend better. However, he was lucid and convinced his daughter that there was no reason for concern. Mr. Suri proceeded to Kabul in the late morning.

The mood in the capital was stern. Most compared Daoud Khan, the most erratic breathing member of the Afghan royal family, to two of his uncles, King Zaher Shah's father and particularly King Zaher Shah's eldest uncle, commonly termed the Machiavelli of the country, who administered Afghanistan with an iron fist for a time. Claims ranging from the most loved leader to someone who was impulsive and capable of pounding flowed among the population. There was, however, one certainty, and that was his strength and stubbornness. He surely dominated everyone else in the family. The creation of Pakistan and its membership in the SEATO and CENTO military pacts had indeed exacerbated the political, social, and even economic situations in the region. King Zaher Shah, his family, and other leaders were all bewildered as to how to maneuver the country between the Soviet Union and the United States, two indisputable giants of the time. The royal family was evidently divided: while the king believed in a neutral Afghanistan, his prime minister, Daoud Khan, deemed that the Afghan-Soviet Union axis would safeguard improved prospects for his country and contribute toward its economic development. King Zaher Shah called on the leaders of the Soviet Union and Turkey in the course of the year 1957. And Prime Minister Daoud Khan toured Austria, Czechoslovakia, Turkey, Poland, Egypt, Burma, and the People's Republic of China, where Mao Zedong personally offered a special banquet in his honor. Both aimed at garnering support for the untenable position of their country.

Mr. Zamir Suri was chauffeured from the south in a vehicle that his friend Ali Khan had offered; he attained Kabul late in the evening and went straight to his house. Abai was waiting and had prepared all the dishes that Mr. Suri favored. She was weeping of happiness and joy, often asking about *Emerald*.

The next day, Mr. Suri was received jointly by two of his friends, Ali Khan, now deputy prime minister, and Naim Khan, the foreign minister of the country, in the residence of the latter.

Naim Khan initiated the talk. "Zamir, we are glad to see you back. His Majesty the King and the prime minister join us to welcome you home."

"Thank you, Your Highness. I am gratified and eager to understand what is expected from me," Mr. Suri replied.

"Zamir is staunch to his reputation, Naim!" Ali Khan joked. "He always ranks work-related concerns first."

"Perhaps this is most appropriate—we will have tea afterward," Naim Khan replied. "We have invited you to assist us prepare the visit of the prime minister to the United States next year. Our independence and the restitution of lost land is our priority. The visit of the prime minister to the United States will be a make-or-break event. We know you can facilitate making it a success. Once this is done, we intend to appoint you as our ambassador to the United Kingdom. As of tomorrow, you will have your office next to mine and directly report to me."

"This is an honor, Your Highness. Indeed, our future will depend on what we accomplish now," Mr. Suri acknowledged.

Meanwhile in the south, the Suri family was waiting for the hint to proceed to Kabul or leave for India. The second morning, Soraya woke up early and noticed a number of young, lofty men dressed in a unique manner. Long rifles and full western bandolier bullet belts hung on their shoulders. They looked handsome and alluring. She was intrigued and desired to learn why they were there and what they spoke about. She hurried in and found her aunt.

"Who are these people, aunt? They have guns on their shoulders," she stated.

"They will serve as your escort, if need be," her aunt innocently replied.

"Our escorts? We will join my father and do not need these people," Soraya maintained.

"We do not know yet! You may still need them," she said while dashing away.

The aunt suddenly realized that she had spoken too much with a curious and intelligent young girl, who was now perplexed and in search of an answer. But it was too late! Soraya then interrogated her aunt's husband to seek clarification. He had no choice and revealed that they might finally go back to India and wait for Mr. Suri to join them there. She did not like the idea but wished to probe her mother. The plan was defined. In case of any hassle, these young armed men would chaperone Mr. Suri's family to Jamnagar in Gujarat via Baluchistan. It was indeed a perilous enterprise, which required nearly a week's journey on foot and by car, camelback, and boat to reach India. Fortunately, they were soon advised that the family could safely proceed to Kabul. The Suri family felt relieved and remained two more weeks in the south, where King Ahmad Shah had at the age of twenty-five become the first Durani sovereign of the country and had formalized the foundation of Afghanistan as a country. His conquests took him to Bukhara, where he received in 1768 the sacred cloak of the prophet Mohammad from the hands of Emir Murad Beg, as well as Delhi, where his decisive victory in the third contention of Panipat in 1761 safeguarded a long-lasting future for Muslims in India.

Soraya's cousin acted as guide to the Suri family. In town, they mainly visited the Hindu Chowk, Kabul Darwaza, Eid Gah, Chowk Charsoo, and tomb of Ahmad Shah, where the cloak of Prophet Mohammad is exposed. Soraya wanted to visit the irrigation dams and nearby villages. The manager of the largest *oeuvre* was overjoyed to see the daughter of the man who had promoted realization of the gigantic power plant. With his new open -top GAZ 69 Soviet jeep, he offered to take her all around. She could not believe that such a green lake could exist in the heart of dry hills.

At her entreaty she was escorted farther south. People lived in a horrible state. There was no clean and potable water. Girls filled their clay jars in a runnel that was also used by animals. Nobody comprehended what school was and why girls should learn, as they were supposed to marry, work at home, and give birth to the new generation. She witnessed in one house an old ill lady being treated by a traditional cleric who was the "doctor" of the hamlet. The ugly bearded man poured a huge quantity of his saliva on the face of the poor elderly woman, spitting all around and claiming that her pains would be released. Soraya did not find it hygienic at all! People did not wish to send their boys to school either as it was far away. Disheartened by the level of poverty and the plight of women and young girls, Soraya was already reflecting on questions to raise with her father.

At the outskirts of the villages, she discerned black tents and animals all around. Ferocious dogs were used to guard both. In torrid heat, she was astonished to see the dark-colored rudimentary dwellings and inquired who they belonged to. For the first time, she learned about Kochis, a nomadic population who moved with their belongings and animals in search of green pastures and earnings. She wanted to visit some. It was not easy, however, as all the men, the decision makers, were out. But as a little girl, she was nevertheless allowed to join a tent. It was pathetic and looked like human beings and animals shared the same space to rest. The women and girls were gorgeously beautiful but in a status of desolation. Everything looked dirty and much like a biblical situation. The scarcity of water made it worse. Soraya was heartbroken and did not know whom to blame for the callous state of these human beings.

Mr. Zamir Suri voyaged himself to convoy his family to Kabul. They had lunch in Ghazni; this mystic city was once the center of art, culture, and might. Mahmoud Ghaznavi was the first emperor of Afghan origin who conquered India, Central Asia, and Iran. His capital, the legacy of his glory, was set afire and burned down by his rival Allaoudin Ghori in 1150, and the engulfed secrets of a splendid past came to an end abruptly. At least sixty thousand inhabitants of Ghazni were massacred in the process.

Mr. Suri's old Hazara friend and colleague Hussein Ali and his family had organized a private celebration in *Balahessar*, the hilltop castle of the city, destroyed by years of conflict and the carelessness of governors. Soraya loved the environment. Red-colored handwoven carpets as well as gorgeous mattresses and embroidery cushions covered the ground under the shade of high walls. The kindhearted couple and their beautiful three children with fine skin and cute red cheeks attracted her admiration. Hussein Ali and his wife offered Hazaragi *pirki,* similar to *bolani,* served with yogurt marinated in garlic and menthe, as well as *dalda*, a sort of crushed boiled wheat with lamb meat, butter, and red fried onion. It was a simple but very earnest gathering that reminded Soraya about the kindhearted and hospitable Hazara population of her country.

In Kabul, Abai was the happiest woman in the world, cuddling and caressing Soraya regularly. She recognized that the little, skinny *Emerald* had now become a beautiful teen with stunningly bright green eyes.

Mr. Suri was occupied briefing the king, the prime minister, the foreign minister, and plentiful other bigwigs. He was entreated to attend every council of ministers' session. Naim Khan judged Mr. Zamir Suri a friend and ally. In fact, he and Ali Khan had shielded him from opponents within the palace. He yearned to persuade the prime minister to back King Zaher Shah in his pursuit of neutrality in the region.

Soraya's mother swiftly linked with old contacts and soon had to split the big house into several quarters to ensure that all who wished to meet her husband—state luminaries, tribal elders, and common individuals—were cared for accordingly. The library once more became the ultimate refuge for Mr. Suri's solemn discussions. This was where Soraya as often as possible sought moments of private chat with her father.

The first Thursday at dusk after Mr. Suri had attended to all the visitors, she joined him.

"Father, I am proud of you," she affirmed.

"What happened, my child?" Mr. Suri inquired.

"I visited the gigantic dam and irrigation system in the south, and the manager took me all around. It is so beautiful," she exclaimed. "He explained to me that without your involvement, nothing could have been realized. I also went to several villages too and conversed with nomad girls."

"Yes, the dams and irrigation system were good projects," he avowed. "Were you with your mother?"

"No, my cousin took me. But, Father, women and girls have a horrible life there," she lamented. "They are prisoners of their brothers, husbands, and other male members of their families."

"It is the same everywhere in this country, my child! And it will take time to transform the culture," he acknowledged.

"It is sad, Father! Someone should help them."

As usual, a lengthy discussion ensued, and finally she gave an earnest kiss to the forehead of Mr. Suri before proceeding to her own room. She vowed that when she grew up, she would care for those who had no protection.

September 1957 was a hectic month for the Suri family because of the Afghan Independence Day festivities, during which practically all their relatives were dropping in from Logar, south, east, and north to Kabul. Afghan cultural doctrines imply that they are to be lodged by kinfolk who dwell in the capital. Abai and her daughters were engaged in the kitchen the whole day, while male servants took charge of the provisions and attending to visitors. The residence of Mr. Suri looked like a hotel. Though Afghans acquired their self-rule from the British on August 19, celebrations were taking place for ten full days nearly a month later to have more clement weather.

Afghanistan has always been at the crossroads of legendary invaders. They have all been enraged because of the ferocity of the inhabitants of this land to defend themselves. Consequently, the human, economic, and cultural burdens of every conquest and subsequent independence have been ruinous. Total demolitions of ancient wonder cities such as Bactra, Kabura, and Varmayana, as well as Bamiyan and Ghazni, are just a few illustrations of the ruthlessness of culture and value destroyers. These cradles of civilization were too simply maimed. This is why in the nineteenth and twentieth centuries amid Russian-British rivalry, neither wanted to stay in Afghanistan, though the tsars appeared more astute. It was an excellent buffer zone where the "great game" was played, and it has been so ever since. While Russians never defied Afghans before 1978 on the battlefield, the British confronted them three times during their occupation of the Indian subcontinent, modeling the current geopolitics of the region. Mr. Suri loved probing the corollaries of British deeds, and Soraya was a most devoted listener.

She learned quickly that the recent history of Afghanistan had been determined by these three battles, which would still forge the stances of generations of Afghan and British administrations to come. The conquest of India by the British Empire primarily commenced indirectly in 1757 through the East India Company and its private armies; it endured for a century. From 1858 on, London took charge of the precious colony directly for nearly another hundred years. The shattering crush of the East India Company troops in the first Anglo-Afghan war, known also as Auckland's Folly, certainly prompted a major change of policy.

Amir Dost Mohammad Khan from the Barakzai Durani Pashtun ethnic group ruled Afghanistan twice, from 1826 to 1839 and from 1845 to 1863. In 1837, he lost his winter capital, Peshawar, to the valiant Ranjit Singh of Panjab and asked futilely for British help; the Romanov court proffered backing and dispatched an envoy to negotiate modalities. Lord Auckland, the governor-general of India, dreaded the arrival of Russians and orchestrated an invasion of Afghanistan in 1839, ousted the king, and enthroned his puppet Shah Shuja of the Sadozai Durani Pashtun tribe. Dost Mohammad sought refuge in Bukhara, already deemed a Russian zone of influence. His young and heroic son Akbar Khan, who had gained fame by facing Ranjit Singh at the age of only twenty in the Battle of Jamrud, near Peshawar, led the resistance against the British. The arrogance of the British envoy Sir William McNaughten and his peculiar affront to Akbar Khan triggered the fury of Afghans that resulted in his death and the massacre of four thousand five hundred British and Indian army men as well as their twelve thousand followers. Only the assistant surgeon, William Brydon, was spared to apprise Lord Aukland. Shah Shuja, recognized as a traitor, was booted and killed too. This was perhaps the chief defeat of the British Empire.

Subsequently, Queen Victoria took charge of India directly, seeking vengeance. Three years later, Akbar Khan was murdered, apparently at British instigation and with the silent consent of his father. Afghans viewed it as an unpardonable tragedy and offense. Soraya asked why Lord Aukland did not face punishment or disciplinary measures by the queen for having caused such a disaster, both to Afghans and to his own people. She was thunderstruck to learn that most political and military mistakes went scot-free, even in developed countries. However, like all Afghans, she considered Akbar Khan as a valorous hero and Shah Shuja a spineless weakling, bowing to the exigencies of his masters.

The narration of the second Anglo-Afghan war provided to the twelve-year-old teen a different picture of geopolitics of her country. It lasted from 1878 to 1880 when the British Empire construed that

Dost Mohammad Khan's favorite son and successor, Sher Ali Khan, was stepping closer to Russians; he had rebuffed their *diplomatic delegation*, while the emissaries of Tsar Alexander II were received earlier. Learning from their debacle of the first Anglo-Afghan war, Lord Lytton, viceroy of India, ordered General Sir Frederick Roberts to muster nearly fifty thousand armed men. The Afghan king was vanquished and died of despair in the northern parts of the country while seeking Russian support. His son Ayub Khan led the Battle of Maiwand. The folklore tale relating to the killing in July 1880 of Malala on the battlefield by the British is perceived as another reprehensible calamity. Malala's poem states:

> *If you do not fall in the battle of Maiwand*
> *by God, my love, you will be remembered as a symbol*
> *of shame.*

It endures to be an eternal recitation among youngsters. Malala became the symbol of resistance against the British Empire and a cherished name for Afghan girls. Knowing the limitations on women in her society, Soraya queried how Malala fought the enemy as she was a girl. Her father candidly explained that she might not have taken part on the battlefield, but she encouraged warriors by her poems to the extent that the British considered her harmful to their interests and eliminated her. He emphasized to his daughter that words are also weapons used in a struggle, conflict, or war and often prove as efficient.

However, the third and last Anglo-Afghan war was the most captivating for Soraya as it involved the king and queen that she had just met in Rome. In April 1919, the British Empire army deliberately slaughtered over a thousand Indian nonviolent protestors in Amritsar, triggering an unprecedented strain in the subcontinent. The newly proclaimed king of Afghanistan, Amanullah Khan, under the political stewardship of his father-in-law, Mahmoud Beg Tarzi, and military advice of Ghulam Haidar Khan Charkhi and his sons, took advantage of the Amritsar Massacre and decided to invade British India. The young king in his maiden address asserted that, contrary to his ancestors, he would not accept orders from the British.

> *I have declared myself and my country entirely free, autonomous and independent both internally and externally. My country will hereafter be as independent a state as other states and powers of the world are. No foreign power will be allowed to a hair-breadth of right to interfere internally or externally with the affairs of Afghanistan.*

No one in the past had the courage to confront the British in their own yard. The initiative of King Amanullah Khan was appraised suicidal by many. He gambled and struck on May 3, 1919. Though he could only marshal fifty thousand soldiers, the fact that the British India elite troops were still scattered in Europe following the First World War and the fear of some twenty to thirty thousand skillful tribal men joining Amanullah Khan's army played to his advantage. British and Indian casualties soon became hefty and compelled the viceroy, Lord Chelmsford, to negotiate. The armistice was proclaimed on August 8, 1919, as an upshot of which the British Crown conceded total independence to Afghanistan within the Durand Line.

King Amanullah Khan was a modern ruler and instantly pioneered social, economic, and political reforms, particularly constitutional equal rights for women. Schools were unlocked to girls, educated women were bestowed jobs in different fields, and Afghan women commenced going into politics. Public libraries were opened to serve the common people. Queen Soraya became the icon of modernity and female emancipation. King Amanullah Khan's accession to the throne also coincided with the rise of Mustapha Kemal Ataturk in Turkey, whom the king's father-in-law admired as a modernizer and reformist in an Islamic society. New development plans were defined for Kabul, Kandahar, Jalalabad, and Mazar-e-Sharif. The famous

Darulaman Palace was constructed and connected to the city by a *Champs Elysées*-type wide avenue.

The king, however, propelled his reform program too far and fast in a deeply orthodox society that was not ready to embrace such revolutionary development steps without hurdles. European attire and hats were imposed on all, particularly the government workforce, virtually the only employment institution in the country. Women were *forced* to unveil just a few years after an independence war that was geared along national and religious values. Some even ridiculed him by placing empty half watermelons on their heads to demonstrate that while some aspects of the reforms were compatible with their customs, they could not afford their financial burden.

Unfortunately, King Amanullah Khan did not pay attention to the growing unhappiness and journeyed to Europe for several months between 1927 and 1928. He met with leaders of Egypt, Italy, France, Germany, the United Kingdom, Poland, the Soviet Union, and Turkey before returning to a tumultuous Afghanistan. It is believed that fearing the influence of the Soviet Union on the young Afghan sovereign following his state visit to Moscow, the British engineered the dropping of leaflets with the queen's picture in low-necked clothes, which stunned the ultraconservative religious leaders. The innovative king was openly criticized, and soon tens of thousands of people openly expressed their disdain. Some even alleged that London was again after retaliation for their defeats. Therefore, they fomented through their loyal religious leaders that the king and queen had become *kafir*, an expression also used for Muslims who turn down their religion. The king did not have ample time to defy the plot that definitely enjoyed the support of some members of his own larger family. He was finally ousted on January 14, 1929. With his exit, progress in Afghanistan halted. Mr. Suri had to console his daughter as Soraya wept for the destiny of so many good people. She was impressed by the kindness and simplicity of the former royal couple. In her own world and mind, she determined to study in the

United Kingdom and comprehend better the knots of international politics from a British perspective.

Mr. Suri was passionate about Afghan-British rapport. Throughout the independence festivities, his guests were relating to the three Anglo-Afghan wars with their own slants and soliciting his analysis on what could happen next. Some elderly still had fresh memories of their battle for independence. On the first day of celebrations, Soraya accompanied her father to the Ghazi Sports Stadium to watch a buzkashi game that was depicted to world public opinion by Joseph Kessel's *The Horsemen* and a 1971 Hollywood movie of the same name. She was staggered by the ability and agility of the riders as well as their animals and even scared for their safety. Each equestrian pushed his horse and his own talent to the limit of life and death. It was dazzling to observe the two competing teams struggling with a load of nearly ninety pounds while their horses galloped at a speed of over forty miles per hour. A simple gaffe meant fatality or at least paralysis.

She was also taken out two nights and enchanted by the illuminated city, huge crowd of people that ambled all around, and piles of fresh fruits, as well as the mobile food sellers with their offerings on large platters supported by wooden stools proposing most popular delights, while at the background she could see the smoke and inhale the sense of unforgettable Afghan kebabs. She noticed the illuminated mausoleum of King Zaher Shah's father on the hilltop. As the car drove by, she was astonished not to see many women, and those who partook were escorted by male members of their families. Huddled in small groups under their heavy veils, they resembled pieces of colorful rocks. The second evening, she was driven around the celebration area surrounded by large tents belonging to major government institutions that offered diverse forms of entertainment. In some, there were acrobats from neighboring countries, artists, and performers. She attended a concert of the famous Indian singer Mohammad Rafi in the main theatre—he had specially composed Dari songs for the occasion—before joining the family for a candid dinner.

Mr. Suri enrolled Soraya once again in the Malalai School. She was now a mellow young teen, who often reasoned with her instructors to get to the fundamentals of matters broached. Her eye color had turned into a mixture of green and blue, something very special. She was irritated that the teaching was perfunctory. Students had to recite word by word in their notes what the educator had stated. The stress was not on comprehension, but recitation. There was no opportunity to deliberate. However and perhaps contrary to other girls, she had her father and the enjoyable evening parleys, when he fostered substantive conversation. Teachers were respectful of Soraya, always fearing a challenge from this courageous child. Her fairness was recognized so much that some even sought her judgment and urged others to follow her example. She had made her mind up about Malala Maiwand and Queen Soraya; their ordeals were most deplorable. She knew Malala's poem word by word and was proud of having met the brightest queen of Afghanistan.

Mr. Suri attended plentiful closed-door get-togethers for preparation of the prime minister's visit to the United States. He counseled that the closer India-Soviet Union bond, compelling the United States to further back Pakistan, must be kept in mind by the prime minister. Around December 1957, the leadership of the country finally agreed that obvious ties with the Soviet Union were not in their interest and that an appeasement gesture toward Pakistan—"*the US boy*" as they used to call it—to soften the sharp edges of their incongruities was needed before Daoud Khan proceeded to Washington. Naim Khan and Ali Khan were indebted to Mr. Suri for having been a wise man to support the neutrality policy and advocate for a balanced approach between the two superpowers.

In February 1958, King Zaher Shah paid formal visits to Pakistan and India, underscoring in his private and public interventions the "traditionally neutral policy" of his country. Daoud Khan was pretentious, seeking too much esteem from the Americans. His obvious dislike of his ambassador to Washington, Mr. Hashem

Maiwandwal, put more pressure on Mr. Suri to negotiate directly with the Department of State or White House. On June 24 of the same year, the *pro-Soviet* prime minister of Afghanistan finally visited Washington. Vice President Richard Nixon received him at the airport, a significant sign of esteem. He addressed the Senate and House of Representatives and met the President of the United States of America.

President Eisenhower emphasized, "Mr. Prime Minister, your visit is of extreme importance for us. This is why I am joined by Vice President Nixon and Secretary Dulles. We hope that this will be the beginning of a new era in our relationship."

"We hope so too, Mr. President. But everything depends on a shared view about Pakistan," Daoud Khan replied.

"Pakistan and Iran are our allies, and the United States stands by them," President Eisenhower affirmed.

"That is where the heart of the problem is, Mr. President. While we have no comments about the creation of Pakistan, our ancestral land seized from us by the British must be restored," Daoud Khan stressed.

"To the best of my knowledge, Pakistan was recognized by member states of the United Nations, including the government of your uncle, with its existing boundaries. Therefore, nothing can be altered according to international law," Eisenhower insisted.

"Well then, we disagree, Mr. President," Daoud Khan resolutely replied.

President Eisenhower had knowledge about a clear understanding between Prime Minister Winston Churchill and the last viceroy of the British Empire in India, Louis Mountbatten, to sow seeds of discord between Muslims and Hindus, encourage partition of an independent India, and pave the way for the creation of Pakistan, contrary to the vision of Mahatma Gandhi. He also knew about the disdain of British rulers toward *Pathans*, as they used to call Afghans, but he insisted on international legal aspects of the matter, ignoring the devastating political, social, and economic legacies of British Empire withdrawal from the subcontinent. Mr. Suri and Secretary Dulles had to swerve the dialogue to topics of mutual interest, such as economic and technical cooperation and recognition of the neutrality of Afghanistan by the United States. Daoud Khan was frantic. He charged Maiwandwal of leniency toward the Americans and blamed him for the failure of his trip. In Afghanistan, there was already debate about democracy among educated youth. Two opposing doctrines, religious conservatism and socialism as practiced in the Soviet Union and the People's Republic of China, already had fervent sympathizers. Some of their underground leaders started to appear publicly.

Back in Kabul, Mr. Suri was appointed ambassador to the United Kingdom and instructed to proceed to London within two to three months. He finally had time to devote to his family.

Soraya was curious and coveted to visit Paghman, Shakardara, and Panjshir—the summer heavens in the country. They commenced with Shakardara, the land of gorgeous grapes, underground clean water brooks, called *kaarez*, and amazing fountains. They stayed with Mr. Suri's cousin. At nightfall, they all hopped on the rooftop of their dwelling, covered by beautiful red carpets and lit by hurricane lamps, for dinner. The cool breeze was enchanting after the hot summer days, as was the after-feast confab. When other women gathered in a corner to indulge in idle gossip, Soraya moved to her father.

"I saw the mausoleum of King Zaher Shah's father. It looks beautiful. Tell me about him," Soraya said.

"Well, he took over in autumn 1929 from Amir Habibullah Kalakani, who was from the next township over from here and the only Tajik ruler of Afghanistan. The new king murdered him as well as his companions and started a campaign of terror in this area," Mr. Suri narrated.

"Why did he have them executed?" Soraya inquired.

"This has been so throughout our history, my darling. Oftentimes one king gets rid of his predecessor and destroys what he had built," Mr. Suri replied. "Do not forget that history is written by vanquishers. Let us see how long the narrative of ours will last."

Soraya was stunned how people could summarily be killed and their properties and wealth looted or confiscated because they belong to a different ethnic group.

In the mountain city of Paghman, the Suri family dwelled in a friend's home. They had a picnic near Qargha before attaining this small city, at the entrance of which King Amanullah Khan and Queen Soraya had built a beautiful park and a victory arch, a duplicate of the famous *Arc de Triomphe* in Paris, which was surrounded by boutiques of all sorts. This is where the royal family and other affluent people had constructed villas and were passing their summer weekends. The snow-cup mountain, from which blocks of ice were chopped for luxury summer consumption, the gigantic walnut, cherry, and mulberry trees with their refreshing shade and fruits, the tilted green valley that represented the identity of the location, the roaring river with combined white and green colors, and the incomparable view all appeased tormented souls.

Daily, Soraya woke up early and sauntered with her father in the parks and on the hills and mountain bay, chatting about everything: nature, history, the plight of the people, and of course, family concerns. She always took her father's hand and moved a step ahead. Such natters made the father and daughter much closer. There was so much affinity between the two that she read his convictions and he fathomed what was going on in her mind.

The trip to the Panjshir Valley, conceivably the most striking vale of Afghanistan, was just fabulous. Mr. Suri and his family lodged in the government's hostel in Gulbahar. Panjshir is a tight, long gorge. Settlements were erected along the river and linked through an amazing muddy and difficult road. During three days, they visited Bazarak, Jangalak, and Astana and climbed until they reached Khenj and Awdak. The picnics along the river were memorable. The inhabitants were gracious, bringing all sorts of fruits to the Suris and offering *talkhan*, a candy-type blend of smashed mulberry, almond, and walnut. The contrast with Paghman was striking. In Panjshir, the scarcity of land had forced the inhabitants to use the slopes of their mountains. People seemed very poor but knew each other, lived in real communities, and were hospitable. Soraya never forgot the majestic mountains, ferocious river with its eternal dancing clean water, and marvelous folks. Once again she was distressed by the condition of women and girls, though they seemed to enjoy greater freedom than those she had seen in the southwestern corner of the country.

In September, the Suri family was prepared to depart for London. Abai and her family felt most unfortunate, as she firmly believed that it was their last goodbye with the people they loved most. For all those years that they lived under Mr. Suri's auspices, they never felt like servants. They were effectively regarded as members of the family. For days Abai was weeping discreetly and often taking Soraya in her big arms, advising her to be strong and fearless when she had to say the truth.

Naim Khan and Ali Khan organized several farewell get-togethers. The newly appointed ambassador was beholden to them for having persuaded the king and Daoud Khan to honor their promise. Ali

Khan was constantly astounded by the intelligence and emerging splendor of the young Soraya. The deputy prime minister had a particular fondness for this dauntless girl. He had never seen one like her within his own kinfolk.

"Soraya darling," he said the day prior to the Suris' journey, "you resemble your father—bright, spirited, and elegant. I am sure you will have a dazzling future."

"I hope so, uncle! Most women and girls have atrocious lives in our country," she said.

"No, my child, we are progressing," Ali Khan claimed.

"I saw them in their huts and tents, uncle! What I said is true," she retorted, gazing straight into Ali Khan's eyes.

"What I said is also true, my darling. Full emancipation of all will take time," he added.

"Yes, my father said the same. I hope the change will not take too long," she added with a deep breath of sorrow.

"We will do our best, my child. But remember, darling, I have genuinely vowed to be with you when you wed," he recapped.

Though Daoud Khan was a controversial political figure, he made significant strides on female emancipation and development projects. After the abortion of King Amanullah Khan's reforms and the bloody takeover by the father of King Zaher Shah, the royal family addressed the issue of women's education and freedom cautiously. Though most of their kin were tutored, total veil was imposed even on them. Soraya had the bitter experience of wearing it already. However, Prime Minister Daoud Khan encouraged women to unveil while at the same time respecting the religious doctrine of hijab by suggesting they cover their heads with light scarves. During the national day celebration, Afghans witnessed their queen unveiled for the first time since King Amanullah Khan. Daoud Khan's wife and the school headmasters all appeared at the lodge to communicate a strong message that times had changed. In spite of these endeavors, the society still remained patriarchal as men overstepped women at each occasion. In addition, construction of the Salang Tunnel and blueprints of numerous hydroelectric dams, most with Soviet Union funding, were also part of his bold approach to take further steps for development of his country. The tunnel, however, proved harmful for the people of Afghanistan when in 1978 it was used by Soviet Union troops to invade the country entirely.

In London, Ambassador Suri coveted to ensure that his daughter catch up with the school cycle. The Afghan Embassy, on the Prince Gate at Exhibition Road, also served as the ambassador's residence. It was a striking four-story building near the Royal Albert Hall and Hyde Park, designed and constructed by the famous British architect and builder Sir Charles James Freake, who had numerous prestigious edifices to his credit. The building was purchased by King Amanullah Khan in 1925 and luxuriously decorated with mahogany furniture, crystal chandeliers, priceless Afghan carpets, large gilded mirrors, and pianos. Since then, it hosted the diplomatic house of Afghanistan in the United Kingdom.

Soraya was instantly admitted to Glendower Preparatory School for girls, sited at Queen's Gate, not far from the embassy. She relished the atmosphere, the tutors, and her classmates the first day. Their spoken English was so different from Washington. She was again in an environment where she could state her opinion without being interrupted. Instructors had time to listen to and argue with her. At school, she felt at home. She had no knowledge of Latin, but she knew more than others about the British Empire and colonization history. That was unquestionably an enormous advantage. She strived hard on her weaknesses and soon became the favorite of the school administration, esteemed by all.

Some astonishing facts, however, surprised her. She had to undergo elocution courses to rectify her American accent to British. Furthermore, she comprehended quickly that heroes of the United States independence were considered traitors in the United Kingdom. Behind her solemn facial expressions, a stunning beauty was taking shape. No one could precisely describe the color of her eyes. They were simply too bright, mesmerizing, and mind blowing, which pierced interlocutors. Not only was the school ardent to ensure the highest standard of education; it also strictly imposed behavior on the pupils. The stern discipline of the school was conducive for seriousness among classmates. Mr. Suri was the sole confidant of his daughter's intellectual inspirations. She debated with her father first, made up her mind, and then broached matters with others.

At home, Soraya commenced learning *la bonne cuisine* from her mother. The chef was from the Philippines and knew nothing about Afghan delicacies and dishes. Mrs. Suri taught and tutored him expertly. Soraya was twigging every prescription dictated by her mother and was helping her in the kitchen from time to time when an illustrious guest was invited for lunch or dinner to ensure that the cook got everything right. Occasionally on a Sunday, Ambassador Suri himself cooked for his family. He was particularly skilled in innovation and loved perfection; everything was vital for him. His wife was his prime apprentice. The Suri table was acknowledged as the finest by all his pals and interlocutors.

Soraya was also introduced to fashion. Mr. Suri brought home magazines in which the latest Dior, Chanel, and Lanvin designs were exposed, with details about their cuts. Mrs. Suri purchased the material and sewed with additional Afghan-style details and enhancements. Soraya was among the most elegant in her school environment. She did not fancy scrub dresses with wrinkles and favored fitted outfits. Her comrades and peers were often seeking advice from her. They were astounded by her forthrightness.

Mr. Suri impelled Soraya to quickly learn Latin and the in-house history of the British monarchy as it was imperative for her to catch up on the curriculum. He was proud of his daughter's progress and solemnity. Soon she had a clear picture of the ten phases, as she preferred to call them, of Britain's evolution in history. Indeed, the prehistoric, Roman, Anglo-Saxon, Viking, and medieval eras were deemed part of making Britain's path to greatness. But the Tudor, Stuart, Georgian, Victorian, and modern Britain contributed to shape the world—its politics, social structure, and economy.

Soraya was astonished to apprehend that like most Americans, British too were migrants coming from elsewhere. It appeared that not much knowledge was available about the initial settlements, physical separation from the mainland in 6500 BC due to rise of the seawater level, and erection of the first stone circles around 3000 BC. However, great endeavors had been made to connect the dots concerning the arrival of Celtic warriors from Central Europe in the sixth century BC, foundation of London in the first century, Roman conquest in the second century, Christianization, and the withdrawal of Romans after nearly three hundred years of domination that coincided with the settlement of Jute and Anglo Saxons (German tribes), as well as the invasion of Vikings from Denmark.

Mr. Suri searched for more documentation and literature to recommend to his daughter about the Middle Ages, around the eleventh century when the Normans conquered the country, leading to the Hundred Years' War with France. Soraya was puzzled to grasp that Britain was a society essentially composed of French, Germans, Dutch, Danish, and Celtic who were fighting each other for power. Where were the aborigines then? At least in the United States and Australia, they were recognized. Soraya questioned her father in several instances without getting a convincing answer. She was, however, most fascinated by the War of the Roses and the arrival of Henry VII to power, making the Anglo Saxons unblemished victors over the Normans. That was when a country made of immigrants became the most powerful colonizer on the globe. Formation of the Church of England by Henry VIII and the rivalry between Mary Stuart and Elizabeth I particularly captivated Soraya's mind. She was so sorry for the unhappy life and faith of the Queen of Scots and questioned her father about the rulers' thirst for bloodshed. She quickly understood that in politics, only interest counted. This was indeed the basis to comprehend geopolitics.

Soon Soraya turned out to be the most conversant among her classmates about the colonization history of the United Kingdom and the war of religions. She loved to elucidate that, though Henry VIII commenced to trade outside the country, it was his daughters, particularly Elizabeth I, who gave the first golden age to England, at the expense of countless lives. The rivalry between the Court of Spain, fervent Catholic and even promoter of inquisition, and that of England, who had rebelled against the Pope by having their own church, split the world.

Soraya was astounded to realize how politicians and rulers alter religion to suit their interests. The Spanish had *commanded* all Jews and Muslims to convert to Catholicism or leave. They had colonized all Central and South America, as well as Far East Asia, while the English had focused on North America, Australia, East Africa, and the Indian subcontinent, leaving West Africa for their less-prized rival, France. She studied a lot regarding the maritime fights between the Spanish and English mercenaries and the futile efforts of different Popes, particularly Pius V, to help their Catholic associates. Queen Elizabeth I's lovers and rivals were of interest to Soraya. She particularly felt anger and sorrow for the Earl of Essex.

For the first time, Soraya came across the name of William Shakespeare and started to read plays by the Lord Chamberlain's Men. She was convinced that Sir William was inspired by court intrigues. Though he had barely lived in London, his deep understanding of personalities and assumptions of court intricacies were exceptionally remarkable.

She soon ascertained that in 1600 through a royal charter, Elizabeth I sanctioned the formation of the East India Company, paving the way for further prosperity of the 4 million populace of Britain and centuries of misery for the indigenous of the larger Indian subcontinent, including Afghans. She often discussed her disdain of colonialism with her father, who was delighted to see his daughter revealing an acute intellectual personality. He persuaded Soraya to study and understand the British misdeeds in India and their subsequent effects on Afghanistan. Not surprisingly, religion was used as a major tool to justify colonialism and the establishment of zones of influence, though some proved exceptionally opaque.

She deduced that Georgian and Victorian Britain were extremely harmful. The Afghan courts were infiltrated by British agents, and the succession of kings was always marred by family assassinations. The epitomes of a prosperous nation envisaged by father founder Mirwais Hotak were annihilated by self-centered and shortsighted visions of the heirs, who preferred to heed the advice "offered" by the British viceroys. Soraya believed that faith-related rivalries mainly between Christians and Muslims, pagans and Christians, or Muslims and Hindus all aimed at financial, economic, and territorial gains. Furthermore, the drive of different courts to promote slavery and colonialism were part of the shame in humankind's history. Tens of millions of innocent people and countless cities and marvels of the world perished in the process. Her father elucidated that God had never endorsed aggression or killing and none of the holy books advised infliction of misery by the mighty. He had asserted that on the contrary, rulers must be wary of their deeds, as all major calamities on earth had occurred as a result of injustice toward weak and common people.

Mr. Suri was instrumental in shaping Soraya's perception of the world. He was indeed her real mentor, tutor, and protector. Both enjoyed their long hours of conversation. At fifteen, Soraya was already a mature lady. With splendid, heavy, silky, light brown hair, delightful skin, striking eyes, and marble long legs, she designed her own dresses. One day, she ventured into buying a perfume. In the evening, she dressed as usual for dinner and opened the flacon impatiently. The day after, Ambassador Suri came home early and summoned Soraya to the library.

"My darling!" He addressed his daughter with a hand on her right shoulder. "Who bought the perfume for you?"

"I bought it with my pocket money," Soraya replied.

"Did someone advise you?" he insisted.

"No, Father. Is there a problem?" Soraya queried.

"Yes and no, darling," the ambassador replied. "No, because you are fifteen years old, and it is time for you to enter the womanhood stage, have perfumes, choose your dresses, and have your friends and your own opinion on all issues. Yes, because the perfume you wear is not for a lady. Here is what your father recommends," he explained.

Soraya was perplexed, took the wrapped parcel, and opened it. There were two bottles of Miss Dior fragrance, one in an amphora shape and the other was crystal topped. She tried them on the back of her hands and was popeyed. She just loved the perfumes.

In June of the same year, Mr. Suri tendered his daughter to accompany him to the queen's annual reception for the diplomatic corps. She could not believe it and inquired of her mother if it was true. For the ambassador, it was the perfect time to introduce Soraya to the world of politics and diplomacy. She was dressed in a white silk, semisheer, lace long gown. The robe was unique, tailored by her mother and inspired by Christian Dior's black velvet. Soraya looked like a fairy-tale princess. At Buckingham Palace, she instantly felt comfortable. Her father proudly introduced her to his peers, government officials, and the royals. She was enchanted to speak flawlessly of what she knew. Soon the lord chamberlain entered, announcing Queen Elizabeth II in the main hall. Guests were lined up to be saluted by the most powerful woman on earth. Ambassador Suri and Soraya were in the first row.

"Ambassador, we are overjoyed to see you again," the queen said. "We recollect every feature of our recent conversation regarding Islam and the challenges we may face in the future."

"Your Majesty is gracious," Mr. Suri replied. "May I introduce my daughter, Soraya, to Your Majesty?"

"Of course, Mr. Ambassador! How are you, young lady?" The queen attended to Soraya and proffered her hand, while Soraya curtsied to perfection.

"I am fine, ma'am, and honored to be here," she replied.

"How do you find your stay in England?" the queen queried.

"Extremely pleasant, ma'am. I wish the United Kingdom to endure under Your Majesty's leadership a very prosperous and peaceful country."

"Thank you, my dear!" The queen smiled. "We had heard of you through the queen mother but are pleased to receive you in person. Mr. Ambassador, please look after your daughter preciously," the queen counseled before moving to the next guest.

Indeed, Soraya had witnessed a similar situation when the queen mother visited Glendower School. She had quizzed the smart daughter of the Afghan ambassador and was very impressed by her attitude and astuteness, hailing her publicly. Soraya encountered the queen again during her sister's marriage, for which she had received a personal invite from the queen mother. Mr. Suri was observing his daughter and her ability to interact effortlessly and passionately with dignitaries. Often, he thought, *"If Nehru has Indira, I have Soraya,"* and he wished peace and stability for his country so that women like his daughter could flourish.

In school, Soraya excelled in her courses and was the epicenter of substantive political and philosophical discussions, both among mates and with her tutors. At seventeen, she embarked in preparing for her higher education and began exchanging views with her father.

In July 1962, Mr. Suri received a missive from his friend and foreign minister of Afghanistan, Naim Khan, to proceed on summer holidays to Kabul via Teheran, where the prime minister and he would have a state visit. The relationship between the two countries was broken as Iran had accused Daoud Khan for his dubious and twisted policies. Mr. Suri was a renowned authority of Iranian affairs from the time when he assumed the chief justice post and extended determined support to the Helmand River projects. He was also the undisputed expert on international legal affairs. Reza Shah of Iran had appointed a new prime minister, a man who had abetted the exiled monarch to return home and reclaim power in 1953 by counterplotting against Mohammad Mossadegh. The Afghan leaders aspired to reinforce association with the most trusted man of the Shah. Mr. Suri planned to divide the journey by flying to Istanbul and then driving to Teheran. Soraya was excited and had already recommended that only a Mercedes-Benz was fit for a long drive from Europe to Asia.

Mr. Suri and his family arrived in Istanbul on a sunny Sunday of the month of August with a direct British European Airways Corporation flight from London. They were driven by the Turkish Foreign Services to the Ciragan on the Bosporus Sea. Interested in the history of the hotel, Soraya was briefed by the manager. The splendid edifice was constructed by Sultan Abdülaziz between 1863 and 1867. Following its destruction by fire at the beginning of 1910, this Ottoman palace was restored and converted into a hotel in 1989.

The Suris' car, a Mercedes-Benz 220 SE, was already delivered to the hotel. They had a week in Istanbul before moving on to Ankara.

The day after their arrival, Mr. Suri was greeted by President Cemal Gürsel at the Istanbul State House. The exiled Queen Soraya of Afghanistan had personally recommended Mr. Suri to Turkish authorities. The conversation centered on the heritage of Kemal Atatürk and King Amanullah Khan, who both and at the same time aimed at moving their countries forward. While the Turkish progress path had been smooth, religious fundamentalism had defeated the king's vision of a modern Afghanistan. Both were of the opinion that creation of a free trade zone among Afghanistan, Iran, and Turkey would strengthen the peace and security of the region. The Turkish president, however, cautioned about the return of an arrogant shah that would be the sole flag bearer of American interest in the region. Soraya praised Atatürk's effort to modernize his country but did not comprehend why he changed the alphabet from Arabic to Latin script. The lack of some sounds and letters such as "v", "ch", "g," or "p" in Arabic, the language of science, philosophy, and literature, could have been addressed judiciously. She concluded that there had certainly been political rationales favoring such a dramatic transition.

Back in the hotel, Soraya defined their itinerary in Istanbul. Among thousands of valued and prestigious places, she suggested to visit Topkapi Palace, Hagia Sophia, Atatürk, and the Istanbul Archaeological Museums, as well as the Sultan Ahmed Mosque, Küçüksu Palace, and the Grand Bazaar.

The Topkapi complex, built between 1459 and 1465 by Sultan Mehmet II, the conqueror of Byzantine Constantinople, embodied the enormity of Ottoman Empire glory. However, Soraya was astounded by the magnificence of the blend of Byzantine and Islamic architectures when visiting Hagia Sophia, erected with a massive dome in 537 by the patriarch of Constantinople; it served as the Christian Orthodox Cathedral but was transformed into a mosque by the Ottomans in 1453. She asked numerous questions. Mr. Suri expounded that Andalucía and Istanbul were unique in the world as they represented the might of Christian and Islamic values combined. But he considered the Grand Bazaar, construction of which started in 1455, Sultan Ahmed Mosque, edified between 1609 and 1616, and Küçüksu Palace, commissioned by Sultan Abdul Mejid in 1857, as revelations of Ottoman Empire evolution. During the week they also dined in Hünkar and Beyti restaurants, as well as Arch Bistro, to have a flavor of local food. Soraya also wanted to visit Andalucía and considered every trip to Istanbul as a pilgrimage.

The journey to Ankara took a day. The government envoys were expecting Mr. Suri and his family at the State Guest House. Ankara has been the capital of the country only since 1920, but it has been known since the Bronze Age by different names, such as Ancyra or Angora. The following day, Mr. Suri was warmly welcomed by Suat Hayri Urgüplü, the prime minister of the country. The core of discussion was about establishment of the free trade zone. The role of Naim Khan was felt instrumental, and Mr. Urgüplü urged Mr. Suri to assist, referring several times to his friendship with the mighty man in the Afghan government. The Suri family spent only three days in Ankara, visiting the Anitkabir, Mustafa Kemal Atatürk's mausoleum, and the Anatolian Civilization Museum, located in two Ottoman-era buildings near the famous Ankara Castle.

Soraya and her parents attained Tabriz in Iran via the cities of Sivas and Erzurum and spent the night there. Some believed that the ancient city of Tabriz was the site of the Garden of Eden, the Persian poetry and the Tabriz silk carpets implying its beauty. Soraya was amazed by the refinement of the blooming designs. Ambassador Suri had no choice but to respond to the wish of his daughter and buy a large one. The motifs described paradise, where human beings and animals inhabited in peace. Mr. Suri and Soraya spent time visiting famous bazaars and stores, where she received a striking Iranian turquoise ring from her father. Soraya kept fond memories of the crispy warm barbari bread, the amazing and appetizing Liqvan salted cheese, and more especially the unique succulent rose petals jam. The Suri family touched Teheran on time via Zanjan and Qizvin. The Mercedes-Benz 220 SE had responded to the challenge and met their expectations.

The shah's secret services, particularly the wicked SAVAK, were still searching for partisans of Mossadegh. The monarch had hurried to Washington to converse with President John F. Kennedy in April 1962, and Vice President Lyndon B. Johnson had visited Teheran at the end of August of the same year to support the idea of what was later called the *White Revolution*. The paradox of appealing for respect of democratic principles on the one hand and endorsing oppression against Mossadegh on the other was inexplicable on the part of the United States. Soraya quickly understood that for raw-material-rich countries, western industry were the effective policy makers that respected governments implemented.

Naim Khan was impatient to meet his buddy. His brother's policy of friendship with the Soviet Union was not yielding the expected results, and Pakistan, with the help of Americans, was gaining force. The Afghan palace had given Prime Minister Daoud Khan an ultimatum to achieve tangible results without delay. Naim Khan apprised Mr. Suri that the goal of the Afghan prime minister was to convince the shah of his goodwill and expect he would intercede in their favor and get the United States' unhindered support. In exchange, Daoud Khan was prepared to strike a deal on the flow of the Helmand River, henceforth offering water to Iran.

The Afghan delegation, including the Suri family, was lodged in the reputed Gulistan Palace, constructed by Shah Tahmaseb Safavid in the sixteenth century, which had served as the "*cité royal*" of the Qajar dynasty. During the Pahlavi era, it was used for special state events, including hosting elite guests. The palace, comprised of seventeen edifices, gardens, and water pools was a unique beauty. The interior walls were gemmed and adorned with extraordinary marble carving, tile, enamel, stucco, mirrors, and silk textiles. Soraya spent a full day visiting the *Takht-e-Marmar*—the Marble Throne, *Khalvat-e-Karim Khani*—Karim Khani Alcove, *Howz Khaneh*—Pond House, *Negar Khaneh*—Picture House/Gallery, and *Talare Roshan*—Crystal Hall, as well as *Almaas*—Diamond, *Zoroof*—Porcelain, *Aaj*—Ivory, and *Aayeeneh*—Mirror Manors. Each chamber was exclusive and matchless. She could have stayed days in each corner and admired the specifics.

The preparatory meeting with Abbas Aaram, foreign minister of Iran, took place in a cordial and friendly atmosphere. He was a soft-spoken gentleman who knew international politics very well and warned that his shah wanted Afghanistan to detach itself at once from the Soviet Union. In the evening, an official reception was organized by the shah in honor of "*His Royal Highness Prince Daoud of Afghanistan*," as specified in the invite. Most of the nobility and dignitaries of Teheran were in attendance. Soraya was dressed in a Pinterest-style Kochi long colorful robe and a green, light scarf on her shoulders. She was joyful and talkative. The shah was captivated by her bearing, intelligence, and logical buildup of ideas. Most dignitaries voiced their admiration too. Though it was the tradition of the Suri family to have open discussion about topics of the day, Mr. Suri had advised his family to avoid doing so outside their residence. The spies of both countries were diligently at work. But back at their corner in the Gulistan Palace, Soraya joyfully spoke with her father to say how much she enjoyed the conversations and found the people interesting.

The shah received Prime Minister Daoud Khan, his brother Naim Khan, and Ambassador Zamir Suri in the Glass Hall of the Saadabad Palace. Only special guests convened in this chamber, which had two doors; the royal entrance led to the throne, which was positioned several steps higher. Two arches of Andre Charles Boulle-designed writing tables faced the shah. A Louis XV bergère brocade seat was behind each desk. He was particularly affable and, contrary to expectations, invited Daoud Khan to the alcove that was more intimate, where bearers served tea and Iranian confections on silver trays. Mr. Suri was perplexed as the cordiality of the shah did not resemble that of an arrogant monarch. After habitual and pleasant courtesies, during which Daoud Khan conveyed the friendly and warm message of the king of Afghanistan and the Iranian monarch reciprocated, the shah addressed Daoud Khan.

The shah began, "Your Highness, here we are to discuss affairs of mutual interest."

"Your Majesty, we have exceptionally withdrawn Ambassador Zamir Suri from his duties in London to join us in this meeting, as he is our best expert on the matters in question," Prime Minister Daoud Khan said.

"We know Ambassador Suri and had the pleasure to receive his family last night. His daughter certainly has a bright future in your country," Reza Shah stated. We have been briefed about topics of mutual interest but are at Your Highness's service."

Daoud Khan spoke frankly. "His Majesty the King of Afghanistan and I as prime minister of the country need Your Majesty's help in bridging our relationship with the United States."

"I appreciate Your Highness's forthright approach, but we must underline that the recent policy of the Afghan government to align themselves with the Soviet camp has led to irremediable harm in the region and to Iran."

"I comprehend Your Majesty's opinion. But the unconditional military, financial, and political assistance of the United States to Pakistan is also a redline for us," Daoud Khan pointed out.

"Your Highness knows better that only those strong enough can pencil redlines! And this is not the case of your country at this stage," the shah stated viciously. "We can help if you break with the Soviet Union instantly and ratify the water-sharing agreement between our countries."

It was a weird situation. The shah of Iran had obviously ignored Afghanistan's constraints. Mr. Aaram guided the Afghan delegation to their cars. Daoud Khan was angered by the shah's audacity and impertinence. At Gulistan, he received an invitation from the prime minister of Iran for an impromptu dinner, during which he offered details about his ruler's deliberations. He assured the prime minister of Afghanistan that Iran would never interfere in his country's internal affairs, but the Soviet lust was a serious threat to the peace and security of the region as the West would never allow them to bring an iota of additional territory under their influence. Sharing of the Helmand River water between the two nations would bring them much closer. Finally, he assured Daoud Khan that the shah knew about the time span for any change, and Iran was ready to stand by Afghanistan to thrive. Mr. Suri arbitrated on numerous occasions to rectify the legal reasoning and assess the current political and economic realities as well as the strategic visions pursued by the two superpowers. He interjected the idea of a free trade zone in the region, which would allow the countries to swiftly find common grounds for their prosperity. But both prime ministers focused on addressing the immediate challenges.

The next day, the prime minister of Afghanistan and his brother flew back to Kabul, while Ambassador Suri and his family departed for Herat in Afghanistan through Semnan, Sabzwar, Neyshapur, and Mashhad. They attained Herat late in the evening. Soraya had read about the city, which was founded by Alexander the Great and known as the pearl of Khorasan and breadbasket of Central Asia, the crossing point of the Silk Road, and a jewel the rebirth of which was due to Tamerlane, the great conqueror. It had also been home to illustrious poets, philosophers, and artists such as Mawlana Jami, Alisher Navoi, and Kamal Behzad. It was in this city that Mirwais

Hotak founded the Pashtun dynasty, which has ruled Afghanistan ever since.

The Suri family was ardently greeted by the governor and settled in the official guesthouse. Soraya had urged her father not to include government executives anymore in their excursions in order to have their privacy respected. The ambassador had acceded to the appeal. They dwelled two days in Herat, visiting the Friday Mosque, a nine-hundred-year-old vestige with incomparable ornaments; the Gazar Gah, a thousand-year-old memorial, housing the tomb of the famous Sufi scholar Abdullah Ansari; and the mausoleum of Queen Gawharshad Begum, the slain fifteenth-century Timuri queen who made Herat the capital of the empire.

Though all the monuments looked to be at the sagging stage, except the Friday Mosque, Soraya was enthralled. The design and construction of each reflected so much love and staunchness. She wanted to know about the Ghorid kings, particularly Sultan Ghiassoddin, who had built the Friday Mosque; Shah Rukh, the Timuri emperor who, through the actions of his wife, Queen Gawharshad Begum, improved the plight of women in a very conservative Islamic society; Behzad, the master of painting on tools, who was valued by the Timuri emperor; Sultan Hussain Bayeqra; and Ansari, the spiritual wizard who has been adulated at all times.

Mr. Suri advised Soraya that conquerors were cherished by their hangers-on but abhorred by the vanquished, so she must see both faces of the same coin before making a judgment. He further repeated that history was always written by subjugators, even in the societies considered democratic, where the right to free speech was often enshrined in their constitutions. Slavery and colonialism were just two crimes against humanity that will remain unpunished as long as the perpetrators dominate the world. He jokingly used the terminology of being *hero or zero*, depending on who judged.

Ambassador Suri urged his daughter to speak for what she considered the truth and stand by her convictions. She knew that as a young man, he had done so in his beloved land of Logar, when in 1930, King Zaher Shah's father, who had acceded to the throne, murdered innocent villagers with whom he had shared happiness and sorrow. The event was engraved in his mind, and his heart was strained at each remembrance. Any discussion about this particular chapter of his life brought tears in his eyes and revealed his compassion toward victims of the reprisal, who were predominantly of Tajik ethnicity. Soraya was moved on each occasion but also puzzled. What was finally fairness, and who was veracious? She knew that felonies were methodically perpetrated in the name of humanity, the rightness of the victor's "civilization," or God. Ruthless rulers never faced justice!

The father and daughter spoke for hours to eulogize those who went beyond the orthodoxy of their times to bring affirmative changes for their subjects. Soraya deemed that capturing hearts and minds yielded better results than snatching territories. While her father concurred from a human perspective, he advised his daughter that politics was never compassionate and that only minds governed the success or failure of policies.

They also spoke about Muslim artists, writers, musicians, and philosophers. Mr. Suri underlined that Robert Byron described the art of Herat as "*a beautiful example of colorful architecture conceived by man for the glory of God.*" Soraya was an extremely accomplished and fast reader; she had studied a lot about western culture and was surprised to learn from her father that Muslim kings, sultans, and emperors oftentimes venerated and rewarded the avant-garde. She liked Louis XIV, "*le roi soleil,*" for his patronage but was so remorseful for Bizet. He died of sorrow and never witnessed the glory of his masterpiece *Carmen.* So many others, like El Greco, Alfred Wegener, Gregor Johann Mendel, Edgar Allan Poe, Vincent van Gogh, Franz Kafka, and Emily Dickinson, died in grief, only to be loved later on. Behzad was lucky, as his talent was recognized by rulers of the time. Some deem that the splendid silk carpet industry in Tabriz was a reflection of his artistic soul. Soraya thought of the glory of Mughals in India and their exemplary influence on music, art, and literature, but remembered that they had vanquished her ancestors and so many valorous heroes of Rajput, Marathas, Sikhs, and other native kingdoms by the might of their sword. She concluded that Alexander the Great, Jules Caesar, Augustus, Napoleon, Mahmoud Ghaznavi, Genghis Khan, and the Mughal emperors all had the same instinct: conquest and expansion, irrespective of what they implied for the indigenous populations.

Mr. Suri reasoned that while good and evil were undivided parts of the military makeup of empires, culture, art, and literature were rhombuses that lingered priceless even within the darkest of stones. He provided a list of Persian must-read books to Soraya, such as *Rubaiyat* of Omar Khayyam, *Shahnameh* of Ferdowsi Tousi, *Mathnawi* of Jalaluddin Rumi, *Diwan* of Hafiz Shirazi, *Gulistan* of Saadi, and *Diwan* of Bedil Dehlavi, as well as the collection *One Thousand and One Nights*. The books were procured from the Chaharsu Bazaar. Soraya's relinking with her ancestral values and tenets started the same sundown. Mr. Suri read rhymes and paragraphs, and a debate always ensued. Soraya terminated each conversation with the same query: *"Why are people killed and razed in the name of God, who is merciful?"* She was further confounded why rulers in her mountainous country constructed in mud. In England, where there were practically no mountains, historic edifices were made of solid rocks. Why in Afghanistan, an ultramountainous land, was everything constructed from clay? Perhaps rulers discerned that their successors would most probably extinguish what they had built, opting therefore for soft structures.

Amid extremely serious matters that she considered or debated upon, an amazing incident occurred on the last day of their stay in Herat. Soraya found an envelope in her room. Inside there was a big postcard with a stunningly beautiful red rose picture. She did not recognize the handwriting and asked her father for help. He had a quick glance and burst into laughter. She had never seen him in such a hilarious mood and was inquisitive.

"What is it, Father?" she queried.

"My darling, it is the governor who offers you the rose and proposes a marriage," he said, still chortling.

"What? I am only seventeen, and he just saw me once," Soraya mockingly retorted.

She was reminded that in most underdeveloped and conservative societies, including Afghanistan, girls were wedded often at a very young age and without their consent. She felt sorry for them and aggrieved that they could not oppose such inhumane practices.

Departing Herat for the south of the country was very special for Ambassador Suri, as he coveted to have lunch in Gereshk, where he used to consume his favorite kebab in Mehrab's eatery during inspection of the Helmand projects when he had given unreserved positive legal advice, infuriating the Communist poodles. Soraya was proud of her choice of a Mercedes-Benz. The air-conditioning was a notable asset; southwest Afghanistan was awfully hot in the summer and driving for long hours a risk.

The old Mehrab was a Tajik from Panjshir. He took Ambassador Suri in his arms as if a brother had found his sibling after decades and cried. No other personality had ever visited his modest bistro. He wiped and polished the tables himself perhaps dozens of times before welcoming the Suri family in. Everything was simple but clean. Instantly rumors spread, and the ambassador was surrounded by the population of the small city, who all came to salute him. It was a very special encounter for Soraya; she apprehended the popularity of her father. Everyone wished to hail and touch him. Mehrab had his long hour chat, nattering about the past fifteen years and the evolution of the province. Mr. Suri was distressed to grasp that after his departure from the country and the arrival of Daoud Khan to power, the Helmand project was ignored because it was an insignia of American impact. Other hydroelectric dams with the backing of the Soviet Union were considered, such as Naghlu and Darunta in the east. Soraya was a stunning splendor now and received particular attention wherever she went. Her father always had the smile of a proud man on his lips.

Among a myriad of Kochi dresses that Soraya possessed, she used one of burgundy color and a green scarf that day. The lunch was delicious. Mehrab worked to prepare the best kebab and *Karai*, a blend of onion, lamb meat, and eggs, prepared in a searing pot and consumed with fresh, warm, crispy clay-oven bread. Soraya had never tasted such a delicious food in a humble place like Mehrab's. However, she did not comprehend why people were caressing her father, and some tried to kiss his hands. She thought they were asking for alms and some kind of charity as practically all of them were very poor. Mehrab comforted her that people judged Ambassador Suri a saint man who always thought of their well-being. This was how they expressed their feeling, respect, and devotion. Soraya clearly witnessed that her father had the esteem of royals and that of common folks as well.

Mr. Suri and his family attained their Kabul dwelling after spending only two nights in Kandahar. Abai and her family were still there to receive them affectionately. She had aged and moaned about joint and articulation problems. Her eyes did not perceive well anymore. Obviously, she suffered myopia. Soraya was now an unbelievable young lady, a real emerald, ornamented with intelligence, allure, a thirst for knowledge, and incomparable beauty. Abai hesitated to embrace her. But as if Soraya needed her motherly arms again, she mentioned, "Abai, this is me, your *Emerald*. Nothing has changed; I have only grown up." Soraya kissed her hands.

Abai suddenly began weeping and placed Soraya's head firmly on her bosoms. She confessed her delight to see them again and was swiftly energized. Mr. Suri, however, ordered a medical checkup for her. Abai returned from the hospital with a variety of pills and a pair of eyeglasses that gave her a sweel look.

New City of Kabul had transformed. The park in front of Mr. Suri's house was of special beauty. The street in front was paved and full of boutiques, restaurants, and strolling traders. Soraya found the area most astounding and loved the ice cream shops diffusing loud Hindi songs. The maker of the special Afghan version of this delicacy was swinging his buttocks with the rhythm of Bollywood melodies and rotating with his two hands the receptacle, in which milk, sugar, snow ice, pistachio, and cardamom powder, as well as other ingredients, were placed, gradually crystallizing into a delicious product. The savor of Kabul ice cream had always been unique. Farther down was the Blue Mosque crossroad, which led northwest of the city. Countless men and women strolled in front of the park and its alleys. Ambulant kebab booths had sneaked within the green area, and myriad people enjoyed their free time with family members and children, friends, or alone. The smolder of the grilled meat was appetizing. The whole area looked like a zone eternally filled with full weeks of day and night festivities.

Naim Khan was anxious and impatient. The next day, they were convened by Daoud Khan for an insightful discussion. The prime minister was not in a good temper. The association with the Soviet Union had detached him from reality, and Washington was increasingly putting pressure on him for more democracy, political rights, and freedom of speech. The meeting was virtually a monologue. Daoud Khan judged that Reza Shah of Iran was the prime lackey of the United States in the region and said he would never consent to his conditions. Mr. Suri tried to reason with him by recapping that following the quarrel between the two nations as a result of the Helmand River route alteration and the signing of the accord in 1939 between the two kings on the division of water rights, Afghanistan had never ratified the agreement. Daoud Khan claimed that some had oil, others water, and if Iran did not share its oil, why should Afghanistan share its water? Ambassador Suri concluded by advising that if the prime minister persisted with his policy of proximity with the Soviet Union, he then should not anticipate any backing from Iran, Pakistan, and the Western countries, but if he gradually changed his policies and alliances, he could receive the needed support. Daoud Khan seemed thoughtful and evasive at the same time.

Two days later, Mr. Suri and his family had a late morning breakfast and were planning to spend the weekend in Paghman when the domestic notified him of the arrival of Ali Khan, then minister of court, who proceeded straight to the dining room and was stunned at the sight of Soraya. He had never seen such a graceful and striking lady. The skinny child had flourished into a splendid adult. With her lion bouffant hairstyle, dazzling bluish green eyes, and captivating soft voice, Soraya had a gracious way of addressing her interlocutors.

The minister conversed a long time with her and was fascinated by her intelligence and the structure of her conversation. She was carefully listening and developing her arguments meticulously. Ali Khan also discerned that Soraya was not one who would give up easily on her issues of concern. As usual, when addressing people, she looked straight into their eyes. She spoke at length about the books that her father had purchased from Herat and the hard work to learn Dari. While she loved reading the quartet of Khayyam and played with Hafiz to "*predict the future*," she was mesmerized by Ferdowsi's epics in *Shahnameh*, the book of the king. They looked like the warriors' *One Thousand and One Nights*. She was very distraught to learn that Sultan Mahmoud Ghaznavi, the "conqueror," of India commissioned the book for his "glories," promising a gold coin for each verse. However, when it was presented to him, his treasury did not have enough gold to pay Ferdowsi. The king then backed down from his promise, and the most renowned poet and philosopher of his court disappointedly left Ghazni for his native land of Tous in Iran. Later, the sultan recognized his mistake and sent for him, but the poet had already passed away. The envoys brought a piece of paper to the sultan from Ferdowsi's only daughter, on which she had written, *"The reward of the mighty King Mahmoud resembles the arrival of remedy for Sohrab,"* referring to the Rostam and Sohrab epic of the book when the father, Rostam, unknowingly fatally injured his son in combat and sent for the curative drug that arrived after Sohrab was dead.

Khayyam and Hafiz were all about love, and Ferdowsi was depicting the tragedies of war. She often jumped from one book to another to feel the "war and peace" spirit of her country. But Mathnawi and Diwan challenged her mind. The philosophies of reaching the ultimate truth—bad and good, love and hate, superficiality and depth of thoughts, God the merciful and the furious, and so on—were profound. She needed hours of reading and sleepless evenings of debate with her father to comprehend the essence of a chapter.

She had developed an undeniable interest for comparative values of all cultures, but finding out more about the Muslim civilization was her priority. She focused on the Abbasid Caliphate in Baghdad between the eighth and thirteenth centuries, during which sciences and culture thrived, particularly the first three caliphs' reigns, known as the Golden Age of Islam. Development of algebra by Khwarizmi, optics by Ibn Al-Haytham, medicine by Avicenna, astronomy by Al-Battani, chemistry by Ibn Hayyan, Islamic philosophy by Al-Farabi and Avicenna, glass and crystal, architecture, and so on were facts, begetting tears in Soraya's eyes. She had borrowed several books about Muslims in Andalusia, including Alastair Boyd's *The Road From Ronda,* as well as on the glory of the Ottoman Empire. What had occurred to the children of Harun Al-Rashid, Tariq Ibn Ziyad, and Suleiman the Magnificent? Why had the Islamic world degraded so much in such a short period of time? Soraya debated at length with her father, who considered that primarily family intrigues and feuds had ruined the foundation of Islamic powers and the wrong understanding of religion had put an end to the evolution and development of the societies.

Soraya also assessed Ali Khan's stance. The minister had superficial acquaintance with the history and evolution of Islam and changed the subject, apprising Mr. Suri that King Zaher Shah wished to meet him. Soraya was curious and asked countless questions about the palace, the king, the queen, the crown prince, and other members of the royal family. She comprehended that the king resided in the Delkosha Palace, an edifice raised by the father of King Amanullah Khan in 1907, and received in the Gulkhana Palace, both in the same enclosure in the center of Kabul. Occasionally, the king moved to Chehel Sotoon Palace, located in the southern outskirts of the city. She felt upset by realizing that her country's palaces were much humbler than those she had seen so far.

Ambassador Suri arrived at the Gulkhana Palace the next day. King Zaher Shah was courteous and affable. He was accompanied only by Ali Khan. This was uncommon as his son-in-law and cousin General Abdul Wali, who deemed himself the de facto heir of the crown, always attended his encounters. The king invited Mr. Suri to the greenhouse of the palace, where he felt more at ease. The furniture was of fine rattan, with glass coffee tables. Tea and Afghan dainties were served. The king sat restfully on his usual sofa and addressed the ambassador.

"We were briefed by the prime minister about his meeting with Reza Shah," the king said. "We would like to have your opinion, Mr. Ambassador."

"Your Majesty is gracious." Mr. Suri replied. His Highness, the prime minister, has certainly informed you that the Afghan government has to make arduous resolutions."

"Indeed, Mr. Ambassador. But the decision will be ours," the king firmly replied. "Reza Shah is narcissistic and rich. Americans listen to him because of his oil, and we have to trade with him carefully."

"Your Majesty, his unambiguous message to His Highness, the prime minister of Afghanistan, was the one that Americans wish to convey to us," Mr. Suri affirmed.

"We know, Ambassador, and this is why we wish to change our political system."

The king engaged in a drawn-out explanation of the delicate political, social, and economic realities of the country and the fact that ten years of close ties with the Soviet Union had, in fact, been not only futile and dangerous but also against the policy of neutrality of the country. He notified Mr. Suri of the imminence of a parliamentarian and multiparty political system, an open economy, and a liable government. Zaher Shah believed that he could wipe out an eventual fury of the Soviet Union and provided his analysis about regional and international alliances, underlining that his government's closer cooperation with Iran and Saudi Arabia would be more productive, bringing Afghanistan closer to the West and keeping its neutral status. He also hinted that the time for his cousin the prime minister was over and that Afghanistan must enter a new era. After nearly two hours of candid discussion, the king addressed Mr. Suri again.

"Mr. Ambassador, you have been our chief justice and served in renowned senior international positions in New York and more specifically in Washington. You represent us in the United Kingdom currently. We have great admiration for you. We would like you to shoulder leadership of the transitional period," the king suggested.

"Your Majesty's admiration is appreciated," Mr. Suri replied. "What would this mean and entail?"

"This means we will appoint you prime minister," the king replied. "It implies that within two or three years, a new Constitution will be elaborated, political parties formed, parliamentarian elections held, and a new prime minister elected by the Parliament. We firmly believe you can do it for the love of the country and the kingdom," Zaher Shah assured him.

"This is a paramount honor, Your Majesty," Mr. Suri replied. Your Grace's proposal deserves deep consideration."

"Of course, Mr. Ambassador," the king concluded.

The minister of court escorted Mr. Suri to the garden of the palace and urged him to consent to Zaher Shah's offer. Mr. Suri and his family departed the same day for Paghman. They passed through Qargha, which now contained an artificial lake. The ambassador was contemplative and studying all options. The situation was extremely delicate, and he found himself at the center of the royal family feud. Five years older than the king, Daoud Khan pretended since his youth to be more apt to rule the country. He had hardly acknowledged the sovereign for his status. The other cousin and son-in-law of Zaher Shah, General Abudl Wali, who was in the same age range, also aspired to rule the country one day. In addition, the political affiliation of the prime minister with the Soviet Union was an additional disputed issue in the palace, and the king desperately desired to come out of domination by offering the premiership position to an outsider. Accepting the proposal was folly, as Daoud Khan would never concede defeat and tolerate someone else taking over. But declining the king's proposal was also hazardous, with unpredictable consequences.

Soraya did not comprehend her father's silence and loss in thoughts. Thus far, he had shared everything with her. Then what was the worry? She reproached herself for having done something horrid and decided to question her father at an opportune moment. A day later, her mother returned to Kabul for family business. Soraya resolved to stay with her father in Paghman. It was a pleasing nightfall. The two had a simple dinner, *borani*, eggplant with yogurt and garlic, *kofta chalaw*, white rice with meatball sauce, and seasoned *ferni*, rice pudding with green tea. From the patio of the house, the whole city of Paghman was discernible, and far away a sort of yellowish light revealed the capital city of Kabul. Soraya hastily engaged in her usual conversation with her father.

"Father, something has perturbed you the past two days," she affirmed.

"Indeed, my darling. I have the impression of having failed," Mr. Suri replied.

"Oh no, Father! A man of your character and stature will never dwindle," Soraya said.

"I mean we all in the government have failed. You have observed the situation of your country. Poverty and desolation are everywhere. Promise me to finish your studies to the best of your ability and come back and assist the people," Mr. Suri said.

"Of course, Father, but you seem anxious since your call on the king. Is there something you want to share with me?" Soraya queried.

"This is true, my love," the ambassador acknowledged.

Mr. Suri disclosed details of his dialogue with King Zaher Shah. He and Soraya conferred for long hours about the proposal. It was most gratifying. For the first time, her father spoke to her of state affairs as an equal. She earnestly felt like she was in the "court of great people." She loved the title *prime minister* and was of the belief that her father should take the offer. Mr. Suri advised that business and politics were based only on selfish interests and that some in the palace would be merciless even in their "retirement." He went on to elucidate with passion the dogma surrounding the interests of the palace, national regards, regional rivalries, and international games of power and influence. Killing, torture, imprisonment, sanctions, and humiliation were just normal treatment of opponents for centuries in the country, though King Zaher Shah was offering a window of opportunity. For Mr. Suri, it was too little too late.

The deliberation was de facto a fascinating course in political science. She listened vigilantly and as usual asked many questions to better grasp what her father implied. She spoke with respect and ardor. In addition to being dragged into the family dispute, several other factors such as doubt of the loyalty of Soviet-trained military officers toward the system, national disagreement on the Durand Line, and lack of a flourishing private sector to absorb thousands of graduates who demanded jobs, as well as the palace's stranglehold on foreign policy did not leave much space for a prime minister outside the royal sphere to succeed. They both gauged the risks and prospects, concluding at the end that the offer presented serious hazards.

A week later, Mr. Suri had dinner with Ali Khan to brief him about his decision. As minister of court, he was to prepare the king, and two days later, both friends were again at the Gulkhana Palace.

"Mr. Ambassador, we have been briefed about your decision and profoundly regret it," King Zaher Shah said. "But state affairs should not be reliant on any one citizen alone."

"Your Majesty, as Your Grace knows, I suffer from poor health and would not be able to successfully assume the responsibilities that such a function requires," Mr. Suri said.

"I see." The king's voice had softened. "We appreciate your services to the country and wish you to continue your excellent representation to the Court of Saint James."

"Your Majesty is most gracious," Mr. Suri acknowledged.

In March 1963, the palace broadcast that Daoud Khan had resigned as prime minister of the country, and Doctor Mohammad Yusof would form a government of transition, during which a new constitution would be elaborated, political parties formed, and parliamentarian election organized. Like Mr. Suri, Dr. Yusof was not associated with the royal family. For the first time, the palace had entrusted this high function to a commoner. Soon, the names of Noor Mohammad Taraki, Babrak Karmal, Rahim Mahmoudi, and Ghulam Mohammad Niazi were murmured as leaders respectively of Khalq (people) and Parcham (flag), of pro-Soviet Union obedience; of Sholay Jawed (eternal flame), a Maoist movement; and of the Beradarane Musolman (Muslim brotherhood). They constituted the main political parties that acted underground so far and whose antagonism caused decades of conflict, war, and misery in Afghanistan. There were also two minor movements: (a) Afghan Mellat (Afghan Nation), of Pashtun nationalistic obedience, led by Ghulam Mohammad Farhad and (b) Hezbe Democracy Motaraqui (Progressive Democratic Party), of social democracy tendencies, chaired by Hashem Maiwandwal, the destitute former ambassador to Washington.

Soraya's father understood the game of the palace—divide and rule—and was very happy to be away from the conflict zone. With his network of friends within and outside the country, he received dozens of reports, letters, and even phone calls every day. Oftentimes, he disclosed his fears with Soraya during their late evening heart-to-hearts. The format of such dialogues was defined; Soraya reported about her studies first. Then they engaged in an open discourse about social, economic, and political situations of Afghanistan and other hot spots of the world. Never had Soraya had such a wonderful professor and mentor. Her father was her god on earth!

In the first half of September 1963, King Zaher Shah and Queen Homeira were hosted by President John F. Kennedy in Washington.

SORAYA: The Other Princess

The Afghan king aimed at repairing the damage caused by ten years of pro-Soviet policy of his cousin and was amid few heads of states who met this most alluring president of the United States of modern times before his brutal assassination two months later. Though the palace appeared enthusiastic about the outcome of the king's undertakings during the visit, Mr. Suri remained skeptical and saw two impediments, that is, the proximity of Afghanistan to the Soviet Union and the burning ambition of Daoud Khan to accede to the supreme function of the country.

As most young girls of her age, Soraya admired the young dashing Bostonian who had succeeded in the presidential race, deeming him for obvious reasons the most handsome, intelligent, and honest head of state of the world. She read everything about John and Jacqueline Kennedy and argued often with her father. Mr. Suri recapped at each occasion that she should not be taken by glamour and confuse the empathy and good intent of someone with state interests and affairs. He resolutely thought that the end of the Cold War would be the obliteration of the Soviet Union. At the same time, he seemed anxious about the corollaries, chiefly for Iran and Afghanistan, neighboring the *big bear*. Though the king pledged his intention to restore the neutrality of Afghanistan and keep the Soviets at bay, the Central Intelligence Agency (CIA) had inferred that Zaher Shah was a lightweight compared to his fired cousin Daoud Khan. The backing of the ostracized General Abdul Wali was not adequate to avert the much dreaded Daoud Khan from seizing power again. The CIA had catalogued Afghanistan as a third-degree country of interest for the United States. American support was to be only of a development nature. Ambassador Suri was cheerless about his king's feats. Soraya's acquaintance with fundamentals and the art of politics and diplomacy was speedily growing, while in school she shone in literature, economy, history, and philosophy.

She was terribly distraught at President Kennedy's assassination, one of the most furtive state misdeeds. She wept and did not eat for several days, as if the tragedy signified the end of the world. Her father had extensive discussions to take her out of despair, referring to the sad side of being a leader. He mentioned that Abraham Lincoln and Mahatma Gandhi were also great leaders who were killed violently. In each such case, conspiracy theories have a large place in the media. He contended that whether internal bodies of the government or the crime syndicate or even the Soviet _Komitet Gosudarstvennoy Bezopasnost_ (KGB), Committee for State Security, murdered President Kennedy will never be elucidated. Life will go on and the real perpetrators unpunished. Soraya felt sad and recognized why her father refused to be prime minister of his country.

In Kabul, schools and the university had turned out to be the nest of revolutionary activists. The antagonism between the communists and the Muslim Brotherhood was shrill. The two pro-Soviet entities and the Maoist movement tussled too. The social and political environment looked dim. In spring 1964, the draft of a new constitution was finalized, and Prime Minister Yusof traveled to main capitals to seek support. Sir Alec Douglas-Home had been in 10 Downing Street for a few months. Soraya knew that this building of Gregorian architecture was the office and residence of British prime ministers since 1684 and was constructed by several experts under Charles II of England. Dr. Yusof, who had commenced his European tour from Bonn, was zealous to meet him. He had a candid talk with Mr. Suri the night before his face-to-face with Sir Alec.

"Zamir, how shall I broach him?" Dr. Yusof probed. "I ought to impress the man at once."

"Yusof, let me be forthright with you. Sir Alec is not attentive to Afghanistan and considers your visit as a courtesy call," Mr. Suri stressed. "He deals prominently with Soviet influence in Europe, decolonization, and evolution of the Arab world. The queen's foreign secretary deals with other issues, such as ours."

"I am the prime minister of His Majesty King Zaher Shah. My interlocutor is and must be the prime minister of the United Kingdom," Dr. Yusof angrily countered.

"Be calm, my friend. You have no choice," Mr. Suri stressed.

"You see, Zamir, I am the only Afghan that His Majesty has trusted outside his family with the function of prime minister. I am not a nonentity!" Dr. Yusof proudly claimed.

"No, my dear! At least one person before you rejected the offer," Mr. Suri serenely emphasized.

Dr. Yusof was baffled and demanded to know the name of the individual who had the pluck to say no to the king. He was counseled to confer with Ali Khan. Every day Soraya was acquiring more knowledge of how to treat delicate political and diplomatic concerns.

On May 26, 1964, the world faced another political shock. Jawaharlal Nehru, the disciple of Mahatma Gandhi who had governed India since its independence, passed away from a severe heart attack. The world was anxious. Two years earlier, the Indian Army had ferociously faced the People's Liberation Army of China on the mountains of Aksai Chin in Kashmir and Arunachal Pradesh, north of Aasam and neighboring Tibet. The fear was that General Ayoub Khan of Pakistan would take advantage of the circumstance and push Mao Zedong to strike India again. The CIA had warned New Delhi of such a move. The Afghan government was nervous, not only due to its mistrust of Pakistan and the aggressive manner that the flamboyant general was addressing its external relations with the help of the young Zulfiqar Ali Bhutto, his foreign minister, but also due to the fact that the Afghan democracy was too young to face a major military challenge. Bhutto navigated to Beijing several times but could not persuade his smart Chinese counterpart, Zhou Enlai, who had much bigger ambitions for his country.

The much feared second Indo-Chinese war did not occur to the great dismay of Pakistan. Dr. Yusof had meanwhile been charged by the king to consult Ambassador Suri, who had acquaintance with influential members of the Congress Party leadership. Lal Bahadur Shastri was sworn in as prime minister just after Nehru was cremated. The discipline and maturity of the Indian political class staggered those who thought that India was only Nehru. While the world remained calm, Ayoub Khan and Zulfiqar Ali Bhutto were boiling with rage for a lost opportunity to hammer India. The Indo-Sino-Pakistani matters were themes of debate between Soraya and her father for months. While she had great esteem for Nehru, his heir and daughter Indira was deemed impassive. She also felt that Bhutto was destructively ambitious and somehow a carbon copy of Daoud Khan.

In late summer 1964, Princess Belqis Begum, eldest daughter of King Zaher Shah and wife of General Abdul Wali, was announced in London for a private visit. While in European realms, wedlock is sought with other royal bloods, in Afghanistan interfamily marriages has been the practice for a long time, with some noticeable disadvantages. The most defiant opponents to rulers have always been within the palace. For some, such bonds contributed to the salvage of their power. The princess had unreserved esteem for the former chief justice and his family. No state act was envisaged. She was accommodated in the Grosvenor House Suites, located on Park Lane.

Soraya quickly searched and learned that the place was initially acquired by the first marquis of Westminster, Robert Grosvenor, in 1805 and had since belonged to his family, known as the Dukes of Westminster, till the end of World War I. In 1870 Hugh Grosvenor, third marquis of Westminster, commissioned the famed designer and architect Henry Clutton to revamp the property, particularly the state rooms. However, the edifice was constructed anew in 1920 to become a luxury hotel. Dwight Eisenhower and George Patton were its customary guests. Queen Elizabeth II had also learned skating in its great room. The Afghan royal family members were used to staying in this hotel as it was close to the embassy.

The second night, Ambassador Suri received the princess at his residence for a private dinner. The chef, who had meanwhile become a whiz, did not need Mrs. Suri's aid in the kitchen. Soraya and her mother groomed the table and requisitioned name tags. Her father came up in a timely fashion to have a look at the sitting and seating layouts. He was confident that his daughter's education was unique and urged her to act as the host of the family. Soraya was overjoyed. She wore a green shiny Little Mistress embellished maxi dress with black upper lace and sleeve endings and resembled a pearl gemmed with an emerald. It was a memorable evening for the young Miss Suri. Her comprehension of issues, courage, and allure impressed the Afghan princess. They discussed at length about fatwa, a religious order that aimed primarily at restricting women in their rights. A trustworthy bond was undeniably established between the two.

Personalities like Mr. Suri were pioneers of their era. He tutored Soraya to be a free thinker; she loved challenges, argued about ideas, and deliberated on what she deemed truth or sound. While she embodied the ancient aristocracy of the Suri dynasty, Martin Luther King Jr., Mahatma Gandhi, Ernesto Guevara, Ben Bella, Nelson Mandela, and Patrice Lumumba had intrigued her mind. She read about them and felt that nonviolent resistance to oppressors was more efficient to ensure justice for all human beings. Mr. Suri eulogized the peaceful defiance of Gandhi, Martin Luther King Jr., and Mandela. He urged his daughter to make a clear distinction between revolution that destroyed and evolution that ensured steady headway.

In response to his daughter's query, Mr. Suri narrated that according to legends, the Pashtuns were descendants of Quais Abdur Rashid, who had four sons, namely, Gharghasht, Sarban, Bet, and Karlani.

All tribes were their broods. The Sarban and Gharghasht clans settled in Southwest Afghanistan, namely around Quetta, Kandahar, and Helmand, while offspring of Bet and Karlani scattered between South and East Afghanistan, as well as North-West Pakistan. Durani and Ghilji were the most renowned lineages of Sarban and Bet, respectively. It was the Lodhi Ghilji branch, who in the fifteenth century ruled India and contributed to the harmony between Hindus and Muslims. They were crushed by Babur, the mighty creator of the Mughal Empire in 1526.

The ambassador's Suri Ghilji ancestors resisted and ruled north India in the sixteenth century too, though for only a short period of time. Another outlet, the Hotak Ghilji, instituted in Herat the foundation of modern Afghanistan, but they were overthrown in 1738 by the Iranian Turkman King Nader Qoli Beg, known as Nader Afshar. Some conspirators believed that a few Durani officers who served in the court of the Iranian ruler played a role in the downfall of the Hotak Ghilji dynasty. Since then bad blood has eclipsed the rapport between the two rival cousin kinfolks. Ahmad Shah founded in 1747 the Durani dynasty and renamed the country Afghanistan. His family has ruled since. Knowing all facets of the antagonism between the Ghilji and Durani Pashtuns, Mr. Suri apprised Soraya that she would have to fight for a country in which right replaced might and competency substituted for ethnic drive.

In autumn 1964, Mr. Suri was notified of his nomination as ambassador of Afghanistan to India. Though he had fond memories of the University of Bombay and looked enthusiastic, he would have wished the occasion for a few years later as Soraya's future and education preoccupied him. The departure for New Delhi was set for December of the same year. During this period, Soraya gained a Politics, Philosophy, and Economics scholarship from the University of Oxford with full boarding. Realizing the imminent absence of her father, she instantly moved to the City of Dreaming Spires. At the age of nineteen, she represented the proper definition of glamour.

Myriad notabilities, diplomatic bigwigs, foreign royalties, students, and even professors desperately endeavored to court her to no avail. Afghan dignitaries too counseled Mr. Suri to wed his daughter as soon as possible, and numerous proposals were voiced.

Soraya was interrogative why her society was so disgraceful of her ambitions. She was irritated for the attention people were bestowing to her physical splendor. The rapport with her father had changed; it was now the ambassador who anxiously awaited every Friday evening for his daughter to return home. Evening conversations always happened in the library, but on more fundamental philosophical, political, and economic issues. On the eve of decolonization, the essence was about who the revolutionary leaders were and what they aspired to attain. Comparative values of market and directed or socialist economies were deliberated, often till late hours of the evening. The sense of justice for all made Soraya an unpopular student with Paul Brown, a professor of economy who believed that only capitalism was the solution and that it was routine if the frail among human beings perished. She often complained to her friends and classmates. They grumbled to each other about Professor Brown, who displayed a colonial approach. Soraya countered him ragingly for his outdated behavior.

Mr. Suri was soon bested by Soraya in philosophy. She took her courses with Professor Bernard Williams and spent enough time to comprehend different categories of this science. In addition to Aristotle, Plato, Descartes, Kant, and other classic authors, she read in particular the oeuvres of Martin Heidegger, Karl Popper, Friedrich Nietzsche, and Jean-Paul Sartre. She turned out the favorite student of the eminent soul of modern British philosophy. They often took coffee together, arguing and exchanging interpretations. He used to say, "Soraya, your curse is your beauty, and Professor Brown is an idiot!"

She did not comprehend why Professor Williams never used the furniture in his office. He was always lying on the floor reading and writing. Several times Mr. Suri invited the renowned professor and relished conversing with him. He then became a regular weekend invitee at the Suri table and loved Afghan food. His favorite dishes were *dopiaza*, a heavy lamb shank soup, full of onion, coriander, yellow peas, and other essential condiments, and *shola ghorbandi*, mashed risotto with lamb meat with or without sauce. He fondly called Soraya *Miss Dior* of Oxford as she not only continued using the fragrance offered by her father four years back but also was smartly dressed. Her presence was discerned everywhere she went, not only by her stunning beauty but also through her knowledge of topics debated, elegance of character, and choice of dress colors and cuts. She was transformed to simply an outstanding young lady. She captivated all attentions at any given circumstance. Professor Williams became her second inspirational tutor and often told her, "You have an extraordinary presence and aura wherever you walk in, Soraya."

The date of Mr. Suri's departure for India was fast looming. Ali Khan was recurrently calling him to seek advice as King Zaher Shah had urged a *loya jirga*, a grand council of traditional leaders, to convene and approve the new constitution of the country. Mr. Suri was a national figure and renowned lawyer. He was instrumental in recognizing tribal chiefs of Logar, Qalat, Herat, Nangarhar, Badakhshsan, and Parwan provinces, in particular. On September 9, 1964, the country shifted to a parliamentarian system. Some judged it was the end of Daoud Khan's aspirations, while others, in particular Mr. Suri, cautioned.

Soraya was perplexed. All her life, she had been with her father and acquired everything from him. But now she had to carry on without his presence even during weekends. She had sleepless nights. Her father was her confidant, companion, tutor, and protector. How could she survive in the United Kingdom without him? For a while, she contemplated leaving Oxford as, after all, there were prestigious institutions' in India too. Her father had studied in Bombay. But Ambassador Suri emphatically countered the idea and instructed her to behave as a mature person. Soraya had another reason to insist on accompanying Ambassador Suri. She could not bear her father's illness.

However, he said one day to his daughter, "My darling, life and death are in the hands of Almighty God. The certitude of life is death; the timing is the only uncertainty."

That day, Soraya howled in her room and went to inspect every corner of the residence, particularly the library. There she had had tender moments of discussion, debate, disagreement, and appeasement with her father. She cherished every recollection of events and touched repeatedly the armchair where her father had been seated. She had a strange feeling about his assignment to India and cursed the king for taking away the only human being she trusted and loved. Soraya was mature enough to construe that her father was a virtuoso who shone in law, sciences, history, philosophy, diplomacy, and politics. But above all, he was a magnificent father and comrade to her. He utterly understood his daughter's inner feelings. She often detached herself to think and organize her mind for the day her parents would leave for India.

On the eve of his departure, Mr. Suri told her, "My child, the time has come, and I have no counsel to give you, for I know you will cope very well with life and your studies in Oxford. Just be yourself, the way I know you—authentic, assiduous, enterprising, and focused."

He declined further discussion with Soraya, stressing that he had said it all. In early December 1964, Mr. Suri was already settled in the Chanakyapuri quarter of the Indian capital. The embassy was just around the corner. It did not take long for his *agrément* to be granted. He soon became a confidant to Lal Bahadur Shastri, who was open-minded, generous, and less dubious in politics. He had encountered the young Zamir Suri at the University of Bombay during Mahatma Gandhi's lecture long ago. Soraya promptly restructured her life.

She now had a comfortable self-contained studio in the Oxford girls' accommodation quarter, navigating between classrooms, libraries, and her residence.

The year 1965 was remarkably busy for Mr. Suri. Soraya was apprehensive and fretful. She was following the trend of events in the subcontinent. Zulfiqar Ali Bhutto and General Ayoub Khan recognized that Mao Zedong would not engage in another war with the now nuclear India. They hurled their Operation Gibraltar, meticulously prepared by the ISI, striking India in Jamu Kashmir. Lal Bahadur Shastri retaliated by moving into West Pakistan. The bloody war, costing the lives of tens of thousands of soldiers and innocent civilians, continued till September of the same year. Neither side had a clear-cut triumph. The CIA and KGB leaders had convened in Montreux, near Geneva, and resolved that protraction of the war was favoring the Chinese. Americans and Soviets then settled to restrain from further meddling and to compel their respective proxies to end the conflict. Leonid Brezhnev, as the new dictator of the Soviet Union, offered to host peace talks in the city of Tashkent in Uzbekistan. Lyndon Johnson had no option but to press Bhutto and Ayoub Khan to consent.

Meanwhile, Kabul was exceedingly nervous. Daoud Khan probed the king whether his pick of parliamentarian democracy was at the right time. But Zaher Shah endured and charged Mohammad Yusof with the organization of elections for the lower and upper chambers. The king personally oversaw the ministry of defense and ordered troops to be on alert. Mr. Suri had weekly encounters with Shastri to ensure that King Zaher Shah was well apprised and Afghanistan remained neutral in spite of mobilization of its army. The prime minister of India genuinely called him *Brother Suri*.

Soraya exchanged weekly long letters with her father. She usually delivered a full report about her studies and life in Oxford before seeking his advice on plentiful topics. They wrote less about political

126

matters. She was of the opinion that her father's correspondence was certainly monitored, not only by Pakistani, Indian, and other foreign agents, but more importantly by the Afghan secret services. She had no interaction with the new Afghan ambassador's family and was busy with her own restricted circle of friends and professors in Oxford. She now lived on a different planet. Apprehensive of her father's welfare and mindful of the fact that projection of any wrong image would tarnish the prestige of her family, she only focused on her studies.

In Delhi, the pressure on Mr. Suri was immense. He had daily dialogue with his country's joint security team, comprised of ministers of foreign affairs, defense, and internal affairs, as well as the head of secret services, the majority of whom were members of the royal family. He knew that such conversations were scrutinized by many immersed in the Indo-Pakistani crises. His endeavors to persuade the team for face-to-face briefings in Kabul did not yield results. He then resolved to dispatch exhaustive weekly reports to the king through Ali Khan. Every Sunday, Afzal Amir, who was piloting the Boeing 707 of Ariana International Airlines to Delhi, met Mr. Suri at his residence and received a sealed envelope to hand deliver to the minister in person. His reports summarized his formal and informal encounters with Lal Bahadur Shastri and other Indian dignitaries, as well as his colleagues, mainly Pakistani, Soviet, Chinese, British, and American.

Occasionally he featured the presence of Homi Jehangir Bhabha, a Parsi Indian scientist, in the prime minister's residence at 10 Janpath Road. Bhabha was of Mr. Suri's age. They had met at the University of Bombay under the British Empire and shared views about the future of the region. Mr. Bhabha proceeded to Cambridge and initially studied mechanical engineering but shifted to nuclear physics and acquired a PhD under the guidance of eminent scientists such as Paul Dirac and Niels Bohr. He had persuaded Nehru to make India an atomic power and is considered today the father of the Indian nuclear program. Mr.

Suri relished chatting engineering, physics, religion, politics, and philosophy with him. They understood each other. Bhabha proposed to establish a nuclear engineering department in the newly Soviet-sponsored Kabul Polytechnic University, but similar to the idea of a free trade zone, Kabul did not pay attention. The king was only attentive in exchanges between Indian and Pakistani authorities.

Zaher Shah was also fussed about the internal situation. After he sidelined his ambitious cousin and pioneered democracy in the country, the West was pushing for free and fair elections that were finally scheduled for September 1965, just before the Tashkent peace talks between India and Pakistan. The campaign was marred by inducement, nepotism, and meddling of the palace. The leaders of Khalq and Parcham in particular were enraged and called for a public uprising. Some believed that Daoud Khan was hatching the unrest. Of course, high schools and the university were the best spots to instigate and muster against the government. Dr. Yusof was utterly overwhelmed. No one was listening to him. All ministers were relating directly to the palace. General Abdul Wali seemed to be the real holder of power now. Daoud Khan was irritated that the crown prince was so clueless and could not face his foe.

The general gained notoriety among the young officers of the army within the country, while thousands of them who had been spread to the Soviet Union Republics and the Warsaw Pact member states remained loyal to Daoud Khan. Rallies started in July of the same year and were reaping momentum on a daily basis. Each political party shaped its own gatherings. But the communists had the upper hand. More specifically, Babrak Karmal and Rahim Mahmoudi with their senior respective lieutenants orchestrated and led the roars of unhappy students to which common people joined.

The antagonism between the pro-Soviet and Maoist movements was evident from the start. The joint security team took charge of the entire government and began issuing security decrees and orders. Some middle-ranking party leaders were apprehended. This deteriorated the situation further. Mr. Suri, admired by all, was recurrently consulted and urged to speak to various tribal and opposition leaders. The king was concerned about the domino effect of the strife in the provinces. He also instructed Mr. Suri to unveil if India was abetting the opposition parties. Within a few weeks, he became the special envoy for all sides, a role that he disliked; Ali Khan understood his disdain. He wrote Soraya more often and in length. She offered to join her father in Delhi, but Mr. Suri refuted the idea and ordered her to remain, finish her studies, and face the challenges of her life. Though his effective exile had affected him, he felt fortunate to have his family out of Afghanistan. In every conversation with Soraya, he was warning of an imminent and gory situation in the country that would take scores of lives. The election finally happened, and the king seemed happy about its upshot, inviting Dr. Yusof, the interim prime minister, to form a new government.

The amateurish parliament was to convene on October 14 of the year 1965 to rubber-stamp the cabinet. However, Parcham and Sholay Jawed did not disarm. Countless numbers of students decanted on the streets of Kabul, moving toward the Parliament on the famous Darulaman Avenue. They rapidly amassed in front of this newborn body, questioning its legitimacy and authenticity. The king was suddenly fussed and suspicious of his entourage. Why were his subjects so ungrateful? He was giving them more rights, and they were *spitting in the soup*. Vexed and alone, he gave full authority to General Abdul Wali, who ordered the army to open fire on demonstrators. Dozens were brutally murdered. Hospitals were full of critically wounded. A long patriotic and revolutionary poem was quickly smuggled to all dwellings, accusing the mighty general of murder and exhorting justice. Its author was unknown.

To contain the hemorrhage and political turmoil, the palace resolved to put the blame on Dr. Yusof and plump him. He was forced to resign on October 29. A week later, on November 2, the king urged

Hashem Maiwandwal, Daoud Khan's declared enemy, to form a new cabinet. The prime minister designate was a journalist by profession and knew the art of addressing the public. Before even asking for a vote of confidence, he surprised the entire country by appearing in the middle of demonstrators at Kabul University without any protection or specific measures. He spoke to students, acknowledged the mistakes committed, and assured them of remedies. A temporary truce was agreed upon, and he was confirmed by the parliament. Daoud Khan was furious. The man he disliked and had removed from his ambassadorial position in Washington had now replaced him and seemed more popular. His ego could not admit such an affront on his personality.

Mr. Suri received two distinct phone calls in the same week. Dr. Yusof was probing what went wrong and why he abruptly lost the trust of the king, while Maiwandwal was querying what he should do to succeed. Of course, no reprimand was forced on General Abdul Wali or any other shooter. Slowly the situation in Kabul settled, and Mr. Suri's thoughts once again converged to the regional issues.

Meanwhile, under the auspices of the United States of America and the Soviet Union, the Tashkent peace process between India and Pakistan was progressing. Zulfiqar Ali Bhutto and Swaran Singh, foreign ministers of Pakistan and India, were piloting the talks. They both were brilliant, sturdy, and uncompromising. Afghanistan was an observer, and King Zaher Shah had concurred that Mr. Suri backed the foreign minister in the talks when required. It was a weird situation as he flew to Tashkent via Moscow instead of proceeding through Kabul. His appeal to stop in London was turned down. Soraya was advised not to join him in Moscow. The Cold War had its toll on innocent people on both sides of the curtain. Applicants of visas for the Soviet Union were blacklisted by Western secret services, and Mr. Suri had knowledge of the fact. Soraya was saving her mind and queries for the pleasant moments when she occasionally phoned her father. Nothing had changed; she relied as usual on his advice and wisdom. Oftentimes, she started sobbing and required time and comfort to engage in her conversation. She sorrowfully missed her father's presence and chats.

On January 6, 1966, a fit, jovial, and full of energy Shastri unexpectedly called Mr. Suri for their weekly encounter. The Indian prime minister affirmed the success of the Tashkent talks. He was proud of his foreign minister, who had neutralized his Pakistani counterpart on all fronts. He notified Mr. Suri that together with Ayoub Khan, he was proceeding to the Soviet Republic of Uzbekistan for the peace deal. Aware of Ambassador Suri's efforts, he invited him to travel together. But the palace felt he had accomplished his job and urged him to remain in Delhi.

On January 10, the Tashkent Declaration was signed between the two leaders, putting an end to the second Indo-Pakistan conflict. Shastri was impatient to return and personally proclaim the outcome of the talks to the Indian Parliament. There was jubilation in India as Pakistan had to withdraw from the occupied territory of Jamu and Kashmir, a sacred land for both nations. But shockingly and unexpectedly, Shastri died in the early hours of January 11 in his hotel room, leaving the world astounded and his nation orphan. No one in India believed the death of their prime minister was due to natural causes.

Mr. Suri had the sternest time of his life. Kabul was soliciting daily report, his peers were entreating for more words as he was the only foreign envoy who had met Shastri before his journey to Tashkent, and Indian authorities were seeking his opinion, particularly on US-Pakistan relations. He was also distressed by the death of his friend and "brother." He accompanied Shastri's family till the last stages of his cremation near the Jamuna River and strolled side by side with Homi Bhabha. The next day, he expressed commiserations of Afghanistan to the government of India and visited Shastri's widow. Back home, he felt drained and took an early nap. On January 14,

1966, Mr. Suri rang Soraya in the early hours of the day and spoke at length, recounting the Shastri family's mourning, analyzing the situation as if he was no any longer troubled by his conversation being intercepted, and urging his daughter to remain strong no matter what ensued. She was perplexed but felt blessed that her father had called her. However, a strange feeling eclipsed her thoughts. She judged her father was lonely and rushed to Air India and booked a ticket for the next day.

That was the last time Soraya heard the tender voice of the man who represented the essence of virtuosity and goodness. At midday, Mr. Suri was no more! At the age of only fifty-four, he had an apparent horrific heart attack and passed away while being carried to the hospital. Homi Bhabha hurried to the morgue. He was tearful; the man who shouldered him in Bombay, defied his scientific and philosophical intellect, his friend and colleague had died so abruptly. Within hours, the government of India determined to maintain part of their honor guards, deployed for Shastri's funeral, on alert. In Kabul, Ali Khan was notified; he apprised King Zaher Shah and was tasked to organize a state funeral for his longtime friend. Soraya arrived in the early hours of the day. She was escorted by Indian officials to their residence, where Mr. Suri's body was lying in state. She sat next to his coffin, took his right hand in her two hands, and was sobbing of humungous sorrow. She was murmuring incomprehensible phrases, as if she was conversing with his soul. She stared at his visage.

Even in his death, Mr. Suri was dreadfully handsome and had a peaceful smile and saintly face. State dignitaries, ambassadors, writers, musicians, scientists, bookstore owners, neighbors, and common people had lined up to express their condolences to Mrs. Suri. Soraya was in her place, chatting silently with her father, and had the sense that he was responding without being able to verbalize. Many times, she disbelieved his death, but the frozen hands and stiff body left no doubt. When the Indian services came to take the coffin, she acquiescently joined her mother in the car taking them to the airport. Swaran Singh and Homi Bhabha were instructed to accompany Mr. Suri's body. The Indian honor guards were along the streets to venerate a man whose ancestors had given so much to India, who was an exceptional statesman, and whose advice and friendship were always without prejudice and self-interest. Soraya was in her own world, recollecting every second of her life with the man she deemed her god.

At the airport, Swaran Singh addressed Soraya for the first time. "Miss Suri, I am sure he taught you to be strong. This is the only way to overcome the demise of this great man and valiant son of the East."

Soraya was stunned as these were precisely the words her father had stated to her before his exodus to eternity. Bhabha lost his two finest comrades within just three days and was shattered. He was speechless and just gently shook Soraya's hand. She saw tears in the eyes of this great scientist about whom she had so much studied and for whom she had so much respect. Afzal Amir, the trustworthy pilot, saluted Mr. Suri's family. His Boeing 707 was to transport the casket to Kabul. That day, Soraya overheard several people close to her father say that "*he was killed too.*" She did not comprehend the purport of the statement and disregarded it.

They landed at 2:00 p.m. in Kabul. Ali Khan, Hashem Maiwandwal, and plentiful other executives dispatched by the king received the family. There were thousands of people at the airport. It appeared a chaotic scene. Scores were offering their shoulders to carry the coffin. Others had lined up along the airport road as if a head of state was visiting their city. The people were honoring somebody they had heard of as a noble, honest, intelligent, and hardworking gentleman. Most had never encountered Mr. Suri but meant to pay their respects. The entire government had been staggered that a man of his stature desired to be interred in his parental village in Logar. But this was where he was born and grew up. Though his father had hectares of arable land, his own standard was, "*You must live with what you earn.*" As a young man, he had refused family farmers and domestics to serve him. This was where he had his honeymoon, promenading with his wife along the streams excavated to irrigate their crops. And this was where he turned up every weekend to meet his companions and the imam of the mosque where he had so well learned the Holy Quran. Logar was his real refuge to refresh and face the inanities of politics and government administration.

Thousands of individuals had come to this hamlet. Nobody cared about Ali Khan or Hashem Maiwandwal; they all sought to carry Mr. Suri's coffin on their shoulders, an honor according to Afghan and Muslim culture. Delegations of tribal leaders had arrived from Herat, Qalat, Kandahar, Laghman, Parwan, Nangarhar, and other locations. Tajiks, Uzbeks, Turkmen, Hazara, Pashtuns, and others all mourned their great man. The concord and fraternity among this populace was startling. They knew they had lost an exceptional individual and leader. After arrival at the Kabul airport, Soraya instantly comprehended the harsh veracity that the Afghan society had barely cared for women and their views. Her mother was sidelined; all resolutions were made by male government officials, family members, and friends. At burial, she pleaded to see her father's face one last time. It was unusual, and the imam had to be consulted. He finally conceded against his will.

The next day, there was emptiness everywhere. Soraya went to corners of the house where her father used to spend time, hoping that he would speak to her again. She saw him ubiquitously without being able to get hold of or converse with him. He had an exultant and joyful face. The three-day bereavement was unbearable for Soraya. The Suris proceeded to Kabul for the third and last day. King Zaher Shah, Daoud Khan, Naim Khan, Ali Khan, Hashem Maiwandwal, the whole cabinet, and most of royal family members attended the commiserations ceremony in the Eidgah Mosque of the capital.

A week later, Soraya returned to Oxford but had no desire to attend her lessons. Everything seemed disheartening and depressing. She often traveled to London and strolled around the embassy to feel the presence of her father. Her friends were anxious. She was not the same communicative person and often avoided coffee occasions and became reclusive. The adversity was aggravated as after a month, she was notified that there was no money for her education abroad and she had to return to Afghanistan. Processing a pension had been chaotic and lengthy. The skies were falling on her.

On a sunny Monday of March, Professor Bernard Williams invited her for a coffee. They spoke at length about Mr. Suri and the unlimited respect that he had for the "exceptional man," At the end of their conversation, he said, "It would be a pity if you returned to Afghanistan. Your father told you to be combative and realize your dreams."

"Yes, professor, but my scholarship alone would not cover my financial needs; it is not possible for me to continue," Soraya sadly responded.

"Look, Soraya, today students are working to earn money and pay their tuition and other costs. You can do the same," he advised.

"How?" Soraya queried.

"We have a family friend—an old lady. Her name is Lisa Bernstein. She is alone and would love to pay you to spend a few hours a day with her and chat," Professor Williams suggested.

Soraya concurred, and the day to visit Lisa was set. From this instant on, she was a different soul and felt more valued. She had the inkling of having taken her life in hand, pursuing her father's advice. Her mother could not argue and just expressed her blessings and prayers. The conversant, bright, studious Soraya was reborn. She had no time for herself and planned meticulously. Lisa liked her company; in many ways, they looked alike—beautiful, refined, aristocratic, and assertive.

On Monday, January 24, 1966, Soraya learned that Homi Bhabha was killed in a plane crash near Mont Blanc in France just days after he had avowed that India could fabricate an atomic bomb. He was to attend a high-level meeting of the International Atomic Energy Agency in Vienna. What on earth was occurring? Within two weeks time, Shastri, Suri, and Bhabha had all fallen and vanished. Was it curse, conspiracy, or just calamitous fate of a region that dreadfully needed them? She read everything about Air India Flight 101 that never attained its destination. While conspiracy theories arose all over, a CIA operative, Robert Crowley, disclosed later on that his agency was behind Shastri's death, invoking close ties with the Soviet Union and development of atomic weapons. Whether Mr. Suri and Homi Bhabha were victims of East-West rivalry, nobody would ever know. If true, it was the most idiotic and shortsighted endeavor. Not only did India become a powerful nuclear power but also an economic giant. Moreover, Afghanistan's destiny in the decades that followed demonstrated that the country desperately needed a man of Mr. Suri's stature, knowledge, and conviction to save it.

Lisa was also inquisitive and perused books, newspapers, and magazines to be able to converse with Soraya. Actually, she had given Soraya a new life. It looked like a sweet rivalry as to who got to a subject of interest quicker had grown between the two. They traveled most Saturdays or Sundays together to London. Soraya was priming her courses by conversing with Lisa. They often went for afternoon tea to Claridge's. Some companions of Lisa joined them. The meeting of old ladies was both enthralling and heartbreaking. They spoke of their family members and friends who were arrested, detained, tortured, and killed by the German Nazi regime for the simple reason that they were Jews. Soraya was often silent, listening and learning about the cruelty of humankind. Why did Hitler and his

Gestapo scheme to exterminate an entire population? What sin had these millions of innocent women, children, and elderly perpetrated to face such a fate? In a short period of time, Soraya became a second daughter for Lisa. She was reciting her poems, exchanging opinions, supervising the maid in house affairs, particularly polishing the precious silver items, and taking her out for walks or to tearooms and restaurants.

At the university, Professor Brown was nastier than ever. Occasionally Soraya thought he was a remnant of a Gestapo group that had escaped international justice. He did not like non-Christians, even Catholics, brown–colored people, Africans and Asians. Poor people were judged "ash of the society," according to his economic theories. Soraya was defying him openly, asserting the explicit effect of diversity on economic growth. In July, the results came. Professor Brown had allotted Soraya a severely bad mark, and she failed! According to the rules, she must have passed all subjects to succeed for her year. She was dispirited, and Professor Williams was fuming with anger at his *"idiot"* colleague. Mrs. Suri urged her daughter again to return to Kabul; she was primarily disturbed by what people would gossip about her.

Lisa objected and offered a voyage to the Austrian Tyrol. She had already reserved in Hotel Schwarzer Adler in Innsbruck and more distinctively solicited for Tiroler and Hermes rooms. To make the journey entertaining, she had opted for surface transportation, rail, boat to traverse the Channel, and then rail again through Paris, Strasbourg, Basel, Zurich, and Liechtenstein. Soraya was grateful for the thought and packed speedily. Though long, the trip was most pleasant. Both ladies loved conversing on topics of shared concern, such as politics, economy, philosophy, fashion, and nature. They often navigated between their seats and the "wagon restaurant" of the train. After the departure of her father, Soraya had commenced smoking. Somehow it was a means to abscond from depressive thoughts. Lisa's personal recounts about the plight of Jews during the Second World

War all over Europe were most revealing of a scheduled extermination by a devilish man and his demoniac lieutenants. Soraya often asked why other European leaders tolerated Hitler and did not stand against him from the start. If Albert Lebrun and Philippe Petain of France were enslaved by the rapid rise of Hitler, George VI and his prime ministers Stanley Baldwin and Neville Chamberlain had the might. Lisa constantly declined to judge, stressing the resilience of victims and the vigor of survivors.

In Schwarzer Adler, Lisa had the Tiroler and Soraya the Hermes rooms. They did not like the lower dining area of Byzantine-style architecture with plentiful roofs. The upper space was much more luminous, airy, and pleasant. The next day, a couple approached their breakfast table. The man, in his sixties, had a mass of hair on his skull, and the woman, in her early forties, was a refined, slim blonde. Lisa could not believe it and screamed, "Arthur, Cynthia! What a surprise! What are you doing here?"

The man bowed and paid an English-style reverence to Lisa and introduced himself to Soraya as Arthur Koestler. This time around, Soraya shrieked of surprise. "Oh, my God! Arthur Koestler, the famous writer and philosopher?" she asked.

"Yes, my young lady, he replied. "And this is my wife, Cynthia Jefferies Patterson."

They were cordially invited to join them. Koestler and Cynthia knew Lisa; they frequently congregated in spheres of friends. He too was Jewish and a survivor of the Holocaust. Lisa presented Cynthia as Koestler's third wife. They had been married for less than a year and had moved from the United Kingdom to settle in California. Soraya had read his books. While she found the *Darkness at Noon* gloomy, *The Act of Creation* was more of the type she enjoyed reading. Arthur Koestler had sought refuge in Tyrol to write a new book. But his wife pressed him to devote time to Lisa and Soraya. Occasionally they had breakfast or dinner together and walked on the streets of the old town and along Inn River or Sill Stream.

Koestler was amazed by the intelligence, eloquence, splendor, and behavior of this young lady, who did not share anything with Europe by birth but had all the attributes of European aristocracy. They reasoned extensively whether Fyodor Dostoyevsky influenced and inspired Sigmund Freud, Friedrich Nietzsche, and even Thomas Mann. Soraya was affirmative, but Koestler deemed that each had his own style. He further asserted that similar to scientists, philosophers, poets, artists, and novelists were at the vanguard of evolution and new rational and that they were up front to transform society. He was resolutely of the opinion that while Thomas Mann, a Nobel Prize winner, had to hide his inner feeling and only implicitly express it, particularly in his *Death in Venice*, there would be a time when people would speak openly and without fear about what was deemed irrational. There was harmony of opinion about the substance of *Darkness at Noon* as communism had shown its totalitarian face, and everybody comprehended Rubashov and his disillusionment with Bolshevism and Communism. The 1956 suppression of democracy in Koestler's native Hungary, the murder of two thousand five hundred, mainly young and harmless, students, and the exile of over two hundred thousand citizens of the country to West Europe were themselves darkness that spread over Hungarians. But voicing about the despotism of Communism and its revolutionary theories in 1940 was indeed revealing Koestler's genius and avant-garde spirit. Discussing *The Act of Creation* was a distinctive matter.

Soraya frequently disputed with Koestler about theory, reality, and the significance of creativity, imagination, and invention in science, art, or literature. For her, nature was constituted based on defined laws of physics, and scientists were just unearthing them. She further was of the belief that the notion of invention in science and technology applied only to vehicles for expression or implementation of laws, and the best such instrument was mathematics; in art or literature, on the other hand, everything was improvised, and the creator indeed was inventing the substance, through realities observed or imagination or a blend of both.

Koestler was captivated by the depth of conversation. For him, Soraya certainly did not at all exemplify the women of her country. Being British, he had an ambiguous knowledge of Afghans and was of the sense that they were mountainous, coarse, and brutal people who had massacred the entire British army, including women and children, during the first Anglo-Afghan war. Her reaction was unfussy, that actors of every war were merciless, that there were no losers and victors in a conflict, and that all sides were too simply dark horses. She, however, confessed that women were facing appalling conditions in Afghanistan, stating her childhood encountering of villagers all around the country. He believed that only Western education would produce women of Soraya's stature from developing countries as their ancestral culture was rudimentary.

She grinned when confronted with such an impression. In her opinion, all contributed to the well-being or agony of the world, and she firmly opined that her ability to argue with the distinguished writer and philosopher was due to her broader knowledge of East and West cultures. She stated that Afghans have an astonishing sense of friendship and enmity. Further, that they sacrifice everything for those who prove gracious but have overpowered sternly the hostile intention, even when the force disproportionality has been a defining factor. She elucidated that notorious conquerors had tasted the end of their glorious expansion with a defeat in Afghanistan. While other invaders had united the diverse peoples of the country, the British abuse of amity and trust of Afghans for decades led to interethnic rivalries and conflicts. As a result, one group stood against the other, one tribe versus the next one, or even one brother opposed the other. This policy of divide and rule through companionship had devastating consequences in the region. Oftentimes, Lisa backed Soraya while Cynthia supported her husband.

The week passed quickly, and Soraya was enchanted. The intellectual entertainment with Arthur Koestler, Cynthia, and Lisa was so captivating that contrary to her obsession, she did not even perceive how the old city of Innsbruck looked. Not only had she met the illustrious writer and philosopher, but she was able to plow his mind, deliberate with him, and assert her own aptitude. She suddenly felt keen to confront Professor Brown and impede his "economic spits." But the occasion never occurred as he was transferred elsewhere. Arthur Koestler and *The Act of Creation* significantly shaped Soraya's opinion for the following years. She often wished her father was alive to complement its religious aspect. Professor Williams was of no assistance as he did not honestly trust religious doctrines, but Soraya did and profoundly. She was under tremendous compulsion not to waste time in returning to Afghanistan.

Soraya was eternally obliged to Lisa and has kept fond memories of talks, disagreements, and deliberations with that remarkable lady. She declined the waylays of hundreds of smart and handsome men and had only one short-term aim of concluding her studies and returning home. Most Oxford contenders of her heart gently nicknamed her "hopeless case." When it came to debate substance matters, she was most affable, outspoken, and esteemed.

Somehow Professor Bernard Williams had substituted for her father. They were often seen in the cafeteria deliberating arduously on themes of their concern. The point of dissonance was always about religious beliefs. While the distinguished professor considered religion an archaic philosophy, Soraya was of the judgment that it was a combination of rules and means to reach the ultimate of goodness and perfection. Religious books were subject to construal of individuals, and contemporary tomes did not give her as much joy as one hour of intense debate with her late father. She did not see a disparity in scientific, spiritual, and metaphysical delineations of the act of creation and deemed evolution its natural derivative. For her, the definition of life was movement, and as electrons were moving around the nucleus of atoms of all substances in solid, liquid, and gaseous forms, then not only everything lived, but God had made life evolve. Professor Bernard Williams rebuked her frequently. Soraya retorted that death was relative, referring to the general relativity theory of Albert Einstein. In principle, nothing was added or subtracted from the universe. When God pledged life after death, it implied that there is no demise of anything. Williams was content to see his protégée evolving and defying him directly.

The first half of 1968 was devastating for the United States of America. On April 5 of that year, Soraya woke up as usual and turned on her radio; Martin Luther King Jr. had been slain in Memphis in the state of Tennessee while breathing fresh air on the balcony of a motel. He was there in support of Black labors on strike for equal rights and wages. The man who had followed the path of Mahatma Gandhi, promoting nonviolent resistance to White domination and oppression, the one who all his life preached compassion among all races and peoples of the world, the politician who fought for justice and human rights, and the devout man who believed in equality as the best religion of our times was brutally and cowardly murdered. Soraya had great admiration for him. She had actually grown up with King's struggle and rise before public opinion. She was electrified and thought of Sara, Mama, and other African Americans who would now be orphans. They, too, had a dream—a dream of living free of segregation with equal rights in their own country. What would now happen to the dream of Martin Luther King Jr.?

The night before his assassination, he spoke of his death to the crowd of workers as if he knew that some nefarious people wished his elimination. He had told them:

> *I may not get there [freedom] with you. But I want you to know tonight, that we, as a people, will get to the promised land. So I am happy tonight. I am not worried about anything. I am not fearing any man.*

The right cheek that he always offered to his enemies in a sign of fraternity, solidarity, understanding, and common concerns was hit by the bullet of the assassin. Soraya rushed to Lisa for comfort. Both ladies spoke of the cruelty of mankind, exchanged views about divinity, scrutinized behaviors and went through pages of religious and scientific histories to debate why human beings perpetrate the same sins recurrently without learning from their blunders.

Lisa proved, once again, a mother to Soraya, assisting her to focus on her forthcoming exams. However, it was short lived.

On June 6, 1968, Soraya awakened timelier than usual and turned on the radio to learn the appalling news of Robert Kennedy's assassination. She admired the young, dynamic Senator and always feared for him a fate similar to that of his illustrious elder brother. Since the killing of President John Kennedy in 1963, Robert was the hope of those who sought change in the United States. Some believed that his open support for Martin Luther King Jr. and the civil rights advocates, stand against organized crimes and the power of big money, as well as efforts to oppose the hard-liners in the government, may have prompted his assassination. America had become senseless. Soraya was tracking the presidential campaign of Robert Kennedy like many others in the world. Millions of Americans were anticipating that he would win the primary in California in order to get the nomination of his party. The night before, he had indeed won and addressed his supporters in the Hotel Ambassador of Los Angeles. At the end, he was counseled by some of his entourage to take a shortcut through the kitchen of the hotel. His bodyguards had objected in vain. He was viciously killed by a coward who was waiting for him. The only white politician who was cheered during Martin Luther King Jr.'s funeral was no more. It was depressing for Soraya. She did not know where the West was heading. Emotionally drained, she wanted to get her degree as soon as possible and return home, hoping for less violence in Afghanistan.

Her graduation approached fast; she did not realize how time had fled. There was an inexplicable bond of comradeship, sincerity, and loyalty among her, Lisa, and Professor Williams. She always felt attended to. She graduated with honors, and Lisa booked dinner in the famed French restaurant of Dorchester Hotel in Mayfair to celebrate her success and say farewell at the same time—Soraya was instantly leaving for Kabul. The two ladies hugged each other repeatedly, while Professor Williams did not stop smirking.

Chapter 3

Marriage and Early Days of Real Politics

Your friend is your needs answered. Friendship is always a sweet responsibility, never an opportunity.

—Gibran Khalil Gibran,
The Prophet

At the end of July 1968, Soraya returned to Afghanistan. She could not believe how the country had transformed. Signs of modernity and headway in women's rights were discernible everywhere. Above all, some good degree of liberty and emancipation of women was noticeable. She knew that the city of Kabul had an amazing history and geography, affecting even its current political makeup.

The Afghan capital was ringed by the Khair Khana, Asamai, and Sher Darwaza mountains. It had a history of at least three thousand five hundred years. *Rigveda*, a sacred text of Hinduism, and *Avesta*, the primary collection of holy texts of Zoroastrianism, spoke of the Kabul River and the city as a "vision of paradise set up in the mountains." This small city became consecutively the center of Hinduism, Buddhism, Zoroastrianism, and Islamic expansion. It was always deemed a strategic setting between the cold plains of Central Asia and the warm waters of the Indian subcontinent.

The history of this city had been similar to that of the rest of Afghanistan, written with bloody ink. The Achaemenid, Greek, Seleucid, Mauryan, Kushan, Sassanid, and Kabul Shahan were the pre-Islamic empires that governed the city. Each era transported piles of memories and pages of history full of sorrow, joy, conquests, defeats, and manslaughter. And each empire ravaged what the other had fashioned, inclusive of cultural values. The Kabul Shahan erected a wall on the foothills and around the city to protect it from the Arab and Islamic invasion. Perhaps they already had knowledge about the Great Wall of China and its merits. Though of much smaller size, that wall served the purpose, but only for a while.

The resistance to Islamic invasion was exemplary, forcing the assailants to change strategy. The then rulers comprehended how the Sasanian Empire in Persia was defeated by a horde of ferocious Arab combatants who, on the back of their lightning-fast horses, destroyed the endurance of a system rotted by corruption, nepotism, and mismanagement of people's interests and wealth.

Aware of the protective walls and stratagem of the Kabul masters, Abdur Rahman bin Samana, a non-Arab Muslim, infiltrated the city in the late seventh century and was able to convert a minority of over ten thousand inhabitants, opening the way for Ya'qub bin Laith Al-Saffari to enter the city and found an Islamic governing system. Al-Saffari was not an Arab but a smart, brutal, and merciless leader who subjugated Khorasan, Sind, and Central Asia. In fact, the viciousness of the invaders in Persia, leading to the disdain of the population, forced the Arab Abbasid caliphs of Islam, based in Baghdad, to determine and use native commanders for further conquest. Among them, Abu Muslim Khorasani was undeniably exceptional. He even unified the Muslim world by defeating the Damascus-based Umayyad caliphs in 743. But the newly enthroned Al-Mansur Abbasid felt threatened by the might of his incomparable warrior and charged him as being a heretic. He was brutally murdered in 755 at the age of only thirty-seven, and his body was thrown in the Tigris River. The revolts following Khorasani's slaying led to the disintegration of what could be called the Islamic Empire and to the sovereignty of non-Arab provinces and cities, including Kabul. However, in each location, Islam had ample disciples to survive.

Though Kabul played an important role under the domination of the Samanid, Ghaznavid, and Ghorid rulers, it was only with the advent of Zahiruddin Babur, the founder of the Mughal Empire in 1504, that it became the capital of a great king and emperor. Babur, an outsider and offspring of Tamerlane, grasped how to win the hearts and minds of the indigenous people. Kabul became his capital during the summertime. However, others, British and Russians in particular, left indelibly painful recollections of their stay. Geographically, access to Kabul is strenuous due to the enveloping mountains. The Kabul and Chamcha Mast rivers, both springing from the Paghman massifs in the far west, join and divide the city that, in this year of 1968, was a mosaic of peoples, outfits, vehicles, stores, edifices, and many other constituents. The city not only characterized the entire country but also displayed the dominion of free thinking and commerce. Iranian, Indian, Russian, American, German, and French products were competing.

The city was distinctly split into several quarters. The core part inhabited the royal palace, ministries, and central park of Zarnegar. The northwest was the lately rich area of New City, where Soraya and her family dwelled. Poor neighborhoods of old Kabul were situated to the south of the river. In the outskirts of the city, provincials had settled. Two main arteries, the Darulaman and Chehel Sotoon avenues, led to two prestigious palaces of the same names. While the first now housed the ministry of justice, the latter was the official guesthouse of the king of Afghanistan. Driving, riding, or sauntering in the spring and summer on these two lanes, bordered by perfumed acacias trees, was a unique and stunning pleasure. While the scene of the poor, pulling extraordinarily loaded carts, and the ambulant vendors yelling to sell their products for a few coins was distressing, the view of booming trade, girls and boys sharing classes at the schools and university, and the growing number of women having political and important managerial functions were distinctive of a country moving forward. All four corners of the city had their own bus stations, serving respectively provinces toward the north, east, west, and south of the country. The latter, though, had kept its colonial-era name, the Lahori Gate. During the old days, it was from this point that convoys departed to the Indian city of Lahore. The ravaged old military garrison of Bala Hisar, where the British were humiliated during the First Anglo-Afghan war, was located on the adjacent hill.

Soraya was saddened to find that Abai had retired but was happy to see that Khan Ali, her son, took care of the family. Of course, he was trusted and acted as cook and house manager. Her return concurred with the preparation of the festivities of the nation's independence. The difference with earlier years was striking. Major arteries of Kabul were enlightened and ornamented with colorful bulbs. Hundreds of thousands of people ambled in and around the city to rejoice. In addition to the national parade, presided over by King Zaher Shah himself, countless sports and leisure events were organized. Main government institutions had constructed stands around the King's Park, Chamane Hozouri. The best chefs and artists were hired to entertain guests at night. The ministry of education had its own zone, offering opportunity for young student performers, called amateurs, to demonstrate their faculties. Roadside cuisine excelled. Carts of soda water, with amazing red, orange, green, and yellow colors, trolled all along to the great pleasure of children. Bottles were tied up with small glass balls. To open them, someone had to press to depressurize the bottle, releasing a pop sound before bubbles appeared with astonishing flavors. Artists and sportsmen of different provinces were given the opportunity to present their specific talents to the public at large. The King's Camp was reserved exclusively for high government dignitaries and foreign diplomats.

On the music front, the whole country was conversing about Ahmad Zaher, a twenty-two-year-old singer called the Afghan Elvis, son of a well-behaved family. His father was Mr. Suri's peer, friend, and colleague and a cabinet minister who later on became prime minister. Sons and daughters of such families did not engage in music. Therefore,

Ahmad Zaher was a pioneer, a revolutionary, heretical, unconventional, and atypical creation of the society. But millions loved his melodies. He was handsome, fearless, and audacious in his art. Upholding order in his shows was very difficult for security forces.

During the ten days of festivity, the King's Park was jam-packed with souls. Some tried their luck to approach unescorted girls or women who, for their part, pretended to scorn their glances but nonetheless enjoyed being the center of attention. The Ghazi Sports Stadium hosted practically every late afternoon a variety of games. Buzkashi, engraved in the blood and body of the northern populations of Afghanistan, spear launching from the back of a horse, practiced essentially in the south, wrestling, soccer, and other games gathered tens of thousands of individuals. Movie theaters had mushroomed. Old playhouses in the ancient parts of Kabul portrayed Indian pictures, while modern halls were constructed in New City and projected Western flicks three times a day. Cinemas had become the best dating spots for young souls who attempted to escape the rigid family environments. Black market tickets with exorbitant prices had their customers. Thousands gathered each day to watch the favored films. In addition to standard newspapers, fashion and cinema magazines had begun to appear in kiosks. Photos of Indian and Iranian stars were offered at inflated costs, and young girls and boys hurtled to purchase them. Rose postcards had become the trademark of communication between lovers. Countless new schools had been erected or leased. Primary and university education was mixed, while girls and boys were separated at the high school level for six years. Kabul University was a heaven on earth. Ornamented with beautiful flower gardens and vegetation, it hosted all major disciplines, each located on an artfully designed alley. In the center of the campus, there was a small garden and a canteen, where hundreds of students agglomerated at lunchtime. Talented professors, educated in Germany, France, the United States, and even the Soviet Union, had returned and contributed tirelessly to the development of the country. Girls loved the miniskirt dresses, and boys adhered to tightly fitted attire and bell-bottom pants. Private-sector millionaires were now known to the populace. There was a real feeling of liberty in Kabul at least, though major challenges such as equal rights for all ethnic groups, corruption, and nepotism had still to be resolved.

Next to Soraya's house, restaurants, kebab windows, and ice cream shops now required reservations, something new in Afghanistan. Contrary to other areas in town, the eateries of New City did not compel men and women to separate. Every observer would have deduced that Afghans were humble but happy people. However, on the political front, the country was straying in an erroneous track.

Noor Mohammad Taraki, Babrak Karmal, and their respective comrades Hafizullah Amin and Anahita Ratebzad, leaders of the pro-Soviet Khalq and Parcham, were empoisoning the atmosphere with their Marxist-Leninist initiatives and moves. Most in Kabul whispered that they were grasping instruction from some corners of the palace. While Mahmoudi firmly ruled Sholay Jawed, new blood such as Saidal Sokhandan and Noor Tabish emerged, shouting for revolution. Mao Zedong's booklets, ornaments, and brooches, all in a red color, continued to be secretly distributed to students. Amid strong and forceful appearance of communist ideology, the Islamic Brotherhood party was swiftly suppressed. Menhajudin Gaheez, the founder of their newspaper, was arrested and put in jail, but Ghulam Mohammad Niazi and Burhanuddin Rabbani, both scholars and professors at the university, remained in command. They were less visible than the scalding and obstreperous communist leaders. People often murmured their names among sympathizers. The smaller entities did not have any significant impact. The communist factions were vigorous. Schools and Kabul University remained infected by the creed of boycott and abstention. Hordes of ireful agitators, calling themselves the "enlightened," were teeming to overpower teachers and compel pupils to join the mass rallies against the government. Slogans of death to this, to that, to the neighbor, to the shopkeeper, and to whomever the leaders did not like were yelled.

Red- and green-colored banners dominated the respective crowds of demonstrators. Youth were dragged in the rallies like sheep without digesting what was at stake. The government did not use force, and freedom of expression was fully respected. Perhaps the gaffe that General Abdul Wali had committed some years back and Western pressure pushed the palace to be cautious.

Soraya could not make any sense of it. People openly referred to quarreling within the palace that was giving rise to breaches of law and order. Even primary-school kids were dragged into the demonstrations in support of one or the other communist movement. Teachers and professors were frustrated as they could not implement the required curriculum. They warned about a generation that would be raised without proper education. What was surprising was that both communists and Islamists advocated for a revolution in their favor. Slogans and rhetoric were extremely violent.

Soraya was in search of a job and as usual portrayed knowledge and elegance. She always wore Miss Dior in memory of her late father and promptly found a solution for her wardrobe. Among numerous tailoring shops that she visited, Master Hassan appeared the most endowed. She gave him fabrics and sketches, inspired by the latest fashion magazines of renowned brands that she received from a friend working with Ariana International Airlines. The talented Master Hassan was able to tailor any outfit as it was fabricated in Paris, London, or Milano. In a matter of weeks, the entire high society of Kabul was conversing about the stunning young Suri, who was distinctive and seemed more British than Afghan. Contrary to other females of her generation, she dared to address all men, stare straight into their eyes, state substance and logic, and refute unsubstantiated claims. Her style was unique, and she was a firm, humble, and courteous person who always kept her distance with people she did not know well. She was heartened by the emancipation of women, at least in the capital city. But soon she grasped the insurmountable disparities.

Economic, social, and cultural fractures were divisive, even in her own surroundings. She had impassioned debates with her interlocutors. Yes, the country was on the right track in spite of defiance, acutely on the part of communist and revolutionary dogma, but she felt so remorseful for Afghan women in general and those who lived in rural zones in particular. The Afghan democracy was too new and fragile. The government needed to address disparity and illiteracy quickly and engage in comprehensive social support programs, not only to ensure the vast majority but also counter efforts of extreme leftists. She quickly discerned that since her childhood trip to the villages of Southwest Afghanistan, little had changed for Afghan girls and women outside major cities. Her three paternal cousins attended her like *mousquetaires*—protectors. United Nations agencies, banks, and international firms were her focus, as pay and standing were much loftier than government institutions.

In the first week, she had three interviews. Among the encounters, the meeting with the president of a renowned bank was an eye-opener. From an eminent self-made family, he greeted her in his spacious office on the top story of the famed Spinzer edifice. He had studied on the East Coast of the United States.

"Let me give you the background of my studies at Oxford, sir," she suggested.

"I have studied the application carefully and know your background, madame," he replied.

"What do you mean, sir?" Soraya inquired.

"I studied at Cornell when your esteemed father served in Washington and New York. He gave me precious advice that I will always remember," he calmly stated.

Soraya quickly grasped the reverence of the refined man toward her father. She had witnessed the admiration of tribal chiefs and poor villagers, but knowing more about the great Zamir Suri from a highly talented and educated person was like a pleasing fresh breeze in her face. He categorically advised her to seek a job in an international organization, describing how public administration was rudimentary and frustrating.

Back home, the eldest of the three mousquetaires-protectors was chuckling at Soraya and counseled that she required more time to determine the great challenges that her country and its new democratic system faced. For him, women had a long way to go in Afghanistan, as no effort was undertaken to fight prejudiced customs. Most reprimanded the British for the misdeeds. While she granted that the former colonial power had a devastating policy of divide and rule, not all in the world could be due to their transgressions and indigenous leaders had a large share of the blame. Indeed, the British Empire skillfully employed religion and spiritual conservatism to dominate their colonies, and Afghanistan as a zone of influence was no different. It even appeared that some of their military intelligence agents served as imams in the principal mosques of key Afghan cities, particularly Pule Kheshti in Kabul. It also seemed that those who managed this top religious edifice of the capital in the first half of the twentieth century contributed to the downfall of King Amanullah Khan. Their role in bringing to power Zaher Shah's father seemed crucial. Millions of innocent and ignorant populace were rallied in accordance with London's policies and plans of action. Of course, intellectuals, impartial politicians, and opinion shapers who favored national interests were sidelined or directly targeted. It was enough that a religious figure tag someone as an infidel for the palace to undertake the rack.

The eldest uncle of King Zaher Shah molded the intelligence services of the country and applied them most effectively in defense of his family and clan. His unequivocal approach to Afghan politics was distinct. To illustrate it to royal youngsters, it appeared that one day he summoned them all to his farm on the way to Paghman. He asked them to observe that the starving turkeys were tailing the gardener obediently no matter what he gave them to eat. A week later, the same group discerned that the glutted turkeys were not obeying the farm caretaker even if he propounded the best seed. His insinuation was evident: keep the people famished, and they will be gratified with little of any low value—but as soon as they are satiated, your leadership will be at jeopardy as they will have the luxury to think about state affairs. Though in 1946 after over sixteen years, he had vacated the position for his younger brother, the ruthless ex-godfather of the Afghan spy agency still terrified those who disputed the privileges of the royal family. They had an absolute right to be generals, ambassadors, and ministers, no matter their competence.

Indeed, since 1929, the country had regressed in terms of women's rights, civil society emancipation, and freedom of the press and expression. Even in the palace, men decided and women shadowed. Tribal leaders were pouring in to offer deals to the "regent" and to get rewards for keeping their people more ignorant than ever. Politics, finance, and economy were men's affairs. Moreover, any controversial issue or criticism of the regime was not tolerated and was conducted in whispers. But since 1963, commoners had made some significant difference. Soraya was puzzled though politics was in her blood flow. On the surface, all seemed serene, including women's emancipation, but underneath Afghanistan lived anxious historic moments. Many times, she was wedged between two massive groups of demonstrators without being able to discern who said what!

Her cousins had counseled her to keep a low profile and stay away from politics; two years after his death, Mr. Suri and his family were still feared. Soraya resolved herself and found a temporary job at UNESCO, the United Nations Organization for Education, Science and Culture. She was promptly noticed by the country manager, a British citizen, who empowered her with the portfolio of field coordination. She undertook valuable assignments and missions to Ghazni, Kandahar, Herat, Badakhshsan, Faryab, Mazare Sharif, and Bamiyan. Her emphasis was on the salvation of cultural heritage and girls' education. Her reports were impeccable. She soon became the model staff member and developed policy papers. Soraya, however, had heated debates on the political evolvement of the country with one of her Afghan colleagues, the nephew of a famous leftist leader whose political stature was questioned. Some trusted his sincerity, while others considered him a man at the service of the palace. His revolutionary nephew was a pompous young man who thought Soraya was ignorant of local cultures as she had been abroad all her life. This was absurd. Her grasp of the country, its history, geography, cultures, social, political, and economic realities, as well as ethnic composition were profound. However, the attitude of the young man revealed how in general the male population, though educated, perceived their female colleagues.

On a Thursday afternoon, the manager invited Soraya into his office.

"Sit down, Miss Suri! I have been observing your work and tireless endeavors for a while. You should definitely have an international stature. I have looked to job availabilities within the United Nations," he proudly mentioned. "You may wish to compete for an interesting one!" He smiled.

"What do you mean, sir?" she inquired.

"I suggest you apply for a position in the Policy Department of the United Nations Executive Office. Then you go to Paris to brief our headquarters about the lamentable conditions of the Bamiyan Buddhas." He smirked.

"I will have a job in Paris, sir?" Soraya asked.

"No! Only the selection process will take place in Paris. If selected, you will work in New York. Knowing you, I have no doubt that you will come in first," he concluded.

Soraya was flying with delight and could not believe that at the age of only twenty-three, an Afghan young woman could have an international position with the United Nations. The following morning, she went to Logar to the grave of her father. She was weeping of joy and praying for the soul of that great man who forged and taught her honesty, hard work, belief in her ability, and service to a broken country. She was conversing with him the whole afternoon and had the feeling that he was next to her, but she could not see him. It was irritating as she wanted once more to take his hand as she used to do so long ago. The confab was intense, like in London. She reasoned with him, exchanged thoughts, agreed, differed, walked around the village, and giggled with him. At dusk when she left the cemetery, her father had shared a thousand opinions and approved her Paris trip. She was blissful, though she could not touch him. The mere fact of sensing him around was enough.

By the evening of the day after, she had already applied for the job. She then joyfully joined her larger family and announced the imminent trip to Paris. She spoke with enthusiasm and poise. If successful, as an international United Nations staff member, she would acquire the best experience in the world and help her country in a more affirmative manner without fear of misjudgment or ignorance. She could advocate for the education of rural Afghan girls and fulfill her late father's wishes. Soraya already had pictured a plan for her voyage. She would begin with acquiring a passport, as the one she had was taken back by government services. She would then fly to Paris, fulfill the task entrusted to her, undergo the interview process for the job, and visit Paris before coming back. Her immediate admirers were dismayed at the thought that once abroad, she might never return. Each one had a longing without sharing it with the others. Within days, everything was settled.

In Paris, she stayed at the Mayfair Hotel, between Concorde and Vandôme. With the famous *Paris Métro*, it was not arduous to navigate. Her presentation about the woeful situation of the Bamiyan Buddhas was exceptionally well received. Bamiyan was perhaps the most imperative epicenter and melting point of the famous Silk Road, bringing the Roman, Chinese, and Indian civilizations together. Between the third and sixth centuries, when the gigantic statues and countless caves were sculptured, the entire region of Bactria, which encompassed the current territories of Afghanistan, was Buddhist. Chandragupta was the key Mauriya emperor who spread Buddhism throughout this region. Ashoka, known for his particular brutality and an amazing transformation in his life to religious principles, following which he became a devoted and pious Buddhist, bolstered it. Buddhism was further developed in the region by the Kushan dynasty, which had supplanted the Mauriya. The assault on Bamiyan in the year 1221 by Genghis Khan and the demolition of the city that ensued after the murder of his grandson Mutukan Khan by the population did not affect the colossal effigies and grottoes. Alexander Burnes, the famous British spy in Afghanistan, had pictured them in 1832 intact. However, King Abdur Rahman Khan, known as the Iron Amir, smashed them irreparably between 1888 and 1893. Most "whizzes" in attendance did not know that the statues were purposely knocked down by a king that the British cherished. Similarly to the Egyptian Sphinx, obscure religious motivations were used to disfigure the Buddhas centuries after Afghanistan converted to Islam.

Soraya had already concluded that the despicable act had a different motivation. She spoke with real knowledge about the history of the Buddhas, unique jewels of the cultural heritage of the country, and did not dither disparaging the Afghan government for its dearth of interest. She also spoke of the likely collapse of the four Herat minarets, part of the Musalla Complex, constructed by 1417 with so much love and care under the guidance of the famous Queen Gawharshad Begum, as well as the Jam Minaret, erected between 1174 and 1193 and deemed the pride of the Ghorid Empire of

Afghanistan. Finally, Soraya spoke of the Bost castle and its famous triumph arch in southwest Afghanistan. She had a bond and love story with this part of the country through her father's undeniable support to the Helmand River projects. Bost signified the glory of the Ghaznavid dynasty of Afghanistan, those who had put an end to the Arab domination in the tenth century and propagated Islam in India. Their glorious Sultan Mahmoud Ghaznavi ordered Ferdowsi to write the book of the king. Bost was destroyed brutally by Genghis Khan and blasted by Tamerlane in 1383, but the arch somehow survived. She proudly informed her audience that the Bost Arch was nine hundred years older than the *Arc de Triomphe* in Paris and labeled the devastated monuments in Afghanistan as part of the heritage of the world and urged UNESCO to take action. What captivated everyone was that this young, bright, and alluring lady spoke fearlessly and determined that ignorance, misjudgment, and reluctance of the government were also dangerous nemeses of culture in Afghanistan.

The interview with senior staff of the Executive Office of the United Nations who attended the same gathering then became a formality. The same day she received a positive predetermination and was thrilled. She was proud of being the first female Afghan to reach such a distinction, and she rushed back to the Mayfair. It was the greatest achievement of her young life, and she wanted to share it with everyone. In her room, she opened her wallet and kissed her father's picture. She was pleased about her education, courage, and background, but realistic at the same time. Indeed, hard work, intelligence, talent, and a great ability to read and write were in her blood. But would these qualities ensure success? When she called her manager in Kabul, he already knew the outcome of the interview, congratulated her warmly, and advised her to fly as high as she could. She was, of course, flattered but remembered her father saying, "My child, when you fly the highest, try to keep your feet on the ground!"

She walked along the Champs-Elysées, enjoying the boutiques and window shopping. This majestic avenue and the *Arc de Triomphe* at its end were part of the identity of Paris, the "bride of all cities of the world," as some described it. She took a taxi to reach the *Champ de Mars* and the *Tour Eiffel* and join a group of colleagues. She climbed to the second floor of the tower to dine at the *Jules Verne* and have a view of Paris by night. The sight of the city from this place was unique. She gazed at it from all possible angles. Every single slant of the view was just exceptional.

Soraya called her mother with joy and enthusiasm. She chatted extensively about her presentation and interview. She apprised her that she would probably have a job with the United Nations Executive Office. As she spoke, an implacable silence loaded the atmosphere. After nearly fifteen minutes of monologue, she queried whether her mother was listening.

"Yes, I am," she replied.

"What is wrong then, Mother?" Soraya inquired.

"I am so glad, and your father is certainly proud of you in his rest, my love," her mother replied. "However, what would society think?" she calmly continued.

Her mother voiced her fear that in case she moved out of the family sphere before marriage, Kabul folks would gossip and invent theories. She protested and called for her mother's understanding as it was the fortune of her life. But the credence of Afghan tradition, deeming women as house objects to labor and reproduce, was too crippling. This was a line that she should not cross. Of course, the whole family coveted a dazzling future for Soraya, but the worry of what others would gossip about the daughter of a great man haunted them more.

As the job offer took some time to be processed, she was instructed to return instantly to study all aspects of an international career. The night was sleepless. At dawn, she took a walk along the Seine

River, wondering if her father would have made the same decision—certainly not, as he had the erudition, strength, and audacity to stand against obscurantism. She had never felt otherwise and venerated his courage to say no to what he believed was wrong. She was whispering as if he was walking alongside her, lamenting what had transpired the night before. She recalled people speaking of so many women maimed by their husbands or nucleus family members, thousands of young girls thrashed to death because they had displayed their liking for someone or millions of forced marriages in which the girls had no choice but to follow their uncertain destinies. This was in total contradiction to the religious instructions that required acceptance of both. Honor-killing victims were overwhelmingly female. Men were never or hardly ever "punished." It was paradoxical as graduation from Oxford did not have any relevance compared to the exigencies of an orthodox society. All around the country, so many young and inspiring souls were neutralized through cultural barriers, crippling the society's ability to soar. Significant numbers of scholars believed that such deeds were not practiced by the ancestral communities of the country but introduced through invasive foreign cultures.

This was the time she desperately needed her father to overrule the decision. After all, as an international civil servant, she could have fought against inhuman practices and traditions. But she could only speak to him and feel his presence—nothing more! Her heart was broken, and her dreams looked shattered. She ambled for a long time, pondering whether to call her mother and express her disobedience—but only if her father approved! She had an appalling feeling. She was persuaded he would, but she heard no voice to say, "*Do not worry—I will approve.*" Her throat was compacted. She meant to scream, but curious people along the river and near the Jardin d'Erivan would notice. She had no choice. As of this moment, nothing was appealing in Paris, and she decided to return to Afghanistan the next day.

Back in Kabul, her mother was gloriously pleased. She knew that Soraya had the audacity to express a categorical *no* to her exigency and take the job or abscond for Oxford, where she would have the backing of Lisa and Professor Williams to settle comfortably. But she was beholden to her daughter for having assented to her inner appeal. The Afghan ambassador to UNESCO had transmitted his account on Soraya's outstanding lecture and was of the view that the Bamiyan Buddhas would soon become the focus of the organization's special attention, once the so-much-debated Convention Concerning the Protection of the World's Cultural and Natural Heritage was agreed upon. The whole city was speaking about it—and Mrs. Suri was eager to give her own description of her daughter's success to friends and family members. The Suri name was once again on people's lips.

Soraya's manager was perplexed. He had earnestly toiled to get the bright Soraya out of her cultural prison and did not wish her to surrender so easily when all opportunities were there to let her fly high. He had assumed she was stout enough to decide for herself.

"What is going to happen now, Soraya?" he asked.

"I do not know, sir," she replied.

"Do you have any idea?" he insisted.

"No, but I hope the divine will help—I still have some time," Soraya gently explained.

"I understand. Sit down, please."

They conferred for over an hour. The manager was still hopeful, though the clout of Afghan culture was arduous. Women and girls in this country needed perhaps numerous additional decades to flourish. It was horribly sorrowful for Soraya, as she was educated in the best schools of Washington, London, and Oxford. Now she might subjugate herself to the might of conservatism and custom. She could not reason with anyone that her father would have consented to let her fly. The entire family was fretful of what others would say.

It was so pitiful that nobody cared about how she felt. Her cousins, the three musketeers-protectors, became her confidants. Each one aspired to impress her. Soraya enjoyed conversing with them. Afghan families resembled lion prides: in the absence of a mighty male father, all members were vulnerable. Since the sudden demise of Mr. Suri, his wife's main concern was to protect the reputation of her family and ensure the integrity of her only daughter, in spite of blunders made in the process. Soraya loved her job and had more substantive responsibilities. Though she never lost her smile, the limitations imposed on women by the society in Afghanistan were inhuman and unbearable. She recalled Professor Williams reminding her that her beauty was her curse, but her intelligence and studiousness were also scourges in a country the love of which was inculcated to her mind and soul by her late father. It looked like everyone among her close relatives had an inspiration on how to manage Soraya's life. She was enraged and exhausted. Since her return from Oxford, she had to comply with countless traditional requirements to the extent that she questioned her own personality and ability to be what she wanted to be. The tragedy was that men enjoyed all possible liberties, but women, even with the best education, had to be restrained from their basic rights due to fear of misjudgment by others. And the tongue of gossip among Afghans was very long and destructive.

Most of the United Nations agencies were in one edifice, adjacent to the Marble Palace, headquarters of the foreign ministry of the country. The next day, she strolled along New City Park, moving in front of a cinema of the same name. There were huge posters of *Arabesque*, a movie with Gregory Peck and Sophia Loren, on the front walls of the theater hall. Closer in the screen boxes, there were pictures of the movie. She was stunned; Gregory Peck resembled her father in his youth. She had a strange feeling and decided to watch the movie that evening. Then she passed a large number of restaurants, shops, and boutiques to reach the Zainab Cinema. Here the situation was different. *Neel Kamal*, an Indian picture with a Shakespearian triangular tragedy scenario describing the theory of reincarnation, was projected. People had lined up at this early hour of the day to purchase tickets, most of which were reintroduced in the black market by dealers. Bollywood or Indian and Iranian movies were most popular in Afghanistan. Some watched the same picture two or even three times a day.

Afghans shared history, culture, and even language with the Indian subcontinent, Iran, and Central Asia. These regions were part and parcel of one geopolitical, social, and economic body. For a while, she thought of a free trade zone and its significant positive impacts for the region, particulary for women of her country. But quickly her attention was drawn to young girls, dressed in black skirts, white scarves, and black socks, hastening to Malalai School. Each certainly studied hard for an emancipated future. Soraya questioned whether what she observed was a social mirage or a hallucination. Was women's liberation authentic in Afghanistan or just a social and political dusting?

She had grasped long ago that it would take sustained efforts for Afghan men to effectively consider women their equals. She thought of her own situation. If an Oxford-educated woman could not raise her voice because of social barriers, then what would happen to these girls, most of whom would only benefit from rudimentary basic education? When would the government and Parliament pass bills to protect the rights of women effectively? Though Kabul and main cities such as Herat, Jalalabad, and Mazare Sharif gave promising pictures, the truth was utterly different. Rural young women and girls were whipped, forcibly espoused, murdered, and even swapped for the sins of the male members of their families. The latter, called *badla* in Pashto *or bado por* in Dari, was one of the most shameful traditional praxes, whereby a young girl was proffered by offenders to the victim, his brother, or his family to be espoused. She was then used as a sex and labor slave for the rest of her life. Soraya's head was full of incongruities when she arrived in her office.

On a Thursday afternoon, the beginning of the weekend in most Muslim countries, she received a solemn marriage proposal. So far, she had refused dozens, perhaps even hundreds, of young, talented, handsome admirers, including the president of the bank, who had courteously hinted to send his parents for the purpose. She firmly desired to forge a career. She remembered her father warning her not to rush and do anything that would jeopardize her future. But now the situation was different. She paced along Wazir Akbar Khan Road to attain Malik Asghar Square, where the National Library was situated. She admired the foreign ministry marble building and its gardens. Soraya conceded that all these years, she had not been focused on her private life to meet her father's counsel. And now, she was at the crossroads of a very vital resolution. What should she do and whom could she consult? Her father was no more; Lisa and Professor Williams were far away. She could not trust anyone else. The librarian recognized her and sprinted to help. She took numerous books about international diplomacy. Her cousins waited for her in front of the cinema and had already purchased tickets for the late afternoon showing of *Arabesque*. She found Gregory Peck most handsome and a talented actor and liked the movie; it had a taste of both Western and Arab cultures. But her mind was focused on the proposal.

Her week was troublesome, and often she was isolating herself to reflect and weigh the pros and cons of a decision. On the one hand, marriage was an eventual permit for freedom. But it could also put an end to her aspirations for a bright career. She finally said yes to the marriage, and her mother was elated as she had always feared Soraya's strength and pluck to marry outside the family's norms. The notion of *siyal,* equivalent or within the standard, had been a cornerstone of the obsolete parts of Afghan tradition. Countless young people had been sacrificed and their lives shattered simply because they were not deemed worthy of the ones they loved. The segregation benchmarks could be based on social, political, or economic disparities, but more importantly on ethnic and religious diversity. Soraya valued knowledge, honesty, and hard work. That was how her father had achieved and taught her. Among friends and colleagues, she was most respectful of individuals who met her own norms—but this was not how the society as a whole deliberated matrimonial matters. Moreover, she believed that friendship and camaraderie could exist between boys and girls. But in Afghanistan they were either sisters and brothers or lovers. She was distraught and so sorry at the same time for the girls of her country.

Within days, the rumor of her *fiançail* spread throughout the entire city; the most gifted, stunningly beautiful, and courteous lady had at last decided whom to marry. The bridal event was fixed. The next Thursday afternoon, she hurried home, needing to meet with Master Hassan. She was stupefied to find Ali Khan, still the minister of court affairs, chatting with her mother. He was thrilled to see her.

"My gorgeous lady," he exclaimed. "I knew it from your childhood."

"Your Excellency is gracious," Soraya replied.

"My darling, your father and I were like brothers; you know this."

"Yes, sir. You have always been a true uncle to me," Soraya replied.

"I am so sorry that your father cannot be here to give you away. But I will be honored to stand for him."

"Thank you from the bottom of my heart, uncle. I am sure my father will witness the event from the skies."

"And now, my dear, listen to the good news. The foreign minister has today appointed your future husband to our representation in New York," he proudly announced.

"I cannot believe it, uncle. Please kindly thank the foreign minister on behalf of my family," Soraya blissfully responded.

A week later, the manager in her office was all smiles. New York, as they called the United Nations Headquarters, had formally offered Soraya the job. She was joyfully stunned. The silent and painful deliberations with her father's soul were not in vain then. She believed that even in his death, he had interceded for God's favor.

The foreign minister, as usual a member of the royal family, had deftly perused the report of the Afghan ambassador to UNESCO, who was, not surprisingly, his cousin. He had further reviewed minutes of the debate involving the Bamiyan Buddhas salvation. After all, they were the most momentous cultural legacy of Afghanistan. Kings became notorious for their destructive potentials. Sultan Mahmoud Ghaznavi razed Nagarkot, Mathura, Thanesar, Chandela, Kannauj, Kalinjar, and Somanath in India between 1023 and 1025; Alaouddine Ghori defeated the Ghaznavid dynasty and burned Ghazni in 1151; many others committed the same type of follies. Therefore, historic heritages were considered just rubble in Afghanistan. The mutilation of the Bamiyan massive Buddha followed the same philosophy. Soraya had slammed the vicious instincts of such rulers who used religion as a shield to justify their barbaric acts. The foreign minister had shared her views and engaged personally to make the Buddhas a recognized part of the world cultural heritage. He succeeded later on. But no one ever spoke of a young and dynamic Afghan lady who had defied and pushed the international community and the government of her own country to do so.

The Afghan tradition imposed a heavy and lengthy process before marriage. It entailed expenditures of different natures by the groom. Oftentimes in order to meet the exorbitant demands of the family of the bride, the poor man borrowed money from friends and relatives that destroyed the basis for a harmonious future life at its inception. Soraya overruled the traditional steps and desired a simple event.

The wedding took place on a lovely evening in the month of May 1969 in the Baghe Bala Palace and Restaurant, situated on the hills of Karte Parwan. Surrounded by vineyards, the white edifice was built at the end of the nineteenth century by King Abdur Rahman Khan, destroyer of the Buddhas. Soraya could not comprehend the dual character of such folks. On the one hand, they ruined human heritage that had aged thousands of years, but at the same time they excelled in the creation of such jewels. Master Rahim Bakhsh, vocalist of the court, performed his best melodies. Princess Belqis Begum and myriad other dignitaries of the regime were in presence. Ali Khan indeed acted as the bride's godfather. It was a memorable evening for all. Master Hassan had tailored an Afghanized replicate of Christian Dior's organdy cotton wedding dress, designed by the British Royal Couturier Sir Hardy Amies. The simplicity and allure of the wear was exquisite.

The gentle pace of the customary Afghan nuptial song when the bride and groom are joining the guests, "Ahesta Boro," was very special. Soraya had altered the text and devised her own. Master Rahim Bakhsh was most inspired by the vibrant wording. The buffet dinner around the pool was exceptionally refined and joyful; the chef from the renowned Khyber Restaurant had made a miracle. It looked like everybody desired to be the best. Mr. Suri's closest friends, who were or had been in important ministerial positions, attended with their families. Soraya had opted for a public ritual and lowermost dowry. People were amazed about her resolve; even the judge several times demanded she reflect and confirm. She stood firm, believing that the success of a marriage did not depend on money. In such circumstances, the families argued between themselves away from the eyes and ears of their invitees as if the bride was for sale. She did not bow to the exigencies of the convention and left the scene immediately after the official ceremony.

A week later, the young couple reached New York, and it was the start of Soraya pursuing the path of her father and being exposed to real politics. It was also the beginning of the development of a brilliant brain that only a few had the opportunity to recognize in the country as her stunning beauty was given more importance than her dazzling intellect. While in advanced societies, governments, business communities, and social entities, all headhunted at universities and specialized institutions to pick up the best and brightest brains, Afghanistan still had a long way to go. Over 90 percent of foreign ministry high officials were members or affiliates of the royal family. It was a weird situation; positions seemed reserved like seats in a cinema theater.

The first irritation was rental of an apartment on Broadway. Unexpectedly, it was not furnished. And Soraya did not appreciate the noise and flashing lights penetrating their small dwelling all night. She craved a serener dwelling in the "city that never [slept]" and found one in upper East Manhattan. But at work, she shone instantly. Though she received detailed briefings upon arrival about her responsibilities, the essentials of politics, diplomacy, and dealing with people circulated in her veins. Soon she felt at ease with the new environment. Soraya was tasked to follow matters related to security, as well as economic and social concerns more specifically. Asia was her geographic portfolio. She assisted in all United Nations debates and meetings with respective dignitaries. Her father had bestowed to her the black Montblanc and golden Sheaffer fountain pens in London before he moved to India. Perhaps his sixth sense had pushed him to do so. She adored employing them. The quality of her work and professional ethics were just impeccable. Some even called her *"Madame Perfect"* candidly.

The ambassador of Afghanistan to the United Nations was an icon of Afghan international diplomacy. For a long time, no one had been so efficient at the roots of the country's representation in the world arena. He knew that Soraya was the flawless shadow of her father and would soon acquire the respect of the bigwigs. However, he urged her to assist in shaping and shaking his executive office.

She offered to devote her weekends to train staff. She lectured employees about reviewing draft reports and speeches, examination of their compliance with foreign policy of the country, and above all, scrutinizing the logic behind the words. The ambassador was thrilled by Soraya's willingness, and the staff was gratified.

Within weeks, momentous progress was manifest. She assigned legwork to drafters and coached them to acquire the art of scripting logically. For the first time, the ambassador had an Executive Office that functioned effectively according to the required standards. She also introduced the notion and practice of briefing notes and talking points. She suggested to the ambassador a protocol based on which staffers presented openly and without fear their input on subjects discussed in different bodies of the august organization. Hence, he was properly briefed and knew what points to raise in the plenary, special, or bilateral sessions. She advised employees of the representation that diplomacy and emotions were two opposing phenomena and assisted them to establish a library where staff spent time to research and get their texts presentable. She commenced looking for Mama, Maggy, and Sara, her early-day comrades in Washington, DC, and was pained to discover that the first had passed away, while the latter moved to California. As for Maggy, she had retired and frequently traveled to different corners of South and Central America. However, using her days off, she still occasionally went to Washington to sense again the atmosphere of her infanthood in Georgetown.

In memory of her father, she sporadically visited the Dickinson Law School at Pennsylvania State University. On a sunny Sunday of September, she sat on a bench in the garden of the university near Adams Hall and was gazing at the surroundings while her husband had gone to buy some sandwiches. A man of about her father's age approached her.

"Young lady, are you a student?" he inquired.

"No! I wish I were. Are you English?" Soraya exclaimed, noticing his distinct British accent.

"Yes, indeed. But I am now settled here in the United States and teach at Dickinson. I am Professor George Booker," he informed her.

He sat beside her, and an enriching conversation began. She found a man of her father's caliber facing her. Surprisingly, Professor Booker knew "the young Professor Williams" and admired him. He comprehended promptly that the smart lady on the bench had been a product of the University of Oxford and worked with the United Nations luminaries. The conversation turned to world affairs, the development of international legal frameworks, and immediate noncompliance of some states to what they had agreed to. Professor Booker had sharp criticism toward the United Nations, and Soraya defended that the world body reflected only the views of its member states. The scholar, however, was of the opinion that executive leaders of the body should be more assertive when states violated rights. After a long time, Soraya had the opportunity to engage freely in a discussion and express her opinion without being disrupted or cautioned.

Professor Booker was in real surprise when Soraya revealed that she was from Afghanistan, for he had never encountered such a clever and stunning Afghan lady. His eyes were open wide when she mentioned her father's name. He remembered Zamir Suri as a bright man with great ambitions for his country and was not surprised to learn that the young lady on the bench was his daughter. Soraya was enchanted when he apprised her that he was the dean of the Dickinson Law School. She was amazed to grasp that any discourse with lawyers and engineers was structured and based on logic. Oftentimes, they wanted to close the circle in a deliberation, leaving nothing open-ended, as if it was a PhD thesis. Reaching a conclusion or verdict had always been of prime meaning to them. She pondered that they made better and more honest politicians, looking for solutions to the challenges. She further believed that scientists easily mastered the world of art and politics.

Her husband joined the conversation. He had two beef on weck and two club sandwiches. Professor Booker contentedly joined the improvised lunch. By late afternoon, they were still debating. He inquired about Soraya's ambition, and she expressed a deep interest in undertaking graduate studies. She was encouraged to apply for an evening session scholarship. He apprehended Soraya's eagerness to do as much as possible when she had the opportunity. Professor Booker often called on Soraya for a quick coffee in Aroma Expresso, near Dag Hammarskjold Plaza, or a nice dinner at home. She had become an able cook too. Her mother and own curiosity of cooking were instrumental. What she prepared had no recipe anywhere except in her own mind.

In the office, she was now a renowned, bright young staffer who had pushed the excellence of an executive office to the highest level possible. Heads of agencies fought to have her in their teams. Nearly three months later, Soraya received a job offer with a higher grade as executive assistant for the director-general of an agency based in Geneva. The option of flying with her wings was at her feet. That day, once again, she was the most contented individual in the world. The direct Swissair flight would permit her to work five days a week in Geneva and spend the weekends home in New York. She did not need the consent of anyone. However, this optimism was short-lived too. The Afghan ambassador, who often played with his pipe while speaking, wished to meet with her.

"I understand you received an interesting job offer from a United Nations agency in Geneva," he began.

"Yes, sir, and I am delighted. It will allow my husband and I to develop our respective careers. He will flourish under your guidance, and I will do my best with the world body," she happily replied.

"Have you thought of what people would comment?" the ambassador asked.

"This is not my worry, sir," she replied.

"But your country and I do care! The reputation of your great father, Mr. Zamir Suri, is directly linked to the prestige of our country," he resolutely underscored.

Once again, the game was over; Afghan women had to always worry about how society judged them. Nobody seemed concerned about their plight, inner feelings, and legitimate aspirations. Somehow she reenergized herself. Her late and beloved father always guided her so that in moments of despair, there was always a gate open, and the impossible did not exist. Hurdles just needed time to be overcome.

Developments in the late 1960s and 1970s molded not only Afghanistan's decades of history to come but also regional alliances as well as global affairs between the Muslim and Western worlds. Meanwhile, the rowdy state of affairs was evolving rapidly in Kabul. Political affiliations and opposing views among the populace, particularly youngsters in Kabul, were coming to a clash. In addition to pro-Soviet Khalq and Parcham as well as the Maoist Sholay Jawed parties, the Islamic drive was taking deep root in the political arena of the country. Perhaps it corresponded to the famous dialectical plan of thesis and antithesis. Mao Zedong of the People's Republic of China had called it "contradictions" in a society that did not follow the usual pattern of evolution.

The philosophy of Sayed Qutb, a United States-educated Egyptian Islamic scholar, had its disciples among the Afghan religious intellectuals. More students of the Faculty of Theology and Abu Hanifa School in Kabul were exploring to study at the Al-Azhar University in Cairo. At the same time, Ghulam Mohammad Niazi, also an Al-Azhar-educated professor and dean of the Faculty of Theology, formally formed the Muslim Brotherhood movement, based on Sayed Qutb's thinking. In his determination, he continued to be seconded by Burhanuddin Rabbani of the same institution. Other parties of small scope and influence still remained insignificant. Indeed, as of the inception of parliamentarian democracy in Afghanistan, the communist and Islamic opinions emerged as rivals and leading social and political factors, particularly affecting the young people at schools and universities. One side craved to inflict with foreign backing Marxism-Leninism on a society that was profoundly entrenched in its moderate Islamic tradition. The other struggled not to permit it to happen. Their enmity sculpted for a long time the history of this land. Weekly, if not daily, strikes and street rallies continued to be organized. Any reason was enough to justify a slowdown. With an overwhelming majority of illiterate inhabitants, extremely fragile youth misled by political parties, and lack of information about the exact situation in the Soviet Union, the People's Republic of China, or leading Islamic countries, favorable assumptions led opinions. The country was politically adrift!

People learned of new figures. In addition to Saidal Sokhandan of the Maoist party, Golboddin Hekmatyar and Ahmad Shah Massoud of the Islamic Youth seemed very outspoken. While the West appeared optimistic about the future of Afghanistan due to a parliamentarian political system, the Soviet Union seemed nervous. Alexei Kosygin, their prime minister, and Indira Gandhi, leader of India and a most trusted ally of Moscow, visited Afghanistan three times in a year, insinuating sustained support in military, economic, and cultural fields. The tension among the Muslim Brotherhood and the communist party culminated to an agonizing intensity. And those at the palace were unaware that their fumbling would shove the country into decades of bloodshed, killing, misery, and tragedy. King Zaher Shah opted to shut down schools and universities in June 1969 and proclaimed new parliamentarian elections for September of the same year. The road to democracy seemed challenging for the regime. The public believed Daoud Khan was the instigator of significant defiance toward the government and the sovereign in person. He wanted his cousin, the "soft monarch" of the country, out. It was a political debacle. Conservative and traditional chieftains gained the overwhelming majority of the seats in the new Parliament.

It was true that one of the central accomplishments of six years of democracy since 1963 was undoubtedly some degree of women's emancipation in the few large cities. Most girls attended school. Women parliamentarians and ministers were vigorous. The university continued to be blended. Afghan tailors, particularly Master Hassan, had become fashion designers. The May 1968 events in France had their unequivocal upshots in Kabul. Mini and tight attires were the favorite dresses of virtually all young educated women. The Afghan *chadari*, a horrible body cover foisted on women, was slowly waning. Recreation spots such as Kargha, Paghman, or Jalalabad in the winter were full of young, liberated people. Art and culture did not endure in seclusion. Countless playhouses were created. School and university boys and girls coined groups of amateur artists. They instantly dethroned the conventional singers who had been performing the same melodies for decades. Concerts were organized predominantly during the ten days of merriment for the independence of the country.

In addition to Ahmad Zaher, other new stars emerged. Courting entered as was the wont of youth—though it was not trouble-free. But astuteness made it doable somehow. The most plausible places for dating were university refectories and lawns, school vicinities, ice cream shops, and cinemas. Kabul and key cities of Afghanistan appeared to have spun the page of women subjugation. The evolution was not overpowering as laws had not been altered and the rest of the country was still observing archaic imperatives, so there was anxiety that the country would skate back. The reform program of the prime minister of the country was scorned by the new Parliament; he had no alternative but to back down and resign.

It was true that until 1963, King Zaher Shah was retaining members of his own family in key government positions, but since the amendment of the Constitution in 1964, matters were different. Nonetheless, vital ministries, particularly foreign affairs and defense, remained the guarded zone of the royal family. In July 1971, the father of the renowned and adulated artist Ahmad Zaher, who was a medical doctor and close friend of Soraya's father, took on the remits of the premiership. This was not rare. Dr. Yusof and Maiwandwal were also "commoners" who were entrusted with the same tribute earlier, but the pick of Foreign Minister Mousa Shafiq from the eastern province of Nangarhar, the man whom Soraya had greeted long ago with her sweet skinny hands full of mud, was the first of its kind. He had transformed to a brilliant man with degrees from the famous universities of Al-Azhar in Egypt and Columbia in the United States. It was most astonishing; the foreign ministry had never before been handed over to a commoner.

Mousa Shafiq was, of course, a sympathizer of a moderate but more intellectual Islam, which could also get purged of charlatanism, infiltration, and misguidance that had amplified over decades around religious beliefs. Years back when Soraya's father was sidelined and kept under house arrest by the palace, the young Mousa was the messenger of his father to assure Mr. Suri of the tribal leaders' support. He was then recognized as a bright future talent by Mr. Suri. The foreign minister was distinguished not only for his knowledge but also fashion. He was short and dressed extremely well.

Soraya's workload amplified indirectly as embassy staff visited her daily in her United Nations office for preparation of diverse reports to the new minister on the world body's affairs. He had more specifically instructed the ambassador to trail and track debates and deliberations regarding the liberation of East Pakistan and the struggle of its overwhelmingly majority Bengali population to have their own state. Mahatma Gandhi, who had experienced segregation in London, Pretoria, and Johannesburg during his bright studies and practice of law, opted nevertheless for nonviolent actions for the liberation of India and succeeded. However, he always considered creation of Pakistan and separation of a significant number of the Muslim population of India a personal failure. East Pakistan, nearly two thousand kilometers away from the mainland, was a calamity of Louis Mountbatten's harmful efforts, not only to impose partition but even split the Bengalis of India. Undoubtedly, India of Indira Gandhi supported the aspiration of independence of East Pakistan as a new nation. The issues had serious impact on Afghanistan due to the direct involvement of Pakistan and India. Meanwhile, over ten million Bengali refugees who fled the Pakistan Army's extortion and exaction, led by the notorious ISI, were hosted in India. The United States, the People's Republic of China, and the Soviet Union were all at work for different purposes. In fact, the Pakistan military faced its most humiliating setback. Under the guidance of Zulfiqar Ali Bhutto and General Yahya Khan, the new and yet another military ruler of the country, they endeavored to craft an East-West confrontation by bombing north India. But the strategy did not succeed. The United States and the People's Republic of China, two of the sturdiest allies of Pakistan, did not fall into the trap. In retaliation, the Indian Army intervened in East Pakistan and obfuscated the ISI. Bangladesh, the land of Bengali, was born! New York was the theater of extensive diplomatic efforts for international recognition or denunciation of this newborn state.

Soraya ran in all directions to get the facts and prepare reports, briefing notes, and talking points for the United Nations leadership. She was the victim of her own commitment and endeavors, working till late hours in the office. She had thoughtfully observed Bhutto during his futile endeavors in the Security Council to persuade the world to back his country's position. Not at all impressed by his intervention, she discerned him as refined but deadly ambitious.

The independence of Bangladesh was undoubtedly an extraordinary failure of the Pakistani rulers, but more specifically of the ISI. However, the international community was just short of averting another tragedy that loomed in neighboring Burma, now called Myanmar, as it was directly related with the history of the Bengali population and the British India. For centuries, East Burma or Rohang, now denominated Rakhine, was populated with Muslims, who according to some experts were "utilized" by the British Empire as timber business laborers. They called themselves Rohingya, inhabitants of the Rohang. Before the independence of Bangladesh, the ISI futilely supported separatist movements, cultivating bad blood between Muslim Burmese and other communities living in the country. The 1962 military takeover in Rangoon was the beginning of one of the most tragic segregations of modern times in Southeast Asia. Over three hundred thousand Rohingyas were driven out, and about half a million of them who remained in the country were deprived of their citizenship and properties. Soraya's reports about the plight of the Rohingya population were factual and well documented, revealing and highlighting the traumatic human aspects of a political issue that could have been easily addressed. It seemed that nobody sought to disrupt the discrimination machinery of the generals in the Burmese capital. The United Nations leadership remained silent. U Thant, the supreme leader of the organization, was himself a product of Burmese nomenclature and military setup. For Soraya, it was an obvious cover-up of crimes. She was dismayed, disappointed, and disheartened by the realities of international politics. Mousa Shafiq had determined Pakistan's direct liability in both cases.

Within weeks, the ambassador was apprised that the foreign minister would attend the United Nations General Assembly in September of the same year. His arrival at John F. Kennedy Airport was late in the day. The ambassador and senior staff rushed to pick him up. He had opted to stay at the Waldorf Astoria and after a long journey desired to rest, urging the ambassador and his senior staff to meet him at the United Nations delegates' lounge for breakfast the next day before his encounter with the leadership of the United Nations. Soraya was tasked by the Chief of Staff of the United Nations to greet and guide the minister for his meetings. She had appended some new ideas to her briefing notes, such as an unambiguous position of Afghanistan regarding Bangladesh as well as preservation at all costs of human dignity and rights of refugees in India and their safe return. She had intelligently broached the Afghan position on the Rohingya tragedy, alerting that the minister might criticize the United Nations for their lack of action. She had also included some broader topics, such as the requisite for a stout and independent civil society to judge the actions of the Afghan government as well as opposing parties. As a perfectionist, she constantly endeavored to further improve the text of her briefing notes and talking points. The Montblanc had always and smoothly followed her thoughts on the paper. Sometimes she thought her father was whispering ideas to her through his favorite fountain pen.

As an Afghan, she preferred to salute the minister in the Afghan representation first as per the customs of her country. There, she was informed that everybody had directly proceeded to the Blue Building, as they denominated the headquarters of the United Nations. Soraya thought the minister was unwise not to come to the representation first and hail junior staff. But she cut the conversation short with the employee of the representation and turned to rush to her office in the Blue Building. A refined and silent man of about forty years of age was standing behind her waiting. He was elegantly dressed and wore a nice fragrance that she could not distinguish. The man thought Soraya was a staffer of the representation.

"I would like to meet the ambassador. We are old friends," the gentleman requested in Dari.

"Unfortunately, I do not work here, and it appears that they are all out to receive the foreign minister in the Blue Building," Soraya replied in the same language.

"Who are you then?" the man queried.

"I am an Afghan working with the Executive Office of the United Nations and had come to greet and accompany the foreign minister for his meetings. But now I have to rush, sir," she stated.

"Please wait a minute," he persisted.

At the same moment, there was hurly-burly in the corridor. The ambassador sprinted in, sweating. He seemed very nervous.

"Oh, my God! Excellency! We were looking for you everywhere in the Blue Building," the ambassador exclaimed.

"No worry, Mr. Ambassador," the man assured him.

Soraya was stunned to realize that the refined man was the foreign minister of her country. He was so young and alluring. Mr. Shafiq opted to walk and asked Soraya about her job. She depicted in detail her duties and the challenges that the United Nations encountered, particularly with the tense Bangladeshi situation. She elaborated on solutions and lamented the old-fashioned diplomacy and lethargy of some countries. She was of the opinion that the shape of the world was in the process of changing significantly, and most developing countries would miss the boat if good governance was not implemented earnestly. For the Southwest Asia region, she anticipated a stronger Pakistan, mighty Iran, and an always suspicious Soviet Union. The minister was judiciously heeding, arguing, and contributing to the conversation. As usual, Soraya treasured being defied and spoke with passion about her convictions.

Mr. Shafiq praised the ambassador's reports, briefing notes, and talking points, which according to him were concise, profound, and to the point. The ambassador informed the minister that Soraya had assisted the representation to be compliant with modern exigencies of a diplomatic mission. The week with the foreign minister was most rewarding for Soraya. The brain game between the two was captivating, and often he concurred with her views. She was flattered to realize that after her father and Professor Williams, Mousa Shafiq was the third man in her life who admired her mind. In him, she discovered a profound person with real conviction that Afghanistan could play a pivotal role in the region, among the Muslim world, and internationally in support of peace and security. While he conceded that the dispute with Pakistan over the Durand Line was of a more intricate nature, the Helmand water crisis with Iran could be resolved. Mr. Shafiq asserted that it was the right of the Bengali population of East Pakistan to have their own state, and recognition of Bangladesh would not jeopardize the neutrality of his country, which was the best card in his hand. He, however, was distressed for the forgotten Rohingya population and blamed the United Nations leadership for their laxity. He seemed extremely apprehensive of the escalating tension between the Soviet Union and the Western world, dreading that Afghanistan would turn into a battle arena again. When he left New York for Kabul, Soraya felt the vacuum of substantive discussion.

During the same period, Afghanistan was affected by the worse drought of its history. The northern parts of the country were hit more sternly. Prices of grains had rocketed up. The intensity of the tragedy was such that people ate grass, and families were literally forced to vend a child to rescue the remainder. Providers of humanitarian aid to the country could not offer more wheat and maize. The Soviet Union, a major producer of grains, had commitments toward countries of their own sphere of influence, particularly in Africa. Animals were perishing of thirst. The government was stranded, and its public information strategy was calamitous. Radios were proclaiming the advent of aid before even the negotiations with a party that would lead to something promising. Opposition newspapers were jeering the government. A cartoon became the symbol of how the government handled the challenge. In a picture, a goat that had the silhouette of Afghanistan was exposed in agony, and the owner, which resembled the prime minister surprisingly well, was uttering, "My dear animal, do not die as the maize will soon come from America." The king was still a respected figure, but he was failing his people too. The crown prince was considered spineless. General Wali and former Prime Minister Daoud Khan were already dreaming of succeeding Zaher Shah. Tens of thousands of people and millions of animals croaked in the process. It was so apparent that the policies of all Afghan governments had not aimed at rendering the country self-reliant. On the contrary, achievement was due to loans from diverse institutions and governments, and reimbursement of those loans had drained the already insignificant treasury of the country.

Shafiq desperately aspired to host the Extraordinary Session of the Conference of Foreign Ministers of the Organization of the Islamic Conference. The king was not enthusiastic as it would have made neither the Soviets nor the West pleased. The foreign minister argued that the country could use this occasion to solicit assistance. The monarch finally conceded. He was grasping that his country was at the crossroads of a major transformation but did not comprehend which course it would take. The conference in September 1971 was a victory for the foreign minister. He spoke fluent Arabic, which impressed his counterparts. The level of assistance pledged by major oil producers, though, was still not adequate.

International East-West politics were dominated essentially by the Vietnam War and the conquest of space. Bangladesh did not seem to be a controversial issue anymore; Pakistan was routed both politically and diplomatically. The new president of the United States, Richard Nixon, seemed more hawkish than his Democratic predecessor. Since the brutal murder of Martin Luther King Jr. and Robert Kennedy, Soraya was not interested in American politics, as if with those assassinations, the American dream had died. But she recalled her encounter with Nixon long ago and her surprise that as vice president then, he had not met with Martin Luther King Jr., the icon of civil rights and the Mahatma Gandhi of America. The infamous Vietnam War was going nowhere, and countless innocent people had been slain. The use of chemical and prohibited weapons by a country that had the courage to abolish slavery was incomprehensible. Ho Chi Minh of North Vietnam, Leonid Brezhnev of the Soviet Union, and Mao Zedong of the People's Republic of China, who all supported the Viet Cong, were foiling Americans. Amid Vietnam shame, the United States, however, was triumphing in space. The Soviet Union was comprehensively overpowered, but already voices were raised whether resources were not wasted as the moon did not present any economic value.

In Afghanistan, Gaheez was murdered at the beginning of 1972. The communist leadership was suspected of sponsoring the crime. At the same time, the Muslim Brotherhood determined to be better organized. The movement had become mightier than the two communist parties combined. Rabbani, who asserted more responsibilities, was a soft-spoken gentleman. From his Tajik ethnic background, he was perceived a moderate Islamic scholar. The palace was anxious, and behind the scenes some were scheming to justify apprehension of the leaders of the movement. Meanwhile, schools and the university had been unlocked again in Kabul. In an altercation in the summer of 1972 at the Kabul University campus, it was alleged that Golboddin Hekmatyar, the most harsh Islamic hard-liner of all times, killed the Maoist Saidal Sokhandan personally. He was detained and incarcerated. The occasion was propitious to go after leaders of the Muslim Brotherhood. Professor Niazi was arrested too. But Mr. Shafiq intervened, and he was later on released. Meanwhile, at the Parliament, discontent about too much liberty given to Marxist-Leninist parties was growing. The Soviets too put pressure to ensure that their protégés were given the required political, social, and economic space. At the same time, Western countries were concerned about respect for fundamental human rights.

Soraya accompanied many leaders of the United Nations to various sessions, scrutinized obligations of member states in accordance with international conventions to which they had agreed, studied anew the governments' policies for better interpretation, wrote reports, and got the latest news from all over Asia. She was wary of ethics and the accuracy of her reports to different councils and commissions and was of the belief that the United Nations must remain honest and reveal facts. On private ground, she used her love for constructive debate and introduced *gardaab* by hosting Afghan students and expatriates at her modest residence in New York on Saturday evenings. She was inspired by the French *salonnières* such as Marie Thérèse Goeffrin, Suzanne Curchod Necker, Marie-Jeanne Roland, Sophie de Condorcet, and many others. It was a risky enterprise as the monarchy in Afghanistan never valued free debate in society, and the government spy agency was very efficient. But New York was far away from Kabul. Discussions were startling and lasted long. Occasionally they got passionate, and she had to use all her ability and charm to soothe the most excited orators. Within months, political groups in Kabul were nattering about Soraya's intellectual circle in America. She demonstrated her independence of thought during debates and expressed frank and honest opinions. One Friday evening, Professor Booker came for dinner and appeared excited. He announced that Soraya's application for evening graduate studies had been scrutinized by the board. His opinion was sought, and she was granted a scholarship for the next academic year. She was very excited and was already considering how to marry her professional and academic aspirations.

In November 1972, the pressure on the prime minister of Afghanistan was at its zenith. Economic sternness had been added to political turmoil, and he resolved to quit. The king recommended Mousa Shafiq as the new premier, and the Parliament endorsed him immediately. A hilarious incident occurred, though, demonstrating the incompetency of the system and those who represented the people.

A prominent member of the Assembly was snoozing while the nominated prime minister delivered his inaugural policy speech to get the vote of confidence. At the end of a paragraph when Mr. Shafiq was taking a breath, the neighbor of the illustrious deputy shoved him gently, woke him up, and suggested, "Say no."

He swiftly stood up and yelled, "No! No! I do not agree!"

The entire chamber hooted; this was when he grasped the joke of his colleague. At the same time, it revealed the caliber of those who were in the realm of politics. The new prime minister continued managing the foreign ministry. Two weeks after, Soraya's husband was appointed to a higher position in the capital. She was offered the position of assistant to the prime minister, who urged her to help him in all matters related to the foreign ministry too. She had no choice but to return to Kabul in January 1973, leaving her international career and prospects of graduate studies behind. And Professor Booker was heartbroken!

Soraya opted for an office in the Marble Palace, a place she had long liked. She also resolved not to stay at her parental house and rented an apartment on Zarghouna Road near the New City Park. Khan Ali, Abai's son, was of great help in settling her down. Daoud Khan, whose ego was known to the country, fumed and feared Mr. Shafiq's knowledge and ability. He was undoubtedly the brightest of the four commoners who had so far assumed the function of prime minister. A man of his stature was a challenge to the future ambitions of the self-centered prince. For help he called one of his closest associates, who assumed the position of liaison at the Soviet Embassy on Darulaman Avenue. The new ambassador, Aleksander Puzanov, had a very strong intelligence upbringing. He recurrently met with Parcham and Khalq leaders but cherished most encountering Daoud Khan's envoy, to whom he had labeled Taraki as fatuous, Karmal as frail, Ratebzad as a Barbie doll, and Amin as vicious. Puzanov recognized Daoud Khan's envoy as more of his own caliber. The Soviet ambassador was seen at all fronts, demonstrating that members of communist parties enjoyed freedom of expression. He had tripled financial backing to them. The fact that the Afghan army operated with a Soviet arsenal justified Mr. Puzanov's repeated visits to military garrisons. The decision was made for a takeover with the help of military officers who had been propelled to the Soviet Union more than a decade ago by Daoud Khan himself when, as prime minister, he shifted alliances.

Meanwhile, Prime Minister Shafiq persisted with his reform process within the country and battled to solve bilateral rows. He instructed Soraya to consider all aspects of the Afghan-Iranian dispute over the Helmand river water. Indeed, Afghanistan, a landlocked kingdom with high mountains, disposed of a sizable quantity of water that finally drizzled to the neighboring countries. Any hydroelectric edifice in the west or east, not only to irrigate vast segments of the territory in support of agriculture and promotion of domestic products, but to provide electricity and jobs to citizens had not been hailed by Iran and Pakistan respectively.

While dialogue with Pakistan unavoidably led to the Durand Line stalemate, it appeared that negotiations could start with Iran. The prime minister invited his counterpart, Amir Abbas Hoveyda, to visit Kabul for crucial talks in March 1973, and a joint team was tasked to prepare the nub of the impending negotiation. Soraya was charged to advise the prime minister, lead the organization of the event, and keep key members of the Parliament abreast. Mr. Shafiq opted to host his interlocutor in the Chehel Sotoon Palace, perhaps to allude to the common ethos between the two countries and to recall the Iranian Chehel Sotoon Palace in Isfahan. The prime minister was also active on thwarting the effects of the drought. For the third successive year, Afghanistan did not have enough snow and rainfall. With lack of adequate infrastructure to withhold water for local consumption, the situation of farmers in remote areas of the country was pitiable. The arable land needed the water that flowed to neighboring countries.

The prime minister's endeavors yielded tangible fallout. While massive aid by the Soviet Union and United States was supplemented by China, France, the United Kingdom, and India in particular, he embarked on a widespread reform of the agriculture sector, whereby mechanization constituted a pivotal component. It was amazing to observe that a commoner was in the process of curbing the devastating famine. He also introduced some less popular "moral measures" to keep the Islamic movement quiet. For example, women used the front door of a bus, while men used the rear. He imposed separation bars within the bus. However, his widely touted wardrobe and expensive attire, all tailored by famous Italian and French fashion designers, did not correspond to the image of the leader of a developing country. Nor did they correspond to attributes of the son of a commoner. Nevertheless, his friendship with one of the leading religious leaders and strongest supporter of the royal palace was a protection that nobody ignored. He had an undefined affection and respect for Soraya and deemed her a close confidant. Often he spoke of his admiration of her father, who as chief justice had stood alone to defy the palace and succeeded. Hoveyda's visit was getting closer, and the groundwork was intensive. Soraya had multiple ideas on how to make it a success. At the end of one session, Mr. Shafiq urged her to stay behind.

He stated, "Madame, I would like to thank you for your endeavors. You are exceptionally intelligent and hardworking."

She replied, "Excellency, I had the opportunity to study in Washington, DC, London, and Oxford. Very few other Afghan girls had such a luxury."

"I acknowledge that. But your ability is your own gem," the prime minister suggested.

"I disagree, sir! Every Afghan girl has a unique potential. But instead of being educated and allowed to help their country, they suffer from the worst cultural treatment," she argued.

"I understand! But to change a traditional society, you need a critical mass of educated and talented people," he concluded.

"Yes and no, Mr. Prime Minister. In the absence of a critical mass, a leader in your position would strive to create it," she advised.

Soraya used the opportunity to elaborate on a key point that provoked the downfall of politicians. She believed that exercise of power distanced leaders, even if they were born poor, from the people who, like roots of a plant, fed them. She further underlined that privileges often corrupted those who exercised the highest functions. She alluded to the prime minister that her father's effective contact with the grassroots had saved him from the fury of the palace. Finally, she suggested that the theatrical aspects of customs in Afghanistan should be ignored and the government must address its harmful facets. Mr. Shafiq proclaimed at the next cabinet meeting a series of field trips, with emphasis on the situation of women, and urged ministers to go to provinces and report about rural development, which he counted as a national security impediment. Soraya never regretted her forthrightness and was ready to quit had the prime minister considered it contrary to her duties.

In the office, she asserted her authority more distinctively. Soraya reviewed practically every policy paper, rewrote speeches delivered outside the country by high officials, navigated between the Marble and Chehel Sotoon Palaces, and rushed to the Parliament or greeted parliamentarians on behalf of Mr. Shafiq. She worked between thirteen to fourteen hours a day. One evening, she was late for a family dinner and rushed to her car. There was a gift package. Curious, she opened it prudently and was overjoyed. It was the *Prophet*, a fantastic twenty-six-page prose poetry book written by the famous American-Lebanese writer, philosopher, and artist Gibran Khalil Gibran. A simple sentence by the prime minister was on the title page: *"This book cannot replace your thoughtful discussions with your late father, but may serve as food for thought."* She wept of happiness! Indeed, since the decease of Mr. Suri, no one had given her a book, the present she cherished more than anything else. At the same time, she sensed firmly that Mr. Shafiq valued her talent and brain. She felt rewarded for her hard work. Like for all gifted people, simple gestures of esteem and recognition meant a lot to her, while mountains of wealth signified nothing. Both she and Mr. Shafiq had established a bond of mutual comprehension, dedication to the country and service to its populations.

On March 13, 1973, the Helmand Water Treaty was signed between Shafiq and Hoveyda. Every step of the negotiation was impeccable. Behind the scenes, Soraya was most prominent. It was yet another victory for the prime minister and his team. The crisis had soured the relationship between the two countries since the 1870s, flaring again after the river changed course in 1896. Mr. Shafiq proposed a debate in the September session of the Parliament to ratify the agreement. He was convinced of a win. But the next day, communist newspapers denounced the accord and charged Mr. Shafiq as a "water trader." An air of negative apprehension reigned in Kabul.

On an evening of late May 1973, Soraya attended a reception at the Soviet Embassy. It was the usual diplomatic jabber, with everyone weighing what he or she would say. A number of ambassadors and delegates approached Soraya to find out how the prime minister would be implementing his priorities. The emancipation of rural women was well received by Western chancelleries, and they wished to see the action plan. Ambassador Puzanov was poised with the attitude of a conqueror.

When Soraya came out of the building, it was heavily raining. A man strolled along the street without an umbrella; obviously he had also been attending the event. He carefully moved forward in order not to step in small ponds on the road. He struggled with the intensity of the water falling. She stopped the car and offered the gentleman a ride to a safer place and was staggered. It was Babrak Karmal, chairman of the Parcham Communist Party, who jumped into the car thankfully. Of course, he knew Soraya and admitted that his party recognized the Suri family for their integrity, hard work, and fairness, though he did not agree with their political stand. His hostility with the prime minister was sharp. He teasingly reproached Soraya for not being a member of his party. A surprisingly curious dialogue ensued between her and the most notorious opposition leader in the country, during which he insisted on an imperative "soft revolution" to prepare the ground for the "people's takeover of their affairs," which would alter the geopolitics of the world. Soraya questioned how a revolution could be soft. Karmal answered vaguely but mentioned a controlled military option.

The morning after, Soraya had her usual briefing with Mr. Shafiq and informed him about the encounter with the communist leader. She warned the prime minister of her apprehension. In the course of their conversation, she learned that the secret services accounts were submitted directly to the palace. The prime minister only received instructions from the king on major issues related to national security. It seemed so stupid and surrealistic. But then she realized that he was a commoner; perhaps the palace did not deem it necessary to keep him abreast of national security issues. The prime minister altered their discussion to focus on his government's four major priorities for the remaining part of the year 1973; Soraya's report had a deep effect on him. He suddenly seemed concerned but insisted on the Helmand Treaty ratification by Parliament. He wanted an urgent rural women's emancipation plan of action to be developed, his agricultural reforms to be fully implemented, and a government accountability mechanism to be drafted and proposed to the cabinet. These were colossal projects. Though Soraya loved challenges and was devoted to assisting the prime minister, pulling and pushing various government entities was not an easy mission. Several weeks later, Mr. Shafiq was notified that King Zaher Shah was traveling to Italy for a medical checkup.

On July 16, 1973, the prime minister worked late into the evening. He was earnestly preoccupied and called Soraya in. "Madame, I must acknowledge that we are failing," he lamented.

"What do you mean, sir?" Soraya inquired, remembering her father pronouncing the same sentence long ago. "The whole country is speaking of your achievements," she pursued.

"Listen, Soraya. You were so right! I am informed that there will be a takeover of power by Daoud Khan very soon. Details are not known. The chief of staff of the armed forces supports him, and I am helpless. I want you to be calm, stay home, and do not panic. May God bless and reward you for all your support to me and to your country. You may go home now," he concluded.

"But, sir, what about you?" Soraya inquired.

"They will probably arrest me tonight," he calmly whispered.

"You have time to flee, for example to Nangarhar," Soraya suggested.

"Daoud Khan has conspired for a bloodless coup. Let him do it. The contrary would create more tragedy for the country. Now, take your essentials and leave the office."

This was the first time he had called her Soraya, and she felt touched. At the same time, she became fretful and recalled Mr. Puzanov's haughty conduct toward her and Karmal's statement of soft revolution.

Indeed, the next day, on July 17, 1973, King Zaher Shah was overthrown in absentia by his cousin Daoud Khan in a bloodless coup. The prime minister was totally unprepared for an event that was considered the abysm of Afghanistan for decades, resulting in unforgivable tragedies, killings, and destruction.

Chapter 4

Political Maturity and Life under Communist Rule

*The lion cannot protect himself from traps, and the
fox cannot defend himself from wolves. One must
therefore be a fox to recognize traps, and a lion to
frighten wolves.*

—Niccolò Machiavelli, *The Prince*

King Zaher Shah proceeded to Italy on July 8, 1973. Nine days later
was a sunny Tuesday. The history of Afghanistan toggled from a
slow but steady evolution to the uncertainties of a revolution that was
unwarranted and futile, proving harmful for future generations. That
day at dawn, a bloodless military coup began!

It was meticulously prepared. Even the prime minister of the country
sensed it only at a very late stage. Was it in accordance with a palace
covenant or an effective "soft revolution" as some termed it? In fact,
the terminology did not matter so much; it signified the downfall of
the country and its future. At daybreak, all key and senior military
officers were neutralized and apprehended in their slumber. But
nobody ventured to arrest General Abdul Wali, son-in-law of the
king and cousin of Daoud Khan. It surprised many as he considered
himself the true heir of the crown. Perhaps leaders of the coup did
not wish to disturb his sleep.

The commander of the garrison in the south of Kabul, unaware of
deals already made, moved toward the city in support of his absent
monarch. But he was swiftly neutralized and his troops sent back
to the barracks. Colonel Abdul Qader, a Soviet-trained pilot and
member of the Parcham party, was leading the operation. It seemed

that numerous senior officials who ensured liaison between the communist leaders and Ambassador Puzanov excelled in their lethal service. Daoud Khan himself was acting as chief of central command and dreadfully coveted a bloodless seizure of power. He instructed Colonel Qader to arrest his cousin. At 7:00 a.m., when General Wali woke up and attempted to muster the garrison in the west of the capital, only one shell fired at his residence was enough to secure his surrender. A few other generals who had escaped were neutralized in the Chehel Sotoon area. The coup was an impeccable triumph!

At 8:00 a.m., Daoud Khan addressed the nation, stated that he had taken control of the country, and proclaimed that the kingdom was abolished and Afghanistan was a republic. At around ten o'clock, all students comprising the primary grades were induced to come on the streets and rejoice over the "soft revolution." Some were even pulled out of their homes to lead the "celebration." Nobody knew what the future would look like, but they were hopping and swaying. It was pitiful to see people luxuriate over the demise of a king who during his life never initiated any harm to the people. Of course, like all souls, he had his shortcomings, but the country was progressing at a steady rate in tune with the slow rhythm of development that reflected the level of comprehension of the majority about an evolution. The plight of women was given attention, though nothing was substantive as far as effective protection mechanisms were concerned. He remembered how British-fomented religious hostility ruined King Amanullah Khan and his reform route. He had opted for small steps. In the capital, no one cared whether women dressed in miniskirts or traditional clothing; religious orthodoxy valued the restrained approach of the king.

Soraya stayed home and gathered that as soon as she had left the office the day before, the Afghan government spy agency had arrested Mr. Shafiq in his office. She felt fortunate but worried for her country. The bloodless nature of the coup did not matter. The fact that officers of the army took over power, forcefully overthrowing a democratic government, seemed an alarming step and precedent. Soraya was anxious, though the status of the Suri family, predominantly the reputation of her father, Mr. Zamir Suri, was a shield.

A transitional team was revealed the day after, in which Daoud Khan stockpiled the positions of president and prime minister as well as defense and foreign ministers. Obviously, India and the Soviet Union recognized Daoud's coup and pledged financial and military reinforcement, while Western nations waited for further evolution. Daoud Khan abrogated the 1964 Constitution. Two of his closest team members, who were suspected of supervising the liaison with the Soviet Embassy, occupied the most prominent positions of first deputy prime minister handling ideological matters and second deputy prime minister in charge of policy execution. Four members of Parcham were given ministerial posts, and Colonel Qader was appointed as deputy commander of the air forces. Again and in spite of the president's harangues in support of women, none had a leading role in his cabinet. Daoud Khan's moderate and younger brother Naim Khan did not figure in any list. Did that already signify his opposition to the "soft revolution"? Some, however, recognized that he managed foreign affairs policies of the country from behind the scenes. A cousin of the family and long devotee of the newly proclaimed president was designated as deputy foreign minister. He had served as a junior attaché under Ambassador Zamir Suri in London, and Soraya remembered him well. At midday, she was called in to work as the "new boss" aimed to address staff.

The deputy minister of foreign affairs, an unsightly and short individual, wore dark sunglasses in a room that definitely required more light. He endeavored to be a carbon copy of Daoud Khan in his posture, harangued for over an hour about the popular support to the revolution as nobody was hurt, and warned of major policy changes. He particularly blamed the foreign policy and diplomacy of his country under Mousa Shafiq, whom he characterized as inefficient and incompetent. However, he remained silent about the mass of inefficient individuals who as members of his "august" family or linked to the palace had led Afghan diplomacy to a sclerotic status. It was easy to undermine a commoner but still not permissible to pinpoint the facts and criticize his kinfolk. Back in his office, he called Soraya in.

"Soraya, first of all, let me tell you that a lot will change in this ministry. Second, we know that you assisted that son of a religious cleric to be successful and want you to render the same service to us," he emphasized, referring to Mr. Shafiq.

"Sir, I prefer to be called by my family name," she replied. "Moreover, I would like to stress that Mr. Shafiq himself was an extraordinarily intelligent, competent, and hardworking person. I just followed his instructions and advice."

"Then I expect the same efficiency in my ministry too," he angrily replied.

Soraya did not want to continue the conversation and deemed the man was haughty, foolish, and repulsive. She disliked him and instantly apprehended that he would be troublesome. However, the political and security environments were extremely uncertain, so she resolved to "swallow the bitter pill" and keep her opinion to herself for a while. Change of senior management of the ministry and incumbents of most central embassies constituted the primary task of the little man. Meanwhile, as a goodwill gesture, the new master of the country released some prisoners, including Mr. Hekmatyar, who continued with his radical Islamic doctrine and preaching. His adversaries opined already that he was the prime recruit of the ISI in Afghanistan; others nurtured diverse theories. Knowing the dubious personality of Daoud Khan, tribal leaders were perplexed and the rest of the royal family anxious. A covenant was struck.

Daoud Khan permitted General Abdul Wali and those close to the king to join him in Europe or move elsewhere, and the former monarch declared his abdication on August 24, 1973. As anticipated, a new "gigantic" trade deal with the Soviet Union had to be negotiated. The slogan of "*Daa Pashtunistan Zemouge*" resumed again on radio waves, alluding to the hostility of the Afghan government to the Durand Line. Zulfiqar Ali Bhutto, who had just shifted from the presidency to the premiership of Pakistan, opted for robust retaliation. Both leaders had similar personalities: ambitious, ambiguous, selfish, and obstinate. Islamic countries, and more specifically Saudi Arabia, urged restraint between the two neighbors. The mounting role of Soviet experts in internal Afghan affairs was deplorable.

Soraya was irritated. During a time when the "soft revolution" and East-West rivalry endowed prospects with crucial social, economic, and political platforms, no proper policy guidance was issued or even communicated verbally to allow her to discern where the country was heading. People looked all around as they ran. Each high government authority bleakly sought to embody the president. With Daoud Khan assuming the responsibilities of the prime minister from the palace, Soraya's role altered. She was contained in the executive office of the deputy foreign minister to review policy papers. She loathed futile deliberations with a man who was not even browsing an essential report about which he engaged in a debate. Soraya began despising the environment. But at such an uncertain period, no one had the stamina to confront the republic.

Within the new cabinet, the minister of internal affairs, who also led the spy agency of the country, was one of the most notoriously ruthless individuals. He closely ganged up with the second deputy prime minister to "impose" the new regime's "vision" by all means. In September of the same year, the deputy minister prepared to attend the twenty-eighth session of the United Nations General Assembly. Soraya had massive work on her desk—review, revise, and even rewrite senseless and unconnected discourses, coordinate matters with the Afghan representation in New York, mold briefing notes and talking points so that the deputy minister did not muff the essence, and so on. She was fortunate, as the ambassador in New York displayed compassion, understanding, and backing toward a formidable lady that he recognized was practically left alone to shape and shake issues. Nearly nine hours' time difference with the East Coast of the United States did not make matters trouble-free, particularly when she had to confer with the Afghan ambassador himself for apprehension of issues. In New York, the Afghan delegation was warmly greeted by the Warsaw Pact member states and India, as if the country had already entered the Soviet Union sphere of influence. However, Western representatives voiced their fear and cautioned that the country would face serious defiance if it did not remain neutral. Daoud Khan, because of his temper and known affinity, signified a gloomy future for his country.

On Monday, September 9, Soraya woke up promptly and sensed a weird atmosphere. From the top floor of her apartment, she descended to the kitchen, prepared a coffee, and began to smoke her first cigarette of the day. She did not feel comfortable and had the same premonition as in London when John F. Kennedy, his brother, and Martin Luther King Jr. were murdered. Perhaps she had a pronounced sixth sense, and she looked for her small portable transistor radio. A coup attempt had been neutralized, and its presumed leaders—former ambassador to Washington and Prime Minister Hashem Maiwandwal, as well as the retired Air Force general Abdul Razaq—together with many officers had been detained.

She could not comprehend the gist of it. The former premier of the country was known for his pro-Western stands and had never established a reliable association with a pro-Soviet army. She had known the frail man very well in Washington when her late father served as a senior international lawyer; he never concealed his social democrat stand and had even created a political party. He could not attempt a coup against the top and most feared man of the country, who hated him since his time as ambassador in Washington, DC. At this moment, Yusof, her cook and house manager, entered and reported that soldiers and military vehicles coursed the streets. She was worried; the "revolution" would probably not be as "soft" and bloodless as they had pretended. It may have had inertia, but now those who were deemed opposed to Daoud Khan or the big neighbor in the north had to disappear.

For an instant, she thought of her father. What would have occurred if he was still alive? The ruthless minister of interior and his secret services heavily tutored by the KGB apprehended a sizable number of innocent individuals. It was public knowledge that the second deputy prime minister and the interior minister commanded the terror and oppression squad of the new regime. Nearly forty years of peace and steady evolution was suddenly interrupted by a republic that people did not grasp. Soraya pondered about an Afghan proverb, a vehicle of knowledge transmission in the region, that "*the charge of blood is blood.*" Daoud and his team did not comprehend that detention of power was provisional and violence was the generator of vehemence. For her, the axiom described the basic and scientific principle of proportionality of action and reaction. Maiwandwal, gifted and refined, was also a commoner. There were already questions as to why General Wali, who attempted to organize armed opposition at the time of Daoud Khan's coup, was allowed to go scot-free, and the former prime minister was apprehended and charged with treason. He had devotedly served his country in the United States, United Kingdom, and Pakistan before becoming minister and prime minister. Certainly he demonstrated some talent to be trusted by the former king for such sensitive responsibilities. Now, indicted of being a CIA agent, he faced death.

For many, the whole plot appeared Soviet style. It was so absurd that nobody trusted the theory disseminated by the government. Communist cants employed cynical notions to substantiate his "capture" and appealed for the purge of counterrevolutionaries.

Daoud hardly valued opposing views, even within his own family, and scrapped ferociously those who aspired to reach the top of the power ladder. People were worried for Maiwandwal. Daoud's conduct with Malik Khan in the 1950s was in the mind of all. He was capable of pounding those he considered foes to his power and authority. To counter the eventual fury of Western countries, the Afghan government opted for a hands-on communication strategy. Soraya was ordered to draft silly diplomatic directives to Afghan embassies in the West. Soviets and India were supporting Daoud Khan. Maiwandwal was detained in the underground of the ministry of interior. On the morning of October 2, 1973, the entire country was outraged to learn that he "had committed suicide" in his cell. Government and communist outlets published anti-Mainwandwal accounts to defame and present him as a guilty and shameful person who had no other alternative but to take his own life. The people did not trust a word of what was claimed on radio waves; they knew he was simply murdered! Western chancelleries and the United States in particular hunted to comprehend exactly what had occurred to such a prominent character.

In consultation with the "soft revolution" leadership, the deputy minister of foreign affairs urged Soraya to summon ambassadors of Western countries, with their Japanese and Australian counterparts, to the Marble Palace. The atmosphere was drab. Foreign high representatives were thunderstruck and anxious to understand what exactly had happened. Armed with a heavy folder that the spy agency had provided, the deputy foreign minister conceitedly displayed pictures of the deceased former head of government on the table. There was an acute streak around his neck. The little man affirmed that he committed suicide with his tie for "having perpetrated a disgraceful act against his nation." The partakers grabbed a series of pictures and left the room without posing even a question. They had concluded collectively that the government had perpetrated an assassination.

Only Puzanov exchanged a few words with the deputy minister, who felt offended by the lack of attention of the West in his "bright explanation." The deputy foreign minister was prepared to "give them a punch in the mouth." Back in his office, he called Soraya in.

"These ambassadors are dull. I think we were comprehensively convincing," he told her.

"No, sir, you were not! They seemed unconvinced," Soraya replied.

"What do you mean?" the deputy foreign minister said.

"If you allow me, Excellency,"—Soraya urged while observing the photos—"Maiwandwal was a very tall person, and everyone knew that the cells in the basement of the ministry of interior were low-pitched. It appears impossible that he committed suicide unless he was forced to kneel. Moreover, how could he still keep his suit and tie in his cell since his apprehension nearly a month earlier? The ambassadors went back persuaded that he was tortured and killed," she concluded.

The little man grabbed his coat and converged to the now Presidential Palace. An hour later, he reappeared and instructed Soraya to call for another meeting, this one with representatives of Islamic countries as a "sovereign nation does not need to explain internal matters and bow to Western delegations, as only friends and Muslim nations count." Indeed, Maiwandwal was tortured systematically for several days. It was alleged that the interior minister himself suffocated him with a cord. Soraya remembered her father and grasped why he never desired to be prime minister! Somehow, she felt relieved that he was no more. How many additional valorous sons and daughters of the country would be robbed using singular and dubious manners was the question in the mind of all citizens. Soraya thought that Mr. Shafiq and even the Suri family could have encountered the same fate. For a while, she imagined being in a prison cell. The mere thought was horrifying. She was marching on the edge of a very sharp blade; any false move could cause her demise. She resolved to search other professional options.

In the summer of 1974, Soraya gave birth to a gorgeous daughter, Selina. She was also an adorable green-eyed skinny girl. Her mother was in heaven and a most blissful person. Somehow, with this tiny angel, Soraya felt better protected. Selina was strikingly beautiful. Some of her features perceptibly reminded Soraya of her own father, such as a large forehead, loftiness of her body, beautifully tailored ears, and refined hands. She had never been so ecstatic. The little girl was a new light in her life. Oftentimes, she had suffered from her husband's prolonged absence. But now she had someone to rely on in the future. Selina was a quiet infant and did not bawl as often as other babies do. Perhaps her mother anticipated when to nurse her. Her eyes were vivid and discretely followed Soraya's movements; Soraya instantly felt so proud of her child.

Meanwhile, the president embarked on the "either friend or foe" doctrine. Some named their newborn kids Daoud or grew long moustaches perpendicular to the corners of their mouths as testimony of their sympathy to the regime. From the nasolabial angle, one side of the fuzz resembled the figure two and the other the figure six in Arabic, employed also in Afghanistan. Combined, it presented the number twenty-six. Daoud Khan's glory and accession to the supreme leadership of the country tallied with 26 Saratan in the Afghan calendar. Therefore, such an appearance became the symbol of the "soft revolution" partisans. As Daoud Khan's dogma largely targeted independent, liberal, or Islamic scholars and movements, communists endorsed the policy. However, the Maoist Sholay Jawed seemed solitary as the victory was on the Soviet Union side. They did not subjugate themselves and sustained mustering students. Their leaders, particularly the Mahmoudi brothers, were oftentimes incarcerated and then unconfined.

President Daoud, now confident of his power assertion, embarked on a five-year development planning program and expected Soviet and Indian subsidies. Upon conclusion of the first draft plan in June 1974, he resolved to visit Moscow. The Parcham and Khalq leaderships were at the zenith of their joy. When Daoud met Brezhnev, he received an intense kiss on his lips as was the Soviet tradition of the time. He was disgusted and nearly vomited in the Kremlin. The Soviet leader conditioned his willingness to provide assistance and asked for a dramatic reduction of Western experts in Afghanistan. Daoud Khan did not appreciate it and stressed that as a sovereign state, it was the prerogative of the Afghan government to decide. It seemed that his interlocutor apprehended from that instance that he might finally not be a trustworthy ally and had in fact manipulated Parcham and communist army officers to grab power. Senior members of the pro-Soviet communist parties who accompanied Daoud Khan were stunned and concluded that he could not be maneuvered to serve their interest. Both sides found themselves in a catch-22 situation. The much anticipated projects lingered since Soviet and Indian funding did not come as expected.

Upon his return and in an attempt to persuade Moscow of his seeming allegiance, Daoud Khan instructed the arrest of Professor Ghulam Mohammad Niazi, the icon of the Muslim Brotherhood in Afghanistan. Nobody understood the gesture as he had released the most radical Golboddin Hekmatyar a year earlier under an amnesty order. It was a massive blow to the movement. They were destabilized, and a split emerged between radicals and moderates on how to respond. Communists were scratching their hands.

Soraya was following the evolution through newspapers, which all embodied the view of the government. Though President Daoud feigned to champion the cause of women, as he had done long ago as prime minister of the country, the slow path of his ancestors and steady approach was preferred by his presidential government. It is true that women gained immense liberty compared to the 1930s, but their prosperity remained shallow. No one ventured to transform discriminatory customs. A woman could be ditched without any social or legal protection if her husband just verbally declared three times that he divorced her. On the other hand, she did not have the same privilege. This practice was in sharp contradiction with divine instructions. But an absolute lack of knowledge about the essence of religious doctrines by the people due to illiteracy had given rise to abuses of all natures against women and girls. Male brutality in rural areas was reported on a daily basis. Acid was pitched onto the faces of university female students.

Of course and perhaps on justified grounds, the government accused the Muslim Brotherhood of hosting radical and extremist sticklers, led by Hekmatyar. He had been on the run since his release. Practically everyone in the country believed that he had already absconded to Pakistan, well regarded by the mighty ISI and even active to destabilize Daoud Khan and his regime. Soraya bemoaned that the democratic process initiated under King Zaher Shah was aborted because of the peculiar ambition of his cousin. She was convinced that Mr. Shafiq was on the right track.

Some believed it would take centuries for Afghan women to evolve. Women and girls were the prime victims of any political turmoil and conflict, won or lost! Most contemporary hurdles were attributed to the Durani-British connivance. Skeptics were also of the view that Afghans would languish for the reverses they inflicted to the British as long as the United Kingdom remained a superpower. Winston Churchill's instruction to Louis Mountbatten to punish *"pathans"* was recounted in family spheres. The myth of love and hate between Afghanistan and England would then last for generations. Right and wrong were always parted by a gray area. But for sure, British commanders and chief agents perpetrated outrageous blunders that resulted in the downfall of their empire. *The Man Who Would be King*, played by Sir Sean Connery and Michael Caine, depicted so well the viciousness of one and the innocence or silliness of the other. One major motive of Afghan rage was the abuse of women. The British also smeared the policy of humiliation through sexual exploitation and abuse of Afghan women. It created most ferocious reactions. Amid Akbar Khan and William Macnaghten's confrontation during the first Anglo-Afghan war, the head of the British Intelligence, Sir Alexander Burnes, was ferociously massacred by the population for the very abuse of Afghan women. Mr. Suri always reminded Soraya that she should not be fooled by the so-called democratic nature of a system. Outside their territories, victorious troops dealt with the occupied or vanquished the way they fancied as finally history was written by them and democracy was just an illusion. However, the utmost hurtful enemy of Afghan women had been their own society and archaic customs. In the course of history, they were regarded as objects. Their human dignity and rights were proclaimed when they served a specific political purpose. In this regard, all Afghan governments had behaved hypocritically.

In the autumn of 1974, Soraya resumed work half-heartedly. All of Kabul had knowledge of her as a stunningly intelligent, superbly fashioned, and unequivocally hardworking being. Women in government institutions endeavored to imitate her, at least in their attire. She was undeniably the "top model" of the city. Master Hassan could not cope with so many new customers. He would rush home whenever Soraya needed him. Selina was also growing astonishingly. The deputy foreign minister's frustration culminated as Soraya had no time or patience to listen to his delirium. She hurried home as soon as her daily tasks were completed. Moreover, she could hardly make sense of Afghan foreign policy. She was, however, approached in all diplomatic congregations by ambassadors and envoys to comprehend her analysis of the situation. She was not shy of disapproving of the government and believed that lack of harmony within the president's team would make it practically impossible to have tangible upshots on any front.

President Daoud was disillusioned fast; the Soviet Union did not wish to salvage his republic. The only flourishing issue was hostility toward Pakistan and the claim that *"this Pashtunistan is ours"*! He had meanwhile convened a *loya jirga*, a grand assembly of Afghan tribal chieftains, to endorse his new constitution and proclaim him president of the republic without an election. Only a handful of women were in attendance. The scene was silly! There was a theatrical arrangement whereby all delegates pleaded with him to accept the presidency. For his part and similar to his uncle, the father of King Zaher Shah, Daoud Khan pretended reluctance. But the partakers implored him again to do so. He then made it appear that it was at the great insistence of the Assembly that he conceded to lead the country. People who followed the deliberations on the radio waves were smirking, and some even felt insulted by such a foolish approach. Western diplomats recounted a "remarkable mockery" to democratic principles. Even a child would have jeered. But Afghan rulers had succeeded so since the making of Afghanistan, and their "godfathers," the British, fostered such practices at the expense of seeking people's opinions.

In the same period, a profound split within the Muslim Brotherhood took place. Followers of Golboddin Hekmatyar asserted their independence and extremist view from the main trend, while Ahmad Shah Massoud remained with the more moderate faction, led now by Professor Rabbani. He, however, engaged in a revolt against Daoud Khan in the northeastern part of the country, behind the mountains of Hindukosh. But he did not succeed and escaped temporarily to Pakistan. The Soviets had immediately assisted in the rescue of Daoud Khan's government. Within opposition circles, rumors of Hekmatyar's failed attempt to assassinate the twenty-two-year-old Massoud spread quickly, leaving him with no choice but to return to his Afghan mountains. Most, if not all, Muslim orthodox scholars and politicians, particularly the notorious Jalaluddin Haqani, were already in Peshawar, under careful watch and care of the Pakistan military spy agency. The instant was propitious to use them against

President Daoud and his policy of "*Daa Pashtunistan Zemouge.*" As of this juncture, the cities of Peshawar and Quetta became cradles of Afghanistan's ruin and destruction and the centers of radicalized Islamic movements. Nobody would ever comprehend how Zulfiqar Ali Bhutto, the master of Pakistan who portrayed his democratic identity exaggeratedly, permitted establishment of the poisonous bees' nest on his territory.

By the beginning of 1975, President Daoud twigged that the Soviets would not rescue him. Their tactic was obvious: let him flop, so communists could prevail and take over! He determined to swap alliances once again. His obstinacy was to the extent that he often disregarded Naim Khan's advice. On an evening of April 1975, the deputy foreign minister imposed a working dinner to prepare President Daoud's impending visit to Iran, where he anticipated to obtain a significant grant. The occasion was candid. Numerous executives of the foreign ministry were also in attendance. Soraya articulated her opinion frankly while the executive assistant took careful note of the deliberations. Since her arrival in the Marble Palace, she had imposed strict rules that every official movement and statement of the foreign minister was recorded formally. The basics of the trip were agreed upon quickly, and it was time to "smoke cigars," But Soraya persisted, as something perturbed her. "Excellency, what if the shah of Iran does not accede to our president's expectations? You have not considered this possibility," she quietly suggested.

The deputy minister stood up and arrogantly pointed out that no one could deny "his" president's request. But Soraya had a precise recollection of Daoud Khan's visit to Iran when he was prime minister and grasped the finesse of the Iranians' diplomacy during the Helmand water agreement. She remained puzzled, though, by the amateurish attitude of the deputy minister. The shah of Iran indeed refused to accord any grant and offered two billion dollars credit with the condition that the Afghan government distance itself from the Soviet Union. Not prepared for such an eventuality, once again Daoud Khan was furious and fumed. He could not counter the Iranian proposal and finally had to give in. The deputy minister of foreign affairs put the blame of unpreparedness on his senior staff. Soraya was appalled. Her decision was made: working with such an individual could prove life-threatening. She recalled her father, who often quoted the Prophet of Islam that "when you are faced with an aggressive fool, change your path." The next day she offered her resignation; the little man, however, declined to receive it and "ordered" her to continue with her work. In any civilized society, he would have been blamed for the diplomatic flop, but in Afghanistan, those linked with power and the palace were immune from justice and the rule of law; only commoners paid high costs.

There was no other alternative; support of the virtual Foreign Minister Naim Khan was indispensable. Two days later, she was received at his residence.

"Excellency, you have always been a real uncle to me," Soraya started, sipping her green tea perfumed with cardamom.

"My young lady, your father was an exceptional man. He understood before anyone else the games of the superpowers," he replied. "We appreciated him very much, and indeed, I personally considered him as a brother."

"I am resigning from my position. My family has enlarged, and the government salary is not enough," Soraya apprised him.

"We are aware, Soraya, and do not appreciate the inefficiency of the foreign ministry. But you see, we have nobody else to run it," he emphasized.

"There are very competent people, and Your Excellency may know most of them. But I also understand the constraints," she underscored by looking straight into Naim Khan's eyes and referring to family ties.

"Please proceed; we will instruct the deputy minister to acknowledge your resignation," Naim Khan softly assured her. "But we hope to rely on your cooperation in reviewing sensitive documents and deliberations inside or outside the country when called upon," he proposed.

"Certainly, uncle!" Soraya gladly replied.

The next day, Soraya was out of a job. She had the sense of having been freed from a penitentiary. As an outsider now, she was certain that President Daoud Khan lived in a castle of cards and his megaprojects were just dreams. He had irritated his two strong neighbors and the West. More tragically, he demonstrated that power can be snatched by the use of force and weapons. This last point brought calamity, carnage, destruction, extremism, and foreign interference and extended the very existence of rampant political corruption for decades to come in Afghanistan. Practically 85 percent of the credit given by the shah was earmarked for the construction of a railroad to connect Kabul with the Iranian networks. This indeed became Daoud Khan's surprise priority as Pakistan declined to permit Afghan commercial commodities to transit through its territory unless the country clogged its enmity. Systematically, Indian leaders' state visits were followed by those from Pakistan. President Daoud could not comprehend the substance of the intricacy of Indo-Pakistani rapport. The fact that he had squandered Afghanistan's privileged neutral status left him with no protection. Moreover, he overvalued his own credibility.

Soraya soon faced the challenge of reviewing policy papers that did not mean anything or rewriting senseless speeches that were out of context. She strived often to merge what was logical and the government's opinion. There was no sense of strategy and direction; the focus was on retaining power and privileges. Her annoyance was mounting. Financial impediments once again pushed her to seek a job, and she was hired by the British-backed Afghan Insurance

Company. Moving from an intense diplomatic environment to a purely business sphere was a defiance that she joyfully consented to. However, she continued voicing her judgment and deemed that in a country where basic services were not delivered to the majority of its population, particularly women, an unregulated private sector had its limitations. She was given a horrible, humid office in the basement of the building, with only one hanging bulb and mice running around. Descending from the Marble Palace to the cellar of such an edifice was unfair for a graceful lady. Her friends questioned whether it was a punishment induced by the little man. But she faced it with dignity and humility. Three months later, at an evening social event, a refined and polite gentleman approached her.

"Madame, I am dealing with development strategies in the ministry of planning." He introduced himself. "Since your departure from the Marble Palace, the minister has been looking for you. I was tasked to find you."

"Thank you, sir, for your consideration. How can I help?" she inquired, noticing at the same time that the gentleman stuttered occasionally.

"Well, we have a group of foreign advisers and would like you to join them," he politely answered.

"What type of contract and salary range would I have?" She continued with her inquiries.

"You will be the highest ranked Afghan staff, mover and shaker of the policies, strategies, and action plans. Your payment will be in accordance with international rules for local staff," he replied.

Once home, she wept extensively. For three months, she had been pushed to the limit of humiliation and faced the situation with calm and honor. She was so grateful to God for having saved her. Selina felt the joy of her mother. With her sweet, elated eyes, she followed Soraya in every room, hugging and kissing her abundantly.

On a magnificent day of spring 1976, when sunshine and a tender breeze wandered the city's atmosphere, Soraya emerged into the building of the ministry of planning on Darulaman Avenue. This was the finest time in Kabul. Blossoms of fruit trees, flowers of all varieties, and the marvelous acacia saplings were pouring their perfumes into the air, giving an indescribable ambiance. Those who knew Soraya were stunned; they never thought of sighting her in this edifice, and folks in the corridor instantly stirred aside to let her walk to the office of the minister and his international advisers.

And this is when I encountered her! She was dressed in an emerald-green combination. With strikingly bright greenish eyes and lion-styled hair, she moved with grace and allure. She had a remarkably noble grin on her lips and wore the most suitable fragrance; I believe it was First of Van Cleef and Arpels. She was simply too regal and a perfect reality of what poets describe as splendor. For two years, I had assisted the same experts during my free university hours and had never seen such a wonder, elegance and glamour, in my life. She moved upright with measured steps and responded graciously to every greeting. Within the team, I steered the opposition to engaging royal family members in the office, due to sour past experiences of abuse and categorical exploitation of other national staff. Thinking hastily that she was certainly coming from the palace, I hurried to the manager, a Swiss citizen of Hungarian origin, who as a young opponent to the Communist regime in Budapest had to flee his country following the 1956 repression and reach Switzerland on foot. He looked like a much taller and stronger Kevin Costner, with a short boxed beard.

"Sir, a remarkable lady is here. It is conceivably for the highest position," I informed him. "Allow me to underline our opposition once again to hire someone along considerations that have created serious discord in the past," I pursued.

"My dear colleague," he replied. "Indeed, I am expecting her. Rest assured that in the appointment process, nobody will be dismayed. I am informed that she is an extremely competent person," he affirmed.

The international experts were accommodated next to the minister of planning, perhaps the only bright individual in Daoud Khan's cabinet and the most decent one that he had fetched. It was alleged that he had ties with the Soviet Union, perhaps because of his Uzbek origin. Within an instant, the entire ministry learned that Soraya Suri had now joined the minister's foreign advisory team. Due to my own family context, I had a strong disbelief in the Soviet Union and communist system and was outspoken about it. Oftentimes, I received threats. Therefore, most high-level shoe shiners and those with "26 Saratan" mustaches did not appreciate me, and my social interface was limited. Soraya and the manager remained in the minister's office for a long time. This was already a good indication as the minister did not waste his time with idiots. Another long tête-à-tête encounter between her and the manager followed. They spoke not only of implementing the minister's guidance and instructions but also of Arthur Koestler and Soraya's delightful weeklong discussion with the great philosopher in the Austrian Tyrol. While we anxiously waited to see how this recruitment would affect the national staff, only one among us, who claimed to be a cousin of President Daoud, said that she was his friend.

The same day, she relocated the entire office to much larger and decent spaces at the end of the hallway, far away from the minister's office, with authorization to use his lavatory, something of great significance in Afghanistan to the extent that his chief of staff was the custodian of the key of the venerable location. Soraya believed that being next to the minister did not imply prominence as it had to be demonstrated by tangible outcomes of entrusted tasks accomplished. An incident occurred that possibly sealed a reverential bond between Soraya and me. She began scouring the office carpets, actively shaking them and urging others to join her before moving to the new location; everybody, even employees of the ministry, rushed to help. I did not and still thought she was a bigwig, recommended by the palace!

"Sir, who are you?" she inquired.

"I am in your team, madame," I replied.

"Then why do you not help?" she asked.

"It is not part of my job description," I insisted.

She was certainly surprised but, contrary to my expectation, ignored my arrogance and let me be alone in my corner. I looked ridiculous and absurd.

Within days, Soraya reformed the modus operandi of the office based on a formal agreement between the minister and the manager. It affected the way staff functioned. Resources were not squandered anymore to favor authorities or their acquaintances. A strategic direction and a plan of action for export sectoral development had to be formulated and proposed to the minister. In addition to the Swiss manager, the group of experts comprised an American, a Brit, and a Soviet of Russian origin. The latter, Piotr, was more prominent and noticeable. He "handled multiple issues," disappeared most of the day, and often returned before closure of the offices. Apparently he had daily exchanges with the Soviet Embassy and justified it as negotiation efforts to open a land transportation corridor for Afghan exportable products to Western Europe through the giant neighbor in the north. He pretended that the embassy did not wish to bargain with other foreign experts. It was a strange situation but tolerated. Within two weeks, the foreign advisers had their distinct status. Experts yakked about broader policies, domestic production, and consumption strategies, as well as elaboration of annual goals that encompassed field project implementation monitoring, elaboration of quality control mechanisms, and advising the minister on bilateral and multilateral opportunities. Soraya recommended development of a catalogue of exportable artifacts, and a renowned Swiss photographer was hired in Geneva for the purpose. In addition, she opened a fully equipped library within the ministry for staff to further their knowledge about areas of concern. There was a wholly new and dynamic environment. Coordination and consultation sessions with internal and external actors were systematically held, and the minister received weekly briefings and reports.

Amid these manifest upturns and intensification of activities, I was notified that my services were not required any longer. I was then dismissed! It was a big whack to my morale. Like Soraya, I grew up in a family environment where honesty, hard work, and fairness were inserted to our blood and circulated in our veins, arteries, muscles, nerves, hearts, and minds. Over a decade of systematic and fearless struggle against injustice that we confronted had made me popular among my larger family. Though I direly needed to have an income, there was no reason to argue. I left the office, walking along backstreets toward the university compound and considering other options to earn some money. The weather was extremely nice, and the physical effort comforted me somehow. My good friend and classmate Mirwais invited me for lunch at the cantina of the campus, and in the afternoon I was a different person, more resolved to find another part-time occupation.

Several weeks later, while I was attending physics courses at the university, the lecture was halted by an intruder that I knew. Afzal, the driver of the manager, appeared and spoke to the professor for a good while. Soraya had called me back to the office. My first retort was an uncompromising rejection to the invitation that revealed the hurt of my inner feelings. But the professor, who valued me, hinted to me to be judicious rather than emotional, and I was permitted to leave the class.

Soraya greeted me with her characteristic and trademark smile. "I understand how angry you may be at us," she started. "But there was a corruption network within the office. I had to dismantle it."

"Then what is the outcome, madame?" I inquired.

The self-proclaimed "cousin of President Daoud Khan" and Soraya's "friend" had been sacked. Not only had he collected commissions from all the suppliers, but in connivance with them, he had charged inflated rates to the office. It was the rebirth of my confidence and the commencement of over four decades of cooperation, fellowship, shared views, respect, and fights for justice, fairness, and human rights with this wonderful lady who, in my opinion, has been one of the most beautiful minds of Afghanistan. It was a demanding challenge for me; some days, I had to hurry back and forth between the university compound and the ministry several times on the back of my bicycle, which looked like an old donkey.

Within a few weeks, I realized what a noble person Soraya was. Unquestionably, she was a perfect image of Mr. Suri. As a teenager, I had knowledge and heard praises about the former chief justice through my own father, who respected him and regarded him as a true leader. Both men were from Logar and had passed away in the same year of 1968 at the same age. Zamir Suri was venerated as a hero of the province. Those disenchanted by the regime befriended Soraya quickly. Serious, bright, rational, astute, beautifully dressed, and down-to-earth, she gained the hearts and minds of practically everyone in the ministry. She had time for all and could deliberate about every topic. The highest executives were ridiculed in meetings where they had to offer solutions, but many resolutions were suggested by Soraya; she was such a quick thinker. For an extremely complex issue, she could think of several options within seconds. Not only was she trained so, but her deep acquaintance with issues and the aptitude to research and read gave her a further edge. She was also a rapid reader. While presidents of departments perused reports word by word, she was capable of digesting them much faster. Her talent to synopsize was startling. She summarized bulky policy documents in just two or three pages. The most astounding fact that dazed me was her proficiency of the English language. Oftentimes she substantially amended texts drafted by English-speaking experts. She appeared busier than the minister himself and had barely any spare time in the office. Every morning she entered the building with a number of broader government papers to review. She was indeed a human robot!

The year 1976 was acutely grim for the country. The government efficiency and power base were dwindling, and natural calamities put more stress on the system. Visits of foreign heads of states and governments as well as their diplomatic endeavors aimed at hauling Afghanistan to the arms of one or another superpower and thrusting for extraction of its natural resources. Soraya was solicited by Naim Khan to help. Certainly the minister of planning and his advisory leadership had consented. She also desired to comprehend more than her diplomatic and political orbits. I accompanied her to the university compound, where she lunched for the first time in front of a street eatery and in poor quarters at the outskirts of the city. She was devastated to see that around town, people lived in slums. Even living circumstances in rural areas were more decent, for sure!

We often conversed on politics. While she knew enough about the pro-Soviet communist parties and leadership, her knowledge about the pro-Chinese Sholay Jawed was limited. Within the ministry, she did not welcome one particular "26 Saratan" mustached who held a senior position and oftentimes appeared in her office to try in vain to impress. He seemed nasty, intimidating staff of the ministry. However, she was particularly considerate of two employees in the building: Agha Saheb, the slim and smart librarian who was handpicked by her through a fair interview process, and Mr. Hashem, a rather short and chubby individual from the Shia community. She ascertained a lot from Agha Saheb about religious movements and their resistance strategy. There was open conversation about Pakistan harboring the alleged Islamic hard-liners. However, the moderate faction had remained in the country and opted for skyscraping massifs of the Hindukosh Mountains, more specifically in Badakhshsan and Panjshir, to seek protection and organize themselves.

Daoud Khan's squad tracked putschists who now and then attempted to topple him. Since the murder of Maiwandwal, no one believed in the honesty of the leadership and the integrity of what they claimed. Consequently, he encased himself with acquaintances, kinfolk, and sons of buddies, the sort of individuals who did not have the guts to tell him the truth; he fancied not to be contradicted and was pleased to hear "the good news." Afghans learned for the first time about their country as a sort of "banana republic." Daoud Khan did not honor appeals by Gerald Ford, Harold Wilson, James Callaghan, Helmut Schmidt, Valerie Giscard d'Estaing, or even Anwar El Sadat to release Mr. Mousa Shafiq and Professor Niazi and allow them at least to proceed to Egypt and live in exile. Moreover, he seemed afraid of legitimizing his presidency with a transparent and fair election. He lived in his own imagination. Naim Khan was dreadfully annoyed by an elder brother who had long ago lost touch with reality and his people. He consistently counseled Daoud Khan to take time, reflect, consult, define a policy, and then deploy all means for its implementation. Once, he privately warned him of the whole family facing slaughter if he persisted with his fantasy world! His big brother apparently stared at him and nodded with an acerbic smile.

Soraya frequently argued with me. For her, I embodied revolutionary ideas that were not conducive for progress. Oftentimes, she depicted me a comparative study of revolution and evolution. And in spite of my ferocious counter reasons, she was most convincing. Accomplishing colossal duties of extremely high quality within a few hours was her characteristic attribute. She despised a task pending for the day after if there was no compelling reason. As usual, she enjoyed using either of the fountain pens to revise manuscripts and then passed them to me. I became expert at reading her handwriting and realized that her fingers could not keep up with the trend of her thoughts, which were much faster. Therefore, on paper, words and sometimes sentences were missing. This steered me to construe her mind. It was a fascinating period!

I was taken out of a restrained philosophy of revenge against rulers of the country to a much wider dimension that included the interest of society even at the expense of individuals including myself. We spoke about what ruined the foundation of a state. Corruption and nepotism were at the top of our list, followed by incompetence. In a debate, she was fearless. Her office was the pivotal lieu of exchange of ideas; junior staff had to vacate when the most senior executives of the establishment entered. It appeared like the *gardaab* that she hosted in New York; the distinction was that it happened during working hours, and there were no invitations. She always offered her preferred green tea to visitors. The manager could not breathe without seeking her views. He had horrendous handwriting. She taught me the technique of most plausible extrapolation, which permitted me to browse the unreadable scriptures.

In early spring 1977, Soraya called me into her office. "There may be fundamental changes soon in the country," she confessed. "The current situation is unbearable for all. I do not know which way it will go. But you must leave the country; you do not seem to have many friends in this place, and they will kill you."

"So far, I have had two scholarships from Western universities, and on each occasion, I was interrogated by the secret services about my relationship with them and why I did not go through government channels," I informed her. "There was no other choice than abandoning my dream."

fundamental improvements in which modification of customary and legislative laws would have been the centerpiece. Promoting more rights for women was obscene; authorities demonstrated an utterly unconvincing defensive attitude.

In midspring of 1977, Soraya encouraged me to apply for a scholarship and pass an entry exam for the famous *Ecôle Polytechnique Fédérale de Lausanne* in Switzerland. In early July of the same year, I was accepted! This time around, I owed my fortune to her. She never explained to me how, but she had done a miracle as the doors of my luck had been closed long ago. The previous two aborted opportunities had traumatized me. Still, I thought of another interrogation. Worried about unpredictable repercussions, I disclosed to her the fear of government fury and the likelihood of another setback. Two days later, she accompanied me to the foreign ministry—her former Marble Palace office—to meet a refined and attentive man. I believe she had already negotiated the gentleman's accord. Subsequently, he agreed to ignore the issue and shelve the file. But I had to find my way out of the country without seeking their support. For this unique instance in life, I bribed authorities to acquire a tourist passport, valid only for a few months.

Prior to my departure for Europe, I urged Soraya and her family to visit the deeper parts of our common ancestral land of Logar, where my family dwelled. Zamir Suri was a great son of our region. Hosting members of his family was a real honor. A strategic route for British invaders in the eighteenth and nineteenth centuries, Azre and Zarghoun Shahr presented the shortest distance between Lahore and Kabul. The father of King Zaher Shah had utilized the same path to attain the Afghan capital, oust Amir Habibullah Kalakani, and viciously overturn his regime. We proceeded to my village, next to Azre, where the husband of my aunt, an army officer and professor at the military academy, had taken charge of receiving the distinguished guests. The dinner was arranged at the riverbank. It was a pleasing afternoon.

221

The news of Soraya's visit quickly spread. Villagers gathered along the Kabul-Gardez motorway. Since her father long ago, no Suri had visited the nearby villages. There was a curious and friendly atmosphere, and I could not dampen the enthusiasm. My cousins and distant relatives desired to see with their own eyes the young Suri about whom my family often spoke. Upon her arrival, Soraya saluted everyone like a queen merging with her subjects. People invited her to their humble dwellings. This was a standard cultural practice, and she promised a tour. Over thirty minutes was needed to convince them to disperse. She then moved straight to the brook. The transparent water, up to her knees, was refreshing. She had waded in it so often with her father long ago. The touch of smooth, shiny, colorful stones with her feet appeased her soul. At home, she solicited my grandmother to escort her to some families to meet young girls and women of the village. The grandfather drove all the men to tread the vicinity. The lush valley of Logar is enveloped by high mountains and irrigated by a river of the same name. Similar to Kohdaman in the north of Kabul, hundreds of kilometers of natural underground water network, the kaarez, lope underneath. Only the elderly knew where to excavate to unearth the path!

The dinner was a fiasco. My aunt's husband overcooked the meat; in fact, he had actually burned it! But the ensuing dissertation about the condition of young women, as well as the sentiments of military officers involving the state of affairs in the country, was fascinating. Soraya felt sorry and saddened that there was no means of education for girls in the area and learned that people stashed and confined their women and young sisters. She realized an ardent longing on the part of people she encountered to do more than perish at home in expectation of a husband appearing. She firmly assumed that restrictions on women from social and public life were implanted due to the lack of education and knowledge of people at large of religious instructions. The principle of "learn, even if you have to go to China" was never taught to the villagers in rural areas, and all imams hibernated on this issue. Historically, perhaps potentates had, contrary to the instructions of Islam, dozens of women in their harems and alcoves and did not want them to be attracted by other men. This was certainly why they not only inflicted full coverage of their bodies and minds, but also gelded all males who performed a duty in the female quarters of their palaces.

On her way back to the capital city, Soraya was reflecting as to why in her society only boys and men mattered! Women were prodigious mothers, sturdy sisters, magnificent daughters, and staggering wives; then why did everybody want a son and rarely a daughter? Was it iniquitous to be born a girl? If so, then people must seek accountability from God, as he has not made a distinction between male and female in any of the holy books received from the skies. In Afghanistan, people were pompous of their mother tongue, considering it a national pride; why not of their women?

Soraya seemed thoughtful and concerned about the assertion of my aunt's husband that discontent with Daoud Khan in the army was mounting. It was rumored that his loyal first deputy and Ambassador Puzanov secretly congregated with pro-Soviet ringleaders in the army, especially at the military academy, and that the demise of the "first republic" was simply a question of time. Allegations of who did what had always tarnished political stands in the West. But Soraya comprehended that in Afghanistan, rumors were constantly tied up with some type of reality.

Soraya's enchanting visit to my family encouraged me to organize, a week later, another excursion to Zarghoun Shahr, the land of marvelous grapes, perhaps the only site in the world where subterranean trout existed in kaarez. Since they were considered sacred, nobody consumed them. My cousins hosted us. They had received devoted attention from my father after theirs was murdered during their childhood. The eldest was a devout, pious military officer. Like Azre, Zarghoun Shahr was victim of the brutality of invaders who rushed to Kabul from British India. The horde of King Zaher Shah's father crossed the area twice, leaving indelible sorrowful memories. They had massacred opponents and looted the little "green city" ferociously. Their charge to capture Kabul was as harmful for the population of this tiny jewel as the retreat back to their tribal areas. Soraya was intrigued to apprehend why the Afghan army was split between traditionalists and communists. While Afghanistan was certainly a country, its citizens barely felt a national bond due to prejudiced policies practiced in the past. Equally competent Turkmen, Uzbeks, Hazara, and even Tajiks occupied secondary positions in key government institutions. It was likely that history books were biased and jaundiced. Therefore, the sense of belonging to an ethnic group was deeper than belonging to a country. And communists advocated for nation building around their materialism dialectic and internationalist values.

I left Kabul in August 1977 for Switzerland by road. Not only had I no money left to purchase an air ticket; the fear of being apprehended at the airport haunted me. Eighteen days and nights were adequate to attain Lausanne via Iran, Turkey, Bulgaria, Yugoslavia, Austria, and West Germany.

Meanwhile, Daoud Khan reshuffled the cabinet. Though the communists lost most of their ministerial posts, the first and second deputy prime ministers remained immovable. Disappointed with the result of his trip to Iran, President Daoud decided to travel again to Moscow for help. It was a make-or-break attempt. He concurred to receive once again a despicable kiss on his lips from Brezhnev. The outcome of his dialogue was a debacle. It culminated in an open row. The Soviet leader grumbled about the rising influence of Iran and Western countries in Afghanistan and directed him to implement a preprepared script of actions. Daoud Khan was deeply offended and made it clear to Brezhnev that he did not receive orders from anyone for affairs related to his country; then he left Moscow. The subsequent divorce from the Soviet Union was inevitable.

Though President Daoud had his sympathizers, thought-provoking questions have been raised about whether he did not prevent the country from a steady headway due to his imprudent drives. He dreamed to place his indelible features in the history of the country in much brighter ink than any of his predecessors. His change of alliance in 1953 propelled the country into Soviet arms. Once removed as prime minister, his obstinacy to undermine the democratic process was unforgivable. His reckless act of deposing King Zaher Shah to be himself at the realm of power again impelled the country to years of uncertainty, paving the way for decades of crises, war, and devastation, inflicting massive human and financial tolls. Finally, his political zigzag between the protagonists of the Cold War was amateurish, futile, and fatal for himself, his family, and the country. Thus, four decades of peace and measured progress were shattered, with foreign military interventions spurring an upsurge of extremism and terrorism.

Soraya began to distance herself from those who embodied the inner circles of power. Agha Saheb and Mr. Hashem briefed her regularly about the rising likelihood of an armed conflict. The minister of planning frequently exchanged views with her. He also alluded to the grief of traditional supporters of President Daoud. The ugly "26 Saratan" mustached had now adjusted his tactics. He praised Soraya, noting that in a "different political milieu," she would be granted the maximum liberty to light up even more. For her, the contest between superpowers was clear. While the West, through their Iranian and Saudi allies, sought for Daoud Khan to sever ties with the Soviet Union prior to receiving support, Brezhnev goaded Parcham and Khalq to unite against Daoud Khan. Some believed that President Daoud never made true friends within or outside Afghanistan. He was squeezed and had no way out. An air of "each for self" reigned. In Afghan high political and commercial rings, people agonized and explored moving out with anything they could.

The second half of 1977 was marred by ferocious demonstrations. Ambassador Puzanov triumphed; the Khalq and Parcham parties fused to found the sole pro-Soviet communist entity PDPA—People's Democratic Party of Afghanistan. No one conversed about the Maoist Sholay Jawed; they were deemed insignificant now. Rahim Mahmoudi was too old. Their bright youngster, Sokhandan, was murdered, and other leaders were apprehended. But the concern of a coup by traditionalist officers, espoused by the Muslim Brotherhood, was privileged; and Kremlin propaganda endorsed the assumption. Daoud's new minister of interior opted for more tyranny. The government spy agency reclaimed its notorious status of a terror and repression body. Soraya abstained from voicing her opinion or providing advice and hurried home earlier to spend time with Selina. In spite of the minister's attempts to plow her mind during these asphyxiating moments, she remained cautious. Her father had lectured that "dead heroes served no purpose."

In March 1978, Daoud Khan traveled to Switzerland and instantly decided to meet Anwar El Sadat, the Egyptian leader, another most trusted ally of the Western world. Daoud Khan looked like a drowning individual who grabbed every twig! For Soraya the latest developments announced the death of the regime. Very few people knew what exactly transpired between the two heads of state. But upon his return, Daoud Khan and his inner circle decided to neutralize communist leaders. Ambassador Puzanov, who sympathized with the minister of planning, oftentimes articulated his exasperation; now he determined that the endgame loomed.

On a Friday at the beginning of April 1978, Soraya and her family were in the summer residence of a friend in Paghman. It was a pleasant social event, and everybody was doing something to make the outing interesting. Suddenly the guards alerted her that Naim Khan was approaching. In the Afghan culture, people do not inform close friends of their visit; they just appear. Abruptly the atmosphere became sober. Naim Khan was most affable, but something was worrying him. Soraya let the opportunists do their usual display to impress him. He was having his lemonade juice under a jasmine bush when she approached him.

"Excellency, how are you doing?" she inquired.

"Things could be better, but I am doing fine," he replied. "I understood you are now working with foreign advisers of the minister of planning."

"Indeed, Your Highness. I was left with no choice," she courageously pointed out.

"Please call me uncle, Soraya. As I told you, your father and I were like twin brothers," Naim Khan said.

"Then, uncle, what is going on?" she asked.

"The situation is not conducive, and the country faces serious danger. We need the help of someone like your father. Unfortunately, he is no more!"

"Well, under the current circumstances, why do you not ask Mr. Shafiq to help?" Soraya suggested. "After all, he has been under house arrest for five years and is available," she continued with the utmost seriousness.

"No, no! He is unpopular within the highest decision-making circle," Naim Khan pointed out.

They engaged in an intense discussion that nobody had the audacity to interrupt. Soraya was lost in thought. Daoud Khan had molded the army for over two decades to assist him to grab the supreme authority. He managed to avoid elections, the foundation of a republican regime. And now there was panic on board! She opined that the power liked only lickspittles, who were of no use. Naim Khan, with his fatherly attitude, conceded that blunders were committed, but he stressed that wasting time about the past would not help anyone—neither the power nor the victims. Then, Soraya came to her favorite theme of history and grumbled that the truth had always been tampered with and that people were duped. In her opinion, rulers underestimated the grief of the people and the severe aftermath of the autocratic manner in which state affairs were conducted. She noted that not only had earlier facts been distorted but even the modern history of Afghanistan did not reveal the verity. In her view, successive governments misjudged the power of the verbal transmission of knowledge and information in Afghanistan. Indeed, conquerors author history and rulers put whatever they wish in the scripts, but the people have their own version of facts, spread by their parents to them and by them to their children, who then take the flambeau at their own account. This is why different reports circulated about the Charkhi family, Abdur Rahman Ludin, Amir Habibullanh Kalakani, Malik Khan, Hashem Maiwandwal, and countless more valorous sons of the country who were killed for dubious reasons since the father of King Zaher Shah had taken over.

It was time for departure to the city. Naim Khan concluded the discussion. "Soraya, nobody knows who will be where tomorrow. I wish you good luck!"

There was no doubt that even Naim Khan grasped that the end of his brother's regime was near. On April 17, 1978, Parcham's theoretician and the so-called "Suslov of Afghanistan," Mir Akbar Khyber, was assassinated. Some suspected Islamic hard-liners, while others believed it was orchestrated by the communists themselves. However, Ambassador Puzanov discerned exactly what had ensued and accused the government for failing to protect prominent politicians. Contrary to Afghan and Islamic rituals, his body was not buried instantly in order to call for and garner sympathizers for a gigantic rally of partisans. Two days later during his funeral, a massive number of people were on the streets of Kabul shouting slogans against Daoud

Khan, America's CIA, and Iran's SAVAK. Khyber was himself a military officer and played a weighty role in the conscription of army officers to embrace the cause of Parcham. Daoud Khan was worried. In despair, he conferred with his brother Naim Khan.

"I do not understand these stupid people! You know how much I have done for them. Moreover, they killed their own man!" he angrily argued.

"Daoud, time seems over for us," Naim Khan replied, using his elder brother's first name, contrary to the established family protocol. "Please let the family go out of the country immediately," he implored.

"No way!" the president ferociously argued. "We are not going to lose to a bunch of bastards. I made them—they have no pluck to revolt against me."

"You are wrong, Mr. President," Naim Khan replied. "I beg you to let the women and children leave at least!"

Daoud Khan refused to let his family depart the country for safer destinations. On the contrary, he instructed apprehension of all communist principals. The government spy agency was swift in action. Puzanov had full knowledge of the president's determination. No doubt most people were aware of the fact that Daoud Khan's reliable and trusted first deputy updated the Soviet envoy recurrently. All communist chiefs were detained within hours except Hafizullah Amin, a Colombia University graduate and deputy of the Khalq Party. It is whispered that Daoud's first deputy prime minister recommended to put him under house arrest rather than in jail as "he is a CIA agent and could prove helpful." The president was fooled, as Amin charged a leading army communist officer, a member of his Khaq Party, to trigger the coup. General Abdul Qader, commander of the air force and senior member of the Parcham Party, who had placed Daoud Khan in the driver's seat five years earlier, joined the forces against him. Though both communist parties had united, Khalq officers commanded the coup in the operation theater.

On Thursday, April 27, 1978, the eve of the weekend in Afghanistan, the chief of staff of the minister of planning scuttled to Soraya's office and ordered her to go home without further details. Instantly, she thought there had been a family incident. Afzal, her faithful friend and driver, moved quickly, as if he realized what was happening. Her preoccupation was what might have occurred to whom in the family. The road to the city center was closed. Abnormally, there were no police—just soldiers carrying automatic machine guns. He headed toward the western part and then north to reach Karte Parwan. Again, access was not granted. He engaged on small mountain alleys, full of dirt and people, to reach the main vein behind the soldiers. Luck was on their side as no one was hurt! But again the Ansari crossroads was inaccessible. From the Panjshir Valley, he had a perfect map of the city in his mind and, once again, battled in tiny pedestrian lanes to gain Soraya's residence. She hastened in. Everything seemed normal, but Selina was missing. Once more Afzal hauled his car as fast as he could through small back paths to reach the kindergarten. The institution was completely empty except for Selina. Her back up against a wall, she looked around with lost green eyes and a pale face. She shivered. There were countless bullet holes just above her head. Thanks to the height of the child, the shooters had missed her. Soraya was horrified and kneeled, crying like a baby and thanking God. The child hurled herself in the arms of her mother, kissing her extensively. But Afzal grabbed her and urged Soraya to move on. There was no time for emotion.

Meanwhile, columns of tanks progressed from Pule Charkhi in the east of Kabul toward the palace. Air force jets soared over Daoud Khan's office to display might. The president and his close circle assumed that the airplanes glided the air in support of the regime. He instantly called in all women of his nucleus family who were outside the palace for diverse reasons. Assailants stepped quickly and fired some shells at the ministry of defense, adjacent to the palace, and neutralized the command center of the army. The Khalqui coup leader then admonished President Daoud to surrender.

"Who is this bastard to ask me to capitulate?" Daoud screamed!

President Daoud summoned everybody to his office and disclosed that the moment of truth had come and that they must defend themselves. It was a woeful scene. Naim Khan was next to him, together with their spouses, children, and grandchildren. They were all terrified to death. No one had the nerve to pose a question. Meanwhile, the coup chief was unrelenting. He announced an ultimatum and warned against entering the palace at all costs. Daoud Khan was convinced that the presidential guard would protect him properly. He, nevertheless, dashed to a spot and ordered every individual to hold a Kalashnikov rifle and tussle in case the insurgents pierced the space. His wife was apprehensive.

"We do not know how to use this device," she pleaded.

"There is a beginning to everything. If you cannot defend yourself today, you will not be able to protect the country tomorrow," he angrily replied.

"But please, think of the children and babies!" she insisted.

"What do you want me to do? Surrender? Never in life," he retorted. "We'd better be dead than prisoners of these whoresons!" he concluded.

All observers agreed that when Daoud Khan ceased listening to his younger but wiser brother Naim Khan, state affairs began to go out of hand. Notwithstanding the controversial character of President Daoud, he had a decent family. His sons and daughters had commendable behavior in the society. No one had ever witnessed or gathered any criticism about them. His youngest daughter was studying contemporary arts at the university and was a beautiful and timid young lady. It was unwise to compel such decent men and women to take guns in hand and make them targets of putschists. But it is alleged that each adult had one in hand that day.

The youngest daughter, scared, approached her mother. "Mother, we would better not carry guns in our hands," she implored.

"Your father has given his verdict," she replied. "We live or die together. This is the destiny of royals."

The scene embodied a Shakespearean tragedy! The presidential guard resisted ferociously; Daoud Khan and his closest associates scurried from one window to another. Surprisingly, the first deputy prime minister was not among them. Ambassador Puzanov and Amin monitored every move of the army. The defiance of the presidential guard was unpredicted and alarmed all the communist strategists. Their ground forces fretted as the day was coming to an end. The order was given to bomb the palace! The Mikoyan-Gurevich MiG-21 and Sukhoi Su-7 jet fighters that Daoud had purchased from the Soviet Union slithered with supersonic velocity. Within hours, the presidential guard was neutralized and their chieftains surrendered. Daoud Khan could not reach any of the military garrisons to seek aid. His communication network was defused. He was desperate and stranded.

In the early hours of April 28, 1978, the gates of the palace were smashed, and soldiers with machine guns ran into the yard in search of Daoud Khan and his team. His family did not know what to do, and he was short of solutions; his only advice was "Defend yourself!" His kinfolk were shivering. Some of his youngest grandchildren slumbered in the arms of their parents as if nothing were occurring outside. The coup team leader had now loomed near the building, and his orders were overheard. The agony had reached its apogee.

232

Women and children were clasping each other without pronouncing a word. Only the sound of intense respiration imparted their anxiety. Their stares conveyed what they dreaded. The assailants attained the stairs, and the tread of their boots was heard. They shot and murdered whoever emerged on their way. Children were woken up, and some began sobbing. It was evident that the enemy would discover them soon. Adults put their hands on each weeping mouth. When they perceived the voice of the assailants, President Daoud and Naim Khan left their confidants to unite with the family. It was over.

Naim Khan took a deep breath and addressed his brother. "I had warned you," he pointed out.

President Daoud gazed at him without pronouncing a word.

At this precise moment, the door was rammed, and the team leader, a medium-ranked military officer, ordered, "The revolution has succeeded, and you are all under arrest! Surrender yourselves."

There was an implacable silence; everybody looked at President Daoud. He screamed that they would never surrender, and the attackers fired. Countless bullets went out of their guns' barrels. Within a few minutes, Daoud Khan, Naim Khan, and their respected family members present at the scene were all assassinated. Daoud's close allies faced the same destiny. The rooms were full of blood and crammed with bodies. Walls were pierced with shells. Young children were murdered in the arms of their parents. Women lay next to each other hand in hand as if they wanted to undertake this last journey together. It is said that some in the palace attempted to vault the wall and seek refuge in the adjacent French residence, but they were shot at and slain too. The scene of the massacre was horrible. Most faces were terrified even in their deaths. It was so unjust, but politics does not know fairness. Moments later, military trucks arrived; Amin wanted the corpses of the victims to disappear.

In the same early hours of April 28, 1978, tanks were positioned in all strategic spots of the city. There was an apocalyptic atmosphere. Nobody spoke, but everybody sensed the country sliding one step closer to the abyss. Like always, there will be controversy over how it transpired, who stated what, and what may have caused a given circumstance, but murdering opponents and their families of women and children was beyond every Afghan's belief. Though they were not bestowed the rights they deserved, physical protection of women had always been part of the Afghan traditional code of conduct. Long ago, Daoud Khan's uncle and father of King Zaher Shah had exterminated rivals in Kohdaman, Zarghoun Shar, and elsewhere, but he did not slaughter their women and children. They were just exiled. The spoken stories would prevail, and each individual would have his or her facts. It was also undetermined how much the internal enmities among royal dignitaries hurt Daoud Khan. He, indeed, did not benefit from the pity of all members of his own larger family. Dethroning King Zaher Shah, who was harmless, was an unwise and uncalculated blunder.

The Khalqi coup leader proclaimed on the radio and television waves that their revolution had succeeded and that Daoud Khan and his inner circle had all been removed from power. President Daoud's once spiritual son, Abdul Qader, now presided over the revolutionary military council till the establishment of a new government. It seemed that his betrayal was planned five years back. Once Hafizullah Amin was assured of the massacre in the palace, he conferred with Puzanov to seek direction about the former prime minister Mousa Shafiq and the charismatic religious academician Ghulam Mohammad Niazi. The Soviet envoy urged patience; he did not fancy many fronts of defiance to the gory takeover. To assert authority over the country, formation of an inclusive PDPA government was the highest priority. Soraya remained home the whole day, calling and receiving phone calls. She understood that practically all the senior lieutenants of Daoud Khan, including the deputy foreign minister, were executed alongside their president except the first deputy prime minister.

The same evening, the entire nation watched for the first time the prime leader of the revolution, Nour Mohammad Taraki, chairman of the Khalq faction of the PDPA. Babrak Karmal of Parcham was proclaimed the second-in-command, while Hafizullah Amin both scrutinized from behind the scenes and handled the foreign relations of Afghanistan. Taraki was instantly described as the "Genius of the East" by his PDPA comrades—which already began to give a strong negative hint, as in the history of Afghanistan, all inefficient and deranged rulers had the most glorious superlative denominations. Though Soraya had never encountered Taraki, she vaguely recollected the face from when he served in the chief justice office under her father. She had not gathered anything singular about the man. In expert circles, he was effectively known as stupid and the one who used to finish all the liquor bottles before going to sleep. It is recounted that due to the stench of his feet, guards "stifled" his shoes in a fridge! But in subjugated countries, competence was never a virtue for those who assigned rulers. Whoever served their interest was valued and governed. The British had initiated the concept, and now the Soviets practiced it too. Soraya was already questioning who would be the morons that the next invader would employ. The next day, she was summoned to resume her duties.

Soraya was three months pregnant but reached her office as usual. The new minister of planning called for a meeting with foreign advisers and introduced the new "luminaries" of the ministry. All of them were novice in their functions and appeared alike, with heavy whiskers and straight, dark-colored hair on their foreheads. They were all products of the same "time machine"! It was the occasion to reward PDPA members and associates. Thank God, the "26 Saratan" mustached was not part of the leadership of the ministry. She was relieved. Piotr was shining, while other advisers seemed perplexed. As was the tradition of communist leaders, the new minister harangued for over two hours, blaming the corrupt power of Daoud Khan and vowing that the revolution would overhaul everything. At the end of the event, he instructed Soraya to remain behind.

When they were alone, the new minister said, "Madame, we know you, through your work, family, and distinguished father. You must understand that the revolution has been carried out by the courageous and nation-loving part of the PDPA. The lazy sons and daughters of nobility did not assist," he continued, alluding sharp criticism to his Parcham colleagues.

"I see, Your Excellency," Soraya replied.

"I want you, madame, to help us, and me particularly, the same way you assisted the former minister. We do not trust these imperialist advisers—only Piotr is trustworthy. We have asked for international advisers from member states of the Warsaw Pact. Of course, we rely on you too," he concluded.

She had heard the same from the then deputy foreign minister five years ago when the "soft revolution" of Daoud Khan had succeeded.

The American and British were ordered to leave Afghanistan within a week, and the Swiss manager seemed worried. Piotr gained increasing notoriety. Though apparently united, the split between the Parcham and Khalq was manifest, and Soraya feared a bloodbath between the two. The power was in the hands of the Khalq, and Hafizullah Amin was the authentic communist emperor of the country, and Puzanov began losing a grip on him.

A week later, when Soraya went to use the restroom, she found a gun under the mirror of the washbasin. She understood it belonged to the new minister; he had used the lavatory before her. She took the weapon in her purse and urged a meeting with him. He believed the request had a confidential nature related to their earlier discussion. At the entrance, she took out the pistol, pointed it at him, and advanced with steady steps. The new minister raised his hands, terrified. His face suddenly paled. He started to sweat! Within seconds she was in front of him. There was a deadly silence, and he did not have the nerve to even say a word. She put the gun on his desk in front of him. "Excellency, I believe this toy belongs to you," she calmly said.

The new minister was reborn. He sat down, his breath became normal, and blood started circulating in his veins again. He urged her not to reveal the incident to anyone, and Soraya agreed. From that instant, he trusted her and made his trust known to the senior leadership of the ministry. The ugly "26 Saratan" mustached could not believe it and was even instructed not to interfere in the business of the foreign advisers' office. Nobody ever understood what the rationale was for the sudden confidence of the minister.

A vicious chapter of Afghan history started in which women and children were the prime victims. The communist leadership had decided that they'd better capitalize on the new generation in the country rather than wasting time with those who by age, tradition, and political opinion may have already forged their judgment about them. There was only one woman in the new government, and girls in the schools and university became the prey of the system. In the name of liberty and contrary to a strict tradition whereby young females observed discipline and a certain code of conduct based on obedience within the family, they were dragged outside their homes and family spheres for a variety of celebrations in the glory of the revolution. Television programs were altered; not only was Marxism-Leninism tutored, but more women singers were incited and obliged to perform alongside men for the glory of the regime. These were not well received by an orthodox Islamic society that required more time to transform.

The regime took extra steps by assaulting the religion of the population, considering it the "opium of the people," as Karl Marx had stipulated over a century earlier. They animated young girls and boys in the schools to spy on their parents, with emphasis on religious endeavors and interactions. Countless family heads ended up in prison because of the innocent and induced mistakes of their own children. Meanwhile, the West was looking into the faults of the regime. The antireligious propaganda of the government, abuse of children, and an obviously provocative exhibition of young girls and boys in the public arena and on television shows exacerbated the population. Practically everybody had a sense the liberty was fake.

Though the fall of Daoud Khan was a relief for the ISI, Pakistani leaders feared new challenges. The Afghan secret services were restructured and were now headed by merciless individuals under the direct supervision of their KGB protectors. In all corners of the country, popular unhappiness was faced with repression in the name of a revolution, similar to Daoud Khan's republic that Afghans never wanted. Introduction of vodka at official dinners and youth gatherings further infuriated families and the population at large. There was no doubt that a popular revolt was just a question of time. Women and girls became state propaganda tools. Some even exaggerated their denunciation of the Islamic character of their parents' traditions and called openly for international socialism to be the way forward. The change of flag from a traditional black, red, and green with the Islamic emblem into a carbon copy of the Soviet pennon did not go well.

While Agha Saheb fetched news of the obedient Sunni population, Yusof and Mr. Hashem briefed Soraya on Shia discontent. The country began boiling, and repression was accentuated. For the first time, Afghans at large heard of armed resistance. The names of some commanders were murmured, including Ahmad Shah Massoud. He looked slim, handsome, and charismatic. Soon their braveries were recounted in private and family spheres. And people started sympathizing with them. Afzal, also from Panjshir, was a proud man. When driving Soraya to the office and back, he provided the news of battlefields to her. Meanwhile, the ISI had gathered most religious, fundamentalist, and radical leaders in Peshawar. Based on a carefully crafted policy of divide and rule, each was given enough means to establish his own movement. Unfortunately, from the inception they were tinted in accordance with ethnic, religious, and geographic affiliations. They did not strategize, plan, and act in a united manner. Their differences also turned around their personalities, interpretation of Islam, and a myriad of other considerations. It was the birth of the Afghan mujahideen, holy warriors, who President Ronald Reagan later on labeled "freedom fighters." It became the identity of those who rejected the communist ideology.

Within the country, the situation deteriorated quickly. Pracham and Khalq divorced. People disparaged the government explicitly, and the mujahideen started striking government posts in remote areas of the country. Serious and flagrant human rights violations were reported on a daily basis. Afghan youth began doubting the pseudoliberty and grasped that they were being used as objects in support of a repressive policy. Western countries applied more pressure, and Ambassador Puzanov was extremely irritated. His navigations between the leaders of the two factions did not yield tangible results as in the past. The thirst of both Khalq and Parcham leaders to clutch power and impose their fledglings in key positions was evident. While the first was predominantly controlled by the Pashtun communist bigwigs, the latter pretended to merge the "values" of other ethnic groups in the country with international socialism. The Afghan people heard about more mujahideen commanders who defied the government troops. For intellectuals, it was arduous to characterize them. They did not match the pure definition of guerilla leaders as they engaged against an oppressive regime in the name of their country and religion.

Rumors of American and European backing unfolded rapidly, and Afghans hoped for a quick turnover. But their optimism was short-lived. Several facts were strikingly discouraging. Mujahideen leaders were kept split; there was not a unanimous mature politician who could lead a united front; and international aid was channeled through Pakistan, not allotted directly to the mujahideen. The ISI developed combat strategies, selected commanders, and decided about the quality and quantity of aid to different actors. Those with in-depth acquaintance of the historic Afghan-Pakistani quarrel became disenchanted. Extremist mujahideen factions, particularly Golboddin Hekmatyar, were favored and received more hefty support than others. The new master and strongman of Pakistan, General Zia-ul-Haq, seemed extremely intelligent. Similar to his predecessors, he was part of the British Army during World War II and since the creation of Pakistan had climbed the glory echelons. He had deposed the very ambitious civilian ruler Zulfiqar Ali Bhutto and charged him with treason to establish a strong military dictatorship. Of extreme religious conviction, he had three major objectives for his country. Support to Islamic Kashmiri and Afghan extremists, economic soaring of his country, and possession of nuclear weapons to challenge India, the eternal foe, constituted his prime priorities. To accomplish them, he relied solely on and significantly strengthened the ISI.

Four months after the communist takeover, Hafizullah Amin claimed that a coup organized by Parcham was aborted. Subsequently, several ministers, high-ranked military officers, and politicians were apprehended. Abdul Qader, the "chameleon" military general and the mighty minister of defense who often changed political color and position, was imprisoned on the spot. He had executed to perfection Daoud Khan's coup against King Zaher Shah and had joined the communist takeover against the man who was his mentor. He had not even expressed remorse for the massacre of Daoud Khan's beautiful family. Other Parcham chieftains were simply exiled in small countries of the Warsaw Pact member states. Soon the expression "murdered murderers" was used by the entire population to label those who were victims of internal fights within the PDPA. The Soviet Union dispensed money and advisers to no avail. Hafizullah Amin's frustration culminated with the lack of efficiency of Afghan diplomacy. He was apprised of the pitiable quality of deliveries in the international arena and was counseled to bring back Soraya to the ministry of foreign affairs to draft policy papers and review deliveries outside the country. The communist minister of planning called her in.

"My God, madame, we are proud of you," the minister excitedly said. "Comrade Amin wants you back in the foreign ministry. This is a great honor for you and me! He asked me personally to convey this message to you."

It was a nightmare for Soraya. She had glimpsed the butcher of Khalq for the first time a few days earlier on the street when her car was abruptly barred to allow him to get into the ministry. He had long stared at her! Suddenly, a fearful sensation occupied her mind. As a quick thinker, she notified the minister that she was pregnant, which prevented her from being efficient in the foreign minister's office. Astonishingly, it worked.

"Oh, my God! Indeed, Comrade Amin does not like 'loaded' women around him. I will inform him," he assured her.

Soraya was amazed. On the one hand, they considered themselves atheistic, but they were the first to swear by God—and what was Amin's phobia about "loaded" women? The statement was bigoted, discriminatory, and derogatory. She resolutely thought that her second child salvaged her life from being lugged into the communism creek. In this period when the government spy agency had infiltrated the veins and arteries of the society through their zonal and central committees, people felt asphyxiated. Intellectuals did not argue publicly about the reform on women, farmers' rights, or any other political issues. Manipulation of the flaws of former regimes and the dearth of their own sincerity to improve the blemishes became routine. Moreover, the strategy of compelling girls to shatter the ancestral conventions was certainly foolish. The ugly "26 Saratan" mustached vanished; he may have belonged to Parcham. Soraya did not even bother inquiring about his whereabouts.

Agha Saheb and Afzal supplied scripts portraying the government's atrocities that were then put into stencil and Gestetner machines, purchased by Soraya and installed in the basement of the ministry. Late in the evenings, thousands of copies were printed for delivery as night letters. It was an exceedingly perilous enterprise, but she was determined to help those who fought a totalitarian system. Countless leaflets went out every week to notify the population about what had transpired where in the country. Afzal, Agha Saheb, and Mr. Hashem liaised with distributors during weekends and daylight in order not to invite any inkling of secret services monitors.

In summer 1978, Soraya gave birth to a gorgeous boy, Arslan. He had vivid and cheerful eyes. With a slightly smaller forehead, he was a very handsome baby. From the first instant, he revealed his fortitude and resilience. His mother was joyful. Selina now had a companion, brother, and playmate. Arslan never cried. His attitude already resembled that of a lion cub. Perhaps at birth he comprehended the challenges that his parents, and more specifically his mother, faced, and he did not want to be an additional encumbrance by summoning her in the middle of the night to feed him. He was already a man and had to endure the odds of his very young life. Every day Soraya spoke for hours with her children. While Selina comprehended and was able to converse, Arslan stared at his mother tenderly and tried to say something that nobody decrypted. Only she knew that with a simple gaze or motion, he conveyed all his love and care to his mother. Selina grasped that something disturbed her mother at work. When she came back home, Selina hugged her regularly with kisses and cuddled, pledging in her own language that she would take care of her. Agha Saheb and Mr. Hashem reported about skirmishes in the southern and eastern provinces along the Pakistan border, while Afzal brought news of the northern and central provinces.

The government did not figure out how to handle the widespread discontent. Their strategy of frontal hostility against customs and religious convictions of the population had badly flopped. In early

December, Taraki traveled to Moscow. Leonid Brezhnev's nauseating kiss was waiting for him. As a result of this visit, the Soviet-Afghan Friendship Treaty was signed, based on which the Soviet Union acquired the right to interfere militarily in case of "foreign assaults" on Afghanistan. This was a direct retaliation to mujahideen feats that they considered as Western interference. It was apparent that the support received, mainly from the United States, was affecting the communist buildup, and their leadership was nervous. With the treaty signed, there was some sense of relief within the pretended PDPA. The more the Taraki regime goaded for their so-called progressive political and social policy, the more the mujahideen reacted by expressing conservative opinions. This time around, lip services were provided by the regime to boost women's emancipation, but they seemed trapped between two warring nemeses.

Agha Saheb and Afzal animated a few mujahideen commanders from nearby districts, such as Soraya's own Logar, Kohdaman, Wardak, or even other nearby provinces to encounter Soraya. They required situation analysis and had found the right person! The frequency of such visits was worrisome. Yusof cautioned Soraya and recommended she stop receiving them. Of course, she fretted too, but the concern stimulated a bright idea. Every weekend she invited an admired musician couple as well as a number of former dignitaries who had lost their glory. Mujahideen commanders joined the crowd incognito. While everybody enjoyed remarkable melodies on the ground floor, they moved straight to the third for their secret meetings. Spy agency officers attended the events several times. They were quickly spotted by Yusof, Afzal, and Agha Saheb. However, they swiftly concluded that Soraya organized such leisure for a corrupt community that had decayed and "was in the process of perishing." She had recommended reviewing government policy papers and speeches at home as a way of simulating that she backed the regime. Oftentimes, manuscripts were drafted as if the political system had not altered.

243

Hafizullah Amin had known the honesty, dedication, and hard work of Soraya's father, though he never met him as when he joined Colombia University for the first time in 1956, Mr. Suri was on his way out of Washington. But the former chief justice's status was rock-solid. Amin often liked Soraya's amended documents and instructed his subordinates, "This woman is very intelligent! We do not have such a talent among our own people. Use her as much as you can."

Meanwhile, Yusof fetched the news from the Hazara and Shia fronts. He oftentimes spoke of a political Unity Party, led by Abdul Ali Mazari who, contrary to other mujahideen groups, had opted to stay within the country and face the enemy. Mazari, as representative of the much-discriminated-against Shia population in Afghanistan, advocated for a federal system in the country. The rationale on which he based his arguments was the ethnic, linguistic, and even religious diversity of the country. He believed that the might of the United States, West Germany, Canada, or even India was subscribed in their political system. However, the idea embodied discontent from over two hundred fifty years of Durani Pashtun domination and rule, with almost no meaningful gains to other communities. In fact, not even all Pashtuns were attended to as the priority of most rulers was how to keep the British happy to ensure their financial, military, and political backing to the kingdom of Afghanistan. Soraya was abreast of Tajik, Hazara, Uzbek, and Turkmen griefs, but this was the first time she learned of someone appealing for a federal regime. At the same time and though less publicized, there was more evidence of Iran's involvement in support of the Shia mujahideen groups, further complicating the Afghan puzzle.

Somehow, Soraya's residence became the melting point of all who dissented from the government. Selina lingered longer to listen to "Maamaa Jani," whom she called uncle Jani as she still could not pronounce the exact name of the artist. In fact, most bureaucrats commiserated with the mujahideen—particularly when young girls were constrained to publicly denounce their cultural and religious dogmas. Oftentimes, Soraya gathered from some commanders that in Afghanistan, people were first Afghan and then Muslim. This implied the enormous credence of values implanted deep in the souls and hearts of people, values that had been part and parcel of Afghan life for centuries. They needed to evolve, but the forceful tactics of the communist rulers engendered a ferocious reaction of the people. Refugees started pouring into the neighboring Pakistan and Iran.

At the same time, the year 1979 began with the triumph of the Iranian Islamic Revolution. Ayatullah Khomeini victoriously regained Teheran, where he was hailed by millions of individuals. For a long time, experts had conversed about a secret Western plan, led by American thinkers, to besiege the Soviet Union by religious regimes. The philosophy of this strategy was to impede the expansion of an ideology by fostering other ideologies. Soraya perused numerous assessments and had full knowledge of Zbigniew Brzezinski's viewpoint. Poland, Iran, and Afghanistan were foreboded to be prime experimental grounds for implementation of this policy. While the world compassionately viewed millions of youth who rallied against Reza Shah of Iran, the slaying of his regime's dignitaries that ensued was a massive cold shower to the optimism of some. It is assumed that either the Islamic Revolution was infiltrated by the communist Tudeh Party or its leaders demonstrated overconfidence, lacking vision for recognition of their undertaking by the larger international community. Soraya more closely tracked Iranian affairs since her involvement in the Helmand Water Treaty with prime minister Mousa Shafiq.

The political frailty and wariness of the West concerning the Islamic system in Iran reflected the start of a much wider mistrust. It did not comfort those struggling for justice in Afghanistan. Meanwhile, Ambassador Puzanov was awfully agitated; the communist government was dwindling. The refugee crisis enticed international attention and condemnation. Puzanov insinuated to his friend and comrade Amin to act against the Americans. On the day of Saint

Valentine in 1979, Mr. Adolph Dubs, the United States envoy, was kidnapped by four individuals and hauled to the Kabul Hotel. The government feigned it was a hostage situation; however, most whispered that the Afghan secret services agents, with the help of Soviet advisers, staged the incident. Without conferring with the Americans, the head of the spy agency ordered the storming of the hotel. Within minutes, Mr. Dubs was killed; there was no doubt that he was deliberately murdered. Soraya was informed that the government had dispatched dozens of cable texts of explanation to foreign governments. She recalled sadly the Maiwandwal assassination masquerade. The two calamities resembled each other so much, and the idiocy of the respective Afghan governments was so discernible. It was manifest that with the help of their guardians, the Kabul regime had opted for the policy of an eye for an eye and a tooth for a tooth. Again, she remembered Daoud Khan had pursued the same strategy, which caused not only the demise of his regime but more importantly the extermination of his esteemed family. The real uncertainty was whether the communist chieftains would face the same destiny.

At the beginning of spring, people demonstrated their disdain in Herat and wanted to hunt down Soviet advisers. The government opened fire. The Herat garrison, under the leadership of Captain Ismail Khan, mutinied in support of the protestors. For the first time, weapons were distributed to the people to siege armed revolt against the communist government of Taraki. The entire population of the country greeted the news with satisfaction. In May of the same year, Soraya accidentally encountered Mousa Shafiq in Qargha, where he was "walled" by the government spy agency officers. Surrounded by his "guards," he was in his preferred coffee shop. He had lost weight but looked as bright as ever. The episode did not take more than a minute or two as he swiftly signaled that it was not in her interest to linger longer. He requested Soraya leave him her cigarette pack. Though it was rewarding to again see such a great man in good spirits, she experienced several anxious days, fearing an inquiry by the government against her.

Failure of the PDPA, particularly in rural Afghanistan, and the clout of the mujahideen were themes of daily debate among Puzanov, Taraki, and Amin. The Russian envoy had already deduced that Taraki, the "Genius of the East," was neither a theoretician nor a manager. But they were stuck with him. The Pule Charkhi prison, constructed by Daoud Khan, had become notorious. Whoever was taken in would have no chance of survival and coming out. Rumors unfolded that over eighty thousand people had been incarcerated since the communist coup. Accounts of methodical torture and murder were smuggled out on toilet paper, empty cigarette packs, and even textile fabrics. The government identified anyone who sympathized with the mujahideen as "*ashraar*," troublemakers, counterrevolutionaries, or bondmen of imperialism. Official media harangued more about their achievements in confrontation with the mujahideen. However, people distinguished facts from misinformation.

Irritated by the recurrent operational fiascos, the Soviet envoy and the government leadership resolved to "inflict an injury to undeclared leaders of counterrevolutionaries." At the end of May, the head of the government torturing machine and spy agency received instructions to deal with Mr. Mousa Shafiq and Professor Ghulam Mohammad Niazi, portraying them openly as religious ringleaders and agents of imperialism. Amin was of the opinion that "a wound can only be cured if there is no microbe left." The verdict was crystal clear.

Mr. Shafiq was removed from the guarded house in Qargha to the underground of the ministry of interior, where several officers of the Soviet Embassy in Kabul attended the interrogation. They hounded him to know about the Islamic network within the country. Mr. Shafiq argued that he had been under house arrest since Daoud Khan took over the reins of power in 1973 and did not know anything about such grids. The head of the Afghan intelligence agency himself piloted the "grilling" and determined to use all means to get a word out of Mr. Shafiq's mouth. He tortured him to acknowledge that Americans secretly supported him to encourage the revolt against the regime. The image of Maiwandwal's leaning head and smashed neck was in Mr. Shafiq's mind. He concluded that his time had come too. The head of the spy agency ordered agents to take out the nails of four of his fingers, two in each hand. Blood poured on the floor, and he nearly fainted. The contact of air with the injury was intolerable. He had received punches in the face to where his face was totally swollen. He also had marks of beatings on his chest and back.

In the afternoon of the same day, an officer came in. He was in a hurry. "Sir, there is no time left for you. Is there anything you wish?" the officer asked.

"Thank you! Please search my coat. There is a cigarette pack, in which only one is left, I believe," he replied. "Bring it to me. That is all I want."

It was the last cigarette of the pack that Soraya had given him days before. The butchers of the secret services landed later and carted him off to Pule Charkhi. There he smoked his last cigarette before he was hoisted in front of the execution wall. They fired cowardly at him. Three bullets hit his head and four his chest. One of the brightest sons of Afghanistan, who effectively had every credential to take the country out of hell during such a trying period and lead a democratic process, was brutally silenced, murdered, and annihilated. They may have even ditched him in a mass grave as no one ever hinted where the body of such a prominent man was taken. Among the former politicians of Afghanistan, there were indeed others, but Zamir Suri and Mousa Shafiq were exceptional.

Some resolutely believed that had Daoud Khan consented to the pleas of several world leaders and permitted Mr. Shafiq to leave Afghanistan, the mujahideen would have had the most suitable and true leader, who would have led the resistance to the most needed political stature, unity, and success. The news hit like a thunderbolt, breaking the morale of those who still saw some human quality among the communist leaders of the country. In the evening Soraya learned the fate of her former boss. She sobbed and mourned the whole week. Even Piotr, the Russian expert, consoled her and felt sorry. As soon as rumors of this tragic manslaughter spread, people cursed the government and its leaders. In all private spheres, including the one organized by Soraya during weekends, people recited the famous proverb that "the curse of innocents brings down mighty emperors."

Two days later, Soraya was notified that Professor Ghulam Mohammad Niazi was slain at the same time. Contrary to the former prime minister, the secret services of the communist government trusted that he was effectively guiding the mujahideen from his cell. They tortured him to death. His teeth, fingers, and toenails were taken out. The torturers used every imaginable instrument and technique to oblige the already frail academician to "confess," with no avail. He was the same age as Mr. Shafiq, and both sacrificed their lives in dignity. As for the mujahideen leadership, Professor Niazi was the first prominent "martyr who faced the grace of God in his death." Many acknowledged that he was indeed the real engine of the Islamic movement in Afghanistan.

Agha Saheb and Mr. Hashem had disappeared. Soraya was anxious and did not know whether they were apprehended or killed or had fled. No one had knowledge of their whereabouts until Yusof was apprised that Agha Saheb was pitilessly murdered during his arrest by the spy agency, while Mr. Hashem had tried to escape. Within the ministry of planning, Soraya now relied only on Afzal. The mujahideen were getting sturdier, and the government countered callously. The civilian population paid the supreme cost. Women and children, often wedged in the middle, composed the largest portion of casualties. In direct concord with Joseph Stalin's philosophy, communist leadership was of the opinion that they could build a thriving revolutionary Afghanistan with only one million out of twelve million of its inhabitants. The rest were deemed firewood! The army implemented their policy on a daily basis in villages and provinces of the country, where massive killings took place while secret services heaped up innocents in Pule Charkhi prison and the provincial penitentiaries. Two times Yusof advised Soraya to discontinue the weekend events, but it was too late. Even if she did not invite people, they rolled in. Her home resembled a therapy clinic.

Soon, news of substantiated discord between Taraki and Amin emerged. They indicted each other of mishandling of the situation and lack of competence. Suddenly the spy agency was reshuffled, its mighty and brutal head dismissed, and Amin's vicious brother took over the function. Taraki solicited elucidation, and Amin proposed an evening tête-à-tête session with his spiritual leader and the "Genius of the East" to provide the rationale for the sacking. He arrived on time, and Taraki had already consumed a bottle or two of the best Beluga Vodka, of course provided by Puzanov's men. It was reported that Amin did not welcome the hostile attitude of his president and used abusive language. In response, Taraki assaulted him and tumbled down due to his drunkenness. Apparently Amin took advantage of the opportunity and employed a sofa cushion to asphyxiate "the leader" but at the end had to shoot and kill him. Of course, most Khalqi officers declared loyalty to Amin and forgot Taraki as soon as he was lifeless. Later in the evening, the government media proclaimed that Comrade Taraki was no more and Comrade Amin had assumed the leadership of the country. No one within the Khalq leadership called for an explanation. They assented to the fact, and within a second, the page of the "Genius of the East," murdered by his own brutal disciple, was turned within the PDPA too.

The most repressive period under communist rule in Afghanistan began. Tens of thousands of women, children, and men were arrested and summarily executed and their bodies tossed in mass graves. Pule Charkhi now hosted over one hundred thousand inmates. Professors, students, shopkeepers, and load bearers were all apprehended with a simple hint from a sympathizer. Every prisoner was subject to torture of the most inhuman nature. Screams of desolation were heard in the corridors, and dozens of bodies were taken out of the torture chambers now and then. Insomnia, pounding, smashing body members, nail snatching, scorching, electric shock, sexual abuse, psychological pressure, starvation, thirst, and many other tactics were used. Yusof was also detained and tortured on a daily basis. The government wanted to obtain the list of "special guests" who were invited by Soraya during the music nights. He resisted ferociously and heroically.

One late evening, Afzal appeared in a rush and alerted Soraya that Yusof's condition was perilous and he might not be able to sustain the secrets. He recommended that Soraya and her family leave the country immediately and offered to take them out personally through the mujahideen lines. In his own humble opinion, he firmly believed she could work more efficiently and effectively with the resistance, who desperately needed a woman of her stature. But Soraya was pregnant for the third time. She could not take the offer. About a week later, Yusof too died under torture. He had two fingers torn off and his body demolished, but he perished majestically with countless secrets in the bottom of his chest. His body was not given back to his kinfolk and was perhaps thrown in a dump.

Soraya resolved to leave Afghanistan and demanded a passport. The application was taken to Hafizullah Amin himself for guidance. He inscribed at the bottom of her request that the family should not be permitted to "abscond" from the country. The government put more restrictions on voyage abroad. With the assassination of Agha Saheb and Yusof and the disappearance of Mr. Hashem, Soraya did not grasp how much information had been given to the secret services and whether this was the motive for which she was retained. She consented that in the worst-case scenario, Afzal would assist her to reach a neighboring country through mujahideen lines.

Meanwhile, television programs became more radical in nature. The government killing machine was exceptionally brutal. Ambassador Puzanov evaded his Western counterparts since so many PDPA actions were shameful. A new dim figure in Amin's entourage became notorious with the murder of Ahmad Zaher, the renowned, outspoken, popular song star. Apparently his mistress befriended the artist, and it was intolerable for the mighty man. He orchestrated his killing, portrayed as a road accident. Tens of thousands, perhaps even several hundred thousand, admirers flowed onto the streets during the funeral and chanted slogans against the government. A supposedly "ordinary" killing turned into a massive expression of discontent. For Soraya, it looked similar to the assassination of Mir Akbar Khyber, the communist theoretician who caused the fall of Daoud Khan and his regime.

Hafizullah Amin was fuming and seriously cautioned his brother, who as chief of intelligence services should have unearthed the plot, but the irreparable damage was already done. Soraya befriended the artist's sister. He had often performed her favorite songs if she was in attendance. Every young person was saddened by the murder of this thirty-three-year-old exceptional artist who was loved by millions of Afghans. The news in the country was not good. Hafizullah Amin and Ambassador Puzanov had finally split, and bloodshed was unavoidable! Brezhnev extracted his envoy and dispatched a new one, Fikryat Tabeyev, a renowned Muslim Tatar politician, hoping that he would make the difference with the profoundly religious population of Afghanistan.

Soraya arranged a last event at her residence before the couple musicians departed to India for onward journey to France—a tactic often used to escape the country since getting a passport for a friendly India was easier. It was a moving evening. She was urged several times to reply to expressions of gratitude that people of different sensitivities expressed, while two mujahideen commanders on the third floor were impatient to exchange views and leave the event.

The world quaked on November 4, 1979, when Iranian hard-liners struck the United States Embassy in Teheran and took fifty-two diplomats and staff hostage. It was the most calamitous incident for Afghanistan, as the ensuing four decades of Iran-United States hostility and antagonism yielded devastating consequences on the Afghanistan situation. It seemed the inimical act against the mightiest country in the world was perpetrated by members of the Tudeh communist party. The communist regime in Kabul was rubbing its hands and imagined that Iran would now join forces with Afghanistan in the fight against "American imperialism." Some whizzes considered that the Teheran calamity provoked in fact a review of policy in Western countries. Subsequently, the enthusiasm of encircling the Soviet Union by Islamic regimes altered into a feeling of suspicion, skepticism, and even animosity. Though the collapse of the communist giant remained the highest priority, Islamic philosophy was already deemed an adversary of "Western civilization." The hostage situation in Teheran and the murder of Mr. Dubs in Kabul appallingly tarnished the stature of the Carter administration in the region.

Amid global turmoil, Soraya lived anxiously, fearing government agents at her doorstep at any moment. There was no Friday evening music event and no visit by mujahideen commanders. Though Afzal voyaged regularly outside Kabul and fed Soraya with the latest news of different fronts, she felt the absence of Agha Saheb and Yusof. They were so essential for her state of mind and moral support. The minister of planning was tongue-tied and evaded Soraya in the main corridor of the ministry. When they intersected each other, he speedily responded and rushed either to his office, to the toilet, or to the exit door. This was another source of anxiety for Soraya.

Providentially, she was forgotten as the quarrel between the Afghan secret services and the KGB often culminated in open brawls among agents. There were even tales of killings of agents. All international experts in her office were now Soviet citizens or from Eastern

European nations, members or associates of the Warsaw military pact. Piotr sympathized often, but Soraya was extremely vigilant and did not share any opinions with the man. The mujahideen leadership had already proclaimed holy war from Peshawar in Pakistan against the communist government. Commanders voiced their allegiance to one or the other in various spots of the country. The Pakistan government effectively managed the financial, military, and humanitarian support to the Afghan mujahideen and defined the war strategy. International aid agencies and nongovernmental organizations took charge of refugees, whose numbers in Pakistan alone had already reached a million. The Pakistan of General Zia-ul-Haq determined everything and scrupulously implemented their threefold objectives. From the onset, engaging against the communist regime of Afghanistan had been the prerequisite for acceding to further American massive support. General Zia's long-term strategy for his country left no space for sturdy and internationally acknowledged Afghan figures to lead the mujahideen.

Time passed quickly. The West's attention was consumed by the hostage situation in Iran, and the Afghan mujahideen plummeted deeper in the claws of the ISI. A sentiment of desolation was reigning among liberal and nonreligious circles in Kabul and abroad. The Pakistan-Afghanistan dispute over the Durand Line was recognized. By placing Pakistan in charge of Afghan resistance, the roots and spindles of future conflicts were nurtured and designed. In rare private and succinct talks, Soraya repeatedly cautioned envoys of the Western world. At the same time, neither the mujahideen leaders nor the Pakistani public at large grasped that the prime purpose of the billions of dollars of military and humanitarian aid was to dismantle the Soviet Union, not so much to assist the poor people of Afghanistan regain its independence. Now the dread of staunch Islamic regimes anywhere on the globe was haunting Western capitals.

During his tenure in office, Taraki regularly urged the Soviet Union to intervene militarily in Afghanistan based on the December 1978

Soviet-Afghan Friendship Treaty. He considered mujahideen exploits as foreign intervention.

Alexei Kosygin, the then chairman of the Soviet Union Council of Ministers, unequivocally rejected Taraki's tactics in an internal meeting when he stated, *"We should tell Taraki and Amin to change their tactics. They still continue to execute those people who disagree with them. They are killing nearly all of the Parcham leaders, not only the highest rank, but of the middle rank, too."*

In his response to Taraki's formal appeal, he was firm:

> *We believe it would be a fatal mistake to commit ground troops.... If our troops went in, the situation in your country would not improve. On the contrary, it would get worse. Our troops would have to struggle not only with an external aggressor, but with a significant part of your own people. And the people would never forgive such things.*

But political and military circumstances altered in Afghanistan. On the eve of Christmas 1979, Leonid Brezhnev ordered the Fortieth Army of the Soviet Union to deploy in Kabul. Three days later, they staged a coup, during which Hafizullah Amin, his brother, and his close allies were all slaughtered. Babrak Karmal, leader of the Parcham faction of the PDPA, who functioned as ambassador in Czechoslovakia, showed up in the northern margins of Afghanistan. Within one night of Thursday, December 27, when Afghans planned to have a somehow quiet weekend, over ten thousand Soviet troops, mainly from Central Asian Muslim nations, invaded the country, installing Mr. Karmal at the realm of power. Afghans had never seen such apocalyptic scenes. Tanks were stationed in each bend of the city of Kabul, and strange warriors who did not speak their language ruled. The noise of shooting was heard now and then. They instantly realized that their country had been conquered, their pride shattered, and their honor trampled. Since the Second Anglo-Afghan War, no foreign hordes had ever put boots in Afghanistan. The British were totally destroyed. All invaders flunked horribly in this country. The riddle was whether the Soviets would triumph.

All adherents of Parcham were unconfined from Pule Charkhi and other penitentiaries of the country, and those Khalqi who still lived voiced obedience to Parcham immediately and were spared. It is said that Soviets attempted to poison Amin and his intimate advisers in the new Tajbeg Palace, situated in the southern skirt of the capital city, and fluffed miserably. But Colonel Victor Karpukhin of the Special Forces of the Soviet Main Intelligence Directorate, garbed as an Afghan officer and assisted by one of the most trusted comrades of Amin, the person who had led the bloody coup against Daoud Khan and massacred his family, did not muff his targets when he faced them. One automatic hand machine gun, fully charged, was enough to bring them all down within a few seconds. It is astonishing that Hafizullah Amin and Daoud Khan perished under the same circumstances, gun in hands! Most members of their corresponding families and associates were also slain with them. Both, conceited and ambitious, stained the history of Afghanistan appallingly. Replacing Puzanov with Tabeyev was then part of Brezhnev's strategy. He may have thought that invading Afghanistan with Muslim Soviet soldiers in the presence of a Muslim Soviet ambassador would be easier. But his assumptions proved utterly wrong. That day of the Soviet invasion, all Afghans felt mortified. People moved in a strange way on the streets; some desired to seize the throats of the intruders and choke them. Their aspiration for a better Afghanistan was wrecked.

Soraya could not imagine what had occurred. Ten days earlier, she visited the tomb of her father for her habitual "spiritual reunion." She looked for such privileged moments of her life since the demise of Mr. Suri, particularly when times were arduous. In the twilight of that day, the color of the moon had particularly altered to red. All the inhabitants of the village spoke of the same, saying it presaged a bloody period ahead. The imam of her father's mosque had counseled her to get out of the country swiftly. In Afghanistan, popular creeds are part of the wisdom spread vocally from one generation to another based on experience. She attempted to visualize the corollaries of Brezhnev's act. Why was there such a shift of stance within a year? Though Amin and his crowd of torturers had vanished from the surface of the earth, their system was still in place. The secret services and spy agency was immediately restructured and called KHAD, State Intelligence Services. The KGB entrusted the new machinery's command to their longtime loyal supporter Mohammad Najibullah. Definitely with the Soviet invasion and subsequent popular resistance against aggressors, KHAD became the centerpiece of government brutality.

In January 1980, Soraya gave birth to another gorgeous girl, Serena. She was a perfect image of her mother. Soraya was rushed to the hospital in the early hours of the day. The establishment looked like a ghost house. Everything was missing, and the hygiene was rudimentary. Only a few nurses received emergency cases. They looked demoralized. Since the advent of the PDPA in power, public services were in a lamentable state. The Soviet invasion just made them worse. Most talented doctors and staff had already fled the country. After her delivery, everybody rushed to find an additional blanket as the heating system did not function. But there was none available. Soraya decided to return home in the afternoon.

On the chilly second day after Serena's birth, she had a strange hunch and did not desire to move out of her bed. But children require attention, and she was impelled to do so. After dressing Selina and Arslan and reaching for Serena, she sat in front of the makeup mirror. Instantly she was horrified. The right half of her face was not in its place, and she did not sense any hurt. Soraya had always probed about all possible secondary upshots of childbirth. Nothing like this had ever happened to her before. Then what was it? She strived to speak. Her tongue was not under her command. She tried to flutter her eyelids but in vain; she could not move her teeth or drink water. Her lips did not have the strength to hold her mouth shut. She could not believe that such an atrocious thing would happen to her.

Within an hour, she was rushed back to the hospital. An acute facial nerve paralysis, commonly called Bell's palsy, had affected her. Everybody was querying for causes and remedies. The only doctor was called and determined that the cold weather and vestigial care in the hospital, as well as after-birth physical fragility, must have triggered the viral attack. It was prescribed that while in rare cases it could cure normally within weeks or months, immediate intake of corticosteroid drugs, combined with specific antiviral or antibacterial medication, was the remedy. However, nothing was available in the hospital, and bringing the drugs from Turkey or Europe was quasi impossible due to the government's restricted policies with regard to the free world. It was tragic as, in spite of her reiterated plea for cortisone injection, she was urged to linger in bed for "the natural process to succeed." She never healed properly and kept the sourest memory of this incident. After the decease of her father, this was Soraya's second personal tragedy with significant physical and psychological reverberations. She stayed home the whole month of February. As every day passed, the ruthless veracity that she would not recover revealed itself as inevitable. She felt forlorn and bemoaned her fate. However, the future of her children was more central than what had occurred. An extraordinary determination was born in her. Though beauty and elegance had supplemented her intelligence, she did not care anymore about her face and handicap.

Back in the office, Soraya evaded official diplomatic functions intentionally. Her only source of information was Afzal, who also smuggled foreign newspapers from wherever he could. The foggy day of the invasion, surd roars of airplanes were heard from the sky. She also gathered that Soviet ground troops had pierced Afghanistan from Uzbek and Turkmen Soviet edges. Major garrisons of Herat, Kandahar, Paktia, and Mazare Sharif, as well as civilian and military airports, were subdued by the Red Army. Afghan officers suddenly became subordinates. The international community reacted. Not only member states of the Organization of Islamic Conference but the General Assembly of the United Nations too called for immediate withdrawal of the Soviet troops to no avail. Neighboring countries hosting refugees refused to recognize the Karmal regime, tagging it a puppet of Moscow. The cabinet resembled that of Taraki, with only one woman as minister. Soraya's solace was to see the former minister of planning under Daoud Khan back in business. The entire population of the country countered ferociously. The sound of holy war against the invaders came from all corners of the country. This provided another opportune occasion, particularly for the American and British intelligence services. They encouraged the mujahideen in their jihad against the Soviet Union and provided more funding and weapons. The communist giant was now trapped.

About a week later, Afzal apprised Soraya that the mujahideen invited every individual in the country to come out on their roofs at 8:00 p.m. and shout "God is great" to reveal their disdain of the alien forces and communist regime. The same evening, she leaped up. It was an obscure night, but the population adhered to the advice. It looked like the sky too bonded with the people. Kabul trembled, so much that the squawk seemed strong and harmonized. The spectacle was staggering and unique. No KHAD or KGB agent could ever locate who ascended the roof to join others. For thirty minutes, there was nothing heard but the majesty of hidden freedom of expression.

The next day, she met with the minister, who as usual seemed considerate but fluffed to offer any elucidation as to why a foreign army was ruling the country. He was circumspect but felt helpless and sorry. Soraya barely twigged why such a clever man had joined a disgraceful government. Did he do it willingly? Certainly not! Was he compelled? Perhaps! Was he a mole? Nobody would believe it! These were questions she had in her mind. The minister alluded that she should be very prudent as "things are not like in the past." Did

259

he know about the night letters produced in and disseminated from the ministry? Or had he intelligence about the real drive of music nights? She pondered, with no answers.

Now the West was at war with the Soviet Union through the mujahideen. More soldiers from other republics poured into different corners of Afghanistan. Every day, coffins were repatriated. A number of the soldiers, mostly from Central Asian Republics, disappeared and joined the mujahideen to fight against the Red Army, which they blamed for having subjugated their countries too. Commanders of all mujahideen factions systematically assaulted the Soviets to smash them totally. Some, like Ahmad Shah Massoud, preferred to use the principle of asymmetric warfare and a blend of Afghan traditional and guerilla combat strategies that proved most effective. While the Red Army tried to persist, vital mujahideen figures emerged in the west, east, south, central, and north provinces and even deeper shires of the country with allegiance to different groups grounded in Peshawar and Quetta or Mashhad in Iran.

Soraya promptly comprehended the premeditated lack of coordination among various mujahideen movements and even commanders of the same group. The Pakistan Army, which had now taken charge of the resistance operations, did not wish a harmonized approach. It seemed that they fostered dispute and vengeance. Most military aid was given to their favored extremist and intransigent movements. Rumors unfolded quickly that the CIA permitted such action. Contrary to public opinion, they were considered more efficient in the battlefields. For the first time, conversant circles in Kabul heard of Congressman Charlie Wilson, the mastermind of Operation Cyclone, who instigated the collapse of the Soviet Union. The Pakistan government picked two Pashtuns to command their military intelligence and steer assistance to the refugee crisis. The West, and in particular Americans, did not properly evaluate Pakistan's tactics toward the Afghan resistance in general and mujahideen groups in particular, which proved noxious for the region and even the entire world in the decades that followed.

Some believed that General Zia-ul-Haq and his lieutenants used Western slumber and shut-eye to more ardently pursue their crucial threefold objectives to counter India, their eternal rival and nemesis. Access to the technology and fabrication of nuclear weapons, training and supporting heavily extremist and terrorist groups in Kashmir, and economic prosperity remained national interest priorities of Pakistan and its price tag to engage against the Aghan communist regime. Though the hostage state of affairs in Iran dwarfed the hearts and minds of politicians and their public in the United States, increasing mistrust and disdain toward Islamic views, defeat of the Soviet Union remained the highest priority. The West then tacitly subscribed to Pakistan's conditions.

Soraya had the minister's counsel in mind and withdrew from all political deliberations. Piotr, the Russian expert, now led her office. He often sought her opinion without success. On one occasion, he invited her into the garden.

He argued, "Soraya, you know that I work for my country too. Please share your views and analysis of our occupation with me, even if it is unpleasant for us. I will protect you."

But Soraya soothingly advised that she had abandoned politics and political review in order to focus only on her family.

The policy and perceptions of all concerned were known to Afghans. However, most questioned the rationale of Indira Gandhi's stance. Afghanistan and India had shared history. Afghan volunteers battled alongside their Indian companions during the 1857 mutiny. They braced Mahatma Gandhi in every exploit he engaged in against the British colonizers of India, mainly the 1917 Champaran Satyagraha, the 1930 Salt March, and the 1947 Independence of the country. Then why did Indira, the heiress of Mahatma Gandhi, opt for a reprehensible policy to condone an obvious invasion of a sovereign and friendly country by a superpower? The so-called Indo-Soviet friendship did not illuminate such an incomprehensible attitude. Soraya's assumption was that the unprecedented endorsement by the West of Pakistan's threefold ambitions may have triggered the adverse opinion on the part of India. This country grumbled eternally about Pakistan's sponsorship of terrorist groups operating in the Jammu and Kashmir against Indian troops. Perhaps Indira Gandhi would have determined a dissimilar view if the West had not granted a blank check to their rival. It was the most plausible vindication for Soraya, though the fact will always remain an enigma.

The invasion and occupation of Afghanistan by the Red Army did not beget any positive change but exacerbated further the Afghan people. Mujahideen intensified their raids on Soviet and government troops; the retaliation was brutal and merciless. Villages were totally razed from the surface of the earth. Soviet jet bombers hovered as low as a few hundred meters to hit their targets more precisely. MiG-23 Flogger and SU-24 all-weather supersonic attack jet fighters and MiG-31 Interceptor aircraft were terrorizing machines. Their roar alone was enough to silence some. Shrapnel shells and bombs were employed on a civilian population who massively moved to the neighboring countries of Pakistan and Iran to seek protection. Practically all regimes but the communists abused the status of youth and women. Every drift from morality and ethics was attributed to the promotion of their plight.

At the start of the academic year in late March 1980, students, girls in the front row, displayed their defiance by staging protests at universities and schools. Rallies occurred in all main metropolises; government forces struck back at close range without hesitation. Dozens of pupils were murdered because they exercised their basic right of freedom of expression.

On Tuesday, April 29, a march began at the Kabul University campus. It soon spread to all faculties. The move toward the center of the city was inevitable. The Parchami militia termed "youth" and armed by Soviets and the Afghan government's KHAD opened fire and executed several within the university premises. It did not impede the crowd from continuing. On the way, the youngsters of two girls' high schools merged with their companions. Among them, a valiant eighteen-year-old Naheed with murky hair, magnificent eyes, the silhouette of a mannequin, and genuine leadership aptitude stepped forward. She was the banner bearer. Before attaining the nearby boys' high school, Parchami "youth" barraged again. Naheed protruded. Tens of thousands vociferously yelled anti-Soviet slogans. The whole area shuddered, the voice of justice and denunciation was so sturdy. She moved frontward again, and the communist "youth" receded. In one hand, she held the streamer, while the other fist was raised at the level of her head, guiding the movement. Parchami "youth" appeared vexed. Similar catchwords were already hearkened from the neighboring compound.

It looked a coordinated act; several thousand more students waited to join the flow of resistance. It was silly; hardly a few months ago, the same Patchami "youth" campaigned against the Taraki and Amin governments, deploring the violation of human rights. Today in power, they had machine guns in hand preventing others from the same dues. Naheed stopped for a while as if her inner instinct presaged an imminent danger, but the strain and momentum of the flow was such that she had no alternative but to move ahead. Warning served no purpose. The Parchami discharged countless rounds of bullets on the demonstrators. Several were struck in the front line, among them, a handsome young boy of about twenty years of age. Naheed let the banner down to rescue him. Within a second, he was in her arms. His mouth was wide open and eyes sleepy. A tiny flow of blood emerged from the angle of his lips. She was horrified and screamed, "Do not fall asleep! Wake up."

But it was too late. The head of the youngster descended on her torso. Dozens of others had fallen too. She was enraged and roared that God was great. At this moment, the "youth" fired again. Naheed sensed an atrocious pain below her throat and stomach, but she did not want to collapse. She solicited assistance and did not let the body of the boy plunge to the ground. She still continued to move forward. Others tailed with bodies of their fellow friends in their arms. The Parchami "youth" retreated again. Naheed continued. A third round of bullets went out of the barrels of their machine guns. This time, the shot pierced her head. She tumbled, but a man sprinted from behind and put his neck under her left shoulder. She urged him to persist, and he did so. The outcry intensified. He too was hit. Both plummeted down. The demonstrators screamed, "Death to Soviets, death to Babrak, and death to Najibulla." Within seconds, a river of blood swathed the street. A circle was formed around the bodies. Naheed was still alive but hardly breathing. The Parchami "youth" had banned ambulances, and the nearest hospital was adjacent to the university campus—a long distance to race on foot. There was no hope to salvage the wounded, who all bled to death. A dark cloud appeared in Naheed's eyes. She knew it was the moment and strived to speak. "They will face our fate. Invaders will be out, sooner or later!"

These were her last words. Nobody ever apprehended how many students were assassinated that day—fifty, a hundred, several hundred? Over half of the victims were young girls with remarkable aspirations for themselves, their families, and their country. Their hopes and future were shattered by an invader, an enslaved government, and a merciless KHAD. The brutality of the repression was unpardonable. KHAD and Soviet troops instantly encircled the area, removed the bodies, carted off the injured students to an unknown destination, and ordered the others to disperse. Naheed was the first recognized fallen young woman fighting for the freedom of her country from the Soviet claw. People named her Naheed Shaheed, the Martyr Naheed.

That specific day, Afzal witnessed the rally while coming to pick up Soraya. He updated her and recommended exploiting the back roads to attain the office, but she declined. The diplomatic plate of the vehicle was an astonishing asset. It often provided freedom of movement to the occupants. She was passing the demonstrators when the shooting started. Afzal pressed on the accelerator and drove madly in the paths and alleys of Karte Char. He did not obey Soraya anymore and impelled her to crouch low in the car. Twenty minutes later, he reached the building of the ministry of planning. The news of the shooting and the killing of students unfolded promptly. An hour later, Naheed Shaheed was cherished by the entire country, and her picture was smuggled all over.

For Soraya, it was a perfect example of former victims becoming perpetrators of atrocities. She was ravaged and wished to hasten into Piotr's office, jump on his throat, and ask for justice. She isolated herself and directed the peon not to permit anyone to enter.

Piotr popped in, however, and endeavored to expound that a bunch of young students countered others, and in the course of their contention, a few had been killed. This account was so cynical. The fact that a Soviet distorted evidence was not unpredicted. But how could he undermine her knowledge of the situation? She did not react, but her tearful eyes said it all. Piotr lingered for a long time in her office without any exchange between them and finally left, grasping that millions of people in Afghanistan had the same sentiment. She portrayed a parallel between what had transpired on the eve of democracy in Afghanistan when, over sixteen years earlier, the cousin and son-in-law of King Zaher Shah commanded the army to shoot at a march that Babrak Karmal was piloting himself. Did he ever have a conscience and political morality? But then she recalled her father.

"Remember, Soraya!" he had explained. "In politics, there is no conscience, no friendship, and no side. Only interest counts. Politicians change opinion based on what could seem useful for them."

That day, when Naheed was murdered, the Soviet Ambassador Tabeyev came out of his self-imposed reserve and hurried to Babrak

Karmal. He found Anahita Ratebzad, the only woman of the cabinet, in his office and was enraged. He termed them despicable, ignorant, and useless. The Soviets did not need another hero—and more importantly a female martyr! He bristled particularly at Ratebzad, who pretended to be the mother-guardian of Parchami "youth" and women. Why had her bastards killed Naheed and her friends, the envoy had repeatedly queried. In the battlefields, the government troops were desperate! Most low- and medium-level officers commiserated with the people in general and students in particular who pursued their strikes. Naheed was their hero and martyr! Countless people kept her photo at home in their rooms. She was the symbol of their resistance to the Soviet Union and to a repressive regime.

The world discovered the heroic resistance of Afghans to the Red Army through media of all natures. Though the murder of Agha Saheb and Yusof was a serious setback for Soraya, Afzal was most vigorous and committed, recounting news of all fronts every day when he drove her to the office and back. Now and then he reiterated his offer to extract her through the mujahideen lines if required. Soraya was indebted to this devoted and determined friend. Her rapport with the minister was strange. They conversed with their eyes. While she transmitted her disdain and horror, he looked powerless and sorry. She had subscribed the office to receive British and American journals of political sciences and foreign policy analysis. Soon she was notified that they would no longer obtain even the *International Herald Tribune* and *Financial Times*. Then the lone manner to appreciate international opinion seemed to be through the BBC and Voice of America radio waves. Though some journalists declared themselves "specialists on Afghanistan" after hardly a week of attendance in the combat theater, most predicted the fall of the giant that Lenin conceived and Stalin built with the blood of tens of millions of innocent individuals. She urged Afzal to fetch everything that the mujahideen groups published. It was a perilous initiative but the only way for her to apprehend the philosophy of those who led the resistance in Peshawar. She learned that the ugly "26 Saratan" mustached was a senior Parchami and killed in the first purge of the Taraki government.

The international pressure on Brezhnev mounted significantly. Most Western countries decided to boycott the Moscow Olympic Games of 1980. Some believed it was futile and that athletes of the Free World should have attended the event. They referred to Jesse Owens and his fellow African American buddies, who defeated Adolf Hitler in his own Nazi XI Olympiad in 1936, or Tommie Smith and John Carlos, who hoisted the fists of justice against infringement of human rights in the 1968 summer games. They were confident that most competitors would have denounced the invasion and occupation of Afghanistan. Others supported the boycott and deemed that no opportunity should be offered to Brezhnev and Soviet apparatuses to shine. The Soviet leader offered to encounter the French president in Warsaw. For Soraya, it made no sense; the Soviet Union would not withdraw, and the event was tailored by the propaganda machinery of the Soviet Union. Mr. Suri used to say, "You see, Soraya, the Soviet Union is like a bear who recognizes only total success or defeat!"

The event occurred in May of the same year. As anticipated, nothing tangible transpired except empty diplomatic words. The intensity of the war increased. Every day, the exploits of valiant and stalwart mujahideen commanders were recounted by ordinary people. The names of all valorous commanders were now known to the public. The youngsters in Kabul wished to join the ranks of the resistance. In the summer, a conference of mujahideen leaders with Pakistani and Iranian authorities was organized in the beautiful resort of Mont Pèlerin in Switzerland. I was alerted by Soraya and urged to attend if possible. She had not met any of the actors involved and wished my frank opinion.

I was still a novice in politics and began with the preparatory congregation of Afghans residing in Europe to determine who should represent them in the event. Two former prime ministers of Afghanistan and numerous ex-ministers were in attendance. I opted to sit near the exit door, the list was so imposing. However, in the flow of discussion and debate, the phase shift between the realities on the ground and former politicians became evident. They all projected their past into the future of the country! It was pitiable as they dreamed of paper castles, in which each one felt he was the right king or emperor. In addition, the fracture based on ethnic, religious, and geographic affiliations among contestants was flagrant. The efficiency of Pakistani policy to keep them at a distance from the resistance affairs was striking; they were already redundant for the cause.

I was among those who had to partake in the conference. Security was impeccable, and we disclosed "pattes blanches," as they say in French, to get into the Mirador Hotel. I had never witnessed such an imposing scene. Among the mujahideen chieftains, some seemed sympathetic, others practically inept, and a few frightening. The Pakistani and Iranian foreign ministers shuffled up and down. The sympathetic Iranian was dismayed by the authoritarian patronage of his agitated Pakistani counterpart, urging authenticity on the part of mujahideen leaders as none of them intervened before clearance of the Pakistani attendants. Even in Mont Pèlerin, ISI envoys were the actual and factual playmakers. The substantial upshot of this conference was the concept of indirect talks that the United Nations would sponsor, whereby none of the parties dialogued with the Kabul regime directly. The job of navigation was handed over to the designated international envoy. Most of the Western nations scrutinized the flow of occurrences. The Iranian foreign minister was the busiest man; the Swiss government facilitated secret talks between him and the United States high officials about the hostages. He had another arduous job to substantiate the purge of former Iranian dignitaries, engineered by the iron man and chief prosecutor of the Islamic regime. Reports of summary trials and killings were undisputed; diplomats and the media harassed the soft man of the Iranian revolution. I had individual discussions with each mujahideen leader as well as the Pakistani and Iranian foreign ministers and briefed Soraya, bemoaning the lack of diplomatic skill and sovereignty of Afghan mujahideen leaders.

In the battle arena, commanders pounded the Red Army in all corners of the country. Not only was the Soviet supply chain through Salang Pass disrupted, but elsewhere the ferocity of mujahideen fire pushed them back in their barracks. Frustrated, the Soviets resolved to smash them by all means. On a Thursday morning of the month of September, Afzal was late. It was unusual, but Soraya remained patient. He showed up distraught and shattered and was not in a position to speak or drive. She invited him in and learned about the first Soviet offensive on the Panjshir Valley, with appalling effects on the civilian population. Commander Ahmad Shah Massoud, cognizant of the enemy plan and might, urged and escorted villagers to the loftier mountains for safety. Those who did not or could not follow the advice perished under the bombs of MiG-23 and SU-24 fighter jets, as well as the shells of T-72 main battle tanks and SU-100P destroyers and assault guns. The entire Panjshir Valley was wrecked and houses looted. The war tactic of the Red Army strategists for the high mountains and valleys in Afghanistan was distinct: bomb, shell, and move in. Erase, kill, and occupy were the three words infused in the minds of their soldiers. The Panjshir Valley was their first test ground.

Afzal was not troubled by demolition of his homeland or the number of casualties; for him, any war had its toll. He notified that in the course of combat, Massoud had been wounded in the battlefield. He had no way to get treatment. For a long time, external and internal forces had coveted his skin and plotted for his elimination. Afghan medical amenities were all government run. His most trusted deputy, Fazel Ahmad, was a graduate of Kabul Medical College. The fate of the distinguished warrior was in his hands. Massoud banked on him for everything and retreated to the higher hamlet of Anjoman. His lieutenants envisaged extracting him and his deputy doctor to Skazar or Saresang, the apexes of the Panjshir Valley, if need be. Afzal grew up in Jangalak of Panjshir and shared the primary school bench with Massoud. For him, he was not just a commander, savior, and hero, but a brother in blood. He sought to rush and visit him, but Soraya did not advise that as no one could enter the valley.

As soon as Massoud's mujahideen discovered that their commander was alive and in safety, floods of bullets hit the Soviet troops from the peaks of mountains along the valley. Red Army officers and soldiers freaked! They could neither locate their enemy's positions nor demolish the mountains. They were masters of vacated villages and could only filch miserable values from abandoned houses or those they had murdered. The intensity of mujahideen fire day and night instigated disarray among the Soviets; they retreated, dumping their tanks and guns behind. It was a dishonorable defeat, and Marshal Sergei Sokolov, who commanded the ground invasion of Afghanistan, and Ambassador Tabeyev would have wished not to learn about it. Other commanders in the deepest valleys of the country faced the same situation. The defense was too heroic. No one had a remedy to counter the Soviet anger and atrocities. However, the news of their knockout, particularly in the Panjshir Valley, unfolded rapidly in the country and beyond.

For the first time in its history, the invincible and mighty Red Army was obfuscated by barefoot mujahideen, whose mules seemed more efficient than the Soviet tanks. The curve of morale in Afghanistan reversed, and the demise of the Soviet Union started in this month of September 1980. Experts were now certain, though the timing was still an issue. Mujahideen all over the country sensed they had the upper hand; the government and Soviet armies amplified their carnage, targeting women, children, and the elderly. The Red Army resorted to using multiple chemical agents to terrorize civilian and mujahideen forces. Soraya ascertained from her extended family that in the Kohdaman and Logar areas, people escaped to the kaarez to seek protection from severe bombardments and "vomiting gas." The abhorrence was such that after intense shelling, the armies landed in empty villages and searched for "*ashraar.*" They would then reach the kaarez, discharge barrels of the "vomiting gas," and seal the entrance. Thousands of civilians succumbed in this manner. In the main cities, particularly since the massacre in which Naheed and her fellow students were murdered, neither women nor youth trusted the slogans of the government to promote their plight. The ruling leadership and their senior Soviet advisers were scared of other Naheed Shaheed-type heroic women. They opted for an appeasement policy and did not compel girls to appear on TV shows in support of the Parcham.

For Soraya, Afghanistan had no way out. On the one hand, there was a rejected government lacking credibility and slaughtering its own population by tens of thousands, and on the other hand was a mujahideen leadership with no alternative but to submit to the aspirations of foreigners with defined counterproductive ambitions. Pakistan, Iran, and Saudi Arabia were now known regional powers that assisted and even coached specific mujahideen groups. She despaired for her country and its people. She was simply inconsolable. Afghanistan needed at this precise juncture of its history people of her father's or Mousa Shafiq's stature to unify dispersed mujahideen groups and drive the resistance to victory and the country to its independence. But there were none! Intellectuals and free thinkers were sidelined, excluded, and in some cases even assassinated. Oftentimes, she was tempted to take Afzal's offer and move out of Kabul. But then what would be the place of a woman as smart and intelligent as she was among handcuffed chieftains who were in the process of forging an extremely unpredictable future for their country?

In the international arena, the second half of 1980 determined additional constituents that altered the face and fate of the world. The goriest Iraq-Iran war started in the same month of September. It was recounted that the United States hawks animated the Iraqi dictator Saddam Hussein to grab the oil-rich and Arab-speaking Khuzuistan province of Iran. During the nine years of fierce conflict, called also the war of swamps and trenches, nobody would ever determine how many soldiers on both sides, including children, perished—perhaps millions! However, the economic hurt was guessed at nearly 1.2 trillion United States dollars, almost evenly divided between the two nations that required even more than that to focus on their development and the welfare of their population.

Some experts resolutely thought that the outcome of this tragedy was definitely to the advantage of Iran. Not only was Saddam Hussein forced to vacate the Iranian territory as early as 1982, but he demonstrated his true nature of a dictator and quickly fell out of the West's favor. The conflict permitted Iran to rally its entire population in defense of the Islamic regime, forgetting and perhaps exonerating violations of human rights and the systematic purge of former decision makers. It also allowed the government to strengthen its institutions amid serious worry in the West. Those who had schemed the fall of the Islamic regime in Iran were promptly disenchanted. Certainly the upsurge of the Shia Islamic regime was not what the Salafist and Wahhabi fundamentalists in Saudi Arabia desired. From the inception of the Iranian Revolution, the kingdom of Saudi Arabia and its allies intrigued for its downfall. The West had taken sides against Iran! For many and particularly Soraya, the Iran-Iraq war was the beginning of a new downfall of the Muslim world.

The plight of the fifty-two hostages was unresolved. President Jimmy Carter's scheme under Operation Eagle Claw to extract them by force flopped dramatically. The image, might, and prestige of the United States were ridiculed, and the media was mocking. The most appalling trait of the raid was technical glitches that the helicopters developed in the course of action. The daring initiative to dispatch troops to liberate the captives from the heart of Teheran could not be prepared in such a sloppy manner. Was it internal sabotage? Did external factors play a role? Why was it flaunted over two days and nights? Why were helicopters picked up to fly over a thousand kilometers in "enemy" airspace, yearning that they would not be detected or earwigged? Why did American strategists not learn from the successful Operation Entebbe only four years earlier? No matter the reasons, the American giant was hurt in its deep nerves and veins.

There was an appeal for a radical policy change; Ronald Reagan, the Republican primary winner, embodied the plea and challenged President Carter in the 1980 presidential election. The predicted outcome was bad for the administration. Soraya, in spite of her admiration for the famous Democratic president John F. Kennedy, questioned why they championed a president impugned for having inflicted a severe injury to the pride of Americans. Why did Carter himself, as a gifted and rational person, not withdraw? She recalled again her father's advice that politicians were addicted to power and they would not admit defeat until they faced it unequivocally. Ronald Reagan was the hero of the presidential election, with 489 electoral delegates against only 49 for Carter, perhaps the starkest setback of Democrats in recent history. On the eve of Reagan's triumph, a new breeze of hope in the West and a shade of anxiety elsewhere appeared. It was evident that he aimed at restoring his country's credibility, authority, and prestige. He had all the virtues and fabric. But then what would happen to others? The mujahideen commanders in particular hailed the news of his election with enthusiasm and expectation. His old movies surfaced; "from Hollywood to the White House" became a sort of delightful slogan. Soraya was perplexed as she did not have access to information. "Smuggling" analysis and studies was not feasible. The BBC and Voice of America radio waves were frequently disrupted. She could not perceive the role of hawkish, new conservative elements in Reagan's team. Therefore, like many other connoisseurs, she scrutinized the arrival of Reagan with optimism and dread at the same time.

After 444 days of captivity, the fifty-two hostages were freed on January 20, 1981, the date of President Reagan's inauguration. It was never perceived as a goodwill gesture of the Islamic Republic of Iran, but rather a fear of the new mighty American administration.

The month of September 1980 also witnessed the emergence of Solidarność or Solidarity, the famed Polish labor union, led by a simple but immensely charismatic electrician and car mechanic, Lech Wałęsa. A civil rights organization, Solidarność and its leaders confronted the Soviet-backed regime for both its inconsistency toward the workforce and its dictatorial nature. Wałęsa was a very efficient orator and mobilizer. Within a few months, millions of Polish people adhered to and deemed Solidarność as the appropriate vehicle for freedom. Solidarność epitomized what the entire Eastern European, Baltic, Caucasian, and Central Asian nations desired. Somehow, they also sensed that the end of the Soviet Union was approaching. The cracks in the iron shield of the giant were too evident. Contrary to mujahideen leadership, Solidarność leaders were united, solid, and all inclusive, aiming at the independence and sole interest of their Poland.

Recurrent routs of the Red Army in Afghanistan and victories of Solidarność were more than discernible signs. However, the hope for freedom from the Soviet gaol was nurtured predominantly in Eastern Europe after the election of Polish Cardinal Karol Józef Wojtyła by the second papal conclave of 1978 as the 264th Roman Catholic pontiff. Known as Jean Paul II, he was the first non-Italian pope since the Dutch citizen Adrian VI in 1523. The Catholic papacy had been shared by Greek popes and occasionally a few others, but the election of the first Polish national was unique and broke the Italian hegemony, opening the highest Christian holy function to others too. Jean Paul II strongly backed Solidarność and the Soviet-dominated populations who aspired to liberty, democracy, and self-governance. He responsively conversed about human values, something that his predecessors, Pius XI and Pius XII, ignored when Adolf Hitler engaged in the extermination of the Jewish population. His exceptional personality, public relations ability, energy, and desire to reach all and everywhere were unique. Perhaps conscious of the likelihood of a confrontation at the horizon of the Muslim and Christian worlds, he promoted dialogue with Muslim communities throughout his pilgrimages. Unfortunately the Muslim world was not structured in the same manner, and therefore, trying to find an opposite interlocutor hindered his efforts. Nevertheless, Afghan mujahideen commanders found in Solidarność and the pope two unexpected and most valued allies. Already, Polish and Afghan students in Europe envisaged joint actions.

Soraya, cut off from the world of analytical articles and studies, gathered basic news from the radio waves and did not have an optimistic picture about the future of her country. There was too much inadequacy in running the resistance against a superpower. And there were divides among the Muslim world, with fratricidal approaches toward each other. There were also egoistic ambitions that were self-centered, and there was an absolute ignorance about the concern generated in the West regarding Islam and the requisite compulsion to appease it. For her, releasing the hostages was a decent step forward. Not only were most innocent officials attending their country, but the act of taking envoys captive was not an Islamic tradition. It was never practiced or recommended by the prime leaders of Islam. Then why and by whom was this heinous practice introduced as a political weapon? Even if some of them were "spies," there was an appropriate procedure that mature states used to deal with such circumstances. Amid all these worrisome developments, Soraya was powerless and could not even communicate with her own countrymen and women.

On a cold day of late December, the minister of planning called her in. As usual, he was candid and offered a cup of green tea.

The minister began, "I understand your feelings. We have no choice. There are already over one hundred thousand foreign troops in our country, and they rule."

"Mr. Minister," Soraya replied, "I see this. But what I do not understand is your stand."

"This is a long story! God willing, I will explain to you one day. But the important matter today is that you should leave the country," he emphasized.

"How much time do I have?" she inquired.

"Two months or so," the minister concluded.

The next day she again applied for a passport; the reason given was medical treatment abroad. Her strategy was clear. Should the government decline once again to let her leave, she would then take Afzal's offer. Life was meaningless. Apart from the senseless red flags flopping around, there was nothing left of the government. Their army was defeated in all spots of the country. They had no political recognition outside the Warsaw Pact member states. Economically the country was ruined. The population no longer heeded the unending revolutionary rhetoric. Amid all this, Soraya divided her time between a tedious office and her three children. She was updated through her foreign ministry friends on the evolution of her passport request. The matter had once more been submitted to the "Leader of the Revolution." Amin had rejected it, and she was anxious to know Karmal's reaction. His office had given negative advice, but after he questioned about the petitioner, he called his chief of staff. "This lady was nice to me when nobody else had the courage. She helped me on a rainy day. We may not share the same values; I understand that. But we cannot keep her in the country against her wishes," he concluded.

Soraya was astonished that Babrak Karmal remembered her. Perhaps his learning from royal palace encounters in the past made him human for an instant. She contacted Master Hassan, requisitioned a few dresses, and urged him to find someone who would discretely buy her household items. She gave out family silver and crystal sets for miserable amounts of money, knowing that some swelled from the misery of others. But she did not mind anymore. Afzal was elated. He swore to join the mujahideen the day she departed the country. Soraya meticulously decided about the day she would leave Afghanistan.

On the festive Friday, March 20, 1981, the commencement of the solar New Year in the region, when the entire country was on break, she left Kabul for Frankfurt, eyes gorged with tears. Her heart was tired. Though she spent most of her life in Washington, London, and Oxford, there was something special about Afghanistan. This country loved by common foreigners and dreaded by superpower decision makers had a unique magnetism. Was it its rich and daring history, stunning geographic beauty, undeterred cultures, disregarded pride, or simply the sense of friendship, loyalty, naivety, and ingenuity of the inhabitants? Soraya was praised by kings and queens, prime ministers, ministers, ambassadors, business tycoons, and academia throughout the world, but nothing was comparable to the affection of ordinary Afghans from the deepest corners of the north, south, east, west, or central zones. Yes, there was segregation on gender, ethnicity, religious, linguistic, and physical appearance grounds that politicians and those in power exploited to the maximum of their ability, resulting in conflict, destruction, killings, and ignorance. But something inexplicably matchless enticed the attention, hearts, and minds of foreigners. She lived barely nine continuous years in this country, but it was as if she had been there for an eternity.

Her thoughts sailed in all directions. For a while, she quizzed herself. Is Afghanistan a country? The response was yes as it had boundaries, a seat in the General Assembly of the United Nations, and recognition from all other countries. Did Afghans constitute a nation with common interests and equal rights and opportunities? The response was no! She then revised her reflection as it was crossing a dangerous line. Soraya had no option about the demise of her father, but now she had willingly opted to lose her beloved country, friends, and passions. However, an invigorating sense sparkled that she would not cut bonds with a land that had given her so much bliss and happiness. From political deliberations to diplomatic dinners and galas, from excursions to stunning valleys where the purest water roared downhill, the wildest blossom was observed, and pleasing fragrances were inhaled to incognito visits to the dwellings of Hazara, Nouristanis, or tents of Kochis to share precious moments with people who comprehended little about worldly human beings— all were carved in her memory. The mulberry on a kaarez flank, the "*bolani*" of the university canteen, the marvel of a twirling ice cream maker, the scrumptious peasant yoghurt and salty cheese, the warm and crispy bread of Kohdaman or Logar, and thousands of other glees could not be forgotten so easily.

Contrary to Afghan custom, Afzal gave her a big hug and a heartfelt kiss on her forehead to say adieu as he had determined to join the flow of mujahideen in his Panjshir Valley and fight for his people and country. She already missed everything from Afghanistan, even the smell of the cow poop in rural areas. The eventuality of profanation of her father's tomb by the regime haunted her, though villagers and the imam of the mosque had vowed to protect it. On the airplane, she felt privileged to be alive. Most of her friends and close colleagues were murdered; under such circumstances, she was very fortunate to escape assassination, but she wept for the plight of many Afghan women who were trapped. All regimes exploited and abused them without undertaking any consequential schemes to embrace them effectively in the political, social, cultural, and economic fabric of the country. Perhaps they worried about the credence of an obscure animalistic tradition, whereby females were destined to provide food, procreate, or mind children and house.

She had long before established that intelligent, honest, and smart people had no place in Afghanistan. Her father was forcibly exiled, Maiwandwal and Mousa Shafiq were murdered, and countless intellectuals and valorous citizens were put in jail, tortured, and killed.

The political realities were awfully gloomy and the system corrupt. Rulers had made a mess of this wonderland! She contemplated bright people she had encountered, knew, and esteemed for their honesty, dedication, and willingness to serve the country—professors, students, government officials, and ordinary people—all of them bright, representing inestimable value for the country but savagely eliminated. There was a huge disconnect between the common people and their government. Afghanistan had hardly been suitably ruled; nasty leaders above all served the interest of superpowers or their own families. She questioned whether the hundreds of mujahideen commanders who courageously and ferociously wrestled the mightiest giant of the world comprehended that they were instruments of a new "great game." And at the end, they would be losers. Her reality check was sorrowful and remorseful at the same time.

Her thoughts flew all over the country. She visualized the battlefields and tens of thousands of barefoot, hardly dressed, but determined Afghans who defied the Red Army in the coldest of winters. The casualties were uneven. For each Soviet or Afghan soldier killed on the battlefield, ten to one hundred civilians and mujahideen perished. Though there is no fairness in war, the Soviet-imposed conflict in Afghanistan was most iniquitous. If the West had at least routed military, humanitarian, and financial assistance directly to the mujahideen and granted them some degree of recognition, the state of affairs would have been better. Leaders then would have been based within the country and independent from neighbors' interference. There were enough safe havens to accommodate them.

She remembered a factual story recounted by Agha Saheb. During Amin's terror, a distinguished old professor shared a cell with a young protestor. Every night inmates were seized randomly and taken to torture chambers. Unbearable screams were perceived or heard, and scores never returned. On every occasion, the old professor was brought back on a stretcher, with obvious signs of harm. The young man took pity on him and asked, "Professor, I know the director of

Pule Charkhi was your student, and apparently he respects you. Why do you not ask him to spare you?"

"Son," the old professor retorted, "if you happen to be a slave, then be a slave of the master. Being the slave of another slave is a redline that I do not cross—I would be better off dead."

All heroic guerilla figures steered struggles from within their countries. Mujahideen commanders did the same. Then why did their chiefs reside in neighboring countries? They were then "slaves of the slaves." Yes, there were perils, but confronting the Soviet Union was a damned risky enterprise. She was also reflecting on the ruinous effects of Iran-West contentions and the growing mistrust toward Islam. She thought of the medieval era, during which at least nine crusades were undertaken. Killings, lootings, and systematic violations of human rights and dignity by both sides were perpetrated. Were we going backward and would engage once again in futile religious disputes and follow the path of Cain? Suddenly she became fretful of the future. Would her beloved Afghanistan become once again a battleground to meet the ambitions of others? Would religion be used as a weapon of hate? The most worrisome factor for her was the lack of ability of Afghan leaders of all political sensitivities to place the interest of their country as a prime priority. She was not confident of such maturity.

She did not know the route of her journey, but she felt at ease after nearly two hours of flight. She was certainly outside Afghanistan's airspace and sensed that she was free. She became talkative. Serena was in her arms. Selina and Arslan were seated next to her. She did not have a clear plan as to where she would end up and started consulting her son, who knew little about what was happening. She came out of her country with two suitcases of clothing and three thousand dollars, the amount that dealers had paid for her most precious silver, porcelain, and crystal sets. She should have been disbursed fifty times more and felt duped. But looking at her children, she concluded that it was the only way and worth it.

Once the pilot announced that they had entered the European zone, the anxiety of where to go occupied her mind. At the Frankfurt airport, she finally headed to the Austrian counter and purchased one-way tickets to Vienna. In the evening of "*Nawroz*," March 21, 1981, Soraya and her family landed in the city of Empress Sisi.

Chapter 5

In a Free and Challenging World—The Fight for Afghanistan's Liberation

Human beings are members of a whole,
In creation of one essence and soul.
If one member is afflicted with pain,
Other members uneasy will remain.
If you have no sympathy for human pain,
The name of human you cannot retain.

—Saadi Shirazi, *Gulistan*

At the Mont Pèlerin Conference, the diplomatic limitations of mujahideen leaders and their reliance on regional powers became apparent. Hints were conveyed by representatives of Western countries that they expected to also see Afghans in Western countries structured and mobilized. Subsequently, the Association of Afghans Abroad was established. The body, comprised of full and alternate members, ran matters from the city of Vienna in Austria. The alternate members attended meetings and debates but voted only when the principal member was unable to join. I was elected as an alternate member.

Afghans from across West European countries who were part of the association relished their voluntary activities that constituted for some the first steps in the violent, unfair, and uneasy world of politics. Young students dealt with mobilization affairs. The composition of the association was lopsided. From the onset, personalities, prestige, and appearance seemed more worthy than upholding the interest of Afghanistan or its millions of refugees and trapped citizens inside the country. There was a clear disconnect with realities on the ground and a conspicuous lack of discernment about the world's affairs. Those boosted by their lofty executive or political statuses in the past or who claimed royal blood circulating in their veins considered King Zaher Shah as God's savior of Afghanistan. Others had dissimilar opinions and venerated their own idols among the mujahideen leaders or commanders. Few had a broader vision of nationhood and advocated for equality, collectivity, and collegiality among all ethnic groups in the country and abroad. It was indeed a pallid and frail congregation that could not prove effective, but its merits were in its existence.

The fact that billions of United States dollars were routed to Pakistan produced a euphoric atmosphere among Afghans of all affiliations inside and outside the country. However, no one comprehended or questioned how much of that money was effectively allotted to and abetted the mujahideen to fight against the Soviet Union. Rare were those who grasped the real dogma that Afghanistan was not at the essence of the assistance; the collapse of the Soviet Union was! The main concern of the chieftains of the association was how to get into the corridors of the diplomatic representations in Vienna and other European capitals and acquire recognition. The notion of having achievements before rushing to embassies was brushed aside. Though the initial reception was warm, Western chancelleries became disillusioned as soon as the body could not deal with any substantive matter except occasional demonstrations in front of the Soviet Embassies here and there. Of course, the police did not tolerate anyone getting closer to the buildings than the distance enshrined in their laws. The contest among prominent members soon commenced as to who should represent them at a particular occasion organized in a specific country or embassy, a pathetic contest in Afghan politics, where leaders sacrificed the essence for appearance.

At the occurrence of the Persian New Year, I proceeded to Vienna for a meeting of the association and attended with some young Afghans a friendly and affable celebration. It was a surprise and delight at the same time to see Soraya and her family there. Those who knew her always thought she would end up in New York; coming to a German-speaking country was audacious. The joy of again finding a distinguished woman who instigated esteem and admiration because of her knowledge, wisdom, intelligence, and elegance was exceptional. There was much chatter. It was all about Afghanistan, incarceration of the guiltless, carnage, bombings, destruction, abuse of human rights, frustration of the entire population about a promising prospect, and optimistic expectation for a liberation that would perhaps not show up at the horizon soon.

Two days later, I joined Soraya and her family in a pleasing afternoon. We strolled along the left bank of the Danube River. An Austrian friend then drove and guided us to Innere Stadt, where we walked the stone-paved alleys. Selina and Arslan walked ahead of us. However, Serena enjoyed the majesty of the old city from her baby buggy, looking around carefully as if she wanted to memorize every street and edifice. On the Stephansplatz, Soraya popped into Payot to purchase a few magazines and books in English. Adjacent to it was situated the Philosophen Kaffee, where university buddies and professors loved to have coffee or a bite. Some enjoyed their hot drink with Austrian Milka chocolate full of hazelnuts. Often it constituted their speedy breakfast before hopping in the direction of their universities and colleges. Soraya appreciated the atmosphere. A number of young under- or postgraduate Afghan students expected her. They were future medical doctors, engineers, artists, economists, or social workers. The day looked hassle-free. Obviously, they came to converse about Afghanistan and the associated challenges. They were essentially Hazara, Pashtun, Tajik, Turkman, and Uzbek youth. Bright in their composure, analysis, expectation, commitment, and collegiality, they stunned her.

The nearly three-hour discussion was of the highest intensity and quality. She looked jovial and optimistic. Her greatest attribute was that she could converse about any topic—philosophy, engineering, economy, politics, sciences, and even embroidery, which she had mastered as a family tradition. In the course of a fascinating exchange about how Afghans overseas could contribute to the toil of enlightening those who did not wish to see beyond a simple withdrawal of the Red Army, she was briefed about the existence of the association, the composition of its members, and the defiance it encountered. She recognized some members and was enthusiastic to join the collective and united efforts. But, something unexpected and startling happened!

At the end of the discussion, a distinguished gentleman with gray hair and a firm visage, who seemed to be known to some of the Afghan students, approached Soraya. "Madame," he began. "Allow me to introduce myself. I am Professor Knup, head of neurosurgery at the Medizinische Universität in Vienna. You must be from Afghanistan."

"Yes indeed, Professor. How do you know?" Soraya inquired.

"My father was ambassador to the court of your king, and I visited your beautiful country at my younger age, madame. Moreover, I know some of the young people around the table. They attend my classes, he replied.

"I see!" she said with a look of astonishment.

"I have been observing you for a while. You certainly had a facial paralysis that was not taken care of when it should have been."

"Yes indeed, Professor! It happened about a year ago," she replied.

"I can perform a rehabilitative surgery. It will not bring back your nerves, but it can improve the physical aspect of your face. You must have had a stunning one before the attack," he continued.

"Thank you, Professor. But I am a refugee and cannot afford the cost," she replied. "For the moment, it is not a priority for me," she added.

"Here are my details." He handed over a visit card. "We will find a way, as I have some social support means at my disposal at the hospital," he suggested with his soft voice.

Soraya was crying of joy. It was so unanticipated. In Afghanistan, she had pleaded for help without receiving it. And here someone came out of the blue and offered what she had desperately needed during the past awful year. We separated from the young Afghan students and branched off toward the Volksgarten. The park is a jewel of its kind. Soraya's two eldest children were overjoyed and began running in all directions while we continued our chatter on challenges that Afghans abroad faced.

It was impossible to visit Vienna and not fall in love with this "city of dreams." The country itself engulfed the majesty of nearly seven hundred years of Austro-Hungarian Empire achievements. In fact, Switzerland and Austria are four-season splendors. Perhaps Vivaldi composed his famous concerti after living in these paradises on earth.

Two months later, Soraya was operated on in the *Universitätsklinik*, University Clinic. Professor Knup was not amply satisfied with the surgery. The zygomatic and buccal branches of the nerve had died completely. There was nothing he could do. However, the end result still seemed appealing. She looked much fresher and rejuvenated.

A month after the treatment, Soraya was an alternate member of the association, dealing with political affairs. Members from different corners of Europe gathered the last Saturday of the month in the Landtmann Kaffee, founded in 1873 and one of the central addresses in the Austrian capital. From the first instance of her attendance, she made a significant difference. The metamorphosis was manifest as, contrary to other members, she had fresh information from within the country. Her analysis about the interest of regional powers such as Pakistan, Iran, Saudi Arabia, and India or world giants such as the Soviet Union, the United States, and the United Kingdom in particular was strikingly fascinating. She envisioned the larger picture of Soviet intervention in Afghanistan and mastered the English language perfectly, something that nobody else in the team did. Her profound and multifaceted comprehension of the political and diplomatic apparatus in Europe and North America gave her an indisputable leverage.

Soraya mesmerized everybody in the association. Followers of King Zaher Shah began to court her, always referring to the "glorious" past, not knowing that her concern was the future. Others had discerned her father's unequivocal stance on the national interest of the country and seemed expectant that she would favor their opinions. Her language was frank, gracious, and firm. She could work long hours untiringly to explore, peruse many articles and books, deliberate with members, and offer a vision or strategy. This was indeed very impressive for many. In Afghanistan, uppermost dignitaries were slothful human beings. They only gave orders, and there were many of them in the association. As usual, she was the fastest and brightest thinker in meetings and debates. The entire team was stunned by her ability to instantly provide several solutions to questions posed, while the "brains" still searched to comprehend the essence of a challenge.

The jealousy, scorn, and irritation of former high officials of Afghanistan, most of whom she knew personally, were apparent. They promoted the most outmoded and obsolete ideas and then wished others to work hard to implement them. Soraya defied everything that seemed specious, outdated, and irrational. She associated with youth and women in particular. Her friends and acquaintances noticed the impact of the surgery on her face. She had also worked hard to exercise the essential functions of her lips and eyes in particular. There was indeed a sharp improvement. She had not lost her stunning magnetism and remarkable charm, intelligence, and self-confidence. The glitter of her green and bluish eyes was very special.

Within the association, she did not appreciate the attempts of some to create lobby groups in support of their own agendas outside the collegial and united spirit. Oftentimes, the monthly meetings were followed by private lobby dinners offered by distinct groups. She had no problem with the broader spirit advocating for an issue of national interest. But Afghanistan belonged neither to one category of individuals nor to a distinct ethnic community. Furthermore, all constructive trends of thoughts or political opinions aiming at unity and the withdrawal of Soviet troops were needed. For her, it was time that Afghans of all social and political sensitivities opted for a coordinated approach, formed a united front, and stood together to repossess their country first. The establishment of separate movements such as in Pakistan or Iran reflected the politics of "*dīvide et imperā*," which had been harmful for Afghanistan. It was high time to admit that all inhabitants of the country possessed worthy ideas and intentions for their motherland and that extremism—ideological, political, ethnic, or otherwise—begot grief, qualms, and devastation for the entire region.

She was still hesitant to confide in everyone in the association, but her intercessions were shrill and to the point. Some members nurtured extreme religious opinions without having the ability of expounding on rationales. Others simply believed that the past could constitute the basis for the future. Soon, she became the strategy drafter. Once again, Soraya opted to be the engine, remain behind, and undertake the real endeavors while men dressed well and went for the show. There were several prominent former ministers who asserted understanding the world of diplomacy and politics. However, they proved to be the most oblivious of the world's modern challenges. The hostility among the members of the association was manifest and rising.

On private ground, Soraya's three thousand US dollars were quickly devoured. Vienna was too costly for a large family. With her academic and professional background, she anticipated quickly finding a job in one of the international organizations and tried hard to make an entry. But getting inside these august entities to meet the useless bureaucrats was an unsurmountable challenge. She called "friends" who held fairly high positions. Not only did they decline categorically to meet her, perhaps fearing repercussions by the Soviet Union, but worse, the security officers of the venerable bodies were instructed not to permit her in. Some of the same individuals begged her for support when she was an assistant to Prime Minister Shafiq. It was so pathetic of them! Her political opinion and desire for a peaceful and democratic future Afghanistan were most relevant. She had no alternative but to ask for political asylum in Austria.

She was allocated a two-room apartment on the Wiesengerstrasse, near the Julius Raab Platz. Though it was very small for a family of six persons—including her mother-in-law—she was nevertheless very grateful. Finding a job remained her top priority. She had strain rising between care for her children, focusing on Afghanistan, writing applications, attending interviews, and cooking for the family. When a few association members who appealed to meet her disembarked in Vienna, the apartment was too tight. Contrary to Afghan tradition, she invited them out, to the Motto am Fluss Kaffee on the Donaukanal, for discussion.

One sunny day of June 1981, her phone rang. It was Piotr. He knew where she was and urged her to meet him in the Modenapark. It was not shocking that the Soviets had discerned her whereabouts or that Piotr wished to meet her, but why in a public park? Could he not afford a friendly cup of coffee in a decent place? After all, she was not involved in secret service affairs that would require meeting in unnoticed or secret places. But she realized that the location was close to the Soviet Embassy. The next day, Piotr was exultant to see her and did not hide his emotions.

"How are you, Soraya?" he inquired. "I know your few recent years were tough in Afghanistan. But we have come to help your country against foreign aggression based on the 1978 Friendship Treaty," he added.

"Thank you, Piotr. It has been very difficult for my country and its populations," she replied. "Your country has nothing to do in Afghanistan. No sound Afghan can endorse the invasion, occupation, killings, and destruction of villages and towns that are obvious crimes against humanity."

"Let it be so, Soraya! I am tasked to offer you a senior international position, provided you do not criticize Soviet actions in Afghanistan," he stated.

"Your government would like to buy my silence?" she inquired.

"Not at all. It is an amicable and mutually beneficial proposal."

"You know, Piotr, my blood has always been clean of betrayal germs. I live in a free and secure country and am saddened that you underestimated my loyalty to my people," she summarized.

On the way out of the park, Piotr articulated his desolation as he had a job to do. He urged Soraya not to blame him personally and assured her he would never bother her again. She was vexed, fuming and worried at the same time. The brutality of the KGB extinguishing opponents was well-known. She thought of alerting the Austrian authorities. But her status and dignity were more central than her life. She recalled her father's words: "When you engage in something you believe in, then assume your responsibilities as anything can happen."

She became more determined to involve herself in tangible actions for the liberation of Afghanistan. On Saturday afternoons following

290

association assemblies, she oftentimes hauled her children for picnics along Dechantlacke on the right bank of the Danube with friends. While she set up the equipment and prepared marinated legs of chicken or lamp chops, Selina and Arslan teased with other children and assembled deadwood for a bonfire while Serena looked around with her dazzling green eyes. They did not like gathering firewood but complied as well-educated infants. At the time, it was permitted to enkindle fires on sandy lake coasts, provided they were scoured at the end. The gleam of moonlight on the lake and the bonfire on the shore with the smell of grilled meat and the brouhaha of people around was something unique.

It was so peaceful and serene. People did not know each other, but they were very sociable, tendering their meals and snacks to neighbors. The whole panorama revealed the hard work that Austrians of all social, linguistic, ethnic, and geographic sensitivities had accomplished throughout the centuries to create such a heaven. In many ways, the scene reminded Soraya of a peaceful period in Afghanistan. She loved to listen to the1978 song of Bonnie Tyler "It's a Heartache" to divest her emotions; it was another way she could convey to others that her soul bled for her country and people. After the meal and around a high blaze, deliberations endured on what had transpired in the meeting, analysis of behaviors and proposals, and quests for solutions and strategies on how to ensure impartiality and unity in the next encounter. Selina and Arslan stood, quickly tired of collecting fallen branches of trees, and did not comprehend anything debated upon. Occasionally, unknown neighbors joined to enjoy the splendor of moonlight, fire, and sweet noise of lake waves combined altogether.

Several facts appeared discernible. A handful of members of the association assumed the greatest burden. Some devised and nurtured a colonial attitude whereby a few characterized an extreme vision for the future. Appearance and representation at diplomatic events or meeting ambassadors were assumed more crucial than sketching a project for the future or aiding victims. The improper part constituted of untrue projections of what occurred in Afghanistan. Of course, Soraya personally knew many commanders, and three kept in touch even in Austria and called her frequently as soon as they attained Peshawar for rest and recuperation. Their accounts were dissimilar to what the old leadership imagined and averred. Foreign representatives grasped perfectly what went on in Afghanistan and swiftly deduced that the association was at rift between a number of wealthy who pretended to be aristocrats, each fantasizing salvage of the lost crown, and some others of extreme conviction. A few independent souls constituted a minority group. Soraya was the only lady in the decision-making body. No other female was at the horizon, as if Afghan women had been suppressed by their kinsmen, even in Europe. She was then the only voice for half of the population among the roars of mighty men, a tragic and sad reality of Afghan culture.

The dispute between the royal and fundamentalist camps ended up in fracturing the association; oftentimes, meetings were halted by brawls. Everything curdled over personalities. The voice of Afghans made refugee or trapped within the country was unheeded. In response to Soraya's query, one of the commanders labeled the situation in simple words: "People within the country do not even remember who King Zaher Shah was or who the mujahideen leaders are. Their primary concern is how to evade arrest, bombardment, injury, or killing. Survival is the essence for themselves and their families."

Indeed, with the Soviet occupation of Afghanistan, brutality of their operations, malicious intentions of regional powers, and lack of independence and audacity of mujahideen leaders, as well as economic and social strains, the society had drastically changed. Afghanistan was no longer the striking country that foreigners and hippies visited to encounter a welcoming, bashful, and hospitable population. Inhabitants dreaded each other, and the traditional social structures were completely demolished by the Soviets. Corruption within the mujahideen ranks was slowly nurtured, encouraged, and fortified by the ISI in order to keep commanders under control. Some mujahideen groups and Pakistani authorities also engineered a few "*Hollywood El Comandantes*" to guarantee that most Western media met them and provided "documentaries" to their audiences about recurrent Soviet failures.

Amid such inadequacy, incomprehension, and observed incompetence, Soraya retreated to the Tyrolean Alps occasionally to invigorate and resuscitate her convictions. Perhaps they reminded her of the exquisite memories of encounters with Arthur Koestler or the majestic peaks of her native Afghanistan. She cherished renting high-altitude chalets to witness the real sense of the mountain environment and weather. During her first flight to Europe, she had admired the snowy Mont Blanc and Matterhorn summits from her window seat and wished in her innocent mind to visit them one day. When meeting Queen Soraya, she was fretful of becoming a refugee. Now her fate and destiny had brought her to effectively live among the apexes of Europe with a refugee status. Her family and children liked these escapades to scenic mountains, where they could consume schnitzel with spaetzle or apple strudel and kaiserschmarrn during the winter season. They walked long distances, chatting and discussing about everything and nothing. She had a firm desire to introduce Austria to her children and coveted that they know as much about the country as their native school comrades; her aim was to educate and bring up her children as any other European citizen. Perhaps she already had a premonition that her children would never return to their ancestral land.

In the international arena, the exceptional alliance, partnership, and understanding between two outstanding personalities, Ronald Reagan of the United States and Margaret Thatcher of the United Kingdom, presented an iron front to Soviet ambitions. Whether the sophistication of the Englishwoman complemented perfectly the boldness of the American statesman or vice versa is debatable. Soraya recognized the fine lines of Western and Soviet politics regarding the future of the world. She suggested organization on December 27 of that year of a gigantic demonstration in Vienna against the Soviet occupation of Afghanistan. All gathered at Sigmund Freud Park, in front of the *Universität Wien*, University of Vienna. Perhaps the large number of anticipated participants coerced the authorities to offer a location far away from diplomatic representations. But for Afghans, it did not matter. As usual, dignitaries and former "personalities" came late and were lined up to speak first—the supremacy game was played even in Austria! And there was no female orator. As organizers, the young university students urged Soraya to come up on the stage and speak, not only as a conversant person about the issue at stake, but more specifically as an Afghan woman who was forced to leave her country most recently. She was shy and did not like public appearances but somehow acceded to the request.

It was the most remarkable speech delivered at the gathering. She did not opt for analysis of the situation but rather stressed the requirement for Afghans to be united and create the necessary space for all social, ethnic, religious, and linguistic groups, particularly women, to play their role in the struggle ahead. She underscored that the fight against the Soviet Union and repercussions of its intervention and revival would be long and that religious bigotry made it impossible for mujahideen leaders to acknowledge, among other challenges, the role of women. However, that should not deter Afghan women from mobilizing and advocating for their role in any post-Soviet future that would be designed and defined. She lamented the treason of the communist regimes that used and abused women and their status even more than other governments. Finally, she underlined that the first Muslim convert was a woman who played a crucial role in the florescence of Islam and expressed her hope that mujahideen leaders would honor their religious obligation by allowing women to play their role in forging a future for Afghanistan. It was an address that lasted no more than ten minutes, but it was enormously significant and greatly applauded.

In the next meeting of the association, it was announced that Alexander Haig, the US secretary of state, wished to meet a delegation of Afghans abroad in Geneva, particularly the lady who spoke at the demonstration in Sigmund Freud Park in Vienna. There was a peculiar atmosphere. A former minister greeted the news with contentment but opined that Soraya should not attend such a meeting. He believed that politics in Afghanistan were not women's affair and that her intervention at the rally was "undiplomatic" and that it may have already infuriated mujahideen leaders. The debate was stormy. Young members supported her, while the old guard and hawks vigorously opposed her. In Afghanistan, it was a standard practice that ministers or other high dignitaries abused their power or prestige, but how could someone think so derogatively in democratic societies, where equal rights were supposedly exercised? They hoped to be tagged as open-minded, but their inner organs and brains boiled with the acid of discrimination and prejudice. The intervention of some young members was passionate, counseling the former minister to present his standpoint for himself alone, as a country's affairs belonged to all its citizens, irrespective of their gender, social stand, or political opinion. One even screamed in the hall that without women, Afghanistan moved nowhere and that ignoring at least half of the population of the country was a sin as God in the Koran did not distinguish good and evil based on gender but on virtue and service to humankind.

At the end to the dismay of many, Soraya was taken out of the list. Most of those who were delegated to meet Mr. Haig did not even speak or comprehend English; the former minister obviously tailored the verdict to his own advantage. Though the secretary of state may have had some acquaintance with German or French languages, any translation in serious deliberations diminished the essence of what counterparts or adversaries communicated to each other or even triggered conversion of the facts. The situation was ridiculed by many as the honorable minister always brought his texts to Soraya for correction of substance and format. As usual, she candidly obliged. It was pitiful to see a brilliant woman forbidden by a group of ambitious and ruthless men because of her gender or the expression of what she thought it was correct to say. It appeared that the encounter did not meet American expectations and was shortened. Nobody ever revealed the details of what was deliberated upon.

Soraya's quest for a job with any international organization was futile; Piotr had warned her. She now focused on other English-speaking institutions and enhancing her knowledge of the German and French languages. She consented to assist the *Österreichische Nationalbibliothek*, the National Library of Austria, not only to have access to as many books as possible in all fields and areas but to exploit her structured mind for the common welfare. She felt gratified to have an occupation, though underpaid, and mingle in an atmosphere of academia and research. Within days, her interaction with people and open-minded, honest, and constructive debate impressed. The library was close to the *Wiener Staatsoper*, the Vienna opera house, *Rathaus*, City Hall, and *Österreichisches Parlament*, the Austrian Parliament. Students, professors, politicians, artists, and common people rushed either to look for a desired book or just to spend time strolling alleys and shelves or reading newspapers. She often ended up walking in the nearby gorgeous parks or having coffee at the Hofburg Kaffee, close to the library, or Mozart Kaffee, next to the opera house. For serious matters and discussions, she went with her interlocutors to the famous Trattoria Toscana restaurant on the Dorotheergasse, behind her workplace, as the day's special was always tasty and fresh, particularly the osso buco. Despite the disappointments she confronted in the association and with her quest for a job, she had the status of a queen in the library. People valued her, listened to her ideas, and in most cases implemented her recommendations.

One day, she received an invitation from a young student and her artist boyfriend to attend the *Pelléas et Mélisande* opera show of Claude Debussy in the Wiener Staatsoper. Watching this love-triangle tragedy in the grandiose theater was a dream come true since she had left New York, where she used to go frequently to Carnegie Hall for exceptional shows. With her refugee circumstances, she could not afford to fulfill her cultural aspirations in Vienna. The show was exquisite. The Berlin Philharmonic Orchestra, led by the native Herbert von Karajan, and the players excelled. It was indeed a Shakespearean tragedy, ending in bloodshed. But what she liked most about it was the uncertainty and vagueness as to who among Golaud, his half brother Pelléas, or their common love, Mélisande, retained the truth. The young couple invited her often to the Vienna opera house. It was customary that performers could bring a limited number of friends or family members at no cost.

Often she contrasted imaginary classic tragedies, where usually the good, the evil, and the loved one comprised the main characters, to the vicious real show on earth, with two orders and speeds. While on the one hand dictatorship suppressed the population and slowed down the path for social and economic progress, democracy provided opportunity and extracted the best from each citizen to evolve with supersonic speed. Unfortunately, the majority of the world belonged to the first category. Most ferocious regimes violated the basic rights of their citizens, strangling them to the extent that no opposing voice was heard and robbed the commonwealth. The loved one was definitely missing in tragedies we face on earth! Such constituted the themes of her conversation and dialogue within the association or with foreign friends about Afghanistan. The loved one, the people of that tortured country and their interest, was nowhere to be seen. No concrete idea or project was impelled; Afghans of all political affiliations were unable and perhaps inept to take charge of their future and attain a breakthrough for a united vision and approach.

Soraya finally secured a job with the newly established branch of the Webster University in Vienna in the summer of 1982. She was joyful, and a new dynamism ran through her veins. The office was located at the Leopoldstadt, just at the other side of Donaukanal on the Praterstrasse. She opted to move to a decent apartment on the

Castellezgasse with a very nice view over Augarten Park. During weekends, she loved walking in the gorgeous city of Vienna and discovered on each occasion amazing additional historic and cultural facets.

In the second week of her work, a middle-aged man knocked and entered her office. Soraya thought he was either a professor or a graduate student and urged him to sit down, inquiring what she could do for him. The gentleman introduced himself as Jim and stated that he worked with the United States Embassy in Austria. He invited Soraya for lunch at the Donauturm. It is one of the most iconic places in Vienna. The tower was not old. However, it offered a spectacular view over the Danube River and the capital city. They proceeded straight to the Donauwalzer revolving restaurant, where a table was already reserved. Jim was a refined and astute man. He stressed that he was a senior political officer and pursued subjects associated with Afghanistan, as well as their repercussions on Central Asia, inclusive of humanitarian needs. He sought Soraya's opinion about the situation in her country. She provided an objective picture of what went on within Afghanistan, as well as the political wrangle among mujahideen groups in Pakistan and Iran. In the course of a lengthy discussion, she endeavored to emphasize that lack of unity among Afghans everywhere was a major handicap and one of the biggest impediments to success.

At dessert he said, "Madame Suri, I would like to inform you that we are aware of the Soviets' proposal and appreciate your stand. Furthermore, we carefully follow the mobilization of Afghans abroad. We believe they should better complement the efforts of the mujahideen."

"Thank you, Jim. But please be explicit," she replied.

"We do not want to interfere in what Afghans can do or not," he emphasized. "I am tasked to inform you that we were not pleased that you could not attend the meeting with the secretary of state in Geneva. In addition, we believe a new momentum is needed for Afghans abroad to achieve something tangible for their country."

Soraya was flattered that Americans were aware of her exchange with Piotr. But at the same time, she was distressed to hear that the association was already deemed obsolete by the mightiest supporter of Afghan resistance. This was her first formal encounter with a foreign diplomat in Vienna. She used the occasion to quiz Jim about mujahideen groups, their leadership, and the assistance provided, particularly through Pakistan. He seemed enthusiastic about the ability of the commanders to counter Soviet offensives, but he remained ambiguous regarding the faculty of their political leaders, based in Pakistan, to propel the political, social, and economic agenda headlong. He also bewailed that not only were they divided as ever, but none of them had a blueprint for the future of Afghanistan. Jim's information about mujahideen groups based in Iran was indeed limited. He acknowledged that the regime and their Soviet sponsors exceeded in their exaction of the population, not sparing any means to terrorize them. While the Red Army took charge of military operations all over the country, KHAD and its callous leader, Mohammad Najubullah, was the incubus of urban citizens. When asked why assistance was channeled through the ISI and Iran-based groups did not receive the same attention or what role would be preconized for women in a post-Soviet Afghanistan, Jim stammered and said that he had an urgent meeting and must leave.

The association was clearly paralyzed and redundant. From a promising structure, it soon became a psychotherapy gathering for former high officials to vent their pasts or extremists to express their anger. Soraya and the young members were disappointed and determined at the same time to create a new dynamic body. The Committee of Afghans Abroad was established in Geneva with a fourfold purpose. Advocacy to denounce the atrocities perpetrated and to urge instant and unconditional withdrawal of Soviet troops from Afghanistan was the prime priority. In addition, rallying international public opinion and humanitarian aid to support refugees as well as those internally displaced within the country was considered the backbone of necessary action. Realizing the facts on the ground, it was deemed essential to fervently urge a firm pledge by the West to remain engaged in Afghanistan for a long period, as post-Soviet-withdrawal reconstruction of the country and rehabilitation of the wounds demanded time. Finally, consensus on a national agenda among all mujahideen groups, in which competence and equal rights in a society free of discrimination, corruption, and nepotism, was deemed crucial. Soraya was unanimously designated as vice president, dealing with strategic and political affairs.

I had the honor to be part of the leadership of the committee too. As a friend and former colleague of hers back in Afghanistan, we had nurtured a tie based on trust, affinity of opinion, honesty, truth, and belief in someone's own determination and ability. A new chapter of close cooperation and teamwork between this wonderful lady and a group of young, devoted, assiduous Afghans commenced. They vowed to make the difference from the onset. Soraya, as the brain, maker, and shaker of the committee, recommended an entity liable to the laws of Switzerland, with compulsory annual audit by external experts. She outlined the simple approach of partnering with renowned international humanitarian agencies, henceforth permitting the committee to attain all four objectives. The strategy was to consent with an entity on a distinct project, advocate and fund-raise at the general public level, assist the organization in question to implement the assignment, and report back to each donor, irrespective of the volume or amount of contribution. Using a posting system availed the prospect for us to build up an impressive database of people who were interested in Afghanistan, tracked issues related to this country, and assisted financially to make a difference.

Soraya had close family ties in the city of Calvin and attended the monthly committee meetings personally. Afghan youth from across

Europe joined the effort. She considered the media as the most important partner of Afghan resistance and advised a strict rule of participatory internal information exchange, analysis of the situation in and outside Afghanistan, and appraisal of actions undertaken. At the beginning of each session, she briefed members on diverse political stands and reported on her personal contacts with her friends who led mujahideen operations inside the country to get a real picture of what went on. As a quick reader and sharp mind, she scrutinized all specialized publications dealing with strategic reviews of the Soviet invasion of Afghanistan, newspapers, TV shows, and debates. It was amazing to realize that she could follow several deliberations on different channels at the same time. The review offered was substantive, comprehensive, and realistic. She loathed exaggeration and cynicism at the same time. For her, only truth and reality constituted the basis for a healthy deliberation about and future agenda for her country.

Like their Austrian colleagues, she found Swiss politicians extremely modest, knowledgeable, and available. Local, regional, and national figures sauntered the streets, used buses or trains, and easily spared time with anyone who approached them for a given matter. She was captivated by their humility and sense of responsibility and began educating herself on how Swiss politics functioned and direct democracy was exercised at the municipality, canton, or state and even national levels. The amazing part was to comprehend that Switzerland was the only country where the population at large was regularly consulted on issues of public interest and approved legislative determinations could be overturned through a popular vote. Citizens were called upon several times per annum to exercise their rights and use the ballots for issues of major concern. She recognized that in this country people governed as for any expected verdict, someone or a group of people or institutions collected the required number of signatures to prompt polling, the outcome of which was accepted by all parties. Even as a smart political intellect, she was stunned to perceive that a variety of independent cantons or republics with their own language, budget, administrative systems, and origins molded a country that had sustained stability, prosperity, and peaceful coexistence since 1292, a record in the world!

Another astonishing and extraordinary reality of Swiss politics was "*la paix de travail,*" the peace at work whereby labor unions and governments—municipal, cantonal, and federal—opted to negotiate and refer to the direct democracy process in cases of disagreement. Therefore, while strikes were staged in other countries in Europe, triggering massive losses to enterprises and companies, workers in all parts of Switzerland sustained to deliver and increase their productivity. While elsewhere labor unions tussled to work only thirty-five hours a week, in Switzerland the workweek was increased to forty-four hours. Indeed, the Swiss economy was diverse, but precision technology, chocolate, cheese, banking, watches, and tourism industries constituted the backbone of their prosperity. Quality composed the essence of every initiative.

With some of her Afghan and Western interlocutors, Soraya often broached whether the Swiss federal system could not offer mujahideen leaders some basics to configure a way forward for the future of Afghanistan. In both countries, distinct geographic zones possessed their linguistic and social features and specifics, people were separated by high mountains and valleys, landlocked locations presented fewer options for trade and prosperity, neighbors' might dominated, and a neutral political status was a virtue and provided significant leverage. But in the course of their history, Afghans surely lived in a country but not as a nation. Some members of the committee were too enticed by a decentralized Afghanistan in the future, where each province would elect their own local assembly and government and thereby decide about their concerns such as social welfare, development, infrastructure, and any other local worry. A joyful association was healthier and knotted the population together more stoutly than any forced marriage! Likewise, in a federal political, social, and economic scheme, each part constituted an indispensable member of the larger body—the country or nation. Why should a governor for Kandahar or Badakhshan be designated or appointed by the president in Kabul? People must be permitted to hire and fire their own local leaders as the essence of governing accountability and participation in a real democracy. Contrary to the stance of the hawkish members, such ponderations at an early stage were even essential, twilling decision makers of all zones of the country together to forge a common future, expected to be joyful for all.

On a pleasing day of late summer 1982, Soraya met an eminent figure in Switzerland. An admirer and companion of Jean Monnet, he was judged as one of the father founders of Swiss modern politics and diplomacy from an academic perspective. He had even served as an adviser in the White House of John F. Kennedy. He was captivated by Soraya's astuteness, shrewd analysis ability, and solutions-oriented approach. She was passionate about the struggle against the Soviet Union and presented factual data on their losses, morale, and failed strategies. They exchanged comments about the shortsighted tactics of the West, particularly the United States trusting Pakistan and virtually giving the keys of Afghanistan's future into the hands of this country that had existential dilemmas. She portrayed in detail the three Anglo-Afghan wars and the political mess created by the Gandomak and Durand treaties between the British Empire and their lackey kings in Afghanistan respectively in 1879 and 1893. In addition, the Kashmir problem and the menace of regionalization of conflict in Southwest Asia that would possibly transform the geopolitics of the world, leading to the West losing momentous ground to opponents, were discussed.

He listened vigilantly, and after nearly two hours of discussion, he candidly stated, "I am pleased for this discussion and have found your analysis of the situation most useful. However, what you must bear in mind is that competition between East and West will have serious repercussions. The war in your country may end with one side defeating the other, the consequences of which will affect countries beyond your borders and may change the nature of events as far as Europe. It is too soon to predict how they will be impacted. The outcome will depend largely on the nature of intelligence collected."

"I know, sir," she said. "Indeed, intelligence plays a pivotal role. What I am afraid of as far as my country is concerned is that the postconflict stage will be void of a strategy and we might end up with a situation that might result in further conflicts between my compatriots. I see no evidence of leadership among the mujahideen groups presently based in Pakistan or Iran. I fear a power struggle once the Soviets disengage."

"You are so right, madame! But decisions are usually made based on paid intelligence, which unfortunately provides short-term solutions. Unbiased analysis is rarely taken into account," he replied. "Believe me! I have struggled for years to fight this stupidity on the part of Western intelligence networks, but in vain."

Soraya was stunned! She had heard the same appraisal from her father long ago. On her next visit to Geneva, she attended a dinner organized by this personality, during which she received a lofty offer to work for one of the greatest Swiss industry icons. With a broken heart, she could not assent with the proposal due to family constraints. The refugee status of her family in Austria obliged them to stay in the country, and she could not endure the risk of leaving her children alone in Vienna.

It was clear now that the United States, through the largest ever CIA covert Operation Cyclone, had massively intensified assistance to mujahideen groups and commanders through the Pakistan ISI. Congressman Charlie Wilson, who had initiated the idea under President Carter, remained fully in charge under President Reagan's administration. He was de facto leading "Charlie Wilson's War" from Washington, DC, with frequent visits to the operation theaters inside the country. As an engineer and politician, he had a more pragmatic approach as to how to bring the Soviet Union to its knees in Afghanistan. The mujahideens' feeblest point was the lack of protection from aerial bombardments, particularly of Mil Mi-24 Soviet helicopter gunships, which were capable of flying very low to hit their targets. Charlie Wilson was instrumental for the development, fabrication, and shipment of human-portable anti-aircraft guns from Israel to the mujahideen.

This was the first titanic alteration of might in the Afghanistan war against the Soviet Union. The phase of the conflict shifted, and mujahideen commanders were not only masters of their terrain but of their airspace as well. Now they could bring down and annihilate the most horrible and gigantic butterflies that they had ever seen. The fact that such a marvelous war toy came from Israel did not trouble anyone among the extremist mujahideen groups or Muslim countries, particularly the Pakistan of General Zia-ul-Haq. It was known that Congressman Charlie Wilson had used the power and devotion of women to reach his constituents so efficiently through *"Charlie's Angels"* and pass the Safe Drinking Water Act with the precious help of the American League of Women Voters. But why did he not contemplate a role for Afghan women? Was he of the judgment that they were not worthy of a place in the resistance structures that he certainly endorsed if not designed? Based on sound reasons, Soraya deemed that had the West in general and the Reagan administration in particular, led by Charlie Wilson, advocated for it, none of the fundamentalist or extremist movements would have had any option but to create the required legroom. What was the monitoring mechanism to safeguard that Afghan mujahideen were not dispatched to Kashmir to fight the pro-Soviet India of Indira Gandhi? Why did the West accept fragmented and fractured mujahideen movements and not "enforce" unity among them? These were some of the thorny questions that Soraya and the team in the committee parked for a day when they would have opportunity to interpolate their concerned interlocutors.

The Soviet Union was tearing Afghanistan and its people apart. The Panjshir Valley, Herat, Nangarhar, Logar, Paktia, Kandahar, Takhar, Bamiyan, Ghazni, Faryab, and many other places had become the symbols of their defeat and mujahideen commanders their nightmare. Since September 1980, the Red Army had hurled five additional offensives to capture the Panjshir Valley. On each occasion, they had gains at the initial stages of their assaults, seizing parts of the valley and instantly honoring their military chieftains as heroes of the Soviet Union, only to apprehend moments later their sourest dismay that mujahideen annihilated their progress by showering them from the peaks with bullets and crushing them with stones of their mountains.

The situation was the same in each corner of Afghanistan, where mujahideen commanders displayed the utmost ability in repelling Soviet offensives. The Mil Mi-24 helicopters, as well as the MiG-23 and SU-24 jet fighters and bombers were of no worth; they could not uncover mujahideen and their light weapons behind each rock. In addition, the rumble of their engines gave adequate time to their adversaries to cloak their presence. Indeed, there were casualties on the part of freedom fighters but not to the extent to trigger defeat. No one had exact knowledge of where the renowned commanders were or slept; only a handful knew everything. The KGB and KHAD desperately searched to localize and eliminate them. The valorous mujahideen resisted the pressure, bombardments, and systematic killings imposed by the Red Army. Each commander was in effect and could be labeled a lion of his region or location. Babrak Karmal and his boss, Leonid Brezhnev, became more and more irritated. Not only in Kabul but even in Moscow, the leaderships of the respective communist parties were now overtly disparaged. The Soviet side put the guilt on their Afghan flunkies, inculpating them of disloyalty and cheating, not disclosing to public opinion that the Afghan Army in most circumstances actively or passively cooperated with the resistance.

The Herat Garrison mutiny in 1979 had paved the way for other brave military officers to act against the invaders. Mujahideen leaderships were in disarray in Pakistan. Every attempt to bring them together in view of establishing a united front failed. Accounts of embezzlement and larceny became public knowledge. Bank accounts in the Gulf States of Kuwait and Qatar amassed hundreds of millions of United States dollars siphoned from the international aid to the mujahideen. Each leader had to demonstrate loyalty toward Pakistan strategies and objectives. The mighty General Zia never jested and had proven his resolve by hanging the rival and former boss Zulfiqar Ali Bhutto. The most extremist movement among mujahideen groups continued to receive more magnitude. Though effectively less efficient in the battlefields, Hekmatyar's group received the largest portion of aid from the CIA and the ISI. Allegations were voiced that it even had a parallel penance system and penitentiary in Peshawar. Their leadership and prominent members were branded brutal and merciless. There were rumors of intellectuals kidnapped, tortured, and killed by this particular faction at the instigation of Pakistan. The United States and their Western allies were reproached for their silence.

Under such circumstances, numerous commanders took the initiative to create an alliance inside the country to ensure that their acts were coordinated. But it was too complex. With the efficiency of Soviet intelligence, phones and walkie-talkies seemed useless. The only way to guarantee implementation of such a most desired necessity was to meet personally. With the country occupied by the Soviet Union, the ongoing conflict at each corner of the country, and the difficulty of the terrain, it was practically impossible to accomplish proper coordination. Moreover, money and political manipulation, combined with a deliberate policy not to tolerate unity among Afghan mujahideen, emboldened some commanders within the country to contend with their colleagues. The ancestral traditions and cultures of Afghans, whereby old men or those gray-bearded decided upon and arbitrated all disputes, started showing signs of cracks. Some young and rich extremist commanders defied the outcomes of traditional deliberations that often did not favor their actions. People within the country became more desperate. Millions of refugees now resided in Iran and Pakistan.

In the committee, Soraya recommended a yearly strategy of simple, achievable, and visible nature. Tens of thousands of information and appeal pamphlets were printed and, through the post office, distributed to households all over Europe, but mainly in Switzerland. The expectation was that countless number of receivers would subscribe to the cause of the Afghan people and their struggle for freedom and support the proposed idea or project. Accountability and auditing constituted the spine of trust and partnership with the public. The success of the scheme relied on voluntary support provided by young members. The first step was to support the United Nations High Commissioner for Refugees in the endeavor of immunization of refugee children in Pakistan. Soraya carried out the essential negotiations with the international body to confirm that the committee's subsidy went effectively to acquisition of vital vaccines and was not allocated to administrative or salary costs. It took three months to prepare and launch the campaign that represented the first move to bring to the knowledge of the public at large the prime need of Afghan refugee children. The response was marvelously positive and unexpected.

Soraya was resolutely of the opinion that the committee should engage only in implementable projects. In addition, her comprehension and practice of politics and diplomacy comprised the essence of proximity with people the committee cared about. Her father and mentor traveled to all parts of the country, and his battles were known to movers and shakers such as tribal chieftains, intellectuals, academicians, and even the common people. In her own young political career, she had exercised the same approach by visiting women and young girls in their simple dwellings and tents in Bamiyan, Ghazni, Panjshir, Helmand, Logar, and anywhere else she traveled within Afghanistan.

For her, advocacy and commitment of Afghans abroad in support of their country of origin and its population without direct interaction and reality checks appeared futile and baseless. She often used the terminologies of fiction and factual diplomacy and politics to distinguish a well-wishing attitude from comprehensive engagement. Therefore, the committee opted for propinquity with refugees and internally displaced Afghans despite the safety challenges that encompassed.

In the summer of 1983, I landed in Karachi for an onward flight to Peshawar in order to monitor implementation of the vaccination campaign. The weather was horribly scorching and humid. I had never breathed in such an environment. Once in Peshawar, I opted to stay in the Green Hotel, sited in the middle of the city on the Saddar Road, near a bazaar of the same name. Foreigners also used Deans and Pearl Intercontinental Hotels, which were somewhat isolated. The brouhaha of people and the systematic humming and buzz of auto rickshaws, taxis, and buses, as well as the dusty and stinking roads, were worse than the suffocating noise, smell, and disorder seen and observed in Kabul suburbs. The luxurious part of the city seemed to be located farther west at the university town, where rich people, high government officials, and mujahideen leaders had their villas. However, their offices were scattered in and around the city. The Green Hotel itself was very congested. It had a sort of atrium, where hundreds of people were found chatting and conversing with each other on rudimentary sofas and tables. Some had obvious occupations, among whom journalists and aid workers were evident. But the majority appeared to have dissimilar businesses. Their stringency and easy contact were striking.

The noise of the air-conditioning in my room was awful. I quickly jumped out to visit the nearby bookstores and found a treasure. Most old accounts of British officers in the nineteenth century had been reproduced. Among hundreds of volumes, I instantly acquired *Afghanistan and the Afghans* and *Journal of a Political Mission to*

Afghanistan in 1857, both by Henry Walter Bellew, a British army doctor; *Narrative of the War in Afghanistan* by Captain Henry Havelock of the Thirteenth British Colonial Regiment; the personal narrative of Godfrey Thomas Vigne, alleged spy of King William IV to Ghazni, Kabul, and Afghanistan; *Memorials of Afghanistan* by Joachim Hayward Stocqueler, nineteenth-century British journalist; *Afghanistan and Its Inhabitants* by Muhammad Hayat Khan, who served in the government of British India; *Life of the Amir Dost Mohammad Khan of Kabul* by Mohan Lal, who also served in the British India administration; and the most impressive *Notes on Afghanistan and Baluchistan* by Major Henry George Raverty, senior officer of the Colonial British Army in India. The data and evidence provided were inestimable. They revealed realistic pictures of how the British perceived Afghans and their leaders. I wondered whether any mujahideen chieftain or those who around them inspired to lead Afghanistan in the future had ever perused such extraordinarily available information. Certainly not!

At my first breakfast, a dark-skinned man demanded to sit at my table.

"My name is Hussein," he said, introducing himself. "I work for the government. You are new in Peshawar."

"Yes, indeed. I represent the Committee of Afghans Abroad, which is based in Switzerland," I replied.

"Do you want to open an office in Pakistan?" he inquired.

"No, no! We have no such intention. We would like to provide some humanitarian help to refugees and see if we can send the same inside the country for those internally displaced," I replied.

"Then it is fine, and we are happy," he said. "I advise you to first meet the refugee commissioner. Tell him I referred you to him. He will advise you for the rest. Here is my number in case you need anything," he underlined authoritatively.

"Why are there so many people here?" I inquired.

"Look, my dear," he replied. "You are young but do not look stupid. Most of them are intelligence people from around the world. Be mindful in your contacts," he advised.

It was a shock! Hussein was a senior ISI officer and blatantly frank. It was my first contact with someone of the "venerable" institution that terrified all the Pakistani population and Afghan mujahideen. The picture was exactly what Soraya had depicted. This city of Peshawar was full of spies, and moving around was very hazardous and slippery. It was impossible to determine friends and foes of the Afghan cause. She had counseled not to be garrulous with anyone. In the same morning, I was entertained by the refugee commissioner, to whom I outlined the project. He was a handsome Pashtun. We spoke Pashto, and I must admit having difficulty in some circumstances. The accent and introduction of Urdu words made the Pakistani Pashto specific. But we managed to have a constructive conversation.

Soraya had advised that I also knot ties with mujahideen commanders and leaders, as well as the diplomatic and humanitarian communities on the spot. She urged me to consider predominantly the plight of women and children and seek options of support for people trapped inside the country. Practically all the refugee camps were visited within days. Most of them were located in desert areas of the then North-West Frontier Province around Peshawar. Services were rudimentary, and humanitarian aid agencies could not be blamed as the number of refugees was astronomically huge. The shelter situation was pathetically bad. A camp looked like a gigantic, miserable, dusty, and sickening agglomeration. A massive number of children were out of school. Soraya had briefed us about the bilateral aid mechanism and its low efficiency in Pakistan. Corruption and lack of proper oversight were to blame. This was the reason she aimed at engaging with international aid agencies.

She had explicitly requested a visit to the restricted Nasser Bagh Women Refugee Camp, where mujahideen leadership and the government of Pakistan had hosted widowers and their children. Their huge number signified the hideous veracity of war and shattered lives of those who were killed either in the combat fields or by Soviet bombardments or their butterfly and land mines. Women in Afghanistan already had difficulty conducting their lives, but as widowers, their plight was worse. In every conflict, a female without protection seemed like a gazelle in the middle of a pack of hyenas. It was virtually impossible to intermingle with refugees to ascertain their needs. The obscure and conservative aspects of Afghan culture to isolate women were not the only reasons, but it was distinctly obvious that this "sample camp" was created to attract Western sympathy, attention, and support. Therefore, it was sternly controlled by the government spies and agents. Any other intervention was not embraced.

In discussion with some commanders, markedly two of my own distant cousins, it appeared that discontent on how Pakistan treated mujahideen leaders or commanders and allocated more assistance to extremists was sprouting. They referred to ISI agents in Afghanistan as *"moqamaat,"* signifying authorities who "instructed" them on every aspect. This was chiefly the case in southern Afghanistan. The blame was put on mujahideen leaders who did not have the guts to act independently. Almost all of them recognized the ambitions of Pakistan or Iran but did not comprehend the obedient and submissive attitudes of their leaders. One commander with a blunt style stated that "when chicken grows fat, its ass becomes small," referring to the wealth and courage of those who led the political struggle against the Soviet Union. Every concerned individual grumbled about the great importance given to Golboddin Hekmatyar's most radical and extremist group by Pakistan.

The fact that even Americans did not dissent from such a preferential treatment was annoying. It was astonishing that Western agents who were in touch with commanders did not unseal this malcontent. As was divulged later, their primary goal was to trounce the Soviet Union, and the rest was of minor importance. However, every Afghan, commander, refugee, or mujahideen staff loved President Ronald Reagan. For them, he was the rescuer and the hero. In more closed circles, it was evident that Charlie Wilson was the man to fear or bear when evoking the outcome of the Afghan war, "his war," or the future of the Soviet Union. It demonstrated the mujahideens' naivety to believe that the West was fighting for their country's liberation.

The review of the committee's first major action concluded on an optimistic and encouraging note. It overlay all four objectives. Children received vaccination, the level of public awareness and media interest grew on a daily basis, and the committee's objectives were made known to the Afghan resistance, aid agencies, and diplomatic missions. Soraya judged that the committee needed more concrete achievements to be deemed meaningful by interlocutors. Amid strategizing the next actions for refugees and those forcibly displaced within Afghanistan, she suggested two supplementary and tangible thoughts for advocacy campaigns, as well as public and political mobilization all over Europe. Therefore and in order to widen the political pressure on the Soviet Union, it was deemed important to establish close ties with Polish students overseas. The struggle led by Solidarność embodied the legitimate aspiration of the people in Poland to defeat the Soviet domination by peaceful means. The Afghan and Polish crusades against the communist giant contrasted in many ways, but they were unequivocally complementary. Combined, they both resembled a torrent of water in the foundation of a wobbly skyscraper. The student members of the committee promptly liaised with their Polish counterparts to organize photo displays about what went on in both countries.

Furthermore, Soraya recommended reflecting Afghan refugee children's own and individual accounts and standpoints to the public at large. Drawing competitions and storytelling in refugee schools were the best vehicles for the world's opinion to comprehend their emotions, yearnings, and existential realities. Meanwhile, Soraya negotiated successfully with the Swiss Red Cross to support implementation of a mobile eye surgical unit for Afghan refugees in Pakistan. Finally, she advised to seek and identify credible international nongovernmental entities that delivered humanitarian assistance inside Afghanistan for the committee to establish a wider European network in support of the plight of those victims of the bloody occupation who did not receive enough attention. These provided enough substance for the committee to determine its next campaigns.

In spring 1984, I again proceeded to Pakistan. The Swiss Red Cross had accomplished a marvelous task. The mobile eye surgical clinic, based in Mardan, near Peshawar, swathed all refugee camps. Cataracts and trachoma were devastating diseases among the population, causing total loss of sight. For obvious reasons, the entire medical community was preoccupied with war wounds and engaged with major surgeries of all varieties. The Soviet Union strategists comprehended that mujahideen would not abandon their martyrs or wounded friends on the battlefield. While according to Islamic tradition, a slain combatant was buried immediately with his or her own clothing and simplified rituals, the injured were carried out on shoulders through the pinnacles of mountains or widespread steps to safety in the neighboring countries of Pakistan and Iran. The Red Army realized that numerous mujahideen were required for one impaired friend. Therefore and in order to reduce the fighting power of their nemesis, they used shrapnel bullets to make as many seriously wounded as possible. Hence, countless mujahideen effectively left the operation theaters for days to carry the injured to the nearest safe haven, with a high risk of themselves being targeted. At the same time, Soviet flying machines showered Afghanistan with millions of butterfly mines all over. Their army planted land mines along the main mujahideen supply routes and combat zones. As a result, tens of thousands of people had to endure amputation. Others were simply paralyzed.

The mobile eye surgical clinic was a prodigious supplementary asset that all the medical and humanitarian experts valued. It was fascinating and rewarding to see an almost blind person reclaim her or his sight within an hour in the middle of a grimy and discarded refugee camp or hot and wild desert. For patients, all from deep rural Afghanistan, it constituted a miracle of God. The result was instantaneous! Family members, even the most elderly, attempted to kiss the Swiss surgeon's hands, the supreme sign of respect and gratitude in Afghan culture, much to his annoyance indeed.

The visits to refugee schools were most heartrending. Tens of thousands of kids, girls and boys, studied under extreme conditions. Everything so much lacked; the number and needs were colossal. They all had dreams but did not know when and where they would achieve their goals. In response to a question, practically all gazed at the visitor, sighed, and then remained silent. It appeared that their hopes were murdered before sprouting. Their eyes transmitted anxiety about an uncertain and undefined future. Most had seen bombardments, carnage, and even torture of their kin, family associates, or fellow villagers. They all had a hero, often the mujahideen commander of the area where they resided in Afghanistan. Experts were appalled by the education scheme, which did not proffer any prospect for a promising future as standards did not even exist. The children knew about their doomed fate as refugees. Perhaps they nattered about it in their family spheres. Considering that within vast areas of Afghanistan, the governing structures were paralyzed and educative institutions slammed, the picture for the future of the country looked grim and shoddy.

A few mixed refugee schools were selected for the drawing competition, and sheets of blank paper, pens, and markers were distributed. Pupils were invited to project their sentiments and impressions as they wished. A strict monitoring procedure was in place to ensure that they were not swayed by adult students or tutors. Some two thousand sheets were returned. Half of the kids favored to illustrate their inner hunches through pictures, and the rest preferred to write their personal stories. Each drawing or tale demonstrated the sorrow and suffering that the child had gone through as a result of the killings of their parents, siblings, family members, or friends or shelling of their villages. They also expressed the brutality of the invaders as well as the valor of the mujahideen. Each sheet of paper recounted and summarized a personal history. Some images and texts were shockingly violent, showing mutilated bodies of men, women, and children on the ground while jets and tanks were bombing and shelling. This undoubtedly depicted mass murder committed by the Soviets. In interaction with pupils, the immense degree of trauma was evident. It was also obvious that being a refugee was an immeasurable burden and sorrow for most of them. They missed their homes, villages, schools, and friends. In every picture, the enemy was depicted with a hat and red star. In spite of the modest means that the committee possessed, Soraya opined sponsorship of the Naheed Shaheed Refugee Girls' School in Peshawar.

The director, an old friend of her family, was emotional when he realized that she was fully engaged in the struggle for liberation of her country. "She is the perfect image of her father: intelligent, hardworking, fair, just, combative, fearless, and gentle," he said. "In his absence, I wish she was here with us."

"Sir, there is no place for a woman here among the mujahideen groups," I replied.

"This is true, my friend. It is perhaps intentional." he sorrowfully stated. "But this is not the only misfortune of Afghans. It is now clear that neither Americans nor Pakistanis fight for the liberation of our country. They use lousy mujahideen leaders and the heroic struggle of Afghans to achieve their own goals."

Indeed, there were a handful of women who publicly engaged in support of their martyred country. It certainly demonstrated centuries of cultural and political intimidation. The director of the Naheed Shaheed Refugee Girls' School had a pessimistic picture of the situation. For him, only a few years of rudimentary education provided to the hundreds of thousands of refugee children would not provide them with the appropriate basic skills. There was need for secondary and even university education to raise a healthy future generation. He blamed the mujahideen leaders for their lack of care, vision, and "muscle," as well as concerned aid agencies who, in his opinion, were more focused on their short-term image euphoria than the future of the country. He was certain that most Afghan children "would perish on the streets of Peshawar or other cities of Pakistan" doing miserably small jobs. While the war kept children from their basic rights within Afghanistan, as refugees they could not benefit from the same due to the restrictive policy of the host country and the obedience of caretakers. The director, emotional and unremitting, argued that while compulsory education for Pakistani children was twelve years, refugees attended only six years of primary education. Concerned aid agencies should have applied national norms on refugee children too. Afghanistan so much required a refined generation for a healthy future. He recognized the enormity of the challenge but still believed that the international community could have done better.

A quick visit to any of the classrooms would demonstrate to sound individuals that more than half of the pupils suffered from indelible trauma. Hamida, a little girl of about eight years of age, summarized her situation as follows.

> We were having lunch at home with my parents and
> elder brother. Then there was the noise of helicopters
> and shelling. Within minutes they entered our home

and started asking my father where were the "ashraar."
He did not know. Then blue-eyed soldiers came and
started firing. My parents and elder brother were
killed. I was injured in my legs. They also killed the
imam of the village and many others.

Then she cried.

When recounting her story, Hamida was shaking and shivering.
Another villager picked her up after the slaughter of her family
members, brought her to Peshawar, and took care of her as her own
child. One year after the incident, she still had nightmares, shouting
in the middle of her sleep, "Mother, Mother!" In the classroom she
hardly spoke with others unless obliged by teachers. When blue-
eyed foreigners and donors visited the school, she ran away and hid
herself. In her drawing, there were flowers. She explained that they
were for her mother. Shirin, Parwin, Fareba, Bibi Salma, and many
other little girls had similar stories. The boys, however, seemed more
phlegmatic, underlining that such had been the will of God and those
killed were martyrs and heaven was their place. However, after one
or two additional questions, they all tore into tears and kept silent.

The old and experienced director of the Naheed Shaheed Refugee
Girls' School opined that hundreds of thousands of children suffered
from the same symptoms. More than half of the girls wished to
be doctors to help others, while the majority of the boys wanted
to join the rank of the mujahideen and revenge the killing of their
own. This was an alarming signal, depicting a foggy future for
themselves and the country. No specialized aid agency could have
dealt with the frustration and hate expressed by such an enormous
number of children. Most mujahideen leaders were of the opinion
that "God will take care of them," as their priority was to defeat the
enemy. Few of them had ideas about the future of the country. They
all wanted an "Islamic Afghanistan" but were short of elucidating
what it entailed from social, political, and economic perspectives.

There were already strong rumors of some high-ranked officials within mujahideen groups in Pakistan embezzling huge amounts of money and escaping abroad. At the same time, sales of weapons and humanitarian aid allocated to commanders inside the country were "*un secret de polichinel*," as they said in French. Division among the leadership left no hope for the refugees or the people still inside Afghanistan.

Two days prior to my return, the director of the Naheed Shaheed Refugee Girls' School organized a "working lunch," as he termed it. He was the brother-in-law of the headman of a mujahideen movement and therefore had precious connections and bonds. He had kindly consented to my wish and prepared "*Dopiaza.*" It is one of the most lavish and scrumptious Afghan dishes. Though I had met all the leaders and conferred on their aspirations for the future of Afghanistan, the occasion was propitious to meet some again. Indeed, the so-called two moderate chieftains appeared at the event. Of course, they dominated the deliberations. Grumbles about Pakistan and the United States were discernible as they already felt sidelined to the benefit of more extremist groups. Not only did they reproach General Zia on their underrated plight and role, but they also blamed the "favoritism of donors" that did not permit their commanders inside the country to shine at the level of their valor. Upset with the attitude of the United States, both sought ideas on how to secure direct European support.

As they left sooner than the others, I could finally approach an old friend of our family who was a medical doctor and surgeon. He briefed us about his clinic and the "external fixation" technique used to avoid amputation. It seemed that the primitive methodology was practiced some two thousand four hundred years ago. But modern scientists and surgeons, particularly French, Swiss, Belgian, and American, had seriously contemplated about it as a means of repairing broken bones since 1840. Our surgeon friend employed, however, the Gavriil Ilizarov methodology, exercised in the "*four hundred-bed hospital*" in Kabul, where he gained fame under the direction of a renowned Russian specialist. In summary and since bone can be regenerated in the body, metal rings are positioned around a broken limb. Crossing pins that are inserted in the bone keep them firmly attached. The rings are linked at calculated distances with threaded rods and hinges, permitting the movement of the bone fragments without opening the fracture site. Not only can the fragments be fixed in rigid position until complete healing, but practically the totality of lost bones in long organs, caused by fragmented bullets and radically invasive projectiles or shrapnel, can be regenerated. Someone can visualize pulling a piece of chewing gum from both sides with two hands. The link will not be broken even if it is thin and tiny. This is how surgeons do with bone when using the external fixation methodology. Every day, a shattered organ is extended from both sides by a millimeter or so until its complete recovery.

Though the process prevented amputation of limbs, it was very lengthy. Repairing the broken leg or arm of someone in the Soviet Afghan war context could have taken eight months to one year. The doctor had saved the limbs of many people, but to apply the technique on wounded mujahideen or civilians brought from Afghanistan, he required more than five hundred expert surgeons and a gigantic structure. It was unfeasible, impractical, and heavily expensive; he was desperate. On the way back to Switzerland, the images of splintered families, traumatized children, abandoned widows, and hopeless directors of schools or surgeons dominated my thoughts. It was so difficult to enjoy the in-flight services or rest. My heart ached for a ravaged country and its ruined population.

I visited Soraya in her flat located in the artificial island between Donaukanal and the Danube River. She was devastated when scrutinizing the massive pages of drawings and handwritten stories by refugee children. Each recounted and recapitulated veracities of broken lives and tragedies, as well as an outcry for comprehension and compassion. Her tears did not stop for hours while perusing the silent sheets of paper that voiced the desolation of an entire generation of an ill-fated country. She was furious at the destiny of her fellow citizens, who in the course of their history had been repeatedly smashed by invaders and superpowers. Cyrus, Alexander, Britain, and the Soviet Union, who all claimed to be great, proved so miserable at the end. Their magnitude and conquest never lasted, but their misdeeds remained part of an indelible history. Empires have crumpled chiefly because of their continuous transgressions against innocent people, and there was nothing wrong in acknowledging their faults. She was inconsolable.

We opted for a long walk in the alleys of the Augarten park to strategize about the committee's actions for the years to come. Awareness of European public opinion through exhibition of refugee children stories and drawings remained the utmost priority. Soraya considered that supporting the war surgery hospital of the International Committee of the Red Cross (ICRC) in Peshawar, medical treatment of mujahideen and civilians in Western hospitals, securing leadership scholarships for some talented Afghan refugees in Europe in view of molding the future through competent managers, helping those forcibly displaced within Afghanistan through two of the most efficient European humanitarian organizations, and bestowing indispensable aid to the Naheed Shaheed Refugee Girls' School should constitute the basis of the committee's activities. She took charge of negotiations. Though the success of the committee was acknowledged and remarkable, Soraya believed that in the struggle for liberty, there was no time for rest.

Apprehensive of a political stumble by the West in their search for a solution, young members of the committee amplified endeavors in the field of awareness. It was essential to warn friends of Afghanistan and supporters of the mujahideen about the drawbacks of optimistic and foregone conclusions. They labored after university and school classes to print banners, distribute pamphlets or T-shirts, and attend substantive discussions. They were hopeful that their voices would be heard by mujahideen leaders and the Western allies of the Afghan resistance. During short time-outs, some teased Soraya to disregard her favorite Bonnie Tyler song as it was too gloomy and listen to Stevie Wonder's "I Just Called to Say I Love You." The song was the biggest hit of 1984; they exclaimed that they called their motherland to say they loved her! The committee had already gained tremendous respect. Many interlocutors valued the vision, concrete actions, mobilization of volunteers, accountability, honesty, and impartiality of its members.

In October 1984, Soraya convened a working dinner at her place with a senior delegation of the Indian Bharatiya Janata Party (BJP), the most credible opposition to Indira Gandhi's Indian National Congress Party. The weather in Vienna was extremely nice; people still enjoyed their outings. We sat on her terrace on the sixth floor of the building and were stunned by the amazing colors of trees and bushes in Augarten Park. The head of the team was a man of some fifty-five or sixty years of age. He was a charming, knowledgeable, and refined man who had been imprisoned for his political opposition many times. His scrutiny of Gandhi's policy was fascinating. In his judgment, the West shoved India in two circumstances to the Soviet sphere of influence. When the colonial British Empire grasped the resolve of the Indian people and realized that their independence was inevitable, they planned and incited "separation of Hindu and Muslims" to create the state of Pakistan. However, an ample number of the Muslim population remained where they dwelled, and therefore the hostile strategy succeeded only partially. In a second instance, when between 1954 and 1955 the West welcomed Pakistan as a member of the CENTO and SEATO military pacts, both led by the United States and United Kingdom, India was left out and had no choice but to strengthen its bond with the rival body without being a member.

It was dazzling to listen to this mature politician stressing that even if his party came to power, India's stand with respect to international alliances would not change unless the West ended its policy of favoring the rival Pakistan at all costs. However, he criticized the Congress Party's policy to endorse the invasion of Afghanistan and support its hated and rejected regime. He described his mission as reaching to Afghans all around the world. The same evening, the media of the entire world announced the assassination of Indira Gandhi by her two bodyguards. The BJP delegation was frozen and shattered. They desired an end to her reign but not in the way it occurred! The rest of the conversation had to be curtailed. Though the committee members were enthusiastic about such an expression of solidarity by the BJP and expected a change in the Congress Party, the reality did not alter as Mrs. Gandhi was instantly replaced by her son, Rajeev, who sustained the pro-Soviet policy of his mother.

In the spring of 1985, the committee began its annual campaign. The Swiss and European public and local governments were exceptionally caring and generous. Furthermore, Soraya had been fabulous in her endeavor to devise Europe-wide display of children's drawings and accounts in public and private institutions. She secured the assistance of two wonderful women in the United Kingdom and in Switzerland. The British lady was editor in chief of the Central Asian Survey, an official publication of the Society for Central Asian Studies. This think-tank group monitored and scrutinized evolutions in Central Asian and Caucasian Soviet Republics. Her father was a Russian scholar who emigrated to Western Europe in 1924 and lectured in numerous renowned universities. He had an in-depth knowledge of how the Soviet Union was conceived, structured, and upheld as a superpower. For him, their Achilles' heel was Central Asia, due essentially to the fact that its population was Muslim. Communism and the Russian language were imposed by the brutal dictatorship of Stalin. His successors pursued the same policy, subjugating a group of populations in full contradiction of their values.

Soraya befriended rapidly with her; perhaps their affinity with the United Kingdom, particularly Oxford, somehow smoothed their interaction. They both shared the smoking habit as well as analysis and vision about the end of the Soviet Union. Soraya recommended a profound review of the drawings and written stories of refugee children from the "expression of psychopathology" angle. The editor offered to devote a special edition of her Central Asian Survey to this topic. The first step toward intensive years of awareness about atrocities committed in Afghanistan by the Soviet invaders was taken. The second woman, a devoted and dear Swiss friend of Soraya's, championed to coordinate displays of illustrations and narratives.

Soraya led this triangle of dedicated and committed ladies. Though elated by the predictable success of the exhibition, she did not lose sight of the fact that more was required at the international level to push the Soviets toward an unconditional withdrawal. At the same time, she was concerned about the space granted to religious extremism. The majority in the Afghan society observed a tolerant Islam, living side by side with their fellow friends, who were disciples of Hinduism, Sikh, Christianity, or Judaism. As one of the prime routes of the Silk Road, Afghanistan was a melting point of practically all faiths and cultures. The country was not only endowed by its natural beauty, but by the spirit, forbearance, and broadmindedness of its people. She feared, however, that the religious extremism engrained in Pakistan would have serious negative bearing on the many Afghans who were forced to flee to that country. She would often relate the famous Afghan proverb that we may have sought "escape from the rain only to seek refuge under the drainpipe"! The Samanid, Ghaznavid, Seljuqi, Khawarazmi, Ghorid, and Timurid Muslim courts glorified great scientists, philosophers, poets, and architects. None of them used Islamic orthodoxy as an instrument of their policies. However, it became an efficient tool of repression with the advent of the British Empire in the region.

The news of Afghan refugee children's pictures and accounts spread quickly across Europe. Committee members in Norway, Italy, France, Spain, Sweden, and other countries displayed the documents. At the same time, debates were facilitated about the plight of children as well as the past, present, and future of this loved and hated country. It was an extraordinary success already, but Soraya's vision and anticipation was to hold the exhibition in a few politically vital locations. The situation within Afghanistan and in the international arena, however, did not evolve positively in favor of a peaceful settlement of the crisis.

Yuri Andropov, who had replaced the infamous Leonid Brezhnev, was a pure product of the Soviet secret services, the KGB. The Warsaw Pact leaders were not subject anymore to the horrible kiss on their lips. He grasped that the Soviet Union could not win the Afghan war, but he was scared of "pulling the slab" that would bring down the entire Soviet edifice. Andropov favored covert operations, sparing therefore Soviet casualties, and relied heavily on his loyal former counterpart and notorious head of the Afghan KHAD, Mohammad Najibullah. The Soviet leader was a strong advocate of carpet-bombing of Afghan villages and resistance positions.

At the same time, mujahideen commanders obtained more sophisticated weapons against the Soviet flying war machines. By the end of 1985, nearly one hundred fifty bombers, jet fighters, helicopters, and transport aircrafts as well as thousands of tanks were destroyed. Aware of Andropov's war appetency, Charlie Wilson pondered under the Operations Cyclone to equip the Afghan mujahideen with Stinger missiles, a dreadfully efficient anti-aircraft jewel. Coffins of slain soldiers continued to reach Moscow and other major agglomerations of the Soviet Union on a daily basis. Even in such a formidable dictatorship, families and common people inquired why their army was in Afghanistan and their sons and daughters slaughtered.

Andropov and his cabinet desperately searched for a win-win solution. He impelled the secretary-general of the United Nations, Perez de Cuellar, who personally monitored the indirect talks, to unearth a deal. But the West did not heed him and was now confident of cracks within the Soviet political and military apparatuses. No one counted the talks as fruitful anymore. In the country, Babrak Karmal faded like a snow puppy in warm weather. Anahita Ratebzad did not face the so-called Parchami "youth" anymore, she was so ashamed of her creation. The government did not speak of any rights, let alone women's dignity and respect. The only word was *"ashraar"* and how to snare them. Najibullah's KHAD became the center of counterinsurgency as well as the infiltration and killing machinery. He insisted so ferociously on implementing Andropov's strategy that the nickname of "bull" was attributed to him. And perhaps he liked it. The population did not cooperate, though, and bombardments intensified. Pakistan alone hosted five million Afghan refugees. An additional three to four million resided in Iran.

President Ronald Reagan was reelected in November 1984, winning over 97 percent of the electoral and nearly 59 percent of the popular votes, inflicting a most humiliating defeat to Democrats. Afghan mujahideen seemed very happy. Their friend, the man who called them "freedom fighters," was there to help for four more years. But the success on the battlefield hid a bitter political reality, centered on the interests of essentially two big neighbors of Afghanistan. Those commanders who made the difference on the ground distanced themselves from their leadership. The most renowned ones among them, such as Ahmad Shah Massoud or Abdul Haq, openly expressed their dismay and were "sanctioned" by their party's headquarters in Peshawar or *"moqamaat."* It was evident that the theory of surrounding the Soviet Union by religious orthodox regimes had now shifted to a different phase.

The skepticism about a triumphant Islam swelled significantly in the West. Even within Afghanistan, people were scared of extremists taking over. They comprehended that open-minded commanders received less military and humanitarian assistance to the benefit of their more radical and brutal colleagues. No one ever comprehended why the United States and United Kingdom in particular continued supporting Pakistan in its destructive policy in spite of declared and-well understood skepticism toward radical Islamic movements. Soraya expressed her concern on many occasions. "Extremism has now taken the place of fundamentalism! God knows what will happen next, but it will be brutal and bloody," she used to say.

The committee now attended practically all congregations in support of Afghan resistance in Europe. In an event in Florence, where the so-called moderate mujahideen leaders and the former king Zaher Shah had assembled, the attention was focused on known personalities and what they harangued. As usual, dozens of people ran up and down serving or expressing admiration for the highest in the hierarchy. It was Soraya's first direct encounter with part of the mujahideen bigwigs. None of the "gurus of jihad and religion" had a precise idea about the future. They all put the charge on God, underlining that the Almighty would take care of everything once the Soviets were out. She, however, pointed at a young man, Hamid Karzai, and stated, "We have to watch the evolution of this gentleman carefully. His intervention was above the red line traced for mujahideen by Pakistan. And it was certainly for a purpose!"

The Florence event did not produce any tangible results. Not at all inclusive, it was tailored to favor the former King Zaher Shah and the so-called moderate mujahideen groups. It looked more like a social gathering and shopping opportunity for those who were tired of the dusty environment of Peshawar. Mr. Karzai seemed to navigate well among them. Though it was futile, the committee nevertheless followed the evolution of and focused on the outcome of the indirect talks.

After one of the sessions that took place in Vienna, a group of "Pakistani scholars" desired to meet with some of the committee members for an exchange of views. A special room was reserved in the famous Steirereck Restaurant at the Stadtpark. Soraya and I were accompanied by two other members. At the onset, it was clear that we did not face scholars but a few senior military officers, perhaps from the ISI. In the course of discussion, an obvious animosity and frustration toward India and its support to the communist regime in Afghanistan was evident. In their view, not only should their country be able to challenge their nemesis in Kashmir and Afghanistan, but also on the nuclear ground. They described the moderate mujahideen groups as redundant and incompetent but judged the extremists as "reliable." They manifested an undeniable backing toward Golboddin Hekmatyar and an indescribable hostility regarding Commander Ahmad Shah Massoud. On numerous occasions, they referred to "an incentive" for Pakistan's stand against the Soviet Union. The territorial integrity of their country and a post-Soviet mujahideen government of their choice in Afghanistan seemed nonnegotiable. It became crystal clear that Pakistan desired to get worldwide praise and credit for itself alone in case of a possible Soviet defeat by Afghans. Moreover, they considered themselves as regents of a post-Soviet Afghanistan and openly campaigned in Western countries for that purpose. For some committee members, Pakistan still had an existential trauma, and possession of nuclear weapons as well as domination of a weak neighbor gave them the required tangible assurance. Those Afghan mujahideen principals or commanders who declared independence from the mighty ISI would face a tragic fate.

Two months later, we met again with the so-called moderate mujahideen leaders in Oslo, where for the first time, proof of use of chemical warfare by the Red Army in Afghanistan was disclosed publicly. There were women among the victims who had certainly been encouraged by the Norwegians to come out of their shells and describe their ordeals. Soraya strongly suggested their inclusion in mujahideen delegations that traveled extensively abroad to campaign for the liberation and independence of their country. Even in their mind-sets, no meaningful place and role was accorded to women in shaping the future of Afghanistan. The vision dictated by extremist movements had traumatized others, and there was nothing any reasonable person could do. Soraya seemed thoughtful and anxious. She looked philosophical and to some degree phlegmatic.

"The Soviets will leave Afghanistan for sure," she claimed. "But tragedy will persist. I am afraid of the beams of bullets and cannons that mujahideen would fire on each other."

Most were amazed. Some in the meeting room seemed optimistic. Her concern was not the commitment and honesty of foreign countries. The uncertainties lay with the mujahideen leadership and the madness of the ISI to offer the "Afghan throne" to the most radical of them. From moderate to the most extremist Islamic regime, schemes were on the drawing board for the future of Afghanistan, depending on who expressed their opinion. However, no one knew what a future implied. For the committee members, there was no other alternative except to intensify advocacy with the expectation that their voice would be heard.

Soraya picked a number of the children's drawings and stories. While psychoanalysis of these artworks and their publication required time, organizing exhibitions in the most symbolically prestigious locations constituted an important step. She wanted the first such display to convey a strong message to the international community in general and friends of Afghanistan in particular that the Afghan tragedy would not end with the withdrawal of the Red Army. After ample discussion and final agreement with the city of Geneva, the display took place in October 1986 at the *"Palais de l'Athénée,"* in exactly the same room where 123 years earlier in the same month, the first Red Cross Convention was signed. The dedication of Afghan and Swiss women was exceptional and certainly a major reason for a success that became the precursor of many other such advocacy events in Europe.

It was clearly a unique initiative to see the horrors of Afghan war through the eyes of children. The government and politicians, as well as diplomatic and humanitarian communities, were represented at their highest levels. To raise the devastating corollaries of an unjust war enforced by a superpower on the helpless population of a country in the same room where the Geneva Conventions were rooted was emotionally and evocatively charged and rewarding. Soraya had carefully drafted and crafted the declaration of the committee. It contained three important messages. The first point insisted on the human and material tolls of the war as well as the loss of a generation and the necessity to form future leaders. The second point alluded to the uncertain events upcoming and the need for friends of Afghanistan to remain engaged for a long period even after the Soviet withdrawal, not only to reconstruct properly but also to prevent internal clashes and conflicts. The third point warned that fundamentalism had been transformed into extremism, and in the absence of preventive measures, the success of defeating the Red Army in Afghanistan would change into a disappointing failure marked by terror and violence. Though exceptional acclaim was expressed over the committee's declaration, it produced little effect on decision makers as "business as usual" continued on its track. The conclusion was manifest. Soviet defeat was deemed more important than safeguarding a stable and peaceful future for the people of Afghanistan. And mujahideen leaders had opted for silence!

At the same time, there were talks about a sketch for the future in some unofficial circles that looked worrisome as it calked the past structures. Scholars as well as political affiliates began to argue about it. The stand of the committee was well-defined and based on social, ethnic, and linguistic morphologies of the country. All members were of the opinion that a post-Soviet Afghanistan must be grounded on equal rights for all citizens, irrespective of their number, religious belief, ethnic affiliation, or any other political, economic, or social criteria. The rationale was in accordance with the Holy Book, confirming that *"indeed, the most noble of [mankind] in the sight of God was the most righteous [person],"* implying commitment, fairness, studiousness, hard work, and honesty on the part of those who led the struggle and decided about the destiny of the people. Soraya was of the view that circumventing the blunders of former regimes was an indispensable element for the foundation of any future project. For the peoples of Afghanistan to equally enjoy their basic claims, to contribute to the stability of their country, and to effectively form a nation, she advised careful review of history and considered that a decentralized political structure should be studied among viable options.

The so-called "Iron Amir" of Afghanistan forcibly relocated massive numbers of people within the country during his two decades' reign to secure dominance of one ethnic group and impose a centralized system. However, by doing so, he only fostered further division and discontent, the ramifications of which resonated to this day. It may have been a cheap version of the divide and rule policy inspired by his colonial British protectors. Stalin implemented the deadly idea to its perfection later on in the Soviet Union. The amir's hostility toward the Hazara population caused unforgivable discrimination against this stranded portion of the inhabitants in the central parts of the country. Unfortunately, his heirs, including the enlightened Amanullah Khan, made no tangible effort to change the disgraceful policy. For profoundly rational reasons, giving the choice to the people of each province or state to decide about their local concerns would guarantee a better and balanced future for Afghanistan.

On each occasion, the examples of the United States, Germany, and Switzerland, where cooperation and complicity between local and central governments provided the foundations for all to flourish, were provided as proven realities. In debates, some did not hesitate to tag the committee members as being "too Swiss" or "too Austrian." However, in an environment overshadowed entirely by defeat of a foe, such deliberations seemed futile. The unfriendly policy of alliance with the Soviet Union played by the India of Indira Gandhi, the distrust of the West toward an Islamic Iran, and Central Asian states conquered by the communist titan did not bequeath any space for other neighbors of Afghanistan except Pakistan to enact a meaningful role for their future, which for most Afghans was then very troublesome. Aware of the ISI's policies, some commanders were more determined to assert the right of Afghans over their Islamic future. Even among them, though, the interpretation varied. The eternal rivalry between the two oil-rich Islamic countries of Iran and Saudi Arabia, each claiming religious leadership of the Muslim world, had its direct effect in Afghanistan and offered few options for a united front.

At the beginning of 1987, Soraya met in Vienna with the president of the Swiss National Assembly and urged him to host the exhibition of Afghan refugee children's drawings and accounts within the "*Palais Fédéral*"—the federal palace in Bern, the capital of Switzerland. The edifice housed the federal parliament and government of the country. It is the heart of effective neutrality, good governance, and reaching to people's needs. The request was politically challenging. But ignoring the Soviet atrocities in Afghanistan was also a redline for the distinguished statesman. Though not yet a member of the United Nations, Switzerland hosted its European headquarters and could face the fury of the Soviet Union, a permanent member of the Security Council. Definitely the resolution to hold an event of this nature, slamming a war led by a superpower, could not be taken lightly. Soraya shone once again in her negotiations. In March 1987, the cries of children were lauded at the "*Palais Fédéral*" through a great exhibition of their illustrations and stories.

The occasion was exceptional in its own way, as no event criticizing the acts of a member state of the august world body had been allowed in the past. The Afghan and Swiss women were at the forefront of the action. Federal ministers, members of both chambers, ambassadors, high government officials, distinguished scholars, and many other concerned people attended the event. The opportunity was auspicious to assert the three main points noted in the "*Palais de l'Athénée*" and advise that a neutral, landlocked, mountainous, and diverse country such as Afghanistan, situated in the heart of Asia, had many common denominators with Switzerland and that mujahideen leaders must be encouraged to learn from the country of "Guillaume Wilhelm Tell." The president of the Swiss National Assembly offered his country's willingness to assist Afghans forge a governing structure that would suit all components of the country in the future.

While the committee received expressions of admiration for the "exceptional event," yet again no concrete attention was paid to the substance of its proposals by the United States and United Kingdom, the two kingmakers for the region. The doctor who performed external fixation surgery in Peshawar attended the event as a witness and received a warm welcome from Swiss and Austrian medical institutions. While the proposal for a decentralized or federal Afghanistan was brushed aside, a triangular fight among the radical and moderate Islamic movements and devotees of former king Zaher Shah began. Circles and groups emerged in support of one or the other, revealing again the profound division about a common future. Most committee members felt that the voice of the majority was suppressed and that double-dealings of concerned Afghan and foreign makers and shakers would lead to a chaotic situation. I voyaged again to Pakistan in the summer of 1987 to evaluate the latest developments in and around Afghanistan.

In Pakistan, the entire intellectual community conversed of a tragedy for women. Meena Keshwar Kamal, founder of the Revolutionary Association of the Women of Afghanistan (RAWA), was gunned down in Quetta three months earlier. She was an intellectual from her prime age and an unflagging advocate of women's rights. Under the communists, she established RAWA and edited a magazine to promote the rights of women against the pretentious and deceitful propaganda of the regime as well as misdeeds of a culture that was robbed of its essence and taken out of context. In exile in Pakistan, she persisted tirelessly to pursue her objective. Who had cowardly assassinated this voice of Afghan women may perhaps never be revealed, but she was on the wanted list of both mujahideen extremists and the KHAD of the Kabul regime. Her denunciation of Hekmatyar-CIA strong ties particularly annoyed the Pakistani authorities. Soraya was appalled at the suppression of women's voice, irrespective of their political opinions or social affiliation.

Even for those who sought emancipation within their cultural and religious scopes, Meena's murder was an unforgivable crime. Soraya had encountered her several times in Kabul. Although they did not share political opinions, not only was Soraya stunned by the clarity of Meena's thoughts, but she was impressed by the courage of the young advocate. They both agreed on what was imperatively required to improve the plight of girls in rural and urban areas of the country. Meena's death was a poisonous knife in the spine of all Afghan women. Her short-lived life resembled a Shakespearian tragedy as her husband had been assassinated hardly three months earlier by extremists who received unimpeded protection and support from the host country.

This trip to Pakistan was certainly most significant in terms of comprehending different dynamics related to the follow-up of the Soviet withdrawal. In addition to the usual courtesy meetings, Hussein's impromptu calls to my hotel and even room, and visits of refugee camps, schools, and clinics, three extraordinary and important episodes, perhaps linked to each other, occurred.

One of my cousins who was a commander was wounded in his right leg but remained in the country. I proposed treatment outside Pakistan, preferably in Switzerland, Sweden, or Austria. He refused due to vital antagonism with another cousin, though from the same mujahideen movement. As a lame commander, not only was he inefficient, but he put the lives of "his men" at jeopardy. What was then so important, and why was there such a fracture and rift between two friends and family members? It soon appeared that it was the wish of "*moqamaat*" all over Afghanistan to oppose decision makers against their fellow companions, thus preventing a united front of mujahideen just at the most crucial moment. It was a sickening, depressing, and disappointing reality for the Afghan resistance!

On a Thursday, when offices were closed, a friend recommended an "exceptional visit" far outside Peshawar. In his four-wheel-drive car, there were three heavily armed bodyguards in the back row and two Kalashnikov guns between the driver and passenger seats. He drove himself and laughingly stressed that there might be need for use of the weapons. At the outskirts of the city on the road to Khyber Pass, there was a checkpoint, and the Pakistani officers stopped the car. It was part of a routine procedure. One of the officers came forward and queried if we had knowledge of the notice board. He was not concerned at all by armed men and guns in the car. On the plank, it was inscribed in bold letters that passers penetrated the tribal area and by doing so assumed responsibility for their own security and safety. We plunged ahead some two hours, attaining a sort of semiarid zone with huge mud houses and stopping in front of a gigantic structure. The security guards were unusually alert. One dashed and saluted with the customary Afghan smile, while others had fingers on the triggers of their light machine guns. He urged us to wait for the "boss" to come out.

Minutes later, a middle-aged man came out, greeted my friend respectfully, and virtually summoned us in. At the view of my camera, his face changed. With a leaden voice, he notified me that making photos was strictly prohibited by "*moqamaat.*" Suspicion occupied my mind. In conversation while entering the building, I grasped from his accent that he originated from the same area of Afghanistan as my family and knew my cousin commanders. This helped as he finally conceded to my request to take pictures provided I did not display or use them. There were hundreds of teenagers busy with the "art of war" in a rudimentary manner. They jumped, crossed fires, shot, and practiced all sorts of guerilla techniques. I inquired if the children attended school and were taught language, mathematics, geography, history, chemistry, and other curriculum subjects. The "boss" giggled rowdily, underlining that the boys were war orphans and education as per my understanding was not a priority. He confirmed that there were dozens of such "institutions" all over Pakistan and his job was to train as many fighters as possible. I was petrified. Suddenly my body commenced shivering. I had heard this earlier from young and traumatized Afghan refugee pupils. There would then be tens of thousands of combatants in the "market." How can someone envisage a healthy future for Afghanistan when its youth would not know anything else except fighting and killing? Much later, I was convinced that it was the beginning of the creation of the Taliban. Nobody noticed or did anything but close their eyes! Back in my hotel room and devastated, I could not eat or sleep. For a moment, I thought about a horrific post-Soviet Afghanistan and its consequences on the population.

The next day, I went again to the tribal area to visit my friend and former classmate Mirwais, who had meanwhile become a commander of his native Wardak. We had not met for ten years, and the encounter was most candid and friendly. He had graduated from the Kabul Engineering Faculty but joined the mujahideen group instantly. He offered the same picture as my two cousins. Division, mistrust, and confusion were cultivated among mujahideen commanders and community leaders in Afghanistan. Love for wealth, power, and territorial gain that had deeply gangrened the mujahideen ranks further worsened the interfactional rivalries. The "*moqamaat*" naturally exploited each given situation to their maximum advantage. He was short of identifying the true masterminds of such disarray among the mujahideen and impugned the Soviet Union and the communist regime.

Upon arrival in Peshawar full of dust, I desired to take a shower before dinner. My phone resonated repeatedly, and the receptionist alerted me that many armed men were approaching my room. He was horribly worried. I rushed back to put on my dirty shirt and heard at the same moment a clatter behind my door. They knocked; I opened, and indeed many armed men were standing in the corridor. A slim, middle-size man with a reasonable beard and white turban entered, accompanied by three heavily equipped bodyguards. As per Afghan tradition, I offered him to sit down and asked whether he desired green or black tea. His answer was placid.

"No, thank you. I have come to take you home for dinner," he explained.

"Well, sir, please have a *chai*, tea, first," I hesitantly replied.

"Oh, you do not know me. I am Jalaluddin Haqani, commander of the Khost region. Let us go," he suggested.

Indeed, I had heard of him. He was one of those radical commanders who received significant support from Pakistan and the United States. A recipient of the first convoys of Man-Portable Air-Defense System FIM-92 Stinger missiles, he countered the Soviet Operation Magistral and managed an amazing cave fortress in the Tora Bora Mountains along the Pakistani border. There were rumors that not only had he disposed of tanks in his caves, but even helicopters and aircrafts. Wrong or right, he was the man who fought the Soviets in the South with significant Western military support; he was the commander that all mujahideen leaders feared. The unknown question was the basis for such generosity toward him. Other valorous commanders from the same mujahideen movement were not given such a prominence by the "*moqamaat.*"

At dinner, he asked about the visit to the "school" the day before. It was surprising that he designated as such a religious guerilla training facility. Intellectually, school is a sacred place, where pupils learn the knowledge of understanding their creator, nature, environment, and relationship that ties them with others. Definitely he did not expect an unknown guest to his "*madrasa,*" and it was evident that his anxiety surrounded the use of facts I observed. To my advantage, he did not seem to be aware of the pictures I had taken. For once and contrary to my habit, I played the role of an ignorant person and tried to answer his questions in the most dim-witted manner possible. When reassured, he then submitted a wish list for Khost, such as repair of the road, construction of a clinic, and so on. Not only was it my first and last encounter with a man who became the founder of the notorious Haqani terrorist network, but it gave me a full understanding of the defiance that awaited Afghanistan once the Soviet Union withdrew.

A few days later, I encountered in his office outside the city of Peshawar the mujahideen leader who was much favored by the ISI and the Pakistani political bigwigs. He had an unpleasant face, deep eyes, and a pronounced nose. The discussion started in a candid manner, which continued until I inquired about his plans for the future of Afghanistan when the Soviet Union withdrew. To my astonishment, he began a virulent attack on what he named "so-called educated people and intellectuals" and charged them with enjoying European and American lifestyles, drinking alcohol, and spending time in nightclubs, but expecting prominent roles in the future of the country. He waffled about whether there would be a place for them in a future Islamic Afghanistan. It was shocking. Contrary to Afghan cultural ethics, he did not demonstrate any consideration to me, his visitor, or to the committee members, who were also Western-educated Afghans but deeply involved in the struggle against the communist regime and Soviet occupation. He sustained his harangue for nearly an hour, lecturing how magnificent Afghanistan would be under his stewardship and how great a nation it would become after the Soviets were routed. I had no choice but to remain mute and listen. When finally out of his premises, I jumped in a rickshaw and constantly eyed behind me until Peshawar. I lived the rest of the day in fear of being arrested, imprisoned, or even killed by his men.

Before I departed for Europe, Soraya wanted me to visit the International Committee of the Red Cross (ICRC) surgical hospital in Peshawar. It was, perhaps, the largest such institution in the world, operating on dozens of war-wounded every day. The atmosphere was different. Humanity, dignity, humility, respect for life, and reaching out to the destitute composed the essence of staff thoughts and acts. Devoted surgeons, doctors, nurses, and technical staff had only the well-being of their patients in mind and how to reduce their suffering. Everything was so smooth and organized. Had it not been for the hot weather and gigantic tents, someone would have thought they were in Europe. There were several surgery pavilions, and doctors received, diagnosed, helped, and operated tireless hours day and night. The Soviet strategy had its toll. The shrapnel bullets, butterfly and land mines, and other booby traps caused irreparable fractures. Victims were countless men, women, and too-young individuals. The establishment had four main departments of surgery, tetraplegic, recovery, and artificial limb fabrication. It was agonizing to witness a surgery, as over nine out of ten patients reached the hospital already in desperate and gangrenous condition. The surgeons had no alternative but to cut off the dead member with a saw, like a carpenter slicing and chopping a piece of wood.

In the course of my tour, I encountered a young and very handsome thirteen-year-old boy, Omer Khan. He was wounded by a green parrot or butterfly mine in Kunar Province. He too arrived late, and his leg had to be amputated. Before his operation, he was smiling and reassuring his mother that he would be fine. His story was similar to those of tens of thousands of children. They were hit by this inhuman device because of their innocence and curiosity. They found themselves in front of a green, funny object on or next to the road, in their fields or house yards. As soon as they touched it with their hands or feet, the limb was depleted with an explosion. I was permitted to witness his surgery. It lasted some two hours, and the cut had to be exercised at his upper knee level. I vomited so much due to the noise of the saw and the brutality of metallic instruments working with bone.

The Swiss surgeon put his hand on my shoulder and said, "It was tough for you, but he will survive. Otherwise he would have perished of gangrene."

Omer Khan was lucky, as his native Kunar was near the border. Some attained the ICRC hospital with very little hope of survival. I remained next to him until he woke up. His mother had tears of joy; she had known that Omer was condemned. His reawakening was sorrowful, but the boy was dauntless. As soon as he noticed me next to him, he ignored his discomfort and behaved like a gladiator. It was striking at his young age! Later on, the "Story of Omer Khan" turned into a famous ICRC documentary.

The visit to the tetraplegic department, however, was agonizing. It was the most heartrending area. Practically all patients were young men and a few women. They were struck by bullets or shrapnel at the level of their neck or upper body spine, most probably intentionally to cause irreparable bodily harm and suffering. Independent of any reason invoked, no army in the world has the right to commit systematic annihilation of an entire population; even the severest of wars have rules! All the patients seemed poleaxed on the beds; they could not move at all. Frequently the nurse adjusted their position to avoid keloid scars or feed the patient. Occasionally they were tied up to their beds, put in an upright position, and taken for a "walk."

A mother of some fifty or fifty-five years of age approached and took my head firmly into her chest. "God left me with only him," she said. "He was injured. Now his wounds have completely healed, but he cannot move! Why? He should come home with me. You are my son too. Please ask these foreigners what is wrong with my boy," she urged.

Perhaps even the doctors and nurses did not have the heart to render her hopeless. She did not comprehend that her son would never walk again and, like a piece of meat, would lie and die on a bed. How

340

horrendous would it be for a mother to bear this tragedy for the rest of her life, an existence that was already shattered by the killing of her husband and daughter? Tears were not enough to appease the sorrow of these mothers; only their resilience would. Again, the burden of war levied by the Soviet Union and the consequences of their brutality were on women. Their husbands and adult sons joined the mujahideen, appearing occasionally in the middle of the night to give a kiss on everybody's forehead and leave hurriedly. But women did everything else. Indeed, Afghan society was similar to the prides of lions. While leaving the ICRC hospital, I wondered how many victims of this war were confined within Afghanistan and could not make it to hospitals in neighboring countries. There might be a day when this war would come to an end, but at what cost in human suffering?

As Soraya had foretold, the crisis had indeed swung from fundamentalism to extremism, and with the training of countless orphan children to the art of killing, bombing, and burning, another phase of terror and mass killing would inevitably take place in Afghanistan. The similarity with the French Revolution was striking. Jacobins removed the Girondins from the scene by instating an era of terror. Would mujahideen groups face the same fate?

In the same summer of 1987, we opted to initiate a leadership scholarship program across Europe, launch a public awareness campaign during the Geneva International Festival that took place every year in the first week of August, and cross the ocean to take our concerns to the United States. Soraya recommended that key messages should be communicated to massive numbers of visitors during the festivities in Geneva. Balloons and T-shirts were suggested as appropriate vehicles. Within hours, tens of thousands of flying couriers appeared in the sky of the "*Suisse Romande*" and French "*Haute Savoie*" with slogans such as "Soviets out of Afghanistan," "Equal Rights for All," "Be Mindful of Uncertain Futures," and so on. A sizable number landed as far as 150 to 200 kilometers away in different Swiss cantons and in France. At the same time, thousands of individuals received colorful sweaters with the same messages and Afghan flags. That year, the whole city had embraced Afghanistan and its cause. The success of the initiative was boundless.

A month later, Soraya and I traveled to Washington, DC, to sound the alarm about the increasing militancy in Pakistani *madrasas* and future challenges for Afghanistan. We disembarked at Dulles International Airport. Our first encounter was with Senator Claiborne Pell, one of the finest American politicians, who chaired the United States Senate Committee on Foreign Relations. We both had perceived the impressive Capitol Building from a distance, but had never been inside. It was imposing and inspiring. Its cupola gave a majestic dimension to it. Dozens of people were rushing up and down as if there was an emergency somewhere. It was in sharp contrast with what we had observed in Switzerland or Austria, where people had time for others and daily matters seemed to have a slow pace. Though guides were all over to assist, with a glance it appeared obvious that the Senate was in the North Wing, just opposite to the House of Representatives. Everything was spotless and shining. We had a sense of visiting the *Taj Mahal* of the United States of America. While we were still admiring the gigantic mural pictures, a young man introduced himself as an assistant of the Senator. We trailed him in the long corridors and observed the vigor of all these young people, who enthused in different directions.

The Senator received us gently. He gazed at Soraya for a while and was surely stunned by her elegance. Perhaps he expected a different portrayal. His remarkable and tender look, sparking intelligence and fatherly approach gave us confidence at once. He had knowledge of what we did in the committee. The discussion quickly turned around the main topic of post-Soviet Afghanistan. He judiciously listened and indeed was alarmed to learn that a generation of young Afghans was in the making in remote areas of Pakistan with extreme ideology, acquaintance of warfare, and uncertain repercussions. He acknowledged that the Soviet defeat required careful preparation and that Afghanistan would not face peace at once after a decade of ferocious and multidimensional conflict. He was petrified with the number of casualties, use of deadly chemical and conventional weapons, land mines and booby traps, and shrapnel bullets and carpet-bombing of villages. He was concerned about the social burden of millions of amputated and paralyzed individuals. The legacy of the Soviet invasion and occupation of Afghanistan was not only a totally ravaged country and populations, but also the indelible scars that it would leave behind, needing decades to deal with.

It was a delight to speak with someone who understood every word we pronounced and the emotions behind them. In his view, the problem with policy and politics in the Western countries lay with the term of legislative or executive elections, which were in principle between four to five years. He praised the Nordic countries for their political stability, but Switzerland in particular for its "Magic Formula," whereby the first four political parties that make in general more than 90 percent of the vote form a "Government for All," with opposition parties within the same administration. He also highlighted that the Swiss example was unique and that in other democratic societies, including his own, the legislative pillar of the state contradicted the executive on more than half of the occasions, particularly if they represented opposing political parties. He acknowledged that as a Democratic Senator and due to the fact that the Republicans governed, he could only do advocacy and convey our message to his fellow Senators, but due to the importance of the matters raised and their direct implications for the peace and security of mankind, he would try to facilitate immediate meetings with the most concerned individuals in the House and executive bodies.

Within minutes, our program for the rest of the day was defined. We moved to the South Wing to meet Congressman Charlie Wilson. He had a gigantic office, full of his pictures on the wall. Most were taken with Afghan mujahideen either in Pakistan or perhaps within

Afghanistan. In some, he was dressed as an Afghan, with a turban or "*pacole*," the hat used by the legendary Commander Ahmad Shah Massoud. Indeed, there was a significant number of young female assistants. The office looked very busy, with an implacable order as if human beings had been computerized. Both the serenity of the Senator's office and the dynamism of the Congressman's team were unique in their own way. We did not wait long!

A huge gentleman loomed, inviting us inside. He had an attractive appearance and was dressed in a gray suit, with suspenders around his shoulders. While walking alongside us, his assistants continued rushing and asking questions. He was a master of clarity. Short and precise answers pounded every now and then. He looked like a military commander, who aspired respect and admiration of those who worked for him. We noted his authority over issues raised as well as his warm and collegial approach toward his staff. He honestly looked like a friend. Green tea and some Afghan almond sweets were already on the table. He, too, knew what the committee did in support of those who fought the Soviets. "You have impressed and frightened Senator Pell!" he stated. "He asked me to receive you immediately. This does not happen every day. What, then, is so important?" he inquired.

Soraya presented an excellent overview of ongoing and possible future challenges in Afghanistan. The absence of unity among mujahideen leaders and commanders, the interference of Pakistan and Iran, as well as the lack of a comprehensive program for the future of the country were identified as major hurdles. But she considered that extremist teachings and combat training to thousands of Afghan children and adolescents in remote parts of Pakistan was most harmful. Afghanistan needed an open-minded and healthy future generation. Taking up her theory, I articulated serious concern about the shift from fundamentalism to extremism and warned that, if measures were not taken, the trend might end up in an internal war in Afghanistan, where terrorism and devastation would rule with uncalculated effects. He immediately grasped our skepticism! We stressed that Pakistan's endeavor of fracturing the mujahideen into pieces was a sorrowful reality. At the same time, it opened the door for Iran to enter the race for controlling the future of Afghanistan.

He listened profoundly, then stood up and pulled his suspenders repeatedly. He did not seem annoyed by what we had underscored but rather puzzled what to reply. His hesitation was noticeable, as if he knew something that he did not want to reveal. He took a few steps in his office and turned around, stressing softly but firmly that in each political, social, military, and economic enterprise, doers established priorities. According to him, the mother of priorities in Afghanistan was the withdrawal of Soviet troops, and our concerns constituted issues that would be dealt with once the mujahideen took over. It was most disappointing! How could such a bright person undermine our intelligence? For a while, I thought it was abuse of authority—but then I realized what Soraya often reminded us: that states blindly pursue their interest at the expense of others. Nevertheless, we would have expected a different response.

From there, we were taken straight to the Department of State. Initially we met a central official in the Office of Intelligence and Research. She was located in the basement, with dozens or perhaps hundreds of machines throwing out pieces of paper instantly that were then collected, scrutinized, and dispatched to God knows where. The speed of the action was astounding. Hundreds of people were busy, working like machines. The automation of acts performed reminded me of the "*Modern Times*" of Charlie Chaplin. I admired the patience and resilience of those who repeated the same act dozens of times an hour without getting exasperated. She was an extremely candid woman, listened carefully, and took extensive notes without engaging in an exchange.

We were then steered to the fourth floor for our last meeting. A gentleman of some fifty years of age emerged and sat on the desk, swinging his legs. This was extremely irritating as it reflected a lack of decency toward visitors. While Soraya had the courtesy to remain seated and keep her composure, I stood up as an indication of our dismay; the remaining part of our conversation happened with me standing. He was the top man dealing with Afghan issues in the executive branch of the government. He had been briefed on our meetings, referred to Congressman Charlie Wilson, and underscored that the United States government was committed to accompany Afghanistan in its path to democracy, but only once the Soviet Union withdrew. He did not refute the presence of hundreds of "schools," now known as "*madrasas*," but felt we were amplifying the potential threats that they would pose in the future. He alluded to having a different picture from the visiting mujahideen leaders or their own experts of Afghan origin who assisted them either in the field or through their "intellectual" contributions. In the course of the exchange, we were recurrently reminded that they were a superpower and had their own resource bank, having the same background and knowledge as we did. We were upset. Something did not function properly. An in-depth dissertation on post-Soviet Afghanistan was even compulsory. The euphoria of thrashing and humiliating the Soviet Union overruled any assumption about calamity that was developing. It was impossible to place a motion on other priorities.

The committee members faced a period of emotional depression and moral disappointment. In such circumstances, Soraya received books from some members as a sign of recognition of her just views and deep thoughts. They served as the best tranquilizer. The strongest supporter of liberty for Afghanistan did not want to see the wolves behind the door! Understandably, extreme right movements were defied and even confronted by the West. Why the radical religious entities who plotted an awful future for Ronald Reagan's "freedom fighters" did not matter. Soraya was the engine to alter pessimism into positive energy. She negotiated with renowned Swiss, Swedish, and Austrian institutions to begin a program of forming future leaders for Afghanistan. As a pilot phase, the committee recommended thirty students, ten in each country, hoping that half of them would be young refugee women. Such an important project could not be realized outside the scope and vision of the mujahideen. Soraya carefully followed developments relative to a series of seminars that some intellectuals had initiated in Peshawar about the "Islamic Future of Afghanistan." This was the opportune moment to offer leadership training in Europe for future movers and shakers.

The committee also expected a clear-cut description of what exactly mujahideen leaders desired in a post-Soviet era. She was in touch with her friend and colleague Professor Bahaouddin Majrooh, who in spite of all odds had resolved to establish an Afghan Information Center in Peshawar. The mere fact that free thinkers could stay in Pakistan and even engage in a series of deliberations to determine the future and how to prepare the fitting structures was a tremendous positive step. Mr. Suri was a friend and colleague of Mr. Majrooh's father. They were minister and ambassador at the same period of Afghan history. Soraya respected Bahaouddin, though he seemed an unequivocal advocate for the return of the former king, Zaher Shah. He too had studied philosophy but preferred academic engagement to politics and diplomacy. She had exchanges with him and seemed optimistic about unearthing suitable candidates for the training program. She urged me to travel again in spring 1988 to Peshawar, discuss with Professor Majrooh and mujahideen leaders, organize the suitability exams, and select the most suitable candidates.

But on Thursday, February 11, 1988, when offices formally closed business in Peshawar, Professor Majrooh returned home after a long day of hard work. He had a simple lunch before getting back to his books as he had to write an article for the next bulletin of his center. The guard announced that some visitors would like to see him. He had no choice but to receive them as his presence at home had been confirmed. Hours later, he was found dead, brutally and cowardly murdered. There was little known about how it happened. But he was no more. Who killed him and for what motivation will

347

probably remain a mystery. The news of his death at the beginning of a weekend shocked the skeleton Afghan intellectual community in Pakistan and all of us abroad. He knew the challenges and confronted them bravely. But enemies of liberty and pluralism decided to put an end to his voice and existence. Soraya was appalled. Nobody believed that criminals would go that far. He had no gun, no armed men, no money, and did not pose any threat. Her conclusion was that extremists were more afraid of the power of expression and he would not be the last one to perish.

Just weeks before his demise, Soraya had secured his authorization that the committee use an extract of his book *Ego-Monster* for the publication of the refugee children's drawings in a special edition of the Central Asian Survey. She felt terribly sad. His brutal murder demonstrated again the unwelcoming environment of Pakistan for Afghan free thinkers and intellectuals. Majrooh's killing dissuaded others to pursue open discussion on what the Islamic future of Afghanistan meant. A strangling atmosphere reigned, and uncertainty about a viable future gained more momentum. In spite of numerous pleas and meetings with mujahideen leaders, we could only secure six candidates and no women among the beneficiaries for the leadership training. It was indeed disheartening. Even those considered most moderate opted against women. Soraya was furious. When it came to marketing their image, they highlighted publicly how great our foremothers were. But in real terms, the masochist thoughts would take much longer to disappear from Afghan society. The appalling aspect was that they put all the blame for their misdeeds and discrimination on Islam!

In the international arena, Mikhail Gorbachev, who had taken control of the Soviet Union since March 1985, laid down the foundation of several major policy shifts. After securing power, he concluded that Afghanistan was a lost cause for the Soviet Union, and the sooner the Red Army left this slough and graveyard of superpowers, the better for his regime. He did not trust Babrak Karmal, who shared views and horrible kisses with Leonid Brezhnev. A change of leadership in Kabul became a priority of his government. Realizing the cracks within the Soviet Empire, he opted for a more conciliatory policy toward the West. Did he want to prolong the life of the communist giant or put an end to the most renowned dictatorship? Views diverge. However, with leaders of Ronald Reagan and Margaret Thatcher caliber, he found the right interlocutors to avoid a clash and negotiate the plan of "an honorable" withdrawal from Afghanistan. His "*perestroika—* listen" and "*glasnost*—openness" movement gained notoriety within the iron-shielded Soviet political and military apparatuses.

Perhaps leaders, generals, and marshals knew that the end of the Soviet Union was close. Indeed, the Reagan-Thatcher-Gorbachev triangle worked well. Already in 1988, it was understood that the indirect talks would now come up with something that constituted the basis for the Soviet withdrawal, leaving Afghanistan's future at the mercy of its mighty neighbors Pakistan and Iran. The West focused on strategizing the softest way for dismantlement of the Soviet Union and the Warsaw Pact, as well as the integration of Eastern Europe into the European Union. Gorbachev was in hurry to uncover a new and cooperative leadership in Afghanistan as soon as possible. Their man in Kabul, Babrak Karmal, had disappointed and flunked miserably. The promises under his "Fundamental Principles" strategy did not materialize, except the change of flag. With Soviet troops in the country, none trusted him and his revolutionary thoughts. When Gorbachev briefed the Soviet Politburo, he stressed that "If we don't change approaches [and evacuate Afghanistan], we will be fighting there for another twenty or thirty years … The main reason that there has been no national consolidation so far is that Comrade [Babrak] Karmal is hoping to continue sitting in Kabul with our help."

This was the first time that a world leader spoke implicitly of the necessity of nationhood in Afghanistan. Perhaps he wished to draw attention to the Achilles' heel of the country. The change became inevitable. His pick to substitute for the incompetent Karmal was

349

the one that his predecessor Andropov had identified and relied on, Mohammad Najibullah, the merciless and brutal Head of the KHAD. Under his rule, the killing machine of the Kabul communist regime bloated from a few hundred secret agents to nearly thirty thousand. In his reign over the KGB for over fifteen years, Andropov knew Najibullah very well. They had developed together the execution policy on the eve of the Soviet invasion of Afghanistan. Terrorist acts under this loyal servant of the Soviet Union against common citizens, mujahideen, intellectuals, traders, and students had reached its peak. Contrary to Afghan tradition, he instructed imprisonment, interrogation, torture, and killing of women by KHAD, in particular students. The fear of women as vehicles of information sharing between mujahideen and the population had goaded him to this insanity. Cruel, ruthless, and loyal to the Soviet Union, he was able to adapt quickly to any given situation and present the face of an angel if the situation required it.

In ancestral and pure Afghan tradition, women were sacred. The notion of the motherland, mother tongue, and other highly venerated expressions originated from this status. But they always paid unbearable costs to be holders of such "noble prestige." The communist regime had crossed another barrier of intolerance. Contrary to King Amanullah Khan, who wanted to emancipate them in a conservative society, under communists they were abused and misused in the name of an ideology that was not theirs. Najibullah steered for years the repression machinery of a regime that the people rejected. He had served as Andropov's prime adviser in the policy of carpet-bombing of Afghanistan. As a strongman, he was the right pick to replace the flabby Karmal. Leaving Afghanistan in his hands would delay a takeover by mujahideen, even if the Red Army withdrew. The new master of Afghanistan grasped the Soviet plan to vacate his country. He opted to implement Karmal's "fundamental principles" and engaged in a policy of openness toward Pakistan and reconciliation with mujahideen. But it was too late, as the Soviet Union dismantlement process had already begun.

Amid such developments, aggravated by Washington's stand, most Afghans, abroad or within the country, were disillusioned. The committee members wished to give up. But Soraya quoted Martin Luther King Jr. to galvanize them: *"Our lives begin to end the day we become silent about things that matter."*

She advised that the committee tale its advocacy into the heart of the old continent, centering on the Council of Europe and the European Parliament. With the assistance of some Swiss and Austrian politicians, she could secure encounters with two of the most illustrious French politicians, human rights advocates, and resistance figures, Jacques Baumel and Simone Veil. They were icons of freedom in Europe.

A medical doctor and Gaullist of the prime times, Mr. Baumel was a resistance figure who fought the Vichy regime and Nazi occupation. He led the "Combat" resistance group in the south of France before becoming the secretary general of the United Resistance Movement of his country. Omnipresent at the summit of French politics since 1945, he inspired generations of post-World War II French youth. He greeted Soraya and me in his office of Palais Bourbon. From the first instant, we realized his admiration for the Afghan mujahideen, particularly Ahmad Shah Massoud, who reminded him of his own struggle against a repressive regime and foreign occupants of France. He acknowledged that the end of the Soviet Union was too close to help the mujahideen leaders if they did not already have a common understanding and plan for the future of their country. He was frank to underline that in case of Soviet disintegration, the priority of the West would be to save Eastern Europe, politically, socially, and economically. Mr. Baumel recognized that military training of thousands of young "orphans" presented a serious concern for the future of Afghanistan and the region, but the key to the solution lay in the corridors of politics in Washington and London.

Soraya fascinated him. This was the first time he had met an Afghan woman with such grace, talent, sophistication, and intelligence. He

351

too was embittered by the lack of space for women in any future smattered about by mujahideen movements. Soraya enforced that it was time to raise the voice of reason as the indirect talks had nearly reached a concluding point. The Afghan actors for a takeover from the communists had already declared themselves. In addition to the two mujahideen trends in Pakistan, supporters of King Zaher Shah had persuaded some capitals that he had a role to play in the future of his country, but Pakistan did not see the solution in the same manner and opposed the idea. The Iran-based mujahideen groups did not seem to weigh much. The concern of the committee was not so much who would rule Afghanistan in the future, but rather what political framework and type of government structure would be put in place. Would Afghanistan be democratic? Would women enjoy their basic rights? Would discrimination disappear? Would the government have an all-inclusive nature? The list was long, and Soraya was vocal about it. Moreover, she did not shy from cautioning of a serious uncertainty should the West assign control of post-communist and post-Soviet Afghanistan to its neighbors alone. She was certain that external factors, such as the dispute over the Durand Line, the Indo-Pakistan rivalry, the Kashmir issue, the isolation of Iran, and the strong influence of Gulf extreme Islamic views, as well as internal hurdles such as the lack of unity of mujahideen groups and their unpreparedness to take over, were impediments for a peaceful future. The deliberation was delightful with this profound man who had taken part in shaping France as a major player in Europe and in the world.

Our meeting with one of the greatest ladies of Europe, Simone Veil, was unforgettable. For Soraya she was an example of resilience, resistance, hard work, determination, and achievement. She received us at home, located in the seventh arrondissement of Paris. Her life story was intertwined with the greatest tragedy of our time, the Holocaust. A survivor of the Auschwitz-Birkenau concentration camp and Nazi barbarism and killing machinery, she had succeeded in demonstrating the failure of dictatorship, extremism, and hatred.

Gorgeously dressed, she was shining and beautiful. A huge number of people waited to meet her. It was recognized that she had an open-door policy. Her smile, gentleness, and allure were remarkable.

Being in the company of two of the most fascinating women whom I valued profoundly was exceptional. I knew one personally for having worked with and engaged in the purest struggle for the independence of our native land and the other through books, newspapers, friends, and the history of Europe. These two distinguished ladies had so much in common. They looked their interlocutors straight in the eyes. Their determination and self-confidence demonstrated their ability to handle any matter. They were fashionable, attentive, and attractive. It was absorbing to see them exchange views. I had hardly ever before seen such a mesmerizing scene. They agreed on practically every single item, particularly the uncertain future of the country and the plight of its women. She too envisaged a major role for Ahmad Shah Massoud in the future of Afghanistan; he was admired. She found him honest, efficient, charismatic, and close to his fighters. The Soviet Union had attempted to capture all major commanders across the country, but each one of them had foiled the invader's plans. In the first five and a half years of their occupation of Afghanistan, they launched nine unsuccessful offensives to capture the Panjshir Valley and Massoud. Such flagrant failures resonated the end of the Red Army.

The two French friends of Afghanistan offered to organize the children's drawing exhibition in a European Parliament gathering in Strasbourg. Soraya was most delighted. It coincided with the conclusion of the indirect talks and a road map for Soviet withdrawal from Afghanistan. The occasion was propitious once again to advocate for the right solution, a long-term engagement of friends of Afghanistan, and highlight the defiance ahead, particularly the lack of understanding among key movements and figures that threatened the future of the whole region. The date of the exhibition loomed at the last day of the 1988 summer session, and Mrs. Veil committed to address the event personally.

Soraya, her daughter Selina, a number of young members of the committee, and I arrived in Strasbourg during a pleasant sunny day. Our hosts took us to one of the most iconic buildings in Europe, the Kammerzell House, a medieval edifice, most ornate and admirably well preserved. Built around 1420 in the same area of the Holy Roman Empire, it is located in the northwest side of one of the most prestigious religious edifices of Europe, the Notre Dame Cathedral of Strasbourg. The city has been the symbol of division and unity in Europe. Between 362 and the modern era, it was governed by clergy, France, Germany, France again, Germany a second time, and finally France since the end of the Second World War. It is perhaps the only place in the world that the population revolted against their religious rulers, and after the Battle of Hausbergen in 1262, it became a free imperial city. But Strasbourg's recent history was all about the unity of Europe, its peoples, cultures, and languages. It is a perfect example of the harmony in diversity that Europe is all about. In our discussions, Soraya highlighted many common aspects of this city with her war-torn Afghanistan. Obviously it could also be a relevant example that Afghan leaders could consider to build their country. The city is a jewel of architecture.

The dinner at the Kammerzell was candid. Several key Parliament members surrounded us. They wanted to "hear the different story" that we desired to recount, and Soraya was exceptionally forthright. The event was very special as the presidents of the European Parliament, Baron Plumb and his wife, joined us to urge for an Afghanistan where all citizens would have equal rights and chances to serve, where finally women would find their right place in the society, and where religious beliefs would embody their true values of tolerance, acceptance of others, and respect for diversity. After all, we knew that doubt had been cast on the overoptimistic vision of Congressman Charlie Wilson and the United States administration.

Europe seemed receptive of our ideas but did not weigh much from the military and financial aid perspectives. However, some politicians may have opted for proactive advocacy efforts as a few months later we were again invited to Strasburg to expose the Afghan children's concerns to the larger member states of the "old continent" during a session of the Council of Europe.

Soraya had meanwhile become a registrar of Webster University in Vienna. Working in a prestigious academic institution was a great relief. She was the reference expert on Central and Southwest Asia too. Students appreciated her attitude and willingness to help. Meanwhile, the indirect talks had concluded, and the Soviet combat troops were already on their way home from the hell that Brezhnev had thrown them into. It was planned to be completed by February of the year after.

All statements delivered at the occasion were carefully scrutinized to get a sense of what Reagan, Gorbachev, and Thatcher had agreed upon. The official versions were all euphoric. The United States' George Schultz considered that "history has been made" and believed that the cause of the agony of the Afghan people was "the Soviet military occupation of Afghanistan." The Soviet Union's Eduard Shevardnadze deemed that "only irresponsible political figures can ignore, reject, or violate the norms and principles of the settlement." The United Nations' Perez de Cuellar judged the agreement "a major stride" and was "confident that the signatories will abide fully by the letter and spirit of the texts and that they will implement them in good faith." President Reagan called Gorbachev to congratulate him for a courageous decision to formally withdraw from Afghanistan. What neither Schultz nor de Cuellar admitted was the protection and immunity they would grant to some figures of the communist regime who in principle should have faced justice. Nearly ten million refugees, about two million decedents and bruised, and hundreds of thousands of disabled and paralyzed, as well as millions of forcibly displaced and otherwise affected populations, demanded

355

accountability and justice, without which there would be no peace, prosperity, security, and serenity back in the country.

Together with the withdrawal of the Soviet Army from Afghanistan, the countdown of its disintegration had logically begun. As of that day, design and control of the future of Afghanistan was left totally to Pakistan. A new chapter of tragedy was in the process of being opened in the history of this slain country. The implacable General Zia had attained all his three objectives. He had enriched his country and disposed of the key to the Afghan crisis solution in his pocket. His country meanwhile developed nuclear weapons without the international community exercising the proper monitoring, which would have prevented proliferation. And he had been able to create a deadly extremist layer to fight and sacrifice themselves in Kashmir, Afghanistan, or elsewhere for the safeguard of Pakistan's interest. While the Soviet invasion and the role played by the United States and their closest partners were smartly manipulated by General Zia, unfortunately on the Afghan side there was no leader who could inspire unity and a joint vision for the future post-Soviet era.

But the mighty man of Pakistan was no more needed. The rules of the game had changed. On August 17, 1988, his aircraft, a C-130B Hercules, crashed. There seemed to be tangible reasons to believe that it was shot down by his own creation. Politics in dictatorship was indeed a hard challenge, even at the summit of the hierarchy! The general who hanged his predecessor in spite of local, national, regional, and internal pleas and who sponsored foundation of the first terrorist group in Kashmir, Harakatul Mujahideen, in the mid 1980s was downed himself mercilessly. His killers did not even spare Arnold Raphel, the United States Ambassador to Pakistan, who perished with him in the same incident. The truthfulness of the expression "who dug the tomb was in the grave" applied to all dictators of the developing world.

General Zia's death was also not good news for the mujahideen and Afghanistan. Most committee members were of the opinion that while his human rights records were devastatingly shameful, he had nonetheless forged a trustworthy relationship with the mujahideen leaders over a decade and a strategy for the future of Afghanistan. He could have imposed some sort of unity among them even if it was in the interest of Pakistan. The ISI had a different perception and needed to get rid of their strongman. They desired weak and corrupt individuals at the realm of authority in both countries. They could be better manipulated, blackmailed, and ordered around. An independent Afghanistan, ruled by "freedom fighters" of the world, was not acceptable. The imaginary threat of the revival of the disputed Durand Line loomed in their minds. It was tragic that neither the mujahideen circles nor dignitaries around King Zaher Shah had a real grasp of what awaited to happen in Afghanistan. The euphoria of "beating the Soviet Union" had mesmerized all concerned.

At least, the withdrawal of Soviet troops proceeded without a hurdle. Once again, an invading superpower was forced to withdraw in humiliation and defeat. The mighty Red Army, with their sophisticated weaponry, was overcome by a freedom-loving people who stood up valiantly for their motherland. Mujahideen commanders, including Ahmad Shah Massoud, whom they wished to capture and kill for nearly a decade, demonstrated their class and agreed not to attack them in their defeat. They were allowed to cross the Salang Tunnel safely and go home. The fight of the mujahideen was with invaders, not with those who brought their tails down and surrendered.

The year 1989 was a busy one for the West. By the end of February, all Soviet troops withdrew from Afghanistan, and initiatives to declare the Afghan war a mistake were ongoing in Moscow. The United States prepared the post-Reagan era and was deeply involved in election campaigns. The Round Table Talks in Poland between the government and Solidarność had already paved the way not only for the first free election in the country but also for liberation of

Eastern European nations from the claws of the communist giant. The pressure was also growing on Erich Honecker, the East German leader and the man Brezhnev loved to kiss on the lips, to abandon the ship. For most observers, this artificial country was the "slab" that Gorbachev did not wish to remove. But it was already dislocated, and its total detachment was only a matter of time. Finally, the Berlin Wall, the shameful edifice that separated families, friends, and a nation for decades, was cracking.

While the election of President George H. W. Bush gave much needed assurance to the mujahideen, the collapse of the Berlin Wall on November 9, 1989, defined a new reality for the West in general and Europe in particular. It construed and defined the fall of the Soviet Empire and pushed Afghanistan further into the jaws of the ISI. Surprisingly, the young and inexperienced Benazir Bhutto, who became prime minister of Pakistan in December 1988, increased financial and military support to the extremist training camps. She ignored totally that Afghan women would be the prime victims of her policy. Najibullah's offers of national unity tumbled into deaf ears. Extremist movements gained momentum, and ISI officers, the "*moqamaat*," partook directly in the combat fields within Afghanistan alongside their protégés. The so-called government-in-exile of the mujahideen soon proved dysfunctional and unrealistic, so much so that the ideological and political divide seemed profound among diverse groups.

With political and military developments in Europe and in the Middle East, Afghanistan was no longer a priority for the West. The invasion of Kuwait by Saddam Hussein on August 2, 1990, constituted an additional catastrophe for the Muslim world and the beginning of the end for the strongman of Baghdad. The West was horrified, and the wraith of life without oil paralyzed thoughts of politicians and industry leaders. Saddam's act was as unlawful as his venture of engaging in a dreadful war with Iran in September 1980. However, this time the world retorted, and condemnations showered from all around. At the same time, German reunification on October 3, 1990, was the prelude to the collapse of the Soviet Empire. Europe and Gorbachev did not want a scenario spoken about by Héléne Carrère d'Encausse and opted for an evolution rather than a second revolution. Priorities of Western countries were logically defined for decades to come. They centered around two major issues of controlling production of oil wherever in the world and ensuring a silky dismantlement of the Soviet Union, coupled with absorption of as many countries as possible of the Warsaw Pact to European institutions and the North Atlantic Treaty Organization (NATO).

In Pakistan, the two giant families of Bhutto and Sharif had begun their iconic confrontation and rivalry for power. None of them sympathized with and favored a strong, peaceful, and independent Afghanistan next to their boundaries. The support to extremist groups accentuated at the expense of the government-in-exile of the mujahideen and other national figures inside Afghanistan. Golboddin Hekmatyar was clearly the preferred mujahideen leader of the "*moqamaat.*" He had to take over the realm of power in Kabul.

In October 1990, the forty most charismatic and resourceful Afghan commanders from all around the country and affiliations met in northern Pakistan, away from the much controlled and monitored Peshawar, to overtly articulate their unity for a strong and independent Afghanistan and denounce Pakistan's prejudice, trusting that their Western allies, particularly Americans, would discern their stance and hear their voice. It was a futile exercise as no one cared about this gathering. History was in a rush, and events of the greatest importance for the future of the West occurred successively.

John Major replaced Margaret Thatcher as if she did not appreciate partnering with anyone else other than the much liked Ronald Reagan. In January 1991 and under Operation Desert Shield, some five hundred thousand American soldiers were placed in Saudi Arabia. Days after, an international coalition, led by the United

States, launched Operation Desert Storm and struck Saddam Hussein and his so-called invincible army. Within a few weeks, the notorious mustached was on his knees. His army appeared stranded in its own strongholds. They were massacred in the deserts of Al Basra and Al Muthanna, and the Kuwait monarchy was reestablished. Saddam himself became a paper tiger and ridiculed. He owed his survival and life to a difference of opinion between Americans and French. But a new design for an oil-rich Middle East and North Africa became the mother of priorities.

In May 1991, a horrendous event occurred in India that should have drawn the immediate attention of decision and policy makers as well as strategists in the West. During an election campaign, Rajeev Gandhi tragically faced the fate of his mother. He was blown up publicly by a Tamil female suicide bomber with at least twenty-five more individuals. It was perhaps the first mass killing by kamikaze bombing, which later became the trademark of modern terrorism. The world in general, but intelligence networks in particular, should have given due attention to this tragedy and engaged in eradicating the practice. Alas, it became a routine tool to inflict mass murder on societies, peoples, and governments. Nobody felt concerned about the technique used, as a few months later, Gorbachev notified President Bush and Prime Minister Major that he would disassemble the shaky house of communism. Indeed, on December 26, 1991, exactly twelve years to the day after having invaded and occupied Afghanistan, with shameful crimes committed by their army and security forces, the Soviet Union died forever.

In March 1992, the Afghan communist President Mohammad Najubullah declared that he would step down. Rumors of an agreement with Golboddin Hekmatyar to hand over power loomed. Furthermore, experts and governments discerned plans of heavy bombardment of Kabul by his movement, with participation and guidance of the "*moqamaat.*" It seemed that preparative was on their drawing board since early 1990. Pakistan aimed at fulfilling their outstanding objective of having a regime and leader of their choice in Kabul. Though not much documented, such an ambition certainly prompted Iran to intervene in defense of their interest too. At the same time, it was amateurish not to believe that the new Russian Federation was not concerned about safeguarding the Central Asian boundaries from extremists, a gauge for their own safety. The scenario of an ensuing conflict of regional dimensions was discernible. The "freedom fighters" of Ronald Reagan were forgotten. Western countries seemed senseless, and Russians mocked them.

Soraya recommended another journey to Pakistan, which we considered a last attempt to raise the voice of reason. Meanwhile, the leadership training program of the committee had also failed, as none of the candidates wished to return to Pakistan or Afghanistan, fearing for their lives.

I landed one last time in Peshawar at the end of March 1992. The atmosphere was infested by the dismantlement of the superpower that had inflicted so much misery to Afghans. Everybody seemed confused in their vision of a future. In a meeting with a mujahideen leader, one of his most trusted aides indicated that he had dreamed about him to be on the back of a Pegasus leading millions of refugees back home. I could not retain my laughter. It was obviously fabricated to obtain a favor. In the Islamic tradition, it is believed that a Pegasus took only the Prophet of Islam on the night of his ascension. Similar stories teemed in encounters of leaders with their disciples. The dream of riding a Pegasus toward Kabul infatuated all of them and their lieutenants. Western diplomats and of course Pakistani authorities shared the same optimism. There was an absolute denial of accord for a takeover between Golboddin Hekmatyar and Mohammad Najibullah. The vast majority did not know, some had heard but did not pay attention, and a few who had knowledge did not dare touch the topic for fear of assassination. Refugees prepared to leave Pakistan, and partial demolition of some camps had already began.

One evening, I had joined a small group of friends when a messenger arrived from the Panjshir Valley, announcing that Commander Ahmad Shah Massoud was in the last stages of his groundwork to move to Kabul; it was a matter of days, not even weeks. The apparent rationale was to abort the agreed-upon takeover brokered by Pakistan. Expressions of jubilation lasted for long. I lingered silent. The host inquired the motives for my contemplation.

"Well, moving to and capturing Kabul may certainly be easier at this juncture compared to keeping it safe and peaceful," I stated.

"You are too pessimistic, '*andiwal*,' my friend," he said. "All will be fine. Insha-allah."

I had heard this many times, and it was never fine. I used the opportunity and inquired about a few specifics. The answers were vague, phlegmatic, and optimistic. In reality, the race against time had started for the conquest of Kabul between Pakistan's ISI and commanders within the country who did not desire the upper hands of yet other foreigners.

Massoud's sympathizers did not see who could defy him. He was the lion whose roar was enough to scare his enemies. All responsibilities were put on his shoulders. He was the superman who would conquer Kabul and bring safety, security, prosperity, stability, and a bright future to the country and all its inhabitants after decades of destruction and killings. It was too much of a burden for one person! The clash was inevitable. Experts seemed puzzled by the game that Najibullah played. Why did he not negotiate his resignation with the so-called government-in-exile of the mujahideen but favor only one? Did he want a bloodbath in Afghanistan? Did he opt for an ethnically preferential deal? A man who ran the ruthless secret services for over a decade was so naïve as not to comprehend what his deal meant for the country and its peoples? Some of his lieutenants already negotiated their betrayal to the communist revolution that they ferociously imposed by killing, torturing, and mutilating perhaps millions of innocent children, women, and men. They were given protection in some countries. Others, more intelligent, even secured impressive jobs in the international arena instead of being prosecuted. The Russian Federation of Gorbachev did not want any one of them in its territory. It then looked like Najibullah's game was to save his own skin.

My thoughts were with commanders inside the country and the trap ahead. They had fought for an ideal future, free of violence and subjugation. Their actions and charisma were lauded by all. Their independence had often infuriated some foreigners. They had been inspirational for the people they defended. And now they faced a much bigger challenge than confronting the Soviet army. They would be forced to face each other, open fire, and even kill. Ethnic, linguistic, and religious drives in Afghanistan had not been addressed. And there was no united vision for the future of the country. The madness to grab power at all costs loomed much closer. On May 15, 1992, the communist regime of Mohammad Najibullah collapsed. Though Hekmatyar forces entered Kabul at the same time, Massoud's men outnumbered their rivals. Najibullah desperately attempted to escape shamelessly, like a beaten dog with its tail in between its legs, but was apprehended. His plot did not materialize. At his request, he was taken to the United Nations and remained on their premises with special treatment. Massoud handed over power less than two weeks later to the coalition of mujahideen leaders but regrettably remained as minister of defense. The unanswered question was whether he made a mistake by doing so. Opinions will always remain divided.

Chapter 6

Disappointing Free Afghanistan and the Dark Years of the Taliban Rule

Woman is a ray [of the beauty] of God. She is not that earthly beloved—she is creative, you may say that she is not created.

—Mawlana Rumi,
The Book of Mathnawi

Most experts believed that Golboddin Hekmatyar, confident of the ISI's deal with Mohammad Najibullah, dreamed on sound ground to be the sole owner of the crown in Kabul. However, it appeared that while some of the communist leader's handiest lieutenants who belonged to the Khalq faction backed him boundlessly in this venture, those of Parcham obedience sold him out and disclosed details of the plot to Massoud's liaison officers. It was defined as perfidy toward a man who had all along betrayed his own population. A few even joined the mujahideen. At the same time, leaders in Peshawar had gathered to finally negotiate a political agreement on the immediate future of Afghanistan. Massoud, in an attempt to persuade his adversary not to act alone, communicated with him by radio.

Massoud began, "The Kabul regime is ready to surrender, so instead of fighting we should gather.... The leaders are meeting in Peshawar.... Respective troops should not enter Kabul. They should enter later on as part of the government."

Hekmatyar countered, "We will march into Kabul with our naked swords. No one can stop us.... Why should we meet the leaders?"

Massoud replied, "It seems to me that you do not want to join the leaders in Peshawar nor stop your threat, and you are planning to enter Kabul.... In that case I must defend the people."

Indeed, both rushed to the capital city, but Hekmatyar and his followers retreated to the south of Kabul. They were outclassed by more seasoned mujahideen under Massoud's command. The issue was not about aptness of any given commander or mujahideen leader to lead the country. Nor was it about the unfairness of a mighty neighbor or a foreign benefactor of the Afghan resistance. Unfortunately, it was a defining instant for a second calamity in the country, perpetrators of which were "freedom fighters." Unforgivable crimes were committed along ethnic divides and in the name of "religious convictions." The doomed country that had never witnessed peace since 1978 continued to be the theater of a different and new "great game."

In accordance with the April 24, 1992, Peshawar Peace and Power-Sharing Agreement among Pakistan-based mujahideen leaders that Hekmatyar did not sign, each one had to serve for a period of two months as interim president while the premiership was assumed by a different movement. The formula would last till a new constitution was drafted and elections held. A clear order for assuming power had been agreed upon. The idea was to ensure that mujahideen of all political and religious sensitivities assumed joint leadership of the country till a clear choice of the people was made through ballots. The agreement was born in a rush and at a very late stage of history. After Ahmad Shah Massoud's triumphal entry into Kabul, which the ISI considered a serious defeat in their endeavor to conquer Afghanistan, those who dreamed of riding on the back of a Pegasus saw their glorious fantasia changing into reality.

The sprint to Kabul reminded one of the gold rush era in the United States and the unforgettable Charlie Chaplin movie. Everybody had one direction, Kabul; one objective, grab the power; and one expectation, keep it forever. For most committee members, it was

365

utopian to believe that mujahideen kingpins would value a civilized agreement. Since the late 1970s when they settled in neighboring countries, seeds of fear and discord were sowed among them, preferential treatment was provided, and at many junctures they were used against each other to safeguard foreign interests. The core challenge was division and even hatred among a group of people who, in a collegial manner, were supposed to take Afghanistan to peace, stability, and prosperity. Some did not see any logic behind the deal and dreaded obvious clashes at some point. The only positive element of the puzzle was recognition of the new mujahideen government by the international community. Soraya hoped for delay in occurrence of the horror so that people could forge at least their own mind and way out.

Conscious of the defeat of his country in capturing Kabul, the son of General Zia-Ul-Haq, with the connivance of Saudi Arabia, arranged a meeting of last chance between Hekmatyar and Massoud near Kabul on May 25, 1992. Indeed and contrary to Soraya's prayer, bombardment of Kabul by Golboddin Hekmatyar's extremist group began the same day. This was the start of fratricidal clashes between rival mujahideen groups that lasted till the takeover of power by the Taliban. Hostile and opposing coalitions were composed. Plots of some to endure in power or others to eradicate rivals were put in motion. The plea of many commanders for the respect of the Peshawar agreement on a collegial mujahideen leadership and disarmament of armed groups was de facto rejected. The smell of powder and the noise of deadly weapons with devastating effects were already feared at all corners. The extremists did not even let the first interim president finish his two-month term. Assault on Kabul from the southern outskirts of the city was ferocious. Hundreds or perhaps thousands of rockets fell in various areas of the capital, destroying houses and murdering innocent women, men, and children. The circumstance demonstrated not only the fragility of the accord among mujahideen leaders but also the firm determination of a neighbor of

Afghanistan to have their man and team in command of the country, irrespective of casualties.

Amid such tension and strain, the Iran-based mujahideen groups, who had never been given prominence due to the isolation of the Islamic Republic by the West, claimed a power-sharing deal. Each day, matters became more complicated. Even some of those who effectively wanted an independent Afghanistan unwillingly dawdled essentially along ethnic lines. They became de facto interlocked in a shameful intermujahideen conflict. A few months later, Kabul was encircled by numerous armed groups. Some were strappingly reinforced by regional powers. The Wahhabi faction controlled west of the city; the Shia movement ruled in the southwest area of Kabul; and the Uzbek militia, led by the notorious General Rashid Dostom, accused to serious violations of human rights, occupied the strategic area of the airport, while Hekmatyar maintained his assault from the south. Massoud and his forces commanded in central and northern parts of the city in defense of what they claimed to be the legitimate government and its recognition by the international community. Some obviously served alien interests. All tussled for survival.

It was a chaotic situation that could be described as military feudalism. Despite the prompt interference of neighbors in a country that was already at agony, the international view remained apathetic and senseless. The ISI-backed extremists shuffled unreservedly to and acquired weapons and supplies from Pakistan. Rumors about provision routes from Iran to the Shia movements spread quickly, while the Wahhabi fighters received massive cash from Saudi Arabia and the Persian Gulf emirates. The capital city of Afghanistan looked like a bloodstained, poisonous cake for which power-hungry chieftains battled mercilessly. While the United States, United Kingdom, Germany, and some other countries had bolted from their embassies much earlier, the rest of the Western countries extracted their diplomatic staff as of August 1992, putting an end to their direct monitoring of events.

Instead of pressuring external and internal actors to strike an honest peace deal, incongruously Kabul was left in the hands of heavily armed "freedom fighters" who began to clash with each other in a "free Afghanistan." At the same time and amid shelling of the capital city day and night, the so-called unity of mujahideen groups dried up, and fear of further clashes in other parts of the country loomed on the horizon. Doubt hovered over the minds of those who believed that their efforts and sacrifices would secure a shattered but united and peaceful Afghanistan. Their ideals of a free, independent, egalitarian country were far from realization. With uncalculated collateral damage on civilians, some were now bogged down in a situation that would compel use of force against opposing armed groups, most of whom had earnestly tussled with the Soviet Union. Did they fancy it? Certainly not! Did they bemoan it? Undoubtedly yes!

The Massoud-Hekmatyar rivalry, which had separated them in the 1970s over ideological and ethnic considerations, resumed once again in Afghanistan. All his life Massoud had been within the country, reaching the population's needs to the best of his ability, while Hekmatyar preferred a secure existence in Pakistan. But behind this enmity that dominated the years to come, there was much more to unearth. They diverged in interpretation of Islam and the Islamic future of Afghanistan. Of course, a moderate religion, open to all, was practiced in the country. But years of communist abuse and indoctrination of young Afghans in Pakistani madrasas had changed the dogma and power game. The extremists were much better equipped and received unlimited funding from a variety of sources.

Under normal circumstances and in any society where democracy is in effect, the people would decide about their future. However, exercise of democratic choice lasted only ten years in Afghanistan (between 1964 and 1973), not enough to be rooted as standard practice. Moreover, the populations were exhausted by fourteen years of Daoud Khan's heavy-handed regime and communist dictatorship.

In such a situation, the power of guns and violence dictated the rules of the game. The disputes also depicted the discomfort of part of the population toward a past that they considered discriminatory and unjust, as well as the determination of others to maintain the status quo at all costs and keep the ruling of the country in hand. As with all unfinished wars, facts would disinter much later. It was known that with instigation of the "*moqamaat*," Americans, particularly the CIA, did not favor Massoud and his vision for an independent and free Afghanistan. It is recounted that during the intensive bombing of Kabul, he even considered withdrawing from the capital for his rival to put an end to his folly. It was too late.

At the same time, there was a strong possibility of tragic events that could occur once his men and he left the scene. There was a unanimous opinion that the extremists who continued to bomb the capital would instantaneously slaughter a sizable number of inhabitants on religious and ethnic grounds and move on to the north. Those surrounding the commander recapped for him the deplorable destiny of Amir Habibullah Kalakani and countless people in the north who perished under similar circumstances by the horde of King Zaher Shah's father. None desired the same to happen again and were determined to stand and defend their position at all costs. The dirty aspect of politics in Afghanistan has been constant change of alliances and the eagerness of most politicians and rulers to possess more wealth and power. These chronic weaknesses have been exploited by adversaries to dominate the country directly or indirectly. They have also caused more casualties among innocent civilian populations during conflicts.

Amid the reigning tension, a "national council" decided to extend the interim period of the governing team to two years, infuriating all other movements. Poor areas of Kabul continued to be targets of blind rocket shelling. Tens of thousands hurried in different corners in search of safety with their small children hanging around their necks and others on their backs. Disintegrated human bodies were strewed on the roads and in houses. Families had no time to bury

369

their loved ones. The situation appeared tense in other parts of the country, where diverse mujahideen groups dominated smaller or larger portions of the territory or community of people. But none of them had the upper hand over the vast majority of Afghanistan.

The governing team quickly comprehended that the foundation of an all-inclusive Afghanistan was already in the process of being destroyed. The success of Ronald Reagan's "freedom fighters" was unacceptable for regional powers; it had to be discredited at all costs and the notion of Afghan nationhood buried forever. A huge portion of the population was disillusioned by the West in general, but Americans more specifically. After "winning the Cold War," as described by the *Wall Street Journal*, Afghan mujahideen and Afghanistan deserved a better future and an honest engagement of their friends to assist them in making at least a united and peaceful nation. A surprising fact was that Charlie Wilson was nowhere to be seen. The man who regularly dispatched senior CIA officers to meet with and assure the extremists of their support had vanished. His remorsefulness or joy would never be known to public opinion. Relinquishing Afghan affairs to the ISI, the CIA provided a golden opportunity not only for other regional powers but more specifically for Osama bin Laden to enter the new "great game." His notorious terrorist organization, al-Qaida, founded in 1988, was dramatically strengthened. He had money and could buy as many chieftains and warriors as he wished. His hatred for Massoud and admiration for Hekmatyar were known to all intelligence services. What was left of the Afghan mujahideen government had no choice except to urge Europe to avert and prevent foreign interference in Afghanistan's internal concerns.

One evening in Geneva, I had returned from the monthly meeting of the committee. My telephone rang. I picked up the phone, and a known voice was heard.

"This is Fazel Ahmad," he informed me. I am in the embassy and do not see you. Where are you?"

This was my friend. We had lived on the same street in Wassel Abad of Kabul and shared a bodybuilding hobby with two other buddies. We sauntered to school and returned together, listened to the love story of our other friend endlessly, consoled him that good days were ahead of him, and watched Indian classic movies, even in dirty theaters such as Pamir, Behzad, or Mirwais cinemas. Vyjayanthimala and Dilip Kumar were our favorite actors; we relished observing them on the screen and never missed any of their pictures. Often in the summer we ended up consuming a wonderful ice cream or "*zhala*," a mixture of snow and rice vermicelli perfumed with sugarcane syrup, in one of the coffee shops in the central town. In the winter, we dashed home to be warmer around stoves full of embers or visited our other friend whose love was now promised to a rival. Depressed and glum, he frequently and understandably played mandolin and sang sad songs. We vainly devoted hours to cheering him. Fazel's father was a very decent and loyal army colonel, and his three brothers were younger than he. As the heir of the family, he bore major responsibilities at an early age. He had opted to study medicine. We had not been in touch since the communist coup d'état of April 1978 as he vanished from Kabul and joined Commander Ahmad Shah Massoud. He quickly became Massoud's deputy, on whom he relied totally and unconditionally.

The phone call was an unprecedented surprise and delight for me. His voice was the same. I was impatient to meet him too; he kindly offered to reach me at home for a friendly chat and recollection of old memories. Indeed, he came alone, only accompanied by a colleague and mutual friend in spite of heavy security measures that the Swiss authorities had undertaken. I alerted Soraya and invited her to join us; the opportunity was unique.

Fazel commenced from the start of his encounter with the young Massoud at Kabul Polytechnic during the troubled period of Afghan democracy in the 1970s. They both shared political opinions and struggle methodology. From the first instant, he was captivated by the handsome, slim sophomore with a wide forehead and massive hair, who believed that force was not equivalent or proportional to numbers but depended on combat tactics and strategy as well as the judicious use of the means at one's disposal. A few years later, he attained the Panjshir Valley when Massoud had only a handful of poorly armed and ill-trained fighters. He became Massoud's greatest relief and most trusted friend, confidant, and ally.

For hours, he spoke of the commander, a fascinating person who had more values than people realized or witnessed. In love with literature, Massoud always hand carried a book or two to read on the peaks of mountains, from where he targeted communist and later on Soviet convoys. Whenever his fighters came in desperation to report about an impossible action, his answer was always "*chera namesha*"—why can't it be done? It was a different way to advise, "yes, we can." He explained the sorrow of the entire population of Panjshir when Massoud was injured in September 1980 and described how he was taken to the peaks of Pamir on the back of a mule for safety. Fazel treated him and was surprised how quickly he recovered to take back command of his men. Fazel described the relationship of Massoud and the ISI as nonexistent.

It was enthralling to listen to a man who had been with the greatest figure of Afghan resistance, the renowned commander who defeated the Soviets on each and every occasion that they tried to eradicate him. For Fazel, Massoud was a friend, brother, companion, leader, and soul. He could not breathe without him and claimed that years of following his steps on muddy roads, deep and profound valleys, rock-strewn mountains, and furious riverbanks had been a wonderful addiction. He certainly did not exaggerate and elucidated their defense strategy for every Soviet endeavor to enter the valley. They never gunned down those who surrendered and took prisoners now and then. Amer Saheb, his nickname, ordered to feed and treat them well. As a medical doctor, he emotionally spoke of the times of desolation when there was not even a painkiller to give to someone who had lost a leg or an arm or no ability to reach trapped civilians and save them from heavy and indiscriminate bombardments.

The great commander's ingenuity was how to survive when there seemed to be no outlet. His lieutenants thought of *"chera namesha"* before referring a matter to him. He was surrounded by enemies such as the communist regime and the Red Army, the ISI and al-Qaida, rival groups and even individuals within his own team during the entire period of his struggle for the independence of his country. But on each occasion he found a way to neutralize them and strike back.

Fazel expounded at length on Massoud's dilemma with Hekmatyar, who received the biggest share of international aid and continued to shell Kabul from Char-Asiab, the southern outskirts of the city. Their differences were ideological, tactical, and moral, but not personal, despite rumors of an assassination plot of the commander by his foe. Initially in the 1970s, they both stood against Daoud Khan and his notorious coup d'état but soon diverged as the ISI started to interfere. While Massoud refused Pakistan's patronage and returned to the mountains of the Panjshir Valley, Hekmatyar was comfortably established in Peshawar and given the liberty to have a practical government-in-exile. He confirmed that they did not even share the same perception of Islam. While the extremists threw acid on the faces of young girls attending school or university classes, Massoud advocated for equal rights for all citizens and criticized former regimes for their failures. It appeared that he had scrutinized carefully how Mao Zedong organized his guerrilla fight against the Kuomintang of Chiang Kai-Shek, but he soon comprehended that the two situations and social realities were totally different. He then opted for his own circumstantial "active defense" and "asymmetric warfare" strategy, rendering offenders mad.

Fazel went on to explain the vision and dream of his commander for the future of Afghanistan—a country free from discrimination against peoples. He admitted that Massoud had suffered all his life about prejudices not only against his own ethnic group, the Tajiks, but also against Uzbeks, Turkmen, and mainly and particularly Hazara. Therefore, he promoted the idea of a decentralized Afghanistan, where provinces and peoples would have local autonomy but remain united around national interests and values, with a united army. Then he explained in more detail the commander's love for poetry as he believed that each verse or sentence contained a whole secret philosophy that the reader needed to interpret or even unearth. On the bank of his great Panjshir River, the peaks of Anjuman, or the plains of the Kelagai desert, he recited poems to his men when the war offered them a moment of recess. Fazel developed his thoughts with such passion and conviction that there was practically no time on my part for the standard Afghan courtesies.

After hours of absorbing monologue, the time of dialogue and questions arrived. I had alerted him about the frank and honest language that Soraya would use. She was eager to seek his view on many topics. Her first and foremost thought was of Afzal. She queried whether he had known such a person. Fazel remembered him well. He had indeed joined Massoud's troops and served as liaison with their people in the capital. Then he performed as alternative driver to the commander and was tragically and seriously wounded when they were targeted, perhaps by ISI-backed extremist individuals. He had bravely saved the life of his commander, who frequently visited him in his Jangalak village. Soraya and I were tremendously heartbroken to learn that he became permanently disabled. He was our friend too. He took me around Afghanistan with a group of foreigners when I assisted Soraya in the ministry of planning to develop a catalogue of Afghan exportable products. We had our car broken into in the middle of the night on the way to Bamiyan, stuck in the muddy road to Bande Amir, and punctured in its tires on dusty roads to Maimana. Even in the worst cases and dangerous situations, Afzal had a smile.

Then we came to the substance and realities of the war and the stands of countries of the region, mainly Pakistan, Iran, and Saudi Arabia. He confirmed the interference of all in Afghanistan's internal affairs but seemed most worried about an ISI and al-Qaida alliance. In addition to Pakistan, he appeared predominantly apprehensive of Saudi Arabia's backing to Afghan and foreign extremist groups and individuals. He extensively exposed their financing mechanisms. Fazel elucidated that Iran too endeavored to safeguard its interests, making it practically impossible for Massoud to navigate in a water troubled by so many external actors. Soraya then quizzed him about support provided to mujahideen groups. It was evident that most support, even delivered by Western countries, went to orthodox and extremist movements. Soraya was curious to know if the commander was in touch with his fellow friends around the country. The answer was both yes and no. Communication on important issues was conducted by messengers, taking days and weeks to be efficiently performed. In half the situations, the messenger was either wounded or killed on his way. Fazel acknowledged that a congregation of commanders inside Afghanistan had not been possible since the beginning of the struggle against the communist regime of Taraki. That had unquestionably been the feeblest cornerstone of their struggle and permitted regional powers to pull strings to their advantage.

He apprised us that Massoud had recommended several times the organization of such a meeting in a European country, Switzerland or Austria in particular due to their neutral status. Some neighbors had categorically opposed it, and major supporters of mujahideen had kept quiet. He was disheartened as it validated the hypothesis of leniency of the Western countries to the wishes of regional powers about the future of Afghanistan. Deterrence of any such initiative was undeniably detrimental to the necessity of establishing proper and functional coordination mechanisms. He acknowledged that the utmost priority of his commander was to stay with the population inside the country and fight for their independence and rights. Moreover, he assured that the commander did not have any link with foreign countries, despite rumors to the contrary. However, he had agreed occasionally on temporary truces with his adversaries to offer breathing space for his fighters.

Soraya pursued by inquiring regarding the plight and role of women. Fazel recognized that women and children were purposely targeted within the country by successive communist regimes and the Soviet army. They were also deprived of appropriate protection and education in refugee camps. He was honest and confessed that in spite of willingness on the part of his commander, women were not admitted into the ranks of the mujahideen. He seemed very fretful that extremist movements would finally have the upper hand in the fight for Kabul if Massoud was not properly reinforced. To the great chagrin of all open-minded people, not only would there not be an appropriate space and prominent role for women in Afghanistan but they would face serious religious and cultural discrimination as well as violation of their human rights. His mission aimed at warning the world about it too.

Soraya inquired about Western political and military backing. His response was crystal clear. Some comprehended and appreciated Massoud and delivered support, while the two main drivers of Western aid to Afghan mujahideen had always been skeptical of his independent spirit and vision for a future Afghanistan. Their policy was based on old Afghan facts, not current realities, he emphasized. He lamented their decision to leave management of Afghan issues to the ISI and was of the opinion that the future of the country should not be conceived and built based on the mistakes committed in the past. Afghanistan belonged to all Afghans, who had equal rights to govern in accordance with their competencies. Massoud believed that the time of the disciples of the Iron Amir was over and advocated for a modern new Afghanistan, open to all and democratic in a real sense, where the government reached and served all its populations. He rationalized his commander's affection for France and French-speaking countries due to his background in the French Lyceum in Kabul.

Finally, Soraya probed candidly about the most subtle issue: whether Massoud's conclusion to stay with the mujahideen transitional government rather than opt for a savior status, who could be called upon when difficulty arose, was based on some specific rationale. Fazel remained perplexed for a while and cautiously gazed at her. Perhaps he did not anticipate such a query. He replied with a "maybe" but insisted that the main reason had been fear of a historic tragic recurrence.

It was already late, and we had not even broached and thrashed out one-quarter of the topics. He had to depart and prepare himself before getting back to the embassy. But surprisingly, he urged us to sit down for a last chat and resolutely requested that Soraya and I join their team in Kabul. It was particularly a surprise for Soraya; this was their first encounter. She comprehended his invitation to me based on our very old amity, but why appeal to her? His answer was simple and straightforward. He underscored that whatever she articulated about was refreshing and logical. They needed people of her stature in the country—people who could think, advise, and act rationally based on comprehension of the society and topics as well as total impartiality, fairness, and courage, not emotions, ethnic bias, party leniency, or family bonds. He agreed with her that Amer Saheb might become an actor in this quagmire if robust actions were not underway to prevent foreign and mainly Pakistani intervention. Massoud looked for people who could propose solutions outside the standard process to which mujahideen were accustomed. Moreover, he desired to diversify his team and bring alongside him individuals who could contradict and challenge him.

A new debate ensued on the ability of mujahideen leaders to follow democratic principles and practices as theocracy had been implemented in Afghanistan in its most primitive and rudimentary aspect. He said that Amer Saheb was profoundly a Muslim who believed in modernity and the merits of technology, valued science, and earnestly promoted equal rights among men and women of Afghanistan. Moreover, morality occupied the highest position in his priorities. Fazel smilingly stressed that theocracy and democracy were two views that resembled the warm and cold atmospheric currents. They could produce rain and snow for the benefit of all or end up in lightning and thunder. As for his specific request, Soraya allowed me to take the lead and introduce the subtle aspects of what we had in mind.

"Look, Fazel," I said. "This is so great of you. And we are honored to have such an invitation. However, there are a few points that we have, and your response will determine our stand."

"What are they?" he inquired.

I apprised him of the statements of former Soviet senior officers in Afghanistan that Massoud had struck deals with the Red Army. By doing so, he had put more pressure on other commanders and mujahideen groups. Frankly speaking, Fazel did not expect such a question. But he calmly underlined that temporary ceasefires between warring parties to refresh and rearm were part of the rules of engagement. He confirmed that the Soviets had launched nine major offensives in less than five years of their occupation, led by at least four-star generals, to effectively capture the commander. And their plot had been neutralized on each occasion. He acknowledged truces between the two parties but never agreements to allow Soviets to focus their forces elsewhere. Finally, I informed him about credible indications that since the takeover of Kabul in April 1992 by mujahideen, individuals very close to him committed acts incompatible with what he had just described. The rumors included embezzlement, excessive use of force, and abuse of power. Soraya interceded and inquired whether he would take any action against them. She continued with a second question, which concerned his honest view as to whether a dramatic civil war in the country could be prevented. His answers were too amazingly frank.

Fazel stated, "No, I cannot take measures against my closest people. Some are of my own blood, and others have supported me all along. As to the second question, we cannot guarantee that Afghanistan will not face a civil war. The ISI wants it, the West is silent, and though we are not as strong as people think, we will resist," he concluded.

After Fazel's departure, Soraya and I convened at the Cartier tearoom in Versoix. While Fazel's answers were surprising and predicted a tragic future for the country, they had the merit of being frank and describing a situation faced by all mujahideen. Their maturity was key to safeguarding Afghanistan. However, serving the interest of aliens and fear of sacrificing principles for personal gains, family ties, or ethnic and geographic links was clearly real. It was evident that neither Soraya nor I could categorically discard such an offer after many years of dedication and struggle for a cause that most considered lost in advance, but Fazel's answers did not leave any hope for a space where we could prove useful.

The committee members were updated; they too seemed anxious for their country. No one among the mujahideen leaders or foreign friends was disposed to perceive our point of view and pay due attention to the alarm bell that had begun to ring louder and gaudier over the years. Some members suggested that we put an end to our endeavors as any involvement at this juncture would insinuate support to one or another party and therefore be wrongly interpreted. The debate was extensive. While it was easy to distinguish who among the mujahideen groups followed extremist visions, it was indeed painful not to intervene in favor of others for fear of geographic, ethnic, or religious connotations. Soraya recommended that we take a step back, follow and observe carefully political, social, and military developments in the country, and when the opportunity arose, the committee could act again and enter the operation theater in the field. At the same time, she counseled that we pursue more advocacy efforts, though prospects of achievement were genuinely limited.

Soon after, Soraya informed me that both of us were invited by the circle of "Republicans Abroad" in Vienna to a restricted working dinner at the famous Vestibül, near the Volksgarten and Rathous Parks. I had good memories of the location. In 1981 when I had surprisingly met her among a group of friends, we had indeed sauntered in the parks and admired the majestic edifice of the Burgtheater that housed the restaurant. This eighteenth-century building, constructed by Empress Maria Theresa of Austria, had witnessed glory, destruction, and repair as all other great monuments and artworks in Europe. Repeated wars and conflicts among rulers of the Old Continent had rarely spared one. But all of them were grandly reconstructed afterward. In Afghanistan, rulers and people in command only knew how to destroy.

We comprehended instantly that the guest of honor was a very significant figure of the United States political arena. His visit was impromptu; some Republican lawyers based in the city of Habsburgs had opined that he meet with us. It was a very candid occasion, at which hardly ten individuals were in attendance. Of course, the essence of the conversation was about the forthcoming election campaign for a second term that President George H. W. Bush sought. Everybody around the table trusted that with 89 percent approval rate in a Gallup poll in early March, no one could overwhelm the incumbent of the White House in his quest to prolong his stay in the Oval Office. It was euphoria all around. The young and inexperienced Bill Clinton was believed a lightweight, and there were already arguments about the new cabinet members.

Soraya and I listened for a while before being offered the opportunity to brief the group about Afghanistan. She was blatantly open and frank, stressing that the United States' political and financial ventures were at serious jeopardy should the ongoing civil war persist. She acknowledged the priority of the Western countries to handle the status of the oil-rich Middle East and the outcome of the Soviet Union downfall. Furthermore, she underscored her awareness of skepticism about Islam in the West but maintained that extremism and terrorism witnessed in Afghanistan would become the mother of all problems for humanity. She referred to the training camps and madrassas in Pakistan, warning that the mass of fighters coached would pose serious challenges for the future of the region and perhaps the entire world. She urged an inter-Afghan dialogue in Europe in the absence of all foreign interfering bodies and caretakers the soonest possible. The gist behind the proposal was to provide an opportunity to all Afghan actors, within and outside the country, to consult, underline, listen, and propose whatever they had in mind for unity and a peaceful future in their country, paving the way for foundation of a solid Afghan nation. I recall she intentionally did not even use the word *prosperity* as it was not a priority of the moment.

The Republicans based in Vienna displayed great sympathy and nodded at each sentence we pronounced. They knew us very well due to our repeated advocacy efforts. However, the guest of honor declined to commit on anything tangible, noting that the forthcoming election was crucial and if the administration was to opt for any initiative in the direction of our proposal, it could only be after the president was reelected and a new team put in place. It was true that he could not engage the government of the United States as he was not within the administration, but his relationship and sphere of influence were the greatest of the time.

Nevertheless, just a few days later, Soraya and I were invited again to a sort of weird dinner in a palatial residence on the Danube right bank, just outside Vienna. It was a fascinating gathering of some hundred persons, generally considered "experts on Afghanistan." Pakistani, Europeans, North Americans, and a few Russians attended the event. There were also about ten Afghans convened from around the world. The attendees were seated with about ten people per round table, including one Afghan. No representatives of mujahideen groups, commanders inside the country, or even the government in place were in attendance. Soraya and I did not know on what basis the assortment was made and whether other of our compatriots had delegation authority to speak on behalf of mujahideen or the government about the situation. We did not! It seemed there was also a citizen of Pakistan at each table who did not stop hammering that Afghanistan without the presence of a government that Pakistan chaperoned would be a slaughterhouse. They were a blend of military and foreign-service officers, with deep intelligence background. While disputes often occurred between the Pakistani and Afghan occupants of the tables at this "gala" event, others endured silently as if they watched a tennis game, boxing fight, or ancient-style duel.

The gentleman seated at Soraya's table was pompous and did not stop yakking about Pakistan's desire to see a peaceful and prosperous neighbor. He specifically referred to "sacrifices" his country made to help Afghan mujahideen and refugees. At some point, she was saturated by the nonsense and calmly said to him, "But there are reports of your support to extremist groups in Afghanistan."

"This is not true, madame," the gentleman retorted. "We are a democracy and do not engage in what you refer to," he continued, perhaps forgetting that his country had been mostly ruled by military dictators and that real democracy had often been a mirage for the population.

"There are innumerable intelligence reports about training camps in tribal areas where countless numbers of Afghans and perhaps even Pakistani children are taught the art of modern warfare and terrorism. All media point in your direction about the current slaughter and bombardment of Kabul," she firmly stated.

"No, madame, please! I thought the British understood our position," he stressed, obviously referring to Soraya's impeccable English accent.

"Precisely, sir. I am not British but an Afghan who wishes to see her country respectful and respected among the concert of nations. A free and independent country having privileged, amicable relationships with its neighbors, who indeed helped us during the trying moments, as you said," she underscored.

The man was stunned and kept silent for the rest of the evening. The host was a "private but very rich individual," whose family had ties with power brokers of the world for a long time. It was the most futile occurrence that we had ever appeared in. Discussions were superficial and resembled a disappointing social event that certainly cost a tremendous amount of money. We did not even comprehend what the organizers desired to achieve. At least one fact was clear. The interfaction disputes among mujahideen groups had exacerbated friends of Afghanistan. Furthermore, the two strong neighbors nurtured and exploited the situation to their best advantage.

A refined gentleman, certainly British or Australian, who had extensive knowledge approached us at the end to underline a number of advantages that Pakistan disposed. They were a stable and now nuclear country, had the command and control buttons of extremist movements and parties in hand, possessed one of the most efficient secret services in the region, and counted on an engaged diaspora in Europe and America, which was nourished by decades of anti-Indian sentiments and fear of disappearance. In his view, Afghanistan would face a long battle for its independence and unity.

On the way back and in a state of desperation, Soraya suggested that we take a serious step back, stop operational activities, and focus only on political advocacy. Emotions were high. Meddling of regional powers was evident. Moreover, within the country, veracity was tarnished by family, ethnic, linguistic, and religious biases. The United States and Europe had been explicit and clear about their priorities since they noticed the cracks in the Soviet system. The blame was entirely on Afghan leaders. They did not understand where the world was heading and how they should have played their own cards. The toll on the civilian population was very heavy. Often the main question for us was who would assume responsibility and whether Afghans would see the day when justice would prevail over might and the force of guns. Each leader considered himself wiser than and above the others. The peoples in the country were the forgotten elements in each demonstration of force or attempt at negotiation. Soraya coveted more proactive Afghans abroad to put pressure on respective Western governments. But Afghans abroad were also infested by divides along considerations that alienated their families within the country. No one could defend or mobilize opinion and resources for what took place in Afghanistan. In real terms, there was too simply no united Afghan diaspora in Europe or America.

Events demonstrated that the mission undertaken by Fazel Ahmad did not meet the expected results. Kabul was the battleground of armed groups, factions, and individuals. Alliances were brokered and broken at the same time. It was pathetic. Mujahideen, who should have brought peace, security, stability, and a promising future for their so much martyrized countrywomen and men, were now killing each other and, in the process, countless innocent inhabitants of the capital, trapped in a hell of rocket fire. Secret services of neighboring countries directly intervened to negotiate alliances for their protégés among the mujahideen movements.

In January 1993, Hekmatyar's association with the Uzbek militia of General Rashid Dostom, though short-lived, led to the heaviest artillery and rocket battle in Kabul. The country's aviation and air force were totally demolished. Moreover, the rivalry and proxy competition between Iran and Saudi Arabia was another auspicious opportunity for the ISI to strike a deal with the Shia faction in control of the southwest of Kabul. The Saudi-sponsored Sunni movement of the adjacent areas hit back ferociously. For a while, these parts of the capital were the theater of heavy shelling and killing by all sides. The brokered union caused unforgivable casualties among the civilian population. In fact, such an unthinkable tie between the Shia and the ISI-backed extremist movement pushed the Saudi-backed group to join forces with the government. At the end of the process, everybody fired in all directions. In the Afshar tragedy alone, over nine hundred Shia population of Kabul were butchered and mass murdered at once and thousands more injured and rendered homeless. This was a shameful crime against humanity.

The incongruity existed in the pretention of all to fight the just cause in the name of God. But there was no such legitimacy in murdering innocent and helpless families and individuals. The Holy Koran says, "God does not love mischief." However, the alliance permitted Hekmatyar to capture the government's defense ministry in March 1993. But they were pushed back. A cease-fire and power-sharing administration was agreed upon. But it never functioned. By June 1994, it was reported that at least twenty-five thousand people were killed by all sides in the city of Kabul alone. That represented fourteen hundred innocent children, women, and men slaughtered per month since the dissolution of the communist regime. The Soviets would not have killed that many, some argued. The heroes of Afghanistan liberation and the "freedom fighters" had been transformed into killing machines just for the sake of power, money, and serving foreign interests. In other parts and cities of the country, rival factions kicked each other out with the force of guns to grab influence.

It was tragic for the people of Afghanistan, particularly its women and children. They were the most defenseless and had given so much sacrifice in the course of history. At the precise moment when political leadership could have given them some hope of relief, peace, and security, internal rivalries massacred that expectation. The unanswered question has always been why most often men perpetrated crimes, violated human rights, and instigated ferocious wars. The history of mankind has displayed that men have always committed indignities and outrage against their kin in the name of something we can call anything except God's will, let alone reason, fairness, justice, and humanity. In all faiths, killing an innocent is considered as slaughtering life itself. From Caen to Hitler, Stalin to Pol Pot, or genocide perpetrators in Rwanda, Bosnia Herzegovina, or elsewhere, the unforgivable mass murders and shames to human beings have been inflicted essentially by those who claimed having more muscles than brains. Their fame and prestige were their disgrace hung forever on their necks or stamped on their foreheads. And when other men resisted them, they cowardly went after innocent women and children, who in all conflicts constituted the bulk of the victims. Afghan men were no different! The hope of Afghanistan shattered again, but this time by her own sons. The thirst and love for power and money was so evident in each mujahideen leader who aspired to ride the Pegasus up to within the palace, this horrible spot in which so much assassination and murder had occurred. People did not understand why men of wisdom and vision did not withdraw as a sign of protest.

During this time, Soraya used to say, "This is not the Afghanistan for which we all fought! From a proud people fighting the Soviet Union, the mightiest of invaders, we became shameful individuals killing our own brothers and sisters!"

She often reflected on the rationale of what was transpiring in Afghanistan. The conclusion of each contemplation led to the same painful observation. For centuries, Afghan history has not been fair with its populations. Leaders interspersed seeds of discord, discrimination, corruption, and nepotism at the expense of bodies, properties, and lives of their citizens. While those who had conquered Afghanistan were sternly criticized for their cruelty, Afghan kings who perpetrated manslaughter in other countries were acclaimed. Very unconvincing reasons were given to justify their brutality, ignoring the fact that killing of harmless innocents has no justification in any political system, social structure, or religion. None of the leaders had the guts to acknowledge mistakes committed, intentionally or otherwise. Their followers engaged in what could be called the most senseless cult of personalities. Dictators were presented as saviors. Mass murders were justified in the name of religious expansionism or safety of the "nation." Nepotism was promoted as others were considered less intelligent and tedious.

Perhaps it was the same in all other countries and their history books tampered with, but it had to change in Afghanistan to respect the human values of the mass of populations on whom the tragic realities were imposed. Mujahideen leaders were no exceptions. Could they not stop their bombing and shelling? Yes, they could! Why was it not done? They have to answer one day, hopefully not far from today. For the victims, it did not matter who was shooting for what reason; they were all part of the problem. By August 1994, the ISI-backed extremist movement still scuffled to seize power, and the mighty spy agency was puzzled.

At the same time, it is rumored that weeks later and while in India, reports of Fazel Ahmad's "irresponsible behavior" were presented to Massoud, with emphasis that while his mujahideen sacrificed their lives, his venerable deputy did not follow ethics. The prestigious war hero of Afghanistan was devastated. He could not have expected that within the team, his longtime shadow and a man with whom he shared everything would be targeted. His instinct to ignore the so-called accounts was overtaken by the radical position of some of his lieutenants. It seemed that he often questioned the audacity and ability of those who had undertaken such hostile acts. The Indian DIA, Defense Intelligence Agency, had no interest in creating another division; the mujahideen government did not have the capacity to do so; and the West did not care. Then who executed such an act that put the commander before an unbearable decision? Most believed that he should have admitted then the presence of traitors within his own followers and begun a purge. Perhaps he may even have determined so. Against all odds, Fazel Ahmad had no choice but to quit, and he did so. Massoud stated to his closest bigwigs, "I wish you had spent your precious time and energy to do something more useful than denigrate a battle companion!"

Since the beginning of his fight in the 1970s, this was the first crack in Massoud's inner circle and the beginning of his vulnerability. Who did it? Were there effective moles around him? Time will tell us if he was betrayed by his own that surrounded him. The ISI and al-Qaida had found the flaw and exploited it to perfection. Fazel Ahmad joined the team of former king Zaher Shah. At least he was not rejected by other political circles. Amid the fissures in his rival's team, Hekmatyar could still not attain his objectives, though he maintained his pressure on Kabul from Char Asiab and continued bombing the capital. With such an obvious failure, he was not needed anymore.

In August 1994, a one-eyed religious cleric, Mullah Mohammad Omar, declared from Pakistan the emergence of the Taliban, religious students. They were a ferocious force and could do everything. Killing, burning, torturing, and humiliating constituted the basis of their action strategy. By October of the same year, they had seized several key locations, including the province and city of Kandahar. These were the same kids about whom Soraya and I had warned, paying a visit to Washington to ring the alarm bell. They were now mature fighters. Out of their experimental bottles, like in a science fiction movie, they destroyed all and acted like "Terminators"— sharp, quick, brutal, and efficient. In the winter of the same year, they gained Hekmatyar's positions in Char Asiab. The bombers of Kabul did not serve any further purpose and turned tail, leaving heavy weapons to the Taliban. Their leadership fell to the Islamic Republic of Iran. Government authorities had seemed anxious and were now worried. Despite comprehending the making and shaping of the Taliban, they hardly had information about their modus operandi. The so-called mujahideen government was in shambles and could not reshape the secret services under civil war circumstances. The population in general discerned that the Taliban represented the darkest forces. They had been nursed in strictly men-ruled environments in Pakistani madrassas since a tender age. Most of their fighters did not even know the basics of Islam!

Had the mujahideen government retained communist military and spy networks, perhaps they would have been in a sounder position. But with the euphoria of riding on the Pegasus, mujahideen leaders had given up to Pakistan's demand and dismantled all communist security structures, defense forces, and heavy weapons. At the end of the process, they were left without a professional army and information-gathering services. Most experts compared the circumstance to standing in cold winter on a crossroads without pants and underwear. On the contrary, the Taliban, who received tangible military and financial help and obtained steadfast intelligence, sustained the bombardment of Kabul from the same site and with the same arsenals that their less successful friends had "abandoned." From there, they progressed like apocalyptic forces—light, quick, fearless, and in numbers—to the Shia spots in the southwest of the capital city. Ali Mazari, the undisputed and charismatic leader of the Shias who had faced the Red Army, and his key commanders were trapped.

Though people spoke about a tactical alliance of Mazari with the Taliban under auspices of the ISI and Iranian agents, the Shia leader remained suspicious and at large. However, their whereabouts were revealed in March 1995, apparently by influential insiders and former allies. The Taliban captured them one by one. They were all tortured to death. The event constituted a tragedy for the Shia population and the country. It is recounted that Mazari's body was carried by populations from Ghazni in the south, where he was murdered, through the rasping mountains of Central Afghanistan to Mazar-e-Sharif in the north. It was painful to see such a leader caught so cheaply! The history of Afghanistan proved recurrently that an alliance forged by foreigners would never be sustainable. The fall of the Shia strongholds and the second massacre they faced in two years' time was unbearable. They were caught this time around between the government forces and the Taliban!

What ensued after the collapse of the communist regime in Kabul did not provide any space for the committee to be operational on the ground. Its activities were then completely frozen. Soraya nevertheless assisted a number of underprivileged families. Four of them were from Badakhshan, Kandahar, Daikondi, and Maimana. With their respective Tajik, Pashtun, Hazara, and Uzbek origins, they represented most of the people in Afghanistan. They had worked with her in different capacities in the foreign ministry or ministry of planning as gardener, fruits provider, head cleaner, and mechanic. Each lived in the popular quartier of Qala-e-Shada under the control of the Shia movement. They frequently called Soraya to acknowledge receipt of the modest financial aid and provided an update of the situation in Kabul. From their accounts, it appeared that there was massacre everywhere, reminding a few diplomats and spies still left in the capital city of Saint Bartholomew, Innocents, Latins, Wounded Knee, and other tragedies.

These four families were friends and lived near each other. They had shared humiliation by ministers during their services with diverse governments, labored free of charge in their houses, mended their cars without being paid, and kicked out of offices when they needed help. But their friendship was more sturdy and genuine than the odds of life. Often they brought their food together in one dwelling after the Friday prayer and chatted for a long time. They joked and rescued each other in trying moments by all means. Their youngsters followed the paths of their parents and went to school together. In children's fights, they were unbeatable and even feared. And this is what Soraya remembered of their existence and harmonious amity: during peaceful times, when one required something, another came to present the case and plead for a positive response. She was like a sister to them. And even with the scars of war and desolation, they endured as friends and brothers by bonds. Their offspring had grown up, and as usual, there were newborn babies. The takeover of the mujahideen and the ensuing civil war brought serious divisions among the young buddies of yesterday. But the authority and discipline of their parents prevailed, and they continued as friends, though each one had a preference for a warring faction, accusing the others of committing atrocities, of course.

One Thursday afternoon, heavy shelling from the Asmai hills hit numerous houses. Two adult sons and a daughter of the mechanic from Maimana were slain. His wife and two girls lost their lower members, and their shelter was downright ruined. Together with them, a significant number of Hazara families from Daikondi, Bamiyan, and Yakawlang were hit too, losing cherished members of their families. Scores were injured in the attack, mainly women and children. There was an outcry. For most of the population of this area, it was the Tajik government who committed the crime. Within minutes a huge protest was organized against the "Tajik tyrants." Calling for revenge, a small group surrounded the house of the gardener, whose wife, elderly mother, and children were shocked too. He did not know what to do. Go out and face death? Stay home as a coward shivering with his family? Call for assistance, but from whom? The crowd was getting more agitated and shouting at him to come out and face his fate. They threatened to burn him and his family alive.

At this moment, the Hazara head cleaner and the Pashtun fruit provider rushed into the middle of the mob, yelling "Stop." They urged the furious crowd to be judicious and realistic as the rockets were coming from every direction, fired by all the movements. And it was the will of God that the Tajik family was not hit. The Uzbek mechanic joined them, urging people to focus on burial of those who perished and treatment of the injured, rather than increasing the casualty toll. It was like a man-to-man talk. The next day, the four of them were again shoulder to shoulder, preparing tombs along with other members of their communities. People did not know whom to blame, to curse, to praise, or to ask for rescue. Bullets and rockets were fired from all directions.

Months later, when the area was taken by the Taliban and the renowned leader of the Shia movement was captured with his lieutenants, the "religious students" invaded Qala-e-Shada and brought a huge number of men, women, and children together. While hundreds of cadavers littered the streets, everybody knew that with the Taliban in command, their end was very close. Since they were amassed, including the four friends, in a mosque, all felt safe as no one would kill in the house of God. The Taliban accused the Hazara of being *kafir*, infidels, the Pashtuns of being collaborators, the Tajiks of being enemies, and the Uzbeks of being communists. The four friends were searching for their wives, mothers, and children. Some found theirs; others did not. They were waiting for the end of the harangue to go on their quest.

The Taliban commander, a man of some twenty-five years of age, was accompanied by a mature person to whom he often referred and spoke in Urdu. There was no doubt! He was the real commander and decision maker; he was the "*moqamaat.*" His young puppet had a black turban and massively long, dark hair dancing on his shoulders and upper back. He approached the Uzbek and accused him of being a communist and drunkard, like their chief, Rashid Dostom. The detainees concluded that the destiny of the poor man was sealed. Then he moved on toward the Tajik, slapping him in the face and qualifying him as a spy of the government forces. While charging him with more punches, he swore to apprehend all their leaders and hang them "like Kalakani and his bond." He then grabbed the Hazara and asked him to kneel, took his gun, and started torturing him, shouting that all of them were children of Chinese and kafir. At this stage, a sort of white spit appeared on the corners of his mouth. He was enraged and regularly obtained the approval of the "*moqamaat.*"

He violently removed the turban of the Pashtun and screamed that he was not worthy of it as he was a collaborator and not a Muslim. He placed several knocks on his head and back and then went on to ask all of them to identify their family members. In an amazing gesture of unity, the four stood firm and started narrating the divine sentence that *"there [was] no god but God and that Mohammad [was] the messanger of God."* Then:

"We are all Muslims and not afraid of death, as it would be the will of God," the Tajik said.

"There is one God and one Islam, but different ways of worshiping. This is not sin, and those who consider us kafir know nothing of the holy religion," the Hazara stressed.

"All human beings are equal in front of God, women, and men. Killing is the worst sin. Those who commit it in any name will face the darkest part of hell," the Uzbek warned.

"Afghanistan is one country with different populations and beliefs. It is time that it belonged to all in an equal way," the Pashtun argued.

"You bastards! You communists! You kafirs! You allies of Satan! You must all die with your families!" the Taliban commander screamed.

He sent a group of his fighters to look for the remaining members of the respective four families. A few little kids were found at their homes and dragged to the mosque. There were now some hundred or hundred and twenty people inside. He threw a last glance of hate to all, moved on, and ordered to kill them. Within minutes, the house of God was transformed into a massacre chamber. It was a horrific scene. Some have heard of similar stories in Rwanda, where massive numbers of people were gathered in churches to be burned alive later on. What was this animalistic instinct? How could human beings be so cruel, so violent, with so much thirst for killing? Animals kill to survive—but men do it for power, prestige, money, and even pleasure. Such an expression of hatred became a practice later on when terrorist organizations perpetrated mass murder by exploding themselves in mosques and at public gatherings. Soraya was shattered at the news of the massacre. She could not eat or sleep for days. She had known those families, visited their modest houses, consumed hot bread and milk tea with them, and joked with each one about simple and more complicated matters. For her, they represented the real Afghanistan. At the eve of the twenty-first century and in front of the world's eyes, most Afghans were left alone to perish. That day, Soraya was convinced that the inevitable conquest of power by the Taliban would occur.

At the same period, it was rumored that a group of the Taliban traversed security barriers and reached the heart of Kabul. One of them, a young man, presented himself at the United Nations gate and announced that he had a message for the former president and master of KHAD, Mohammad Najibullah, from his cousins and gave precise references. He was permitted in with the consensus of the butcher of Afghanistan. After a while, Najibullah urged United Nations observers to leave him alone with the visitor. He was notified that the Taliban would sooner or later enter Kabul, and their leadership asked him not to move out of the compound as he would then be safely handed over to India, where he could join his family.

Failing to defeat Massoud forces and seize Kabul, the Taliban altered strategy and captured as many provinces as possible, cutting the Kabul regime from its power bases. In September 1995, they entered massively and quickly to Herat in the western part of the country. The enigmatic commander of the region and strongest ally of the government was defeated and exiled to Iran. Other provinces began to tumble like dislocated rocks from a mountain. A year later, they reached with an unprecedented force to Kabul. Massoud and other government leaders comprehended that the end of the mujahideen era was very close, an era that no one would be proud about.

Massoud did not want more carnage. He appeared remorseful, depressed, and isolated. Perhaps he also bemoaned not having his best pal and companion Fazel Ahmad next to him. Fazel was always the man to challenge him for justified reasons. And now, he had to admit defeat to a ferocious force. It was his first defeat, and it implied the downfall of his hopes and aspirations. He realized how much the mujahideen had lost the trust of common individuals, those who had given the worst sacrifices of their existence. His decision was made. He would not defy the Taliban and engage in street battles at the expense of uncalculated human lives. It was no hurdle to convince the government to leave Kabul for the northern parts of the country, preferably Taloqan.

He ordered the release of all prisoners and dispatched his chief of security to approach the former President Mohammad Najibullah and urge him to abandon the United Nations house and accompany them to the north. When he learned of his refusal, he instructed his envoy to forewarn him about the viciousness of the Taliban and exhort him once more to accept his offer. The former president, a man who mastered spies and ruled with an iron fist, refused categorically. He, who had known the ISI, did not grasp the danger looming. Perhaps he remembered the message of the young Taliban. Nobody comprehended what was in his mind or how he reasoned, but he opted to linger. Indeed the Taliban leadership had designated several of their combatants to rush from the eastern part to Kabul, take charge of Najibullah, and treat him carefully. The essence of the order was clear that he should not be killed. However, it is understood that in Pule Charkhi, these individuals were mysteriously murdered, something that had never happened among the Taliban in the past.

When they pierced the United Nations edifice, the former president greeted them with a smile and seemed ready to depart. One vehemently attacked him.

"You kafir! We shall punish you now!" he screamed.

395

"Are you not the envoys?" Najibullah asked.

"No! We killed them, and we will hang you too," another shouted.

The former president was duped by himself! In the final analysis, he may not have been as intelligent as some thought. He and his brother were dragged out and assassinated in the most humiliating and atrocious manner. Their bodies remained hanging for several days to the extent that carnivorous birds enjoyed attacking the soft parts of their slain bodies. The man who had murdered so many innocent people faced his fate in the most barbaric way. Was it divine justice or just an error of judgment? He would have been alive had he accepted Massoud's suggestion; perhaps he would have even been with his family in India. Indeed, "the one who dug a tomb was in the grave." His death put an end to the life of a man who had deprived hundreds of thousands from living. Perhaps he should not have been killed and faced a lawful justice mechanism with the right to defend himself, something that he had not accorded to his victims.

Months later in Vienna, in a friendly gathering with an ambassador of a very powerful country who had long dealt with Afghanistan, Soraya reminded him of our repeated meetings and alerts. He was candid to acknowledge that he himself did not push the topic too seriously with his capital, thinking that we were naïve Afghans who exaggerated in success as well as in failure.

"But, Mr. Ambassador," Soraya said, "millions have already lost their lives. And there will be more! Who will be responsible for it?" she asked.

"Madame, you know that the powerful have the last word. If common Afghans seek justice, they will have to create a nation united, make it strong and peaceful, and then ask for what they want. They should not forget that time is of the essence," he replied.

Indeed, the Afghan people paid heavy costs over the past four decades, and there is no voice to ask for accountability for the misdeeds. Soraya wished to encounter Charlie Wilson again, look at his face and eyes, read his inner feelings, and determine how he would evaluate the outcome of his battle, the "Charlie Wilson War." Where did he vanish to since the disintegration of the Soviet Union? The one who visited the mujahideen twice or thrice a year suddenly evaporated. Was he remorseful? Was he ashamed? Or did he just do what he had to do, and the rest depended on others?

The so-called Afghan legitimate government moved to the north. The ferocious extremist Taliban regime was recognized only by Pakistan—of course—Saudi Arabia, and the United Arab Emirates. The rest of the world continued business with the lawful but lame-duck government. The outcome of the over four years of mujahideen administration was unfortunately desolation, tragedy, and destruction caused by self-centered interests. Was it due to the complexity of the new "great game," foreign intervention, particularly by Pakistan, Saudi Arabia, and Iran, or simply lack of preparedness, ability, and capacity of the mujahideen leaders or unwillingness of the Afghan people to accept others besides their own ethnic chieftains to govern them, or a combination of rationales that we cannot even discern in university theses and reference books? For sure, nobody spoke of "freedom fighters" anymore. They were just remembered as a bunch of people who had inflicted unforgivable miseries at different degrees to their own people.

There was no progress to report on any front. Over four years of opportunities were lost, hopes shattered, innocent women, children, and men killed, the entire city of Kabul razed, and pride gained during fourteen years of struggle against communism and the deadliest superpower ruined. Under such circumstances, Soraya suggested putting an end to the committee's activities. It was unfair to jeopardize the lives of young members for a future that was in the hands of those who knew nothing but war.

Massoud, in his defeat, unearthed new energy to resist and defy the conquest by the Taliban of the remainder of the country. He was back at his best, on the mountains of Hindukush, plains of Kilagai, or steps of Takhar. He was out of the mesh and gears of civil war and knew the enemy. With an unequal balance of power, unreliable allies, and diplomatic inexperience, he still did remarkably well. It appeared that he often stressed to his team that he would continue to fight foreign interference, even for just an iota of territory to remain independent.

The 1996 to 2001 history of Afghanistan was characterized by three main political facts. Kabul and the south were ruled by an outrageously extremist Taliban regime, allied with even more radical Wahhabis of Saudi Arabia, led by the young and rich Osama Bin Laden. The devilish Haqani Network joined them instantly. They terrorized people and systematically violated basic human rights and cultural values. But they provided security to the people and their properties, a rare privilege that the population did not dispose of for years. On the other hand, Massoud and a legitimate Afghan government exiled in the northern parts of the country still licked their wounds, lamented mistakes committed, gathered and renewed forces, and searched how to gain the will of the people again. A third but much smaller force, the former king of Afghanistan Zaher Shah, gained support and attention in the international arena. The three so-called moderate mujahideen groups rallied behind him. The internal triangle was formed, each corner or apex having its own friends and foes. Hekmatyar and the Shia movements practically disappeared from the scene.

Perhaps tactical reasons prompted such a strategy. The Western world looked like a giant bear that had swallowed the Soviet Union, Eastern Europe, and the oil-rich Middle East and required time for digestion. It did not face any more challenges of major rivals. Out of trouble, it enjoyed a total hibernation. The antelopes such as Afghanistan were willingly left over to hyenas in mankind's life stream. The Taliban aimed at annihilation of what could be considered progress, culture, and modernism. They coveted to take Afghanistan back to the seventh century as that was the image of Islam inculcated in their minds in Pakistani drill and training camps. There had been so much emphasis on developing their agility and brutality that most did not comprehend the basics of Islam even as practiced fourteen centuries ago. Zaher Shah and his team did not represent the future; they were the past of the country. As an elderly person whose reign was peaceful, he was certainly respected. But opportunists around him curtailed to a great extent the fatherly role he could play. The mujahideen exiled government to the north did not represent anymore all those who had fought to liberate Afghanistan from the paws of the Soviet Union and communism.

Massoud and his team had lost their aura and undisputed respectability during the civil war. He knew it and had embarked on a strategy to capture hearts and minds back. His earnest sympathizers believed that he would have kneeled in front of the people and apologized for atrocities committed by all sides. Rare were those who in the history of humans had achieved such an objective. But the mere fact that he acknowledged mistakes of the mujahideen governments and wished to move away from the horrible legacy of that time was laudable. He determined that resisting the Taliban was not only his duty but also an opportunity to prove that he was still a man on whom the country could rely. However, he looked like a lonely lion. Some even spoke of a disconnected team around him. His enemies and their foreign protectors wanted his skin at all costs.

The Taliban era looked like the worst horror reality, particularly for women. The small steps back and forth that had been taken since King Amanullah Khan were annihilated. Women and girls were ordered to stay home, and if they were seen outside without an intimate male member of their families—essentially their husband, brother, or father—then the tyranny rule would apply. Moreover when out, they must be totally covered in order not to face public whiplashes. If there were charges of adultery, the sentence was death by bullet or stoning.

The latter, a horrible practice inherited from very ancient pharaonic times, had indeed disappeared long ago. But its resumption was part of the "purification" that the Taliban implemented, though nowhere in the Holy Koran was its practice advised for any crime. Music, cinema, and cultural activities were banned instantly. Nobody could determine whether the security provided was due to their brutality or an efficient strategy. Certainly the usual perpetrators of crimes feared mutilation of their bodies or slit throats and necks, still practiced by some radical Islamic countries and movements.

Golalai's destiny portrayed the fate of all women in Afghanistan during this time. She was a friend of Soraya's cousin. In her early twenties, she lived with her widowed mother and two sisters in Karte Naw in the eastern part of Kabul city. Her father and two elder brothers were killed during the factional war among the mujahideen. One sad day of autumn 1994, a rocket hit their small dwelling. She did not know who fired on them; it perhaps even did not matter! Only women survived, though her mother lost a leg and her two sisters sustained serious shrapnel wounds over their bodies. Golalai, who could acquire only basic education, was the breadwinner of the family, the one on whom three disabled women relied. She could not have a meaningful job and was a street vendor. Her family members delivered her dried fruits from her ancestral land, such as mulberries, apricots, and raisins, and handicraft items that her eldest aunt, affected by myopia, wove. After months of hard labor and efforts, Golalai had offered her a pair of cheap eyeglasses so that she could continue to hand-contrive the wonderfully ornate shirts. Dressed with a repulsive chadari (all-body veil) and looking like a ghost, every early morning she went to what remained of Sar-e-Chawk with her cart and budged up to the New City, publicizing the items she wanted to market. "Excellent dried fruits, wonderful embroideries with cheapest price possible—come and have a look even if you do not buy," she screamed all day while thrusting her dray.

It was unusual to see a woman on the streets of Kabul alone vending items. She was apprehended several times by the Taliban commanders. On each occasion either her persuasion or a visit to her infirm family or even a small amount of money that she offered ended in her release. As she was entirely wrapped, nobody could guess her age, face, or the shape of her body. On two occasions, senior Taliban clerics came to their house to investigate the veracity of what she asserted when apprehended. Finally she had an authorization on a nappe of paper that permitted her to shuffle alone between Sar-e-Chawk and New City but only in the mornings. The Sulh Road, where she found the largest shops, was her dead end.

Halim, a retailer at the corner of the Haji Yakob mosque, esteemed the courage of this young girl and every day purchased the dry fruits and embroidery remaining on her cart. And she blissfully returned home, moving fast with her "four-wheel drive." It was difficult to discern if the storekeeper did it because of sympathy or due to a tender feeling for this dauntless girl. Winter was particularly harsh as she did not have proper shoes and warm clothing. She pushed her chariot with bare hands, stopping from time to time and warming the edge of her fingers with the fog of her mouth. Halim could not invite her in as the Taliban were all around, but he had a stove ready. As soon as she appeared, he brought her the furnace to keep warm. She may also have been attentive to the gestures of this young man and dragged every day longer to the extent that her mother had to warn her. On some occasions, she was accompanied by the Taliban head of the zone as they could not tolerate watching a woman outside at dusk. Halim never conversed with her. He only inquired how much everything would cost. Then he disbursed the money, took whatever was on the trolley, and ran back to his shop. He kept the dry fruits in his own store, while the embroideries were handed over to his brother, who had a clothing window in the Chicken Bazaar.

One evening for the first time, she jumped into the neighboring boutique before proceeding home. She requested a small flacon of locally made perfume and red nail polish. The owner was horrified and denied having such items. But she persisted, underlining that he knew her and she would not divulge anything if apprehended by the Taliban. He was extremely nervous, as Golalai's presence before him was a serious offense according to the applicable rules. She was not accompanied by any intimate male member of her family. He hurriedly ran behind the small curtain, came out swiftly, and handed over a paper bag to her. She put the money on the counter and ran away. She had the items in her shivering hands. It took her a while to secure them in her side pocket.

At home, it was a joy. Golalai was so thrilled to show them to her mother and sisters. Finally she could afford what a woman loved most, though of cheap quality. Her mother had a feeling of discomfort and counseled her not to wear them as the Taliban would severely reprimand her. She phlegmatically conferred that they would not see her hands and notice her perfume as she would be shielded by her chadari, the shame inflicted on women of Afghanistan by God knows whom. The next morning she poured some perfume on the edge of her index finger and rubbed her ear and neck. Everybody felt the fragrance. Moreover, she had beautiful, shiny red nails. Her mother begged her not to go out that day and to enjoy the scent and tint at home. She had a strange feeling and suspected trouble to occur!

But Golalai left the house. Perhaps it was a misstep by a very young person or the desire to see Halim again. She dashed with her wagon to the same locations, applying the same process. By the time she arrived to Halim's shop, she had hardly sold one-quarter of what she had on the trolley. The young man was cheerful and as usual came out to purchase the rest. But the smell of the fragrance and the observation of red nails disturbed him. He had a pleasant heartache and tried to play the game longer, inhale the odor, and admire the stunning fingers. For the first time, he addressed her and asked for her name. A tender, innocent, simple conversation began. Where do you live? You have family members? Are you not tired? They both forgot the reality of the world in which they lived. The more they exchanged, the more they felt attracted to each other. They loved the feeling and pursued their fond talk. Nothing else mattered at that moment. Within minutes, three black-turbaned Taliban rushed up with Kalashnikovs in their hands.

"You cannot be her father," one shouted.

"Are you her brother?" the second screamed.

"No!" Halim retorted.

"Are you her husband?" the third spit.

"Not yet," he gently replied.

The two were instantly arrested. Matters became worse when the Taliban noticed the perfume and saw her hands. She was accused of prostitution and kept for a trial.

Meanwhile, her mother waited and waited till the dawn. But there was no sign of her loved one. Where was she then? What had happened to her? Why did she not inform them or send someone? Did she have an accident? Was she in a hospital? The heart of the infirm woman was palpitating, and her mind was blown. She already had the strong sentiment that something terrible had occurred to her daughter. At around ten the next morning, rumors spread that the Taliban were going to stone in the nearby Bagrami plains a whore and harlot who resided in this area. The mother shivered. She implored and begged God that her presumptions would prove wrong. She liked neither the perfume nor the red nail polish. People started moving toward the Bagrami playground, as if they wished to see a game. Golalai's mother could not tolerate her anxiety, so she took her crutches and started racing on one leg. She arrived at the grounds.

There were a massive number of people surrounding a hole in which her daughter, her beloved Golali, was positioned. Nobody could cross the rope around it and move in. Gunmen guarded the crowd and kept them under control. There was an elderly "judge" circled by ferocious armed faces. He took the floor and announced that the guardians of Islam had apprehended a prostitute with a man and that there were two irrefutable proofs, the smell of her body and the color of her nails. Then he ordered a group of four individuals to go and verify. They went to the hole and started acting like hyena gauging their prey and uncovered her gorgeous hands with red nails. The proof was indisputable! She was a prostitute, and in accordance with their law, she must be stoned. As to the man, he would receive one hundred whiplashes. Golalai's poor mother was screaming to be allowed to make her case. But she was pushed back by long dark-haired Taliban with the barrels of their guns.

About fifteen black-turbaned men began stoning the young, adorable Golalai without even giving her the opportunity to defend herself or say anything. The mob followed. Rains of small rocks hit her on the head, face, chest, and shoulders. The macabre scene continued for some twenty minutes—and then she was dead! The Taliban justice was rendered.

The crowd started to disperse, and the horrid show was over. It was the opportunity for the lame mother to rush to the rescue of the only one who brought home bread and fed three handicapped women. She reached the hole and took off her chadari. She had the head of her beloved daughter in her chest and was weeping and sobbing. When she realized that her daughter was no more, she screamed and cursed Mullah Omar, the blind Taliban leader. The judge was still there. Golalai's mother was apprehended too. She was condemned to receive one hundred whiplashes for insulting the emir of Muslims and for showing her face to the public. Golalai was buried by two courageous neighbors who had known her for years and appreciated and praised her devotion and determination. Halim did not endure his punishment, and three days later he was dead too.

Soraya cried and was heartbroken for the women of her country. Golalai's family was very poor. Soraya recollected having sent a small gift to her mother when the girl was born. She knew that under the circumstances, tens of thousands like Golalai and Halim would be let perish in order for obscurantism to survive. The madness of public killing was the Taliban's trademark. They often used the Kabul central sports stadium for such purposes. A scholar who lived in the same area had written to a friend that God had created women and men to complement and love each other. They had equal rights and faced the divine justice without prejudice. One was nothing without the other. And what he saw there was but the law of ignorance.

Soraya also remembered the situation of Zarmeena, the mother of five children who was murdered by bullets in front of a senseless crowd of some thirty thousand people under the same circumstances. Her "crime" was to react to a vicious husband who tortured and abused her and the children on a daily basis. Taliban "justice" was summarily rendered by whoever was in charge of the zone, and women never had the right to be defended or express their opinion on the destiny reserved to them. The most horrific and appalling aspect was the voluntary presence of thousands of cheerful individuals who enjoyed the act. Were these men totally senseless and could not realize that one day their own sisters, mothers, daughters, or wives might face the same destiny?

While thousands of experts documented the Taliban's brutality and violation of human rights, in particular regarding the plight of women and girls, some specific and important facts and incidents were strikingly annoying for Afghans during this period. All of them had catastrophic effects on Afghanistan and the rest of the world. It was surprising to realize that some figures, such as Commander Jalaluddin Haqani, who was one of the main receivers of ISI and

CIA support and financial backing, joined the Taliban instantly. The manager of the Tora Bora caves did not construct them with his own money and effort. Haqani was assisted by foreign forces to do so. Perhaps the laxity observed after the withdrawal and collapse of the Soviet Union permitted him to demonstrate who he truly was.

Some other well-known figures of the mujahideen also joined them, and it was a huge surprise for the country. Was there a secret plot that common mortals did not comprehend? Or did Pakistan now have the assurance that their making and shaking in Afghanistan would not face disapproval of their Western supporters, from whom they received billions of United States dollars per annum? It seemed that Pakistan had always ranked as the third largest recipient of American military and development aid after Israel and Egypt. How did they become a nuclear power without the world realizing it? How did they betray the rewards of the fight against the Soviet Union by supporting extremist organizations without being prevented, contentedly training thousands of insular and narrow-minded extremists, and playing a policy of fireworks in the region without being blamed for it?

Another fact that went unnoticed was the intermarriage between extremist mujahideen and Wahhabi fighters who had been released from all the prisons of the Middle East and North Africa. It looked like these countries had identified a dumping spot to clean up their prisons and get rid of their radical citizens. Perhaps their custody in jails appeared politically risky and financially costly. It was alarming. Afghans did not share any values with such a reactionary ideology. But now they had intruded into the inner circles of Afghan kinfolk privacy. In any tribal or Bedouin society, the community was responsible for individuals' safety and security. They exploited the principle to their maximum benefit at the expense of the naivety of their fellow Afghan mujahideen. The most prominent and dangerous of such relationships seemed to have taken place between Osama bin Laden and Jalaluddin Haqani. It was believed that they married each other's daughter. They were then son-in-law and father-in-law of each other at the same time. What an astonishing bond! It was questionable how such a notorious tie went unnoticed by experts and even secret services as it proved extremely devastating for Afghanistan and the rest of the world later on.

In the summer of 1999, Fazel Ahmad visited Vienna, and I happened to be in town. We had a quiet long lunch at the Philosophen Kaffee in town. The luncheon was delightful: Greek salad, sparkling water, filet steak, tiramisu, and green tea for all to save time. Our interlocutor deplored the situation of his former friend and companion Ahmad Shah Massoud. He had taken the initiative several times to rejoin and help him, but he had not received any feedback. He did not know whether Massoud was dissuaded of a positive answer by his entourage or if indeed the crystal of their friendship had definitely shattered. For the first time, Fazel Ahmad seemed seriously anxious for the life of Massoud. He suspected flaws regarding his personal security and openly spoke about it. As for the former king Zaher Shah's surroundings, he did not seem confident of their ability to handle intricate defiance, such as the unity of a dismantled country.

Soraya was implacable in her review of the situation since we had last met him. The ruin caused by fourteen years of communist regimes, four years of mujahideen interfaction wars, and three years of the Taliban theocratic destruction was unpardonable. And the people of Afghanistan wanted perpetrators to be brought to justice. She even suggested that as a gesture of fairness to the country, he should publicly announce his willingness to face the court of law and its verdict.

Fazel Ahmad was astounded by Soraya's blunt, logical, and authentic language. He concurred that wounds would take very long to heal and that tangible efforts were needed to bring people together. He then changed the topic and elucidated that in King Zaher Shah's crew, he was still an outsider. At eighty-five years of age and after being absent from Afghanistan for thirty-six years, he was not relevant anymore.

His staff gave him similar reports for nearly four decades: "The situation is terrible, people love and worship you, Your Majesty is the only possible savior," and so on. Soraya opined that the king's team would certainly be included in any future political discussions about the country and that Hamid Karzai would most probably resurface.

We were both sorrowful for Fazel. He did not appear the sharp person we had met some years back. Often he stirred an object for a long time, as if he thought of something else. He scrutinized his mistakes, but he knew well that seasoned commanders did not ponder about a second chance on the battlefield. This was the last time we met him. He was the buddy of my childhood and adolescence, but our paths in life differed. Sometimes we even had opposing perceptions about the country. His loyalty to Commander Massoud, who remained the only icon standing against the tyranny of the Taliban, was undeniable. Distressed by the loss of most of his bright new team members two years earlier in an aircraft crash in central Afghanistan, the commander strove hard to reconstitute anew his forces, but he never seemed satisfied. Something disturbed him subconsciously. His pledge to fight to the end even for an iota of Afghanistan became the slogan of all who stood against extremism and the Taliban. Disappointed by the American attitude toward him and their blank check to the ISI, he embarked on alerting Europe. It was perhaps already too late.

The August 1998 bombings of the United State Embassies in Nairobi and Dar es Salam left no doubt about the power of al-Qaida, led by Osama bin Laden, protected by his presumed father-in-law and son-in-law Jalaluddin Haqani, the Taliban's sturdiest advocate and supporter. The United States authorities may have bothered innumerable harmless people in their investigation, but they did not seem disturbed by the presence and operation of the terrorist training camps in Pakistan. The intimidations of the sole world giant were considered as blabber by the terrorist production factories in the tribal areas.

About two years later, they hit again in Yemen waters. The attack on the United States Ship (USS) *Cole* in October 2000 was another alarm that should have been given much more significance. Some argued that these two incidents scratched the giant but did not hurt irremediably. However, the technique and practice that led to the assassination of Rajeev Gandhi in 1991, suicide bombing, which became the perfect modus operandi of those who wished to inflict mass murder, should have been given highest attention. It was evident that killing people, violating human rights, stoning innocent women, raping children in madrassas, closing schools, and depriving generations of people from basic education were not enough and did not satisfy the folly of those who committed such crimes in the name of God. They wanted to impress, frighten, and inflict mass murder. The world should have looked into many such incidents and considered them redlines. The fight against modern terrorism should have begun when its seeds were sowed in the late 1980s, and their bases in Pakistan should have been eradicated.

At the beginning of 2001, the Taliban and their associates resolved to further step up their violence and destroy the biggest Buddha on earth, a World Cultural Heritage Site in Bamiyan, as if massacre of human beings was not enough. In fact, for months, the decision had been taken by their leadership and protectors to complete over a century later the job that the notorious Iron Amir, Abdur Rahman Khan, had commenced. On the first of March, several dark-haired high dignitaries, dressed with long black turbans and similar sunglasses, arrived from Kabul to the city of Bamiyan, the cradle of thousands of years of civilization, a city with so much pride and tragedy engulfed in it. They had a mission and a horrific one. They spoke only to the "governor" of the province. The next day, numerous armed men appeared in front of the home of Hussein, an elder of over eighty years of age.

"Come with us, bastard!" one shouted.

"Where do you take me? What have I done?" he pleaded.

"You will know soon!" another one claimed and pushed him out of his house.

"Attention! My bones are not solid," the old man urged.

"Good for you," the commander of the team screamed. "At least you will do something useful before you die like a dog."

Hussein was hauled to the office of the governor. He had served as guard of the Buddhas for decades, earning a meager amount of money from tourists. Since the civil war broke, there were no visitors to Bamiyan, and he was left jobless. The Taliban missionaries were all there and commenced interrogating him. He was terrified and shivering. For some fifteen minutes, they humiliated him; some even slapped him in the face to ensure he understood the words they articulated. Others accused him as the enemy of God, who did not deserve to live. The black–turbaned, long-haired individuals probed him to see how well he knew the largest Buddha, popularly called Salsal, and why it did not collapse when the Iron Amir attempted to trash it in 1890. Scared for his life and frail bones, the innocent man began to give an explanation. But the Taliban were eager to grasp why it did not crumble then. Hussein provided a detailed picture of different parts of the Great Buddha's body, and his adversaries listened very attentively.

After nearly three hours of questioning and elucidation, Hussein was "released" but escorted by two Taliban. Dragged along the Bamiyan River, he suggested he walk on his own as his house was completely opposite from where they were headed. The two long-bearded men told him that they would give him sweet tea with milk. Hussein's body was found by a farmer in the afternoon. He was hit with just one bullet between his two eyes. His right clavicle was broken, and he had numerous hematomas over his body.

The whole day and night, explosives were placed in locations of the structure that the Taliban considered weak. The destruction of Afghanistan's and the world's precious cultural heritage started on March 2, 2001. Explosions were filmed and distributed to the international media, with ridiculous Taliban laughing and mocking what was in effect a tragedy for the history of the country and humankind.

Soraya was devastated and could not believe what had occurred. She, who in her young age defended in Paris with so much energy preservation of the Bamiyan Buddhas, appreciated very well how treasured they were for recognition of Afghanistan as one of the bassinets of human civilization. It was evident that outrage on human body, mind, and dignity was not enough without destruction of their culture. It was silly. Nobody worshipped the Buddhas anymore; they represented no threat to any person or religion, and they were sources of income for poor people like Hussein. The level of insanity was appalling. No one could initiate anything. Even collecting the broken pieces was not possible under such a repressive and reclusive regime.

In midsummer 2001, Soraya and I had lunch at the restaurant of the Weiner Park Tennis Club in Vienna. When needed, I always took the early-day flight from Geneva, and we met there. Located between the Vienna airport and Webster University Campus, it suited both of us. As usual, we exchanged views and compared notes on what went on in Afghanistan and elsewhere in the world.

My cell phone rang. I discerned the familiar voice of a friend from Peshawar and was surprised to learn that he was still there. After the usual Afghan greetings, which lasted no less than fifteen precious minutes on a costly international call, he alerted that the topic was very important. With my pen and notepad in front of me on the table, I was all ears to listen carefully. He notified me that Commander Massoud intended to join the Afghan delegation that went to New York for the United Nations' fifty-sixth General Assembly session.

411

He further elucidated that his main intention was to meet the United States Secretary of State, Mr. Colin Powell, and have a soldier-to-soldier conversation with him.

Indeed, he had embarked on an assiduous sensitization campaign about the true nature of the Taliban and their backers, claiming that despite official sanctions imposed on them, they still sheltered and protected Osama bin Laden. Western companies, instances. and individuals dealt with them directly or indirectly, providing them with millions of United States dollars. In April of the same year, for the first time in his life, he had moved outside his mountains of Afghanistan to address Western allies in general but Europeans in particular. In his address, he had warned "the United States government" of Osama bin Laden's malefic intentions on a very large scale. Europe understood him. But he needed to convince the incredulous. It would have been his first visit to the country that did not value him for being so independent. The commander's view matched Soraya's favorite theory about the evolution of the enemy from fundamentalism to extremism and now to international terrorism. Some did not believe her, thinking that no one could take the United States and their sophisticated intelligence services by surprise again. My interlocutor urged us to assist and advocate for a tête-à-tête meeting either in New York or Washington between "the two soldiers." I was surprised by the approach but committed to do whatever was possible.

Soraya could not understand such a degree of immaturity. "Why call from Pakistan, where the lines are carefully monitored by the mighty ISI?" she underlined with much sorrow. "You see, his intention and plan are now known to his enemies."

We instantly called a friend who had entry at the senior levels in the United States administration, explained about the request, and pleaded with him to advocate for a positive response on the part of the secretary.

On September 9, 2001, I was in Kosovo when my cell phone rang. Soraya had a broken, suffocated voice. She could hardly speak. I had never heard her with such a condition and tried desperately to quickly get to the point and then engage in a discussion. But it was impossible.

"They killed him! They murdered Massoud," she stated. "Please find out more!"

I could not believe it! This was not possible. Soraya must have been misinformed. I jumped on my phone and rang Fazel Ahmad, who had been worried about his friend and companion. He was the only reliable source who could tell me the truth—and he was unavailable. In the course of the day, the verity of the tragic news was confirmed. Afghanistan had lost a valorous son. I had never met, spoken, or written to Ahmad Shah Massoud, but I knew that he fought for his country with great devotion, honesty, courage, and commitment. He was unique in his own way, a handsome, charismatic, efficient, good-intentioned person who glorified the Afghan resistance against the Soviet Union. He was the last rock to stand against the Taliban explosion. Certainly he had weak points like all human beings; he even acknowledged them. But as is always the case with great warriors, someone similar to him would not be born soon in Afghanistan.

Within days, Soraya had perused thousands of articles and listened to dozens of tales. There were so many questions. The first assassination attempt on him had taken place in 1975, when the ISI-supported extremist party aimed to eliminate him, and then the notorious KHAD of Najibullah, the Soviet Union and their mighty KGB, the al-Qaida, and the Taliban all desperately endeavored to eradicate him. For over twenty-six years, he foiled all sophisticated attempts and thwarted his enemies. How could two suicide bombers, staged and dressed as low-level and amateurish-looking "journalists," using fake passports, succeed? It appeared that from the onset, he was distrustful and did not wish to encounter the two men "who did not look like journalists." Why was his suspicion not investigated by his entourage or considered serious by those of his "friends" who pushed hard to secure a "chat" with them? Why, for over three weeks that the two assassins lingered to accomplish the evil act, had their papers, rooms, and equipment not been checked? And finally, why was the one who survived the bombing killed on the spot in lieu of being apprehended?

Some argued that Massoud could not have been the victim of such a well-calculated, simple, and precisely measured plot without possible insiders' help. I often recalled Fazel Ahmad's anxiety for the safety and security of his friend. One of the glorious commanders of the Afghan mujahideen was cowardly murdered. Did the man who always changed locations and countered all odds and conspiracies against him indeed fall into the hands of treason? The history of Afghanistan would require time to establish the facts and researchers to find out the reasons. My friend Fazel Ahmad endured silently and never wished to speak on the phone about this topic.

Massoud had reached so many Afghans in all corners of the country within the last five years of his life to repair the damage caused by the mujahideen civil war. This was to his credit. He recognized blunders and was in the process of succeeding to establish a wider anti-Taliban coalition with his fellow commanders and friends. It is believed that he too wanted justice for misdeeds committed by the mujahideen. Many hoped that his death would not mean the end of efforts to build an independent and egalitarian nation, free of the forces of repression and discrimination.

While millions still mourned his departure within the country and tens of thousands wept in the West, the horror hit the United States just two days after Massoud's assassination. On September 11, 2001, the United States was hit in their soul and body. The entire world was outraged by the same pain felt by Americans that day. It is a pity that Western decision makers did not listen to the voice of wisdom when there was still time to avert the tragedy. And this is why Massoud wanted to have a soldier–to-soldier talk with a person that he respected. Destiny or carelessness, perhaps combined with suspicion of treachery, caused his loss. Years later under the Freedom of Information Act, the report of a classified source was revealed. *"Through Northern Alliance intelligence efforts, the late commander Massoud gained limited knowledge regarding the intentions of the Saudi millionaire, [Osama]bin Laden, and his terrorist organization, al-Qaida, to perform a terrorist act against the United States, on a scale larger than the 1998 bombing of the U.S. embassies in Kenya and Tanzania."* Knowledge of such reports, the importance of which was ignored at the time, would neither bring back the Twin Towers nor millions of lives brutally shattered by al-Qaida and its affiliates.

At the beginning of October of the same year, the United States and United Kingdom launched Operation Enduring Freedom to free Afghanistan from the Taliban regime and capture Osama bin Laden, as well as his senior lieutenants. Days after, Massoud's friend and fellow commander of the eastern parts of the country, Abdul Haq, was mysteriously assassinated by the Taliban in Azre, at the boundary between Logar and Nangarhar provinces. Within the scope of the military operations, he had entered the country for an assessment. He was too seasoned a warrior and had certainly taken precautions. But was he betrayed? Did he have an ambition that countered others? Was his murder a plot? Answers to these questions would also need time.

In November, the progress was significant. The Taliban were on the run. Soraya called for a gathering of friends and former members of the committee. We convened in the Landtmann Kaffee in Vienna. She presented a passionate overview of facts and underlined, "I cannot tell you what exactly will happen in the weeks and months to come. But there will be a new government! And they will need people from all around the world. Those of you who wish to serve the country must now get ready to be called upon or go on your own," she advised.

Weeks later, I was in the house of my American friend whom I had urged to assist in securing a meeting between Massoud and Powell, and images of the Tora Bora bombing were on all channels. He candidly asked me whether they would get Osama bin Laden there and "smoke him out," as someone had cussed. My answer was a categorical negation. Based on Afghan tribal tradition, he should have been under the protection of his family in Khost, where his presumed father-in-law and son-in-law Jalaluddin Haqani dwelled. The bombings of rugose mountains and empty caves were futile. Perhaps it was for public conviction purposes. While dozens of tons of bombs were poured on the rocks of Tora Bora, Osama bin Laden and his protectors, the ISI, drank green tea and laughed at the world's naivety.

Soraya had a very interesting view of the whole situation. While it was understood that the coalition forces entered Afghanistan from the north, where the anti-Taliban forces were very strong, why did they let them flee to Pakistan? In any sound military strategy, when your ferocious enemies were cornered, you do not just let them proceed to their sanctuaries. Within days, all the Taliban leaders, their Wahhabi supporters, and their Pakistani tutors were out. There were even rumors of countless military aircrafts transporting them from northern Afghanistan to safety. Such questions led to numerous conspiracy theories, with justified significance.

Afghanistan has been in perpetual turmoil since Daoud Khan changed the smooth and steady current of evolution, but more specifically as of the communist coup of April 1978. The toll has been very heavy on all populations. But the status of two non-Muslim communities has altered dramatically. In spite of all challenges, the country counted a few Jewish families. They were Afghans, felt so, and were proud of belonging to the country. The caves and ruins of this land provided the oldest, perhaps several thousand years of age, manuscripts of the Torah. In October 2013, a fifty-page Hebrew text was discovered in another cave, dating around 840 CE, that is older by four hundred years than the oldest Torah text on earth. Like the Buddhas of Bamiyan, these texts represent the cultural heritage of the country. Today, though, Jewish Afghans are eradicated from the country. The same applies to the Hindu and Sikh populations of Afghanistan. They were the first non-Muslim communities that spread practically in all cities and provinces. India and Afghanistan have shared history and culture. The Taj Mahal, built by Muslims, and the Buddhas of Bamiyan, sculptured by Buddhists, were recognized World Cultural Heritage Sites. However, practically all members of these two communities were forced out of the country; only a few have withstood the pressures.

The Taliban era was certainly the darkest in the history of the country. Their perception of an ideal society, knowledge of Islam, link with terrorist leaders and organizations, subjugation to foreign countries, record of violations of human dignity and rights, particularly with regard to women and children, destruction of cultural heritage, understanding of justice, and many other practices were in contradiction with international norms and seriously awkward. Though their wish was to take back the country to the initial phases of Islam in the seventh century, their acts did not reflect even an iota of what the leader of Islam exercised. Referring to the early ages of Islam, it became evident that the Hodaybiyyah Treaty was signed to ensure peace between Muslims and pagans. In an agreement with the Jewish community, it was stipulated clearly that *"no believer shall oppose the client of another believer. Whosoever is rebellious, or seeks to spread injustice, enmity or sedition among the believers, the hand of every man shall be against him, even if he be a son of one of them. A believer shall not kill a believer in retaliation of an unbeliever, nor shall he help an unbeliever against a believer."* The Charter of Privileges and Rights granted by the leader of Islam to the Christian community of Sinai, Najran, or elsewhere provided them full religious and administrative autonomy. It appeared that numerous such documents were possessed by the Greek Orthodox Church.

The Taliban practice of killing in the name of God was deplorable. It was obvious that they were an instrument of a policy of domination by a particular ideology through two particular countries. Religion was just an implementation tool like in many circumstances in the history of humankind. It provided for slavery and colonization, crowned by unforgivable crimes, perpetrated in the name of religion. And always, the most destitute among all human beings paid the highest cost. When would humankind understand the real message of God? Millions of Afghans perished since 1978 in the name of a communist revolution that they did not desire, by a giant invader who crashed the country to impose itself, by fratricidal fighting among mujahideen groups for power and wealth, as well as by an extremist religious regime away from the principles and realities of Islam. And it is not yet the end of the history! Who will then be accountable, and when will justice be rendered? Soraya suggested that genocide has been perpetrated in Afghanistan, and the classic definition of the word must be improved to include massive numbers of people killed in the name of an ideology, a political system, or territorial gains. Hence, Stalin and many others would join the notorious list of those who committed such heinous acts.

Chapter 7

The Chagrins of Post-2001 Liberation

We come nearest to the great when we are great in humility.

—Rabindranath Tagore,
Stray Birds

It is not titles that honor men, but men that honor titles.

—Niccolò Machiavelli,
The Prince

The entry point of the Operation Enduring Freedom ground forces into Afghanistan began from the north and progressed well. Often the population grumbled about carpet-bombing due to the sorrow of losing family members or destruction of houses constructed with lifetime earnings or for new brides of the families. But the joy of witnessing the Taliban on the run seemed overwhelming and greater. Slowly, a massive number of troops from some forty countries poured into different corners of the country. Like in Kosovo years back, major NATO countries divided Afghanistan into five regional commands, that is, north, south, east, west, and the capital. The American, British, and French opted essentially to lead the south and east regional commands. The prime objective was to chase and apprehend the Taliban and al-Qaida remnants. Their task included to rush and "smoke them out" wherever they sought sanctuary. German troops were stationed in the north, initially described as an easy location. Italy led the west regional command along the Iranian border. The capital and airports were in the hands of United States troops. A new phase of hope appeared on the horizon.

Soraya reiterated to her circle of friends that the follow-up to the repressive Taliban system would depend solely on how the international presence, but more specifically the United States, coped with the situation and realities on the ground. Her reasoning was plain: no blueprint of a plan of any kind designed at headquarters had so far succeeded in this country; only field realities dictated the right or wrong approaches. Were the foreigners going to be in command themselves? Would they govern by proxy? Or would they assist and accompany Afghans to develop their own democratic system that would ensure sovereignty, security, and safety of the populations, as well as creating a solid foundation for a strong and united future nation?

However and as anticipated, days after the start of the operation, it was clear that the international forces did not aim to assist Afghans to forge a nation but to apprehend those who demolished the Twin Towers and inflicted humiliation on the United States. While public opinion was focused on television screens admiring the use of sophisticated military arsenals and actions of combat forces of Western superpowers against the routed Taliban, an article appeared in the *Washington Post* in early November 2001 reporting aerial support by the United States to "an Afghan opposition leader" named Hamid Karzai. Hardly a week later, a few "prominent Afghan figures" were convened in or summoned to Bonn in Germany to lay down the foundation of the future state. Following biting negotiations, a foggy and blurred map of power sharing and distribution scheme was decided upon.

For most observers, it seemed as if Afghanistan was definitely deceased, and its wealth allocated to a few—some of whom had never been within the country for decades or engaged in any meaningful manner in support of their population. Everything took place in an undescribed rush. Though not the choice of Afghan participants, Hamid Karzai was identified by "foreign friends" of Afghanistan as the interim head. The seeds of discord were already sown as many questioned the process and why no credibility and recognition was given to an Afghan government that assumed legitimacy, at least on paper and by the international community since the fall of the communist regime in1992. Gossip and conspiracy theories abounded. Some claimed that the "legal president" was detained by his own lieutenants at the request of the superpowers to allow the Bonn "cluster of personalities" to strike a deal. At the end of December of the same year, just less than two months after his parachuting and landing in central Afghanistan, Hamid Karzai was chairman of a post-Taliban Afghanistan. The "legitimate president" had to "abdicate" silently!

Though the essence of the Bonn Agreement would always be subject to discussion, it was, nevertheless, greeted with joy by Afghans who saw hope at the end of a very dark and long tunnel in their lives. However, some still stipulated that the foundation of the future Afghanistan began with the wrong stones. The total dearth of Western interest in nation-building endeavors staged the first and foremost uncalculated blunder. For centuries, the peoples of the country did not sense that rulers and governments pursued an all-inclusive policy. In their view, the society hardly offered equal opportunities to its ethnic components. In 2002 after nearly twenty-four years of intensive and bloody conflicts, during which all communities demonstrated and proved their valorous courage, competency, resilience, and love for Afghanistan with extraordinary human and material losses, it was definitely the right time to forge the basis for a future strong nation. The opportunity was totally missed! Even participants of the Bonn Conference who had witnessed actively within the country the dramatic inter-Afghan conflicts between 1992 and 2001 did not raise their voices. They should have insisted on such a prerequisite. But grabbing a larger share of power, money, or specific positions in a future governing body seemed more important than founding a sound future for citizens.

Moreover, for Afghans who had been involved in the struggle in one way or the other, the choice of Mr. Karzai was an unprecedented surprise. He was a member of a mujahideen movement and at the same time part of the circle of the former King Zaher Shah. Most Afghans were amazed with the Washington Post's qualification of him as "an opposition leader." His making appeared to have occurred in a restaurant in Maryland, where a significant number of American politicians and senior bureaucrats congregated for long luncheons and dinners. Nobody desired a strong and unbending leader for Afghanistan. It seems that a specialized company located on Park Avenue of New York City even took charge of developing his image as a leading personality against millions of United States dollars provided by the United States government. Afghans did not care who would lead them, provided the country found peace and stability. Apparently and certainly like many others, the young Hamid Karzai was noticed by the CIA years back in their Peshawar office when he "forcefully argued" regarding the efficiency of their aid to mujahideen groups. He was then preferred to lead the post-Taliban Afghanistan.

The overwhelming majority of the population welcomed his advent. However, in expert circles, his transport to Uruzgan in central Afghanistan by the United States forces was compared to Babarak Karmal's dispatch by the Soviet Union to Tashkent in December 1979. Both were brought by foreign troops who then entered Afghanistan. The difference between the two "manufacturings" was time, exactly twenty-two years later, and legal framework. While Karmal's takeover and the Soviet invasion of Afghanistan were totally unlawful and in contradiction to all principles of international law, Mr. Karzai's accession to power and the arrival of foreign troops in 2001 were based on a well-defined legal charter, enshrined particularly in the United Nations Security Council Resolutions 1383 dated December 6 and 1386 of December 20, 2001. The other fact that distinguished the two men dealt with their political stature. Babrak Karmal was known as a leader of the Parcham faction of the PDPA for decades, but Mr. Karzai was a completely unknown quantity and quality for the majority of Afghan people. This fact was an enormous advantage as over two decades of war and desolation had completely tarnished the image of known chieftains and commanders that some did not hesitate to call "warlords."

Therefore, Afghans wholeheartedly greeted the new chairman and foreign troops for the sake of the future peace, security, and prosperity of their country. There was a feeling that after the Nairobi, Dar es Salam, Yemen, New York, and Washington tragedies, the American administration had finally resolved and effectively embarked on eradicating extremism and terrorism for good. A friend of ours summarized the popular perception in Afghanistan extremely accurately. "They cannot make another blatant gaffe! They will go and 'smoke them out' as they said," he insisted.

The Taliban and al-Qaida were finally vanquished in Afghanistan. However, fear of their return resurged within weeks. Not only were their leaders and fighters given an opportunity to flee to neighboring Pakistan from the southern parts of the country but foreign aircraft were allowed to land and airlift to safety thousands of them and their associates trapped in the northern parts of Afghanistan. What was going on? The right strategy would have been not to bomb Tora Bora fruitlessly but to seal five or six main crossing points along the Pakistani border and fetch one by one all the wanted individuals within Afghan territory. Was it a hidden understanding within the Bonn Agreement to allow the neighbor of Afghanistan that nurtured and supported the Taliban regime a face-saving opportunity and secure their backing for the deal? Was it purely an American decision as they searched for Osama bin Laden and the al-Qaida sharks who may have already sought protection in Pakistan? Did they receive assurance from this country's masters to hand them over once they crossed the border? Or was it a flaw in the strategy? Everything and nothing could be plausible, but certainly a few may know all the details. In spite of hundreds of millions of dollars exhausted in different manners, the international community was not able to capture even one wanted major culprit!

This was how Operation Enduring Freedom was gauged by experts and by most Afghans from its onset. The Guantanamo Bay Naval Base hosted only third and lower categories of captured enemy leaders and some sympathizers. Such an incomprehensible approach allowed the Taliban and al-Qaida to regroup, reorganize, and rearm themselves in the neighboring tribal areas with the very strong hand of the ISI. The fact that Osama bin Laden escaped the United States manhunt and could easily secure sanctuary and protection in Pakistan gave another important boost to the morale of the defeated forces. Some Afghan experts did not hide their pessimism and even panicked with such objectionable errors. Were they intentional or due to lack of appreciation? Whichever it was, there were reasons to be worried about the strategy of the West. Practically all Afghans scratched their heads wondering if repeated warnings were given due attention on time, the political, military, and social pictures would not have been different. But such reflections did not serve any purpose anymore.

Mr. Karzai immediately announced a cabinet that was decided upon in Bonn. It was of purely political nature. Proficiency and the ability to carry on state affairs had not been the rationale for appointments. Similar to the mujahideen takeover in 1992, power and money looked like poisonous cakes that the mighty people fought for. For example, Fazel Ahmad, a medical doctor, occupied the portfolio of aviation and tourism! Soraya and I were happy for him. But barely a few weeks later, we were notified of his shocking and tragic death.

The official explanation recounted that a mob of angry pilgrims on their way to Mecca were not content about their aircraft and struck him. Beaten to death, his body was tossed and hauled on the tarmac. However, nobody believed that people who were on their way to the holiest location of Islam seeking forgiveness for their lifetime of sins would commit murder, the ugliest of all offenses. They knew well that the Holy Book stipulated clearly that *"anyone who kills a soul, it is as if he slew mankind entirely; and whoever saves one—it is as if he salvaged humanity."* Most in Kabul and elsewhere who knew him concluded it was a deliberate elimination as he retained sensitive knowledge on all aspects of the evolution of Afghan history and its actors since 1978. Some suggested that he possessed data about Massoud's assassination. For fear of being unmasked, those involved may have opted to kill him abruptly. It looked indeed extremely strange that among all ministerial figures of the new government and merely a few weeks after being sworn in, he was the only one assassinated. His sympathizers were of the opinion that he was a potential presidential candidate too, election of whom would not have pleased a few countries and some august institutions. However, the fact of the matter was that the accused assassins seemed to be protected in Saudi Arabia.

Soraya and I felt very despondent for we had conversed days earlier with him and inquired if he himself felt secure. Afghanistan's liberation was beginning with blood again! It reminded Soraya of her ancestral village years earlier, when the imam announced a gory future ahead based on the color of the moon. She was apprehensive and seemed anxious for people who had seen nothing but war and destruction for decades.

A month after his ascension to power as chairman of the transitional government, Hamid Karzai commenced a tour of the world. Between 2002 and 2013, he undertook at least sixteen official visits to the United States alone and perhaps hundreds more elsewhere. He was always escorted and shepherded by a massive number of government officials and affiliates. Indisputably, each stopover cost millions of dollars extracted from the public treasury. In a country that had gone through long spans of war, destruction, and desolation in which people hardly obtained a rotten piece of dry bread to gobble, such luxury could not have been justified in any circumstance or manner. It was a mockery and insult to people who wished he stayed within

425

the country, healed their wounds, reached remote corners, and served the people. Some former members of the committee were appalled. One often remarked, "Is he the chairman of the Afghan government or David Niven playing the role of Englishman Phileas Fogg in *Around the World in Eighty Days*?"

His cabinet had a weird composition. The blend of "experts" brought from Western countries as well as some tribal and warring actors did not match conveniently. Everybody around the leadership table knew and either accepted or disregarded each other. As they all felt they were the United States picks, silence and connivance became the rule of the game. Repeated calls to exclude some notorious culprits of the mujahideen factional conflicts, sympathizers of extremist movements, or incompetent dignitaries from his surroundings did not seem to impress him. Perhaps he had no choice and under the prevailing circumstances could be exonerated from having made a deliberate mistake. He then pushed hard to bring back the old monarch Zaher Shah to stand by his side and supplement his stature and prestige. The former king at the age of eighty-eight returned to Kabul to back him.

In June 2002, Mr. Karzai called for a *loya jirga*, the traditional assembly of Afghan chieftains, to give his chairmanship some sort of legitimacy. Without surprise, he was elected as interim president of Afghanistan till a new constitution was drafted and democratic elections were organized. His impulsivity and eagerness to be a great man were noticeable from the onset. Furthermore, he opted for the reckless practice of using rivalries to his advantage and established his own slush fund to strengthen his power base. Regional powers found a golden opportunity to fortify their influence within the Afghan decision-making institutions by subsidizing and refloating the fund, while the West and Americans in particular spent billions blindly. Corrupting, enticing, or inducing influential individuals became the state exercise at all levels. Therefore, bribery, fraud, and dishonesty commenced at the inception of the new and supposedly democratic Afghanistan.

A few acknowledged Mr. Karzai's good intentions and put the blame on the American giant who desired "no one to be dismayed." Of course in any democratic society, there must be opposition as only dictatorships know the sacred principle of unanimity. Rapidly, the president's and other dignitaries' family members became recipients of juicy multimillion-dollar contracts or holders of key government positions. Some even confiscated unlimited portions of public lands or grasped heavy amounts of money from private banks where poor people had entrusted their meager savings. Others in the government followed the practice. Within months, the cancers of corruption, nepotism, and inefficiency had infected the whole body of the new government. The habit sieved down to all lower levels of government, the business community, and even shopkeepers and retailers. If a well-dressed individual purchased an apple from a store and paid for the item, there was a 90 percent likelihood that the owner would say, "Sir, you paid just for the fruit. Where is my own bounty?"

Even beggars on the street commenced asking for dollar banknotes and refused ordinary local money. Swiftly, people comprehended that without offering a "reward" even for public service providers, nothing moved forward. This was an unexpected gift to the Taliban and their affiliates, who carefully observed the situation from across the border. It was very simple to decide on a modus operandi to hit back. Their strategy involved a twofold approach. On the one hand, they bribed government officials to obtain useful and classified intelligence, thereby infiltrating the heart of the Afghan security apparatus. At the same time, in rural areas they assisted victims of injustice perpetrated by government dignitaries and associates using the force of guns and sporadic occupation. The enemy now knew that they could retaliate easily.

A few months later, a dramatic situation completely changed Mr. Karzai's perception of reaching his people. During the first visit to his ancestral city of Kandahar in September 2002, he was the "subject of an assassination attempt," though this official version is disputed now. Experts believe that leaked videos and footage do not comprehensively suggest such a theory. The incident, however, impelled him and his entourage to deduce that he was not secure anywhere in his own country. He then opted to secure the services of American bodyguards only. The man who ruled Afghanistan could not find any trustworthy Afghan to rely on! He then contained himself in the Presidential Palace to the extent that some of his own protectors labeled him later on as mayor of the lieu. To compensate for this weakness, he began touring extensively, even too much, abroad to persuade public opinion of his efficiency. The justification was to "gain international support" for Afghanistan. He did not need to do so. Not only did over one hundred thirty thousand foreign soldiers equipped with the most sophisticated weapons and military needs on earth protect him and his regime but billions of United States dollars flowed into the country without him even requesting them.

Mr. Karzai's vital job was to reach people in the deepest parts of Afghanistan and try to build a nation. No one can construct a reliable building on a faulty foundation. The groundwork for the new Afghanistan commenced on a wrong footing in Bonn. The desire to strike a deal speedily over comprehension of social, political, and economic alterations after nearly three decades of conflict, destruction, and killings as well as calls for remedies to historic unfairness was unwarranted. It looked like *Donald Duck's Golden Eggs*. Bonn was indeed a "quick fix" with unfortunate consequences. What also surprised most observers was that since mid-2002, not only were foreign troops attacked in different corners of the country, but on September 5 of the same year, nine months after the arrival of international military might to "smoke the terrorists out," a car bomb killed more than thirty innocent individuals in the heart of the city of Kabul. The wanted ones felt strong enough to cross the border, run through hundreds of kilometers, reach their target, and demonstrate their ferocity. Some in the country already began doubting the American strategy.

After over twenty-one years, Soraya made her first visit to Kabul in the winter of 2002. As soon as she landed, her heart started aching. The city she had known was a ghost of itself. There were military and armored vehicles in every corner. Buildings, houses, mosques, and even streams and the Kabul River had huge scars of the civil war among mujahideen groups as well as the tyrannical and ruthless rule of the Taliban. Kabul had the real face of *Apocalypse Now*! The exquisite parks of Shar-e-Naw, Zarnegar, and Babur were transformed into ruins. As for individual estates, her ancestral house, the place where her thoughts had always remained, was a shambles, and everywhere the holes, big or small, demonstrated the violence of shooting and fighting. Even in the cold winter, the stench and putrefaction of perhaps bodies and mass graves or other objects under rubble testified to the colossal work ahead. The Presidential Palace had not been struck, as if each warring faction dreamed that their Pegasus would land there one day.

Soraya took the liberty to move around the city and jumped in an unbearably grimy taxi. The driver, who was also the owner, had nicknamed it the Rolls-Royce of the city. Soraya was amused. The back seat was torn apart, and the yellow foam was transformed into a black and oily sort of object. Every place seemed like a graveyard. Inhabitants appeared poorly dressed, pale and tired, but still cheerful and courteous. She knew nobody, not even her own neighbors. There were entire generations of new occupants in the city. Everything was muddled and chaotic. No traffic police were discerned at the horizon to regulate the wild and much contaminated circulation of cars, animals, rickshaws, bicycles, and human beings over the roads that looked like craters. What the hell had been done to this once upon a time gorgeous country?

Soraya went to the Intercontinental Hotel, on the Kart-e-Parwan hill, five hundred meters from the famous Bagh-e-Bala where her marriage had taken place decades ago, to reserve a room. The pearl of all hotels in the capital city leaked from all corners. Rooms were dreadfully freezing. There was no heating system. She had to send the Rolls-Royce owner to buy a local stove with wood. A bonfire was made in her room to keep warm, with the risk of burning the hotel itself. But there was no other alternative; every guest, foreigner or Afghan, did the same. There was not a blanket left at the hotel. The Rolls-Royce proprietor proved useful again and procured several local "*lehafs*," a sort of Afghan cotton coverlet. Of course, he charged much more money than necessary and demanded United States dollars. Soraya felt protected and warm underneath. Basic foods were missing. Guests had to reveal their desires the day before; otherwise they went hungry. Windows were shattered by bullets fired from all corners. The view to the east and west of Kabul city, which was once breathtaking, now represented desolation and martyrdom of the populations.

Soraya had deep feelings for the people of Afshar, which was visible in the west. She remembered the glorious epoch when Kabul prospered, but had now a broken heart and distraught mind. From each corner of the city, the sound and signs of death emerged. She was scared of walking for fear of stepping on somebody's skull underneath her feet. She was desperate and frantic for a few days. There was no system in place. While foreign representations and troops had been very well established and operated smoothly, the Afghan Transitional Administration still struggled to have telephone lines. Billions of United States dollars had already been allocated and perhaps even "spent and devoured," but then why was no tangible improvement noticeable? She asked some government high officials. The only answer she obtained was that there was no capacity within the country. Therefore, not only was aid money kept in private bank accounts outside the country, but foreign entities needed to come in and do the job at a very high cost.

The worst observation at this early stage of international presence in Afghanistan consisted of grumbling in the rural areas about the behavior of "foreign friends" who did not value the culture and privacy of citizens. Uninformed and forceful intrusions by soldiers into dwellings in search of enemies violated the traditional code of conduct. After the Taliban and al-Qaida were allowed to flee to their sanctuaries in Pakistan, people did not understand such a vehement and insulting approach of American and British troops. The fact, however, was that the country had not been cleaned of terrorists. The search for enemies was recognized as a necessity by the population; however, the methodology was rejected. Signs of people's unhappiness and grief were already evident. The Taliban and al-Qaida took advantage and had moved to within Afghanistan, while the Presidential Palace and its protectors dreamed of prosperity, safety, and security.

With such a bleak picture, Soraya still believed that it was the greatest opportunity for Afghan patriots from all corners of the world to do something meaningful for their country. The chance of making a beautiful, safe, prosperous, and neutral Afghanistan was real. Though a lot had changed, her presence in Kabul was not unremarked. Within days, she was received warmly by many bigwigs. Soraya was soon invited to the palace too. An old friend of hers described Mr. Karzai as too sure of himself and somehow idealistic. Her encounter with the interim president of Afghanistan was candid and amicable. He knew who she was but did not have full knowledge of what she had accomplished in support of Afghanistan during the last two decades. He seemed confident that with the help of his American friends, Afghanistan would face prosperity and peace soon.

Her encounter with the foreign minister was amazingly straightforward. He had somehow forgotten that their fathers had been good friends but quickly grasped her struggle for liberty.

"Madame, we need your help. The country is shattered, and we do not have enough competence," he said.

"I will be glad to assist," she replied. "However, I do not even have a place to live. Our ancestral property was destroyed during the civil war and grabbed by some warlords," she informed him.

"Unfortunately, that is a sorrowful fact in our country now," he replied.

She had a warm feeling to be back in the Marble Palace. The good memories of collaboration with Mr. Mousa Shafiq and the less pleasant incidents with the little man all returned to her mind. Her thoughts were divided among several duties. Afghanistan, her job at the Vienna Webster, and her family were all priorities. Indeed, her father's house was snatched by notorious gunmen. She strived to claim it back. However and despite her stature and reputation, practically every individual who dealt with the topic at each government institution openly demanded a bribe.

Soraya met with a friend and former committee member, Omar, who resided in Germany and had returned to Kabul to repossess his parental property in Karte Char; it was also appropriated by a warlord. She understood that almost all her acquaintances found themselves in the same situation. Omar indicated that he had arrived in Kabul with strong references to someone highly positioned in Mr. Karzai's administration in order to assist him to have due process in a court of law. But the gentleman in question had alerted him that he should abide by the rules of the moment in town, not by what he had acquired or practiced in Germany. Omar was threatened and kicked out of the area by gunmen. He had no choice but to return to Europe spluttering. Everywhere, armed men with military sunglasses and tinted four-wheel-drive vehicles ruled.

A few days later, she met another former committee member, Zaher, who recounted a similar story. He lived as a refugee in Switzerland

and came to Afghanistan immediately after the fall of the Taliban regime. He purchased a piece of land in the new area of Khair Khana, near the airport. Nine months later, when he came back with a meager additional amount of money to build a house, he saw a palatial building already constructed on his land. Within an hour of his presence on the scene, several Toyota Land Cruisers appeared with their leader, who inquired what Zaher was doing there.

"I bought this land nine months ago to construct a house for my family," he stated. "And now God has given me an already made house of such beauty."

"Look, man!" the leader stated firmly. "We know who you are and where you came from. God has given you nothing! You understand? Take your flight back tomorrow as I do not appreciate seeing you around," he threatened.

Zaher too had no option but to rush back to his country of asylum. There were innumerable such realities. However, those who had connections at the highest apparatus of the government or security forces regained their properties in full.

Soraya resolved to fight the powerful warlords who had grabbed her dwelling. It was not so much the monetary value of the house that counted but its emotional worth. It was her home. She cherished every corner of the property. The memory of infantile chats and mature discussions with her beloved father was still fresh in her mind. In the process, she had to meet with numerous decision makers of the country to protest about nepotism and venality. Of course, they confessed and clearly avowed that the extent of the scourge was such that no one could fight it.

Soraya wished to visit her father's grave in Logar but was directed by security chieftains not to proceed as the government did not have total control over the area. Her cousins, however, had a dissimilar judgment and persuaded her "to take the risk." The conditions looked the same. There were signs of heavy fighting, wrecked walls, gunshot effects, and even trees expunged to prevent opponents from seeking protection behind them. The intensity and devastation of decades of war and killing had damaged the bodies and souls of people in Afghanistan. She met the very old imam of her village. He was in the final phases of a life during which he had witnessed every horror. Blind in both eyes, he recognized Soraya's voice. Teardrops came out of the dried eye sockets of the old man. In an effort, he stressed that the country was not for her anymore.

Another worrisome fact consisted of the cultivation of opium, particularly in the south. While the Taliban had eradicated the plague of farming it by 90 percent, declaring it un-Islamic, it had exponentially intensified in 2002. The amplification of the calamity attained an unprecedented proportion of the country, culminating to two hundred thirty thousand hectares in 2014. The tragedy was that practically the totality of arable land in Helmand and parts of Kandahar, where the best and most influential international troops were stationed, was devoted to opium cultivation. What then were the foreign troops doing there? Yet again, it provided a gold-plated opportunity for the Taliban and al-Qaida not only to denounce the inefficiency of the international presence, but also to sequester the business—even if they had earlier declared it un-Islamic—for their financial advantage.

Back in Austria, Soraya had mixed opinions and posed questions as to whether the unjustified chaos after a year of independence was deliberate, created by mafia networks to gain from the rainfall of money. She felt hopeful and worried at the same time. For years, she had initiated and undertaken advocacy endeavors with foreign capital and personalities. It was time to work with Afghans themselves, she had concluded. Meanwhile, refugees returned by the hundreds of thousands from the neighboring countries of Pakistan and Iran, putting more pressure on a dysfunctional governing system.

Soraya was flabbergasted by the euphoric attitude of most Afghan politicians and senior bureaucrats, as well as foreign friends. The objectives were indeed very far from being achieved, and the enemy threatened again and very seriously. Mr. Karzai's belief that he could strike a deal with the Taliban and Pakistan to expel al-Qaida, hand over Osama bin Laden, and engage in peace talks was too optimistic; it lacked vision and understanding of his own people. Some thought that he already dreamed of a Nobel Peace Prize and was in a hurry to receive it. True or not, he certainly ignored the fact that foreign backing could not constitute the basis of his legitimacy. He needed to work with his own people to forge it. But at the same time, it has to be underlined that he was certainly and surely in a difficult position. Constantly he received American and British instructions in the form of "useful advice" that he had to implement. Some of his friends were of the opinion that he had to put an end to the process if he desired to be credible or even speak about it publicly; at a minimum, he needed to at least reduce the pressure if he could not stop it.

In addition, the inner revulsion of the families of victims should have been understood by Mr. Karzai. They desired accountability and punishment of the strategists and executioners inside or outside Afghanistan for crimes perpetrated. No new status—whether refugee, alien, or fresh nationality in a foreign country—should exempt a criminal from justice. At the same time, no new position, senior as it could be, should protect a culprit from prosecution in Afghanistan. Within the framework of the United Nations Security Council resolutions, the populations expected no political deals with those who had committed crimes against humanity, war crimes, or deliberate killings. Not trusting their own government, some had already begun to seek international justice. But from the inception of the Bonn Agreement, the Afghan government was considered a lightweight that neither the radical movements nor concerned regional powers deemed free and independent.

Soraya often quoted Martin Luther King Jr. to her interlocutors:

435

*We need leaders not in love with money but in love
with justice. Not in love with publicity but in love with
humanity. Leaders who can subject their particular
egos to the pressing urgencies of the great cause of
freedom.... A time like this demands great leaders.*

Afghanistan indeed lacked great leaders—and had for a very long
time! No one in the highest hierarchy of the government comprehended
that their country was an instrument for implementation of a much
larger foreign strategic objective. Some reasonably judged that their
government's highest dignitaries were recipients of great respect
that the world evidenced for the Afghan people. However, those in
charge barely understood that leadership was not a privilege but a
responsibility with accountability toward the populations. Within
a year, Afghanistan resembled a seventeenth-century feudal land
partitioned among a few notorious families of the most senior Afghan
government officials and political nomenclature. Each power district
had its own interest sphere. People were forgotten, and like gangrene,
corruption infested the veins, muscles, nerves, and bones of the
society.

Soraya and I were dismayed when Bashir, a young former member
of the committee, returned back from Kabul. His story was most
divulging of the unethical values put in place. Based on initial advice
provided by Soraya on the eve of international intervention, Bashir
proceeded from Oslo to Kabul and was appointed senior adviser in a
particular ministry. All went well for the first four weeks or so. Then
he was summoned by the deputy minister to be notified that he spoke
too much in official sessions. He took note of the advice and strived
not to intervene as often as he had in the past, but he continued to
articulate his opinion when he deemed it necessary. A few weeks
later, he was called again and cautioned about the same issue. This
time, the deputy minister and Bashir agreed that the government
dignitary would give him a wink when his advice was required on
a specific topic. Three weeks later and to his great astonishment, he

was summoned once more. It was then revealed that the winking of the deputy minister was due to a scar of wartime, not an invitation to take the floor. In his sixth month, he was summoned by the minister himself for a tête-à-tête.

The minister began, "Bashir, my deputy told you that you speak too much."

"Yes, sir," Bashir replied. "But I am your adviser and doing my job."

"Look, gentleman," the minister said. "Do you have guns?"

"No, sir."

"Do you have armed men with you?"

"No, sir."

"Can you bring me money?"

"No, sir. It is not part of my job description."

"Then you are nothing and nobody," the minister emphasized. "I do not want you to create trouble."

"But I have knowledge and intelligence, sir, and would like to use them for my country through you," Bashir stated.

The minister guffawed piercingly and reminded Bashir that in post-2001 Afghanistan, everybody had wisdom and was shrewd. There were many like him on the streets of Kabul. But he required advisers who disposed of force or fetched money. Soraya was revolted and felt guilty for having encouraged Bashir to go and serve his country. His former agency did not employ him again, and he lost years of credit and hard work. Someone could argue that more than a year, even if the country lived a "dollar deluge epoch," was not enough to make a difference. But in Afghanistan there is a proverb saying, *"Whatever takes place is planned from the beginning."* There was certainly timid progress in the fields of freedom of expression and emancipation of women. However, powerful circles within the government and even the business community seemed above the law. No one could approach the black-tinted four-wheel-drive luxury cars that were followed by multiple private security vehicles and guards. All signs indicated that post-2001 Afghan "democracy" was tailored to serve the interests of a few, not the people.

On the eve of the Persian New Year in March 2003, another most unfortunate event occurred in the international arena that once again drew attention away from Afghanistan. A coalition force led by the United States and United Kingdom invaded Iraq to "eradicate the country's weapons of mass destruction," though the United Nations experts had recurrently warned and alluded about their nonexistence. Some distinguished and valorous personalities were goaded to even provide incorrect "intelligence proof" to the Security Council of the United Nations that outraged other members who possessed enough data to prevent a disaster. The world was split between those who trusted the experts' accounts and those who had definitely opted to topple the Iraqi dictator, Saddam Hussein. To convince public and political opinion, some authoritative leaders even asserted that the Iraqi dictator had "existing and active military plans for the use of chemical and biological weapons, which could be activated within forty-five minutes." Indeed, under such circumstances fear of being attacked dominated over a sound and logical appreciation of the state of affairs.

Aware of the anxieties of the worldview regarding Afghanistan and the unaccomplished tasks, at the same occasion, it was declared that the country was "freed from the Taliban" but still suffered. Saddam Hussein, who was cherished and encouraged by British and Americans to attack Iran some years back, was not needed anymore. Like General Zia-Ul-Haq, he had to be eliminated.

For Soraya, it was yet another setback for the people of Afghanistan. Globally, removal of a dictator from power to put an end to the sorrow and anguish of his people was not disputed, but the method deployed, certainly was. Moreover, this time around, Afghanistan would be left to a group of people who were incompetent, inept, and corrupt. A very knowledgeable Western friend of Afghanistan labeled the superlatives used by Western experts and media about the Afghan leader—such as "world star" or "quick with a quip in a clipped British-Indian accent that conjure[d] up Ben Kingsley as Gandhi"—senseless.

What also characterized this period was the practice of high authorities offering empty assurances to Shias, Hindus, other minorities, war victims, destitute, and even refugees outside Afghanistan without any follow-up actions. Most of them appeared like talking machines, whose memories were erased as soon as they stopped to speak. In 1988 the West left Afghanistan to the Pakistanis, and the consequences were devastating for all. Billions of dollars were frittered away and squandered, perhaps diverted to private bank accounts in the rich Persian Gulf emirates or elsewhere. Thousands of Western servicemen and women sacrificed their lives to get the Taliban and al-Qaida out of the country. Hardly a year after such an expression of solidarity and demonstration of sacrifice, the decision to leave Afghanistan in the hands of amateurish, unprepared, shady, and clueless "administrators" to focus on Iraq was a fatal calamity for the people of the country.

Soraya was so right in her analysis. The Islamic world and the West could not bridge their differences and mistrust. With an isolated and adamant Iran on one side and dictatorships of all kinds mastered by the types of Saddam Hussein, Muammar Gaddafi, and similar leaders in the other hand, the hope for appeasement was a distant wish. Some judged that the Iraq incursion was the start of a unilateral "reshaping of the Middle East." Soraya often underscored that the West needed to have smart, brilliant interlocutors to take over from dictatorships. And Afghanistan was already an unfortunate example. Quickly fabricated new leaders, like any fast food, would not be healthy. And if imposed, then the expected change process would be lengthy and bloody. A professor of Kabul University compared the futility of "efforts to bring democracy" to those of development undertakings. In his opinion, the West must at least succeed in one country before jumping to another leaving the first job unfinished. Otherwise, trust in democratic systems of governance will erode in time.

Though Afghans were no longer structured abroad in support of their country of origin, former members of the committee still pursued advocacy efforts. Soraya tracked developments carefully and had encountered many members of the government leadership during their very frequent European tours. For professional reasons, she also visited cities and capitals in the Old Continent from time to time and had the usual courtesy calls on Afghan ambassadors. Indeed, she was esteemed by most Afghan envoys, who devoted time for her whenever she requested.

June 2003 offered a second opportunity for Soraya and Mr. Karzai to meet in London at the Berkley in Knightsbridge. The Afghan president was in the city to "secure more help for the motherland," as his advisers used to say. She enjoyed this edifice, initially constructed for mail-coach travelers, that became a renowned hotel at the beginning of the twentieth century when the award-winning restaurants served customers. It was close to the Afghan Embassy and Hyde Park, where she had unforgettable memories of her time in London. In fact and since 1968, it was her first occasion to return to the United Kingdom. She was there to attend the funeral of her esteemed Professor Bernard Williams, who had just passed away at the age of seventy-three. His demise had occurred days before in Italy from a brutal heart failure. She wanted to pay her last respects to the soul of this gentleman of great values who had helped her in moments of desperation. Professor Williams was a second and spiritual father to her. Even at the burial, she had a discrete, tender smile on her lips, recalling how much he detested the desk and chair in his office. After the memorial, she sauntered around and tried to discern the changes.

The morning after her arrival, she was having quietly her breakfast. At the next table, there was an old couple. The man seemed agitated, while the woman attempted to calm him. Soraya was nearby and overheard the dispute. He was terribly annoyed.

"I am sorry, madame, for the expression of my anger," he stated apologetically. "We have an important program in town but are retained here because a pasha of I do not know where has to come out of his room. The whole lobby is now a prohibited area."

"I understand you, sir," Soraya calmly replied. Curious to know the reaction of the couple, she inquired, "Who is he?"

"The man with a colorful frock from Afghanistan," the wife retorted.

"Yeah, the guy who looks more hyper than me," the man jokingly underlined.

At this moment, there was a sort of brouhaha outside, and everybody rushed to the door. Soraya too moved on as she had to catch her flight back to Vienna. They were all clogged on the stairs leading to the lobby. Countless heavily armed security officers had barred every inch of the location. The whole area seemed under siege. Within minutes she noticed President Karzai and a huge crowd of disciples running after him, all surrounded by armed security officials. As usual, he was in a hurry and passed in front of Soraya hastily. But seconds later, he turned around and came to shake hands with her, underlining that he wanted to meet her again. Everybody was surprised by this expression of respect by the most guarded man in the world to a lady that they had seen minutes earlier in the same breakfast room—the angry man in particular. She politely replied that she would contact the ambassador for the purpose.

The next opportunity arose only a few months later when she met him in Berlin. Soraya was there at the invitation of former committee members to speak about the post-Taliban situation in Afghanistan. Among those she met, one individual particularly appealed for her attention. He was a Hazara from the Ghazni province of Afghanistan, bright, intelligent, and talkative, holding a *"doctorat d'état,"* the highest valued PhD in France. Soraya exceptionally sympathized with him when she was abreast that his request to meet President Karzai had been turned down several times. Eager to serve his country, he was depressed and annoyed. An old family friend of Soraya worked in the Presidential Palace and was part of Mr. Karzai's delegation. He assisted in securing a meeting with the strongman of Kabul.

"Good day, madame, President Karzai greeted her. "It is good to see you again."

"Good day, Mr. President," she replied. "I would like to introduce to you this PhD thesis of a young Afghan. He is bright, intelligent, and hardworking. He could not reach you directly," she continued.

"Oh! Amazing! But you know I have a heavy schedule. This is the reason," he explained.

"I understand, Mr. President," Soraya gently replied. "You may not have time to read it, and moreover it is in French. My request is to give him a chance to serve his country under your leadership," she pleaded.

"Of course, of course!"

Indeed, the young man was called upon and offered a senior position, but he served in the government for only a few months. He may have found the environment incompatible with his principles. However, he remained in the country and is now a renowned politician.

A week later, Mr. Karzai won the presidential election in the first round, with over 55 percent of the vote in his favor. Afghans earnestly voted for him to see a "new life" and a fresh team of honest, dedicated, practical, and hardworking individuals. He now had the full backing of his people. As an elected president and independent soul, he was expected to deliver. Moreover and despite all odds, he still remained popular. Practically all former members of the committee were his supporters and voted for him. Afghans knew and observed all around the country that Americans and British controlled every aspect of life in their country. Their companies benefited from important contracts. Nobody cared about a fair bidding process as there was none in place. Powerful donors tasked whomever they wanted to accomplish what they funded.

President Karzai's sincere followers believed that he would feel the support of his people, demonstrate his independence, and fight for nationhood, peace, development, sovereignty, and the prestige of Afghanistan. But unfortunately, business continued as usual. He had an opportunity to clean up, reduce the power of Pakistan- and Iran-based mujahideen leaders, distance himself from controversial elements within his own family and ethnic group, and bring together an assembly of competent Pashtuns, Tajiks, Uzbeks, Hazara, Turkmen, Baloch, Hindus, and others to establish the foundation of a solid nation and team. As a leader, he should have demonstrated his impartiality, fairness, and modesty. But injustice, corruption, inefficiency, incompetence, and lack of vision and strategy, coupled with outcries of the population for justice and fairness, characterized the situation in the country.

The Taliban further exploited these facts to their advantage and gained more territory and recognition in the south. Every day assaults on international troops, particularly Americans and British, intensified.

443

Not only did they enter Afghan territory from the neighboring tribal areas of Pakistan, but villages began tumbling into their hands. The international troops, who should have apprehended and "smoked them out," remained inactive. As Soraya had anticipated, with the return of the Taliban, the horrible practice of "caging" women resurfaced in remote Afghanistan.

Everybody in the government followed the spirit of the "Madame de la Marquise" song immortalized by Ray Ventura—all presented positive and promising reports. Therefore, low-ranked officials misled their superiors, who fibbed to ministers, who then deceived the president. And the so-called "international community" did not raise a finger to rectify mistakes. While this could have been expected from a frail regime, the fundamental question was what the foreign intelligence and representations who delivered funding and "military protection" to the country were doing? Conspiracy theories started to emerge. The sincerity of the two major Western countries was questioned. Interference of Iran, Pakistan, and Saudi Arabia in Afghanistan's internal affairs handicapped the system. The fear of India-Pakistan and Saudi Arabia-Iran rivalries leading to proxy conflicts in Afghanistan was growing. Countering the emergence of the Russian Federation and the People's Republic of China as new giants of the world on Afghan soil became the topic of intellectual debates. Denigration of Islam by extremist and terrorist groups and actions became a prime concern of the population as they felt their faith had been betrayed and tampered with. Though she had been in Logar, Soraya requested me to travel to deeper south Afghanistan and get a sense of what was going on.

I landed in Kabul in the summer of 2005. Prior to quickly moving to the south for in-depth observation, I met with a few old friends who were in the mujahideen movements and now had senior governmental functions. A former colleague who worked with the National Directorate of Security (NDS) appeared unequivocally anxious for the future of the country due to foreign infiltration and interference. More specifically, he alluded to Pakistan, Iran, and Saudi Arabia, who continued funding and chaperoning their former allies. As a knowledgeable man, he jokingly referred to General Emilio Mola of Spain, who introduced the notion of the fifth column. He acknowledged that a sizable number of people within different pillars of the government, who should have in principle promoted and acted based on sacred principles such as unity, equality, justice, and liberty in the country, did not demonstrate the required ethics and obviously served "foreign interests." Unambiguously and as a good friend, he even named a few.

Some politicians and former mujahideen figures had explicitly verbalized the existence of a fifth column, particularly in the security and intelligence institutions of the state, and urged robust measures to dismantle and apprehend them. He then elaborated on the uncontrollable and irrepressible scale of corruption and nepotism in the administrative, legislative, and judiciary apparatuses of the country. It looked that everything turned around making more money at all costs. Some most senior officials of the government, who hardly gained a few hundred dollars monthly some years back, possessed millions, even tens of millions. The fuel business was in the hands of sharks who did not value any environmental norms or standards, and establishing "security companies" with foreign experts was deemed the second most lucrative industry. All government institutions, diplomatic representations, businessmen, and rich private citizens hired security firms at high costs for one reason or the other. It looked like insecurity in the country offered unlimited benefits to some. Affiliates and family members of the leadership of the country were prime beneficiaries. The construction sector was also infested. Siblings of dignitaries who lived abroad obtained juicy contracts or were employed in the foreign service without any background checks. Fake diplomas and certificates were produced. My former colleague alluded that in one case, the son of a minister benefited from a several hundred millions of dollars deal that he did not even fully honor.

445

My friend was also extremely critical of the status and power vouchsafed to some former warlords who abused people and resources, tarnishing further the essence of the holy struggle that the mujahideen had carried out against the Soviet Union. Family members of the leadership as well as affiliates snatched public land, in principle property of the government, and made horrendous amounts of money. Security networks, including NDS officers, went after small fish. The real swindlers had full independence and liberty. He acknowledged that the Taliban, supported by the ISI and their al-Qaida associates, effectively gained popularity in the southern provinces due to rampant corruption and injustices inflicted on the people by government officials. He seemed confident that Osama bin Laden moved within the Pakistani tribal areas of Miranshah, Thal, Bannu, and Wanna but underscored that he did not notice a dire interest on the part of international troops to cross the border and capture him.

Finally, he elaborated on the cultivation of opium, in the southwest of the country more specifically. The Taliban controlled the poppy fields, and the whole process of cultivation and harvesting, as well as production of the deadly drug, in order to generate hundreds of millions of dollars in support of their operations. At the same time, he openly questioned what the international civilian and military forces did in Afghanistan. In his opinion, they were closing their eyes to the largest parts of misdeeds and insecurity challenges. It looked like they were more concerned about their own security than providing support and safety to the people of the country. He believed that the country would remain a battlefield among different forces for a long time and a variety of reasons. On personal grounds, he had resolved to resign and seek to move out of the country, preferably to Europe or Australia, to take care of his family and children.

At the same time, one of my cousins who was a mujahideen commander campaigned for his "political party" as the parliamentarian elections were announced for autumn of the same year. He still seemed optimistic, while acknowledging that there were serious problems and that the state was dysfunctional from the top. His feeling was that with a democratic parliament, corruption, nepotism, inefficiency, and the fifth column would be dealt with, but combating the resurging Taliban, drug production, and easy money would prove extremely arduous. His conclusion was based on the inability of the government to defend national interests. President Karzai and he were members of the same mujahideen group in Pakistan. He considered American and British "fabrication of political leaders" unwise.

Two days later, I was in deep Logar with some of my family members. We had a huge assembly on my modest ancestral land. Hundreds of people from far and nearby villages were in attendance. The main topic of the discussion surrounded the stoning of two girls to death and the lashing of several men by the Taliban in Azre, a few kilometers from where we had gathered. Commander Abdul Haq, the famous mujahideen leader of Eastern Afghanistan, was assassinated in precisely the same location four years earlier, just before the ascendance of Mr. Hamid Karzai to glory. The only crime that the teenage girls had committed was to go fetch water unveiled where a few young boys accidentally or intentionally waited for them. The Taliban were merciless. Even the girls' brothers were lashed due to their "lack of control over their frail family members." It was an appalling situation, and an elder of the area was categorical when I asked about people's reactions.

"You see, son," he calmly underscored. "The whole population is abandoned by the government. Every day, outrage is committed either by the officials themselves or by those protected by them. The population has no choice but to refer to the Taliban. The price is unbearable from time to time," he sadly affirmed.

Conversation with elders surrounded a variety of social, economic, and political realities. It was a real eye-opener for me. However, at midafternoon, my nephews and cousins seemed nervous, and I did not grasp the cause. The elder approached me and advised that I must return to Kabul as the night there belonged to the Taliban. They appeared between dusk and late evening prayer, settled in the mosque with their guns, collected all sorts of "taxes," and "rendered justice." A man of the village whom I knew very well was beaten to death publicly three months earlier as he had refused to pay the tax again.

For me, the back-and-forth between the capital and the south lasted several days. Mirwais, my old classmate, had returned to his native Nazak Khel in Wardak. His cousin picked me up from the Kabul Star Hotel where I stayed and accompanied me to meet him again. It was my first visit to the beautiful province of Maidan Wardak. Scars of over two decades of war were visible everywhere. We traveled all day through muddy and difficult roads to reach his village. He presented the same picture. The Taliban had not reached Nazak Khel yet, but in his opinion, it was just a matter of time. He was a member of a moderate mujahideen group and fought earnestly against the Soviet invasion, did not participate in mujahideen fratricidal wars, and defended his area against the Taliban. He was among the brightest graduates of the faculty of engineering and certainly someone who could have helped the country. However, he was jobless and had to opt for farming his ancestral land. I spent the night in his modest dwelling and listened carefully to his analysis. He shared the view that foreigners had their own interests and would not effectively assist Afghanistan. His criticism of mujahideen and Afghan leaderships for lack of civism, vision, and knowledge of internal and world affairs was unequivocal, frank, and honest.

Back in Kabul, I visited a number of international civilian aid agencies. While some acknowledged difficulty in finding competent interlocutors in the government, their main concern was the rising insecurity that prevented them reaching southern provinces particularly.

448

An old friend, Zarif Khan, accompanied me to Ghazni and Kandahar, where we spent nearly a week. While Ghazni had remained a ruined city, Kandahar was booming. The military airport was the second largest base for American and British troops. It had its economic effects on the city. But a strange feeling preoccupied the population of both provinces. While those we met shared Mirwais's points of view, the general public spoke of uncertainties. No one could plan anything. The Taliban and al-Qaida training camps were across the border, just a few dozen kilometers away. The populations, mainly in the remote villages, were afraid of tomorrow. Summarizing my notes in my Kabul hotel room, there was absolutely no doubt in my mind that the Taliban were back with extremely structured forces. They did not seem to be bare-footed individuals who ran in all directions. This time around, they looked well informed and better organized and understood where the flaws and faults of the government were. People appeared split. Some still trusted that with billions of United States dollars flooding the country, some sort of good governance, development, peace, security, and serenity would appear. Others put their faith in the hands of God.

Soraya, some former members of the committee, and I gathered again in Landtmann Kaffee of Vienna for a briefing. Under the circumstances, there was nothing we could do to alter the course of history. It seemed that either we spoke an unknown language that decision makers did not comprehend or we simply fought against the inevitable. Though my recounting of the state of affairs disheartened practically everybody, Soraya insisted that advocacy efforts should continue as they might at some point reach the target.

Regarding the election of parliament members, my cousin proved totally wrong. Most parliamentarians were "selected" to go through the process. Soon they became another layer of corruption and nepotism. Instead of attending legislative sessions, they constantly bothered the presidential administration and ministers to urge favor in support of particular individuals. The prime violators of law were de facto parliamentarians themselves. The overwhelming majority drove black-tinted luxury four-wheel-drive cars with a mass of bodyguards behind. They never respected traffic lights or police instructions. When called by officers to respect the law, their security contingents punished the officers. Beating, removal from the job, and other sanctions were practiced by the venerable "guardians of the law."

Respect for the civic duties imposed by the new Afghan authorities was perfectly described and immortalized by Plato nearly twenty-five centuries ago as *"good people do not need laws to tell them to act responsibly, while bad people find a way around the laws."* People could not find a way out. Sons, cousins, nephews, or other close family members of those in charge or political dealers emerged as a derivative layer of power in the country. Leaders who wished so much to look British or American did not grasp the political culture of keeping their family members and friends away from the doorsteps of power and economic gains. However, speaking with envoys of fund providers, this fact did not seem to bother them, or at least public testimonials did not reveal their dismay. They certainly comprehended that a significant portion of the financial aid went to the wrong destinations, but as one of them had underlined long ago to Soraya, they were trapped in a detrimental mesh. Some experts drew a parallel between the addiction of Chinese to opium before the communist revolution of Mao Zedong and that of Afghans to the green American banknotes under post-2001 administrations. Others believed that the entire society had been "castrated" by foreign aid money.

Soraya continued helping Golalai's mother and sisters as well as some other destitute families in Logar, Kabul, and Kohdaman in particular. In the spring of 2006, she returned to Kabul and finally had her father's home repossessed. It was not an easy process, but her determination and fighting spirit against injustice curbed the wickedness of the "confiscators." The capital of Afghanistan represented a perfect example of chaos theory, not only in appearance but also in political essence. Edward Lorenz, one of the greatest mathematicians of the twentieth century, summarized it so brilliantly as *"when the present determines the future, but the approximate present does not approximately determine the future."* However, people in general still seemed optimistic. My old uncle described the hope of the population as a tiny branch that a sinking man still grabs.

Soraya was busy rebuilding her house, which was even further demolished by some sort of nongovernmental organization. On the third day after her arrival, she received an invitation to meet the new foreign minister.

At their meeting, he began, "Madame, we know your background in this ministry and your good work in support of the people of Afghanistan in the last two decades. Would you wish to work with me and my team?" he inquired.

"Mr. Minister," Soraya replied, "I would love to serve my country. But I am a very open-minded and independent person. Search for the right solutions as well as fighting corruption and nepotism have always been my principles. And if these pose a problem for you and your team, then I would humbly decline."

"No, no! This is certainly not the case. There are a few people who remember your stand and work ethics when you assisted Prime Minister Mousa Shafiq," he argued.

"I have a job in Vienna, and my youngest daughter is going to university for her graduate studies. But I am at your service, Mr. Minister. What can I do, sir?" Soraya pursued.

"I have a few senior positions in mind, within and outside the country. But the decision must be taken by the leadership," the minister gently replied. "I wanted to sound you out first. Now, leave the rest to me. I will get back to you," he concluded.

She called to inform me. Despite my extreme reservations about the ability of the country's leadership to deliver, I was overjoyed. Finally, they would have a world-class woman with full knowledge of issues, the ability to study and speak several languages and do research, diplomatic dexterity, forthrightness, irreproachable ethics, and strong management ability. Moreover, she would not be a "yes-boss" woman and would judge and act based on facts and full impartiality. Knowing her talents, I was sure that she would be the engine of innovation in the government and serve like a true adviser, contributing extensively to push the administration to the right path. She had no other interest in Afghanistan except serving her people and, therefore, could be up-front. In fulfillment of her duties, Soraya had always been concerned about the achievability of institutional objectives to serve the people. Empty promises delivered here and there by politicians had never impressed her. But unfortunately, she did not hear any feedback from the minister. As some friend underlined, the leadership of the country knew that she did not appreciate what the French call "*politique politicienne*." She was certainly stabbed in the back at some higher level. Though dismayed, she soon forgot about it. She had a job in Vienna, and Serena still needed attention.

It reminded me of an important person in Europe with whom I toured a devastated zone in the Balkans. A significant number of media representatives and television cameras escorted us. He embraced victims of the tragedy and promised all meaningful assistance. Back in the office, I presented the list of his commitments to seek advice about departments to task and budget codes to charge. His answer was glacial.

"We have no means! Forget about pursuing what I said," he stated. "People and media quickly move on to other pressing issues and fail to recall commitments."

Soraya had encountered this person in the World Economic Forum in Davos and had jokingly labeled him as an Afghan politician based in Europe, waffling empty words.

While a few remarkable women were members of the Afghan Parliament, the top administrative positions were earmarked for associates of the leadership and remained a distant reality for the overwhelming female population of the country. In the 1960s and 70s, there was slow but steady progress on women rights. Then the communist delirium, excessiveness, and even abuse of them perhaps pushed the mujahideen government to suppress them in retaliation for what Khalq and Parcham did. The ensuing civil war was also an undeniable impediment. The Taliban basically assassinated all rights of women. People, but more specifically women, of the country had great expectations from a government that was totally funded, kept in power, and chaperoned by the international community to embark on a comprehensive program of women's emancipation and equal rights. Yet again, no one seemed to have the courage to take the lead. The First Lady of Afghanistan and wives of other leadership members who should have led social and charity endeavors were never seen in public to do something meaningful, at least in support of the victims of wars. They too were locked at home! And now with the rule of the Taliban in some rural areas, people posed the crucial question as to what would come next.

Avoiding collusion of interests was not in the state's vocabulary. Active involvement of a number of Parliament deputies as catalyzers and agents of corruption and nepotism made the situation worse. It was even further deteriorated by infiltration and intervention of foreign actors. In July 2008, President Karzai was forced to issue a decree establishing a high office for oversight and anticorruption. A close friend of Soraya was appointed as head of the agency. He was a very honest German-educated personality who, despite fragile health, had abandoned the luxury of Western life in 1980 and was among the few who proceeded to fight the Soviet Union alongside the mujahideen in Peshawar. His integrity was beyond any reproach. However, he had no decision-making power. Within months, over twenty high-profile and obvious fraud and venality files were concluded and, according to the rules, presented to the appropriate authority for onward referral to the prosecutor general for judiciary process. Among the files, the most impressive concerned the disappearance of over nine hundred million United States dollars from a private bank. The brothers of President Karzai and the first vice president were among those blamed for the misdeed. Other cases concerned illegal oil business by family members of government dignitaries or high-profile embezzlement. Rumors spread that even venerated international organizations were beguiled and misled. Fake progress reports, receipts, and certificates by imaginary local entities often covered misappropriation of funds. As the security situation did not permit foreign monitors to accomplish their tasks beyond the inner circle of the main cities, the trick worked. The plausibility of government power lords contributing to insecurity themselves could not be excluded.

International aid certainly did not fully reach its beneficiaries and targets. In mid-July 2007, the Taliban had felt strong enough to take hostage twenty-three South Korean young missionaries in the south and killed two of them before reaching an agreement for the release of the others. The incident had traumatized further all foreign representations, development agencies, and experts. They curtailed their field evaluations and relied entirely on local governmental or nongovernmental entities. Under such circumstances, even their headquarters conceded. Different interest circles understood perfectly that any development or humanitarian aid must be spent totally during a funding cycle. Therefore, the insecure conditions offered them golden opportunities. Imaginary schools, teachers, employees, and students under the Taliban-ruled areas or other rural zones swallowed hundreds of millions of United States dollars without any inspections. Even cheating in the security services was noticeable. The wildness of abusing aid money and impressing others was to the extent that some close family members of the government leadership kept at very heavy costs wild lions or countless very expensive horses in their domains to demonstrate their wealth and power.

It was a pitiful way of administering a country that needed every cent to be spent in the service of its population. While tens of millions lived much below the admissible poverty threshold, a few grabbed the entire wealth. Mafia linked to the new "power aristocracy" took control of major economic and financial arteries. Foreign supporters of Afghanistan now questioned the ability of the government. But in the absence of any alternative, the choice to continue with the same failure looked obvious.

In January 2009, the head of the anticorruption agency visited Vienna. He loved going to German-speaking countries whenever he could in souvenir of his much younger age. Soraya organized a small gathering of colleagues and friends to discuss issues related to the challenges in the country. I joined them too. From his account, it was apparent that "the cream of corrupt individuals or groups of persons" were shielded with very solid protection from the judiciary process. Major corruption files were simply ignored.

Soraya asked the noble man, "What mechanism do you use to do your job?"

"Initially, I formally dispatched dossiers to the government leadership," he said. But then I decided to hand them over personally to avoid any negation of reception. But still there seems to be no tangible follow-up."

"Then what is happening in this country?" Soraya asked.

"Look, I cannot state it publicly, but our foreign friends have great responsibility too," he noted. "You see, there was no accountability from the beginning. All those in power got used to the practice.

Now there is no way out, unless you remove them all and bring in a determined, new, and honest team. But they will not do it."

During the same evening, he sought Soraya's view regarding the Economic Cooperation Organization (ECO), a regional entity promoting cultural and economic development in South and Central Asia. As usual, she gave an in-depth analysis of its added values, challenges, and ideas how to improve certain processes to make it effectively efficient. The discussion was profound and demonstrated her knowledge and upper hand about economic realities of member states of this organization, and regional rivalries as well as disputes and how to provide a platform to soften some of the harshest contests. Holder of a doctorate degree in economics himself, he was fascinated by such a wide range of understanding about the region.

When back in Kabul, he spoke highly of Soraya in his usual tête-à-tête encounter with a member of the government leadership.

"We know her ability. The foreign minister also had proposals. She is too forthright and may hurt some foreign friends. This is why the minister's proposals were rejected," the government "luminary" continued.

The result of the autumn 2009 presidential elections was controversial. Mr. Karzai's rival claimed victory in the first round and accused him of treachery. He denounced an impressive and efficient election fraud machinery put in place by the president's team. The concept of democracy put in place by the West at the cost of billions of United States dollars, a portion of which had ended up in private accounts of Afghan and foreign dignitaries, was at jeopardy. Nobody in Washington or London wanted a fiasco and public shame. Pressure on Mr. Karzai's rival accentuated. Western chancelleries around the world engaged in consultation with Afghans whom they deemed knowledgeable for advice. Solving the election disaster in which the American and British choice had lost was the mother of priorities.

At the same time, Soraya and I happened to be in Dhaka, Bangladesh, in solidarity with the plight of the Rohingya population, considered by many human rights activists as the forgotten human beings on earth. For decades they were subject to heinous crimes on the part of their government, Burma, now called Myanmar. Deprived of their identity, they were harassed, murdered, burned alive, and pushed out of their homes to exile. Their only crime was to look different and practice a different faith. In many ways, Myanmar looked like Afghanistan. Composed of a variety of ethnic groups, with countless subgroups speaking diverse languages that affiliated with neighboring countries, the country was a human mosaic. Among them, the Rohingya had always been defenseless. The rulers of their country, even the most revered by the West, did not spare them from the worst treatment. Like Afghanistan, Myanmar was also a victim of the "divide and rule" policy of the British Colonial Empire. Soraya had full knowledge of the issue from her time in New York. While visiting the Delta of Chittagong and refugee camps of Naya Para and Kutupolang in the Cox Bazaar district, we encountered many Western envoys.

Back in Dhaka on a hot and humid evening, we had a friendly chat with three emissaries from the United States, United Kingdom, and Australia. The main topic turned quickly around possible options for a breakthrough in the Afghan election stalemate. The social exchange and amiability turned to an in-depth discussion about where the West went wrong in Afghanistan and the search for solutions. Soraya provided a brilliant update on the situation and election process. Broadly, there was agreement on three capital reasons that soured the feeling of the common Afghans and altered optimistic views into skepticism and even animosity. There seemed to be a total lack of understanding by the Western armies that entered Afghanistan of cultural details that made a significant difference in the perception of the population. The utilization of force and most sophisticated weapons had never subjugated any oppressed people in the world. The mother of all such breaches was breaking into dwellings unannounced, searching of women by male soldiers, and increase of collateral damages.

Corruption was the second most damaging factor. A huge portion of military and civilian aid money had been diverted by Afghan and foreign companies and personalities. While money and corruption could not be dissociated, it was painful for the population not to see a glimpse of justice. The third most significant reason that turned Afghans skeptical was the blind trust of the West in Pakistan and its dramatically efficient ISI. Neither Washington nor London in particular understood the deep wounds that this once very useful country had inflicted on the Afghan population as a whole. For a long time, Pakistan was known as *"Terroristan"* to common Afghans of all corners in the country.

The American, who seemed to be a senior person and the oldest in the team, intervened.

"I am sure our colleagues in Kabul do their job with utmost efficiency, madame," he stated.

"It depends how you define efficiency, Excellency! Then why are we in this mess now?" she replied.

"Though it is not our prime responsibility, all of us in every corner of the world are interested in the success of our policies and troops in Afghanistan," the British representative underscored. "What is the way out now?" he inquired.

"The crystalloid relationship between the 'bearer of democracy' and the population seems broken, sir! The best way is to freeze the process and go for a transitional administration of between three to five years with a few prime objectives, such as ensuring security of the country and population, building nationhood and accountable government institutions, eradicating corruption, developing a comprehensive social, economic, and political plan for the near- and long-term future of the country, and a national healing process for crimes committed in the past." I interjected.

"Well, this looks good. But what about respect for the constitution of the country?" The American intervened again.

"This will not be the first time that a constitution is 'frozen' to be improved," the Australian advised. "Courageous and honest decisions are also required on our parts" he added.

We particularly had the views of the head of the anticorruption agency in mind. It was the first time that we heard words of support from a representative of a major troops and financial contributing country. The only way to give democracy and foreign aid a chance to succeed was to clean house and put an incorruptible transitional administration and team in place. Soraya and I were not sure whether the Australian spoke on personal grounds. Indeed, it was hard for Western administrations to acknowledge their mistakes and the trust they had put in inappropriate individuals. But no house can be cleaned if the dust is put under the carpet. The United States and the British administrations pressured Mr. Karzai's opponent to go for a second round of the election. Frustrated, annoyed, and helpless, he withdrew from the contest. Sympathizers of business as usual within and outside Afghanistan were rubbing their hands with joy. The train of inefficiency, nepotism, and corruption was saved.

The summer of the year after, Soraya and I were in Kabul again. We met our friend, the head of the anticorruption agency, in his modest house, made of one floor of mud bricks, in the western part of the city. As usual, he was most candid and hospitable. His favorite dish, *maash palaw,* rice with broken soya grain, a specialty of his Pashtun Zarghoun origin in Herat province, was on the table.

In the course of conversation, we understood that he was considering resigning as nothing moved on the front of the fight against corruption. He acknowledged that the unwillingness of the government caused him serious additional health hazards. There seemed to be a race for making personal gains at all levels. For some, being a millionaire in United States dollars did not mean anything now. The contest consisted of going beyond tens or hundreds of millions. Honest and efficient people were lost or effectively acted as silent observers. The tragedy was that tireless efforts of millions of government civilian employees, low-ranking security officers, and soldiers on the battlefields, who made huge differences despite all odds, were overshadowed by the illicit actions of a few. Though disliked by society as a whole, they firmly retained the handlebars of power and money.

Amid such carelessness of the rulers, the country seemed to have been forgotten even by God. For decades, there was not enough rain or snow in Afghanistan. Crops did not mature enough to cover basic needs. The green areas quickly transformed to dust-producing sources. The capital city was dirtiest of all. Waste of toilets poured on streets, even in the most modern quarters. People walked and cars drove on it. The wind picked it up and spread the deadliest germs in the sky. The level of cheating was horrendous. For example, each "asphalted road" needed to be done again the year after. There was no investigative body even on the part of major donors. Importance and usefulness were characterized by the number of armored, smoked–window, four–wheel-drive cars and security agents that someone had for their own, family's, and pets' safety. The same applied to mines, particularly of precious stones such as emeralds, rubies, and others. Individuals extracted them with rudimentary techniques for their own benefit.

The Taliban took advantage of corruption and mismanagement of the country to make more progress, not only in rural areas, but also hit Kabul. They learned quickly to multiply their sources of income. In addition to the poppy trade, they grabbed as many mines as possible and transported precious material to Pakistan, which purchased them at the price of less than a peanut. Osama bin Laden's al-Qaida moved to subversive suicide operations within the country through the Haqani network. The Taliban assisted too. Some spoke of poor families being forced to "sacrifice" someone in support of other members. Mr. Karzai himself encouraged the violence by calling terrorist groups "unhappy brothers" and releasing their imprisoned leaders, who instantly joined the antigovernment fighters, committing murders and assassinations again.

The election of President Barack Obama offered a new window of hope and opportunity for most oppressed people. Everybody in the world once again felt American. He was the "dream" that Martin Luther King Jr. had spoken about some forty years earlier. The bright, handsome, eloquent, and honest new occupant of the White House and his equally brilliant and exceptional wife had a lot to offer to humankind of all races, religions, backgrounds, social affiliations, and political views. He took steps to repair the damage caused between the Muslim world and America by terrorist organizations and offered a new vision of coexistence and cooperation. There was a wind of hope! However, Soraya always claimed that two hands were needed to clap. President Obama's openings faced serious reservation by dictatorships in the Muslim countries who realized that their power base and financial gains would come to an end. The Arab Spring that was supposed to be the bridge between "civilizations" was quickly deflected and leapfrogged at the expense of the egoistic interests of a few. Afghanistan was no different!

The post-George W. Bush era corresponded to Mr. Karzai's second term in office. The honeymoon with the United States had ended. The more pressure he received from the Obama administration to curb corruption, nepotism, and inefficiency, the more his response was summarized in incomprehensible growing anti-American slogans, feelings, and acts. Nobody understood his attitude. He who began

461

every intervention by thanking the United States, transformed Afghanistan into a feudal system, and nurtured corruption to the highest level in order to stay in power now slapped his protector. Under normal circumstances, in a country that survived due to American and European funds, no one would be permitted to deteriorate the relationship to the extent he did. Some deemed his attitude insolence toward President Obama personally. A simple twofold explanation circulated among Afghan experts. After ensuring he remained in power for as long as he could, enriching himself, his family, and his friends, Mr. Karzai did not wish to be recognized in the history books of his country as a second Shah Shuja, the shameful king and loyal servant of the British Empire who was killed by the population in April 1842. Moreover, there was a presumption that his underground protectors prepared him for the worst-case scenario in Afghanistan. Therefore, a Karzai comeback to the realm of power was considered plausible.

In the summer of 2010, after retiring from Webster University, Soraya consented to be part of the Eminent Personalities of the ECO, representing Afghanistan. Though it was an honorific position with no remuneration, she embraced it genuinely. From the first instant, she was a mover and shaker, pushing her colleagues to propose reform in different arenas for the South West and Central Asian regions. She met with heads of states and senior officials of the ECO member states several times to discuss reforms and efficiency. However, like most regional organizations, politics and self-interest dominated the debates at the expense of real change that member states desperately needed. She often questioned what was the magic magnet that retained leaders of developing countries in their power seats forever? Why did they leave their functions only upon their deaths and after ensuring that their family members or handpicked would replace them? The situation was more dramatic in republic kingdoms. The father ruled for decades, replaced by the son who would rule till his death, and then the grandson came to continue with the misfits of his ancestors. In Afghanistan, the reality seemed slightly different. It was Americans and British who picked the incumbents.

Soraya and I attended the tenth summit of the Organization of Security and Cooperation in Europe. Held in windy and freezing December 2010 in Astana, capital of Kazakhstan, the two-day event was devoted solely to Afghanistan. Therefore, all heads of states and governments expected the Afghan leader to remain and follow the debates. His desire to speak first and leave immediately afterward astonished his counterparts, who could not understand his behavior. In his seven-minute intervention, he spoke of "a new phase, vibrant economy, strengthened institutions, and respect of the rule of law" in his country. He further announced that Afghanistan was safe and strong enough to take over its security from NATO member states' troops by 2014. Nobody understood his sudden belief that foreign troops were not needed in Afghanistan beyond the end of his own second term. Indeed, in the second half of the first day of the event, he left while other heads of states and governments continued their discussion on Afghanistan without him.

Nevertheless, the occasion was propitious for Soraya and I to meet a number of envoys and discuss long-term perspectives of the Southwest and Central Asian regions. I recall her frank and visionary approach in a meeting with a representative of one of the most powerful countries that assisted Afghanistan. The meeting was restricted. The envoy was eager to know the views of those who followed matters but were not in power. She gave a comprehensive overview of the situation, reasons for the Taliban's progress, corruption and nepotism mechanisms within the government circles at central and provincial levels, deficiencies of international aid monitoring through multilateral and bilateral channels, expectations of the population, and foreseeable threats that went beyond the capacity of rulers in Afghanistan, jeopardizing the peace and security of the whole continent. She was interrupted from time to time for more explanation. The envoy took careful notes and on some occasions argued about the position of Western countries.

But it was Soraya who had the final word on each occasion, warning that the West was losing ground in the region by choosing the wrong horses to carry out responsibilities that were definitely beyond their capacities.

"We do not hear from our Afghan interlocutors such an analysis," the envoy stated.

"I cannot comment on their position and speak to you as an individual," Soraya replied.

"What would you advise, madame?" the envoy eagerly inquired.

"Mr. Karzai is in place and will have to finish his second term," she replied. "But my concern would be about the post-2014 Afghanistan."

"What is that then?" he insisted.

"Our friends should listen to the people's perception. Continuation of personality and leader fabrication would be in no one's interest," she continued.

"What do you mean, madame?" he inquired.

"I mean what I said, sir! Leaders made and designated by the West will prove inefficient and problematic. The people of Afghanistan are your friends and grateful for what you all did. But this time around, please let them have a fair and transparent election," she concluded.

The envoy was astounded. His eyes communicated that he might not have liked the conversation but had nothing to argue about. She was so right. From the post-9/11 arrival of international military and civilian forces and despite valorous sacrifices by servicemen and women of troop-contributing countries, Osama bin Laden was still at large, protected and harbored, certainly with knowledge of all important secret services of the world, in the neighboring Pakistan.

The Taliban regained strength and occupied significant parts of the territory. The country became the largest producer of opium on the globe. Rampant corruption intoxicated administrative, judiciary, and legislative bodies of the country and even the private sector. And people started questioning the essence of foreign aid.

Soraya believed that Western countries should also share the blame for such a disaster as they imposed incompetent, ignorant, and inefficient individuals in key positions. She recalled the earlier statement of a high-level diplomat. "It is our money! We want it to be managed by whom we appoint. Forget about what could be considered fair or unfair."

In addition, Afghans at large were more and more frustrated by the attitude and reluctance of Western countries to put pressure on Pakistan, Saudi Arabia, and Iran to stop interfering in Afghanistan's internal affairs and subversive acts through the Taliban or other groups against the population. No one more than the Afghan people desired terrorist training camps in the tribal areas of Pakistan to be closed instantly. It looked like ordinary Afghans had better knowledge than the most sophisticated spy agencies. Some started shouting where masterminds of terrorism were hiding and operating. They went on to criticize the international community openly and expressed their disdain. However, the success of Operation Neptune Spear, which resulted in the killing of the most wanted fugitive of the world, Osama bin Laden, in May 2011, gave some hope of a new start within the United States administration. For ten years, one specific country had protected, supported, harbored, and strengthened the intelligence and operational capacity of the person who had humiliated America by bringing down the Twin Towers and attacking its defense department on its own soil. And no intelligence services knew about it? He was simply taken to safety near a military garrison to protect his communication mechanisms. There was a new hope that not only terrorist networks would be dismantled, but corruption, nepotism, and inefficiency of leaders in Afghanistan would be addressed too. But it was not the case.

The year 2011 was critical for the apparent cohesion of the Afghan leadership team. The Taliban had made significant progress in northern provinces too, particularly Kunduz, Baghlan, and Faryab. Critics put the blame on the president as after the OSCE summit in Astana, a clear message was conveyed to the international forces to withdraw from Afghanistan. The Afghan National Army and other defense forces were not in a position to take over and face the much more sophisticated Taliban and their strategy to hit, occupy, destroy, and retreat. Moreover, part of the government began to openly accuse some governors and high officials of treason in favor of the Taliban.

The sharp ethnic divide reappeared at the summit of the hierarchy, In March, General Rahman Saidkheli, a prominent figure and companion of Commander Massoud, was assassinated by a suicide bomber in Kunduz, where he fought the Taliban. In May, General Daoud Daoud, who also served under Massoud and demonstrated great efficiency in routing the Taliban, was assassinated in Taloqan. The blast that took his life occurred in the office of the governor. The commander of the German contingent was wounded too and two of his soldiers killed. Four months later, in September of the same year, Burhanuddin Rabbani, former president of the country who presided over the Peace Council, was murdered too. On official business outside Afghanistan, he was urged by the leadership of the country to instantly return and meet with an emissary of the Taliban who, in fact, was a suicide bomber.

Many conspiracy theories were recounted. However, people openly criticized President Karzai for his bias with respect to leaders of other ethnic communities and leniency toward the Taliban. Elucidation of these killings would certainly require time, if ever all the details could be discovered. But, mistrust among populations grew dramatically after them, reaching a very dangerous threshold. For some, they were all warlords, and government could do little to prevent their demise. But for the opposing camps, they represented their resistance and pride. They were simply their heroes! Experts believed it was part of a campaign by the Taliban and their masters to eliminate prominent and promising individuals of the country and that they would soon "go after key figures of other ethnic groups"!

Soraya reminded at any given discussion that animosity and friendship in politics were temporary. No war-torn country faced a reasonable future without a comprehensive healing process. And Afghanistan required one desperately and urgently. She continued advocating repeatedly that Afghanistan needed honest doers, not inefficient philosophers, emotional managers, or fabricated leaders.

The last time Soraya and I happened to be in Kabul at the same time was in 2014, just before the presidential election. She seemed extremely worried. The country was totally in the hands of incompetent people. The Taliban, robbers, gangsters, and drug dealers could do whatever they desired. The trust of citizens had diminished to an alarming level. In her interaction with foreign envoys, she regularly emphasized the famous Afghan proverb that "*it is a mistake to try once more the failed ones.*" The political picture was gloomy. The same known figures who had failed a hundred times and robbed the country of its prestige, wealth, and dignity appeared to be the front-runners. It was obvious that Afghanistan would again fall into their hands. People were caught between inefficiency and carelessness.

I had advised an old American friend to meet and listen to Soraya. It seemed that after visiting the government leadership, he revised his intention and did not follow my suggestion. That said it all. Nevertheless, I invited to her residence a number of other foreign friends to exchange views, though she had her own senior-level contacts. She was now a well-known person among diplomatic and political circles in Kabul. The evening was delightful and the discussion rich. There was an atmosphere of fear among these foreign

467

friends as if they did not wish to speak in front of each other. As usual, Soraya was outspoken and frank, underlining that the time of fruitless diplomacy was over and friends needed to be honest with each other. The number of armored vehicles, respective close protection agents, and Afghan secret services guards that accompanied each one of them revealed the tension and climate of insecurity that reigned.

The most pressing topic was how to ensure a transparent presidential election, realizing that no one was amused by the last one, marred with flagrant irregularities. At the end of the discussion, a French speaker friend asked Soraya whether she had been in a casino. She retorted that she had an image through James Bond movies. He softly said, *"Les jeux sont faits, rien ne va plus,"* "The game is over; nothing else will count." The conclusion was evident: the result of the election was known to some before it even took place.

Undoubtedly, the 2014 Afghan presidential election under international presence and supervision registered as the most shameful in the world. As anticipated, the known figures appeared in each other's lists, including some notorious individuals known for their brutality and criminal records. Mr. Karzai seemed determined to be the "kingmaker." From the onset of the campaign, there was a drive for exploitation of ethnic issues, a suicidal matter for Afghanistan. Empty promises poured like rain during the monsoon season. Naivety and honesty of the population were exploited to their maximum extent. No candidate proposed a realistic and simple plan.

In Soraya's view, Afghanistan did not need sophisticated doctorate thesis types of programs, incomprehensible for the people and inapplicable in nature. For her, simplicity, achievability, and timing were of the essence. People earnestly desired improvement in their daily lives and soon. Despite all odds, they were determined to go to the ballot boxes and provoke change in the governing system. Some candidates declared in remote provinces that they would make them gates of world trade and business as if God would transform their empty words into reality as soon as they were elected. And of course, common people, knowing nothing about requirements for a "world trade gate" as well as the needed timing and efforts greeted such unrealistic declarations with applause.

Living the campaign period was similar to watching a science fiction movie. Nothing appeared realistic. In the second round of the election, fabrication of personality became the trademark of some. Slogans were created such as the "second most intelligent brain of the world"—people wondered who was then the first and the third; "the worrier who will bring the broken vessel called Afghanistan to the shores of safety and prosperity"—and people not knowing that Afghanistan was a landlocked country; "the gladiator who will save the country"—with people not comprehending that gladiators fought and killed; and so on. The methodology of building up some candidates was similar to that of Taraki as "Genius of the East." I remembered Soraya insisting that the policy of personality fabrication had never been successful in Afghanistan. Empty promises and use of superlatives were abundant, however.

One of the front-runners declared victory as a result of the first round. And controversy began once again. Supporters of Afghanistan nevertheless "imposed" a second round. People seemed vaccinated and finally did not care about what the candidates proposed. Their promises reminded me of the enormous number of coconuts falling from the trees along the Atlantic Ocean in Côte d'Ivoire in windy weather without people caring and rushing to collect them. Following the second round, there was no clear winner declared. The entire election was marred with massive fraud allegations. The brainy of the globe, the leader whose election would have ensured the promising future, the "Eliot Ness" and his "untouchables" that would have brought down and put behind bars the like of Al Capone, and the undisputed savior of sinking economies and failed states were all now accused of serious breaches and fraud. It was the biggest treason to the trust of the people who believed that for once, their vote would count. Women and elderly crossed mountain peaks full of snow to cast their votes for the candidate of their choice. Others dared the Taliban's ban on elections at the cost of mutilation, some lost their lives in the process, and the majority desperately waited for a true winner. Experts designated the outgoing president as mastermind of the chaos due to his declared hostility with one candidate.

Foreign meddling seemed to be crucial. Since the end of the eighteenth century, most Afghan rulers had appealed to foreigners to back them and resolved internal issues in their favor. The British Empire, the Russian Empire, and the Soviet Union were regularly solicited to intervene. Now the outcome of the election depended on the United States. This time around, the mightiest provider of military and financial aid had the final word about the winner. Certainly there were many like "the man who thought he could fix Afghanistan" who may have pushed the Obama administration to take a side in an event that required neutrality and common sense. This was the moment to follow Martin Luther King Jr.'s view that *"the ultimate measure of a man [was] not where he [stood] in moments of comfort and convenience, but where he [stood] at times of challenge and controversy."*

Under enormous pressure from the United States of America, the two candidates formed a government of national unity on December 14, 2014, based on a political agreement as if they were both winners. But still, Mr. Ashraf Ghani was selected president and his rival chief executive, a formula of political nature that was unconstitutional. By doing so, the constitution of the country was de facto dismissed and frozen. It reminded me of a famous television show in France long ago animated by Jacques Martin, *l'Ecole des Fans*, in which children competed; at the end everyone was the winner. An unelected president ruled over a government that was not constitutional. This was definitely an excellent example of failing to "fix the flunking." And no "second brain of the world" would have accepted such a prescription for further failure. Soraya and I had sour smiles on our lips. In 2009, we had put forward in Dhaka the idea of a transitional government, composed of a real Eliot Ness and his untouchables to clean up the mess and prepare the ground for an honest election. The idea was considered unconstitutional and brushed aside. Now the mightiest power in the world decided indeed to overrule the constitution. But instead of eradicating the roots of misdeeds, business as usual continued.

Despite all criticism formulated, the government of national unity was still a huge window of opportunity. Though against democratic principles, it nevertheless offered politicians of all sides to come and work together for the safety and prosperity of their motherland and the security of their fellow brothers and sisters. However, soon the war for power began. The main question was not anymore how to help the agonizing country and its dying population, but what ministry or what embassy should be given to whom. Political trading continued, and Afghanistan's strongest international supporters could not or did not wish to intervene more than what they had already done. Each side wished to trick the other. Therefore, for months the cabinet could not be constituted, let aside the political agreement implemented. And again, knowledge, efficiency, and expertise were sacrificed for who provided backing to whom. Disenchantment of the population and their need for basic services did not matter anymore and nowhere. When one appointed his uncle, who was above eighty years of age, as ambassador to a very important country, the other designated his nephew as a prominent minister. Once again, the "loved ones," the tormented people of Afghanistan, were forgotten and sacrificed!

For nearly four years after the implementation of the presumed "Afghan magic formula," little has improved for the common people. Those fabricated personalities could not fix Afghanistan. It continued to face horrible insecurity, arrival of the notorious Islamic State on its soil, capture by the Taliban of over half of its territory, record production of opium, millions of drug addicts, galloping corruption, countless massive suicide bombings, and worst of all, a sharp ethnic rift, encouraged by the rulers that could end up in a ferocious civil war with perhaps millions at danger of losing their lives. Within the seven years between 2008 and 2014, Kabul suffered from seventeen massive suicide bombings, claimed mostly by the Taliban and causing countless casualties. However, in the following three years (between January 2015 to April 2018) of Mr. Ghani's presidency, the city witnessed at least thirty devastating kamikaze attacks. Many more have occurred in the provinces. Thousands of people—women, children, elderly, brave soldiers, security officers, and educated youngsters—perished in such evilly sophisticated, inhuman, and violent acts. Claimed by the Islamic State, the Taliban, and even the extremist movement of Golboddin Hekmatyar, they oftentimes targeted religious and ethnically sensitive locations.

Zanbaq Square, where the most atrocious suicide bombing occurred in May 2017, is a few hundred meters from Soraya's house. She was in, and her windows were shattered, walls cracked, security guards deafened, and even the poor dog disturbed permanently. She witnessed the devastating consequences of such heinous acts that aimed at provoking ethnic rift and internal conflict in this country—as if forty years of carnage was not enough.

The situation was exacerbated further by political manipulation of electronic identification card distribution. Ethnicity once again became the cornerstone of *divide*. Supporters called for expulsion from the country of those who objected. Amid such a mess, rumors of widespread fraud for the next election in 2019 put the darkest shadow on what we could still call democracy. Afghans anticipate sharp intensification of suicide bombings in the year ahead. The folly will certainly continue till the blood of innocents of all ethnic and religious affinities fills the Sind River. The response has been shameful. Instead of uprooting the "fifth column" from their institutions, they just issued senseless commiseration statements and established empty "investigative teams" for each incident, the findings of which were never revealed to the public. Some believed that terrorists were so strongly implanted in the veins and muscles of the government that not only did they plan and commit the heinous acts, but they also participated in the fact-finding panels. Jokes were told that the Presidential Palace and other entities established for the convenience used the same condolence letters for each and every tragedy; only the date changed. Despite daily failures that resulted in hundreds of civilian or security forces slaughtered, none of the government agents in charge were either dismissed or had the dignity to resign. At each instance, the government machinery took the population hostage of their botches by hammering on all fronts that any opposition to them would strengthen the terrorist enemies. But the population's patience has ended, and this noxious "prescription" may not cure their anger anymore.

Soraya used her Facebook pages to express her outrage, call for resignation of incompetent "managers" at the highest echelons of the state, and still beg for unity of people at those precise moments when individuals lost patience. She also highlighted the failure of international aid and support and its misconception, misjudgment, and partiality, as well as the inefficiency and corruption of the teams that it put in place. While she gained respect among Afghan intellectuals, foreign envoys complained about her frank and honest language. An important representative recently expressed openly that while he did not appreciate her comments, he had no justification to contradict her.

Defeat of the government by the Taliban was worsened by the arrival of the brutal and inhuman Islamic State. Very ferocious tactics, such as beheading women, children, and the elderly, were used. The increasing number of suicide bombings, committed either by the Taliban, Islamic State, or others, aiming at ethnic or religious conflict, worry the entire country. Northern parts of Afghanistan that were safest began falling into the hands of the extremists. Accusations of government high officials colluding with extremists and terrorists were never given attention. Efforts to convince Pakistan to stop assisting killers and suicide bombers did not yield any fruitful results. The inflexible position of Pakistan that Afghanistan must remain their protectorate was best explained by Pervez Musharaf, former Pakistani president, as well as Hamid Gul, the mighty head of their spy agency, the ISI. Claims such as "either Afghanistan and Afghans died or were subjugated to Pakistan's wishes," "Afghanistan, part of the Greater Pakistan," and so on surfaced. Drug addicts, including a huge number of women and young girls, reached over two million. Homeless and desperate, they sought shelter under dark bridges. Contrary to Islamic and Afghan tradition, unrelated women and men shared the same horror and place.

The population did not know where to turn. Foreign envoys had blind eyes and deaf ears. Why blame them, unless it was for waste of their money, as Afghan leaders did not care about their own population? Traditional transfer of knowledge in the country taught its populations for centuries *"not to accuse the neighbor for mismanagement of his own house."* The population comprehended that no foreign body could be pointed at as they protected their interests at all costs. Afghanistan was mismanaged essentially by its own sons since the arrival of hope and expectation at the end of 2001. People were fooled for seventeen years primarily by their own leaders.

However, the responsibility of the two "foreign controllers" of Afghanistan relied on the choice of inefficient leaders and managers, as well as lack of attention to impartial views that would have improved the situation and saved lives and money. The triumphant return of Golboddin Hekmatyar, the man accused of pouring acid on school- and university-going girls, masterminding suicide bombing, shelling Kabul and its inhabitants during the mujahideen civil war, and countless other atrocities under the umbrella of "searching peace for the country," did not prove useful. On the contrary, he became the promoter for further ethnic and religious divide in the country. What exacerbated the population most was that while the government could not feed or provide medical care for the most needy, they unearthed millions of United States dollars to assume Hekmatyar's and his team's safety and pay for their expenses. Moreover, several notorious communist leaders, some of whom had performed under Mohammad Najibullah's KHAD killing machinery, became the kingmakers of Afghanistan, hence benefiting from substantial international aid money!

In October 2016, Soraya and I met with a very important leader of the government of national unity in Vienna. Soraya had opted for a relaxed lunch at Vestibül. We also walked for a while in the Volksgarten and Rathous Parks. October in Vienna is a gorgeous and colorful month with extremely pleasant weather. Initially, we spoke about every possible topic to ensure that discussing Afghan politics would not spoil the friendly atmosphere. Of course, the inevitable happened, and we spoke at length about the country's affairs and reviewed the situation away from cameras and bodyguards, who were kept at a distance. He gave a pessimistic picture from within the power circle. Government officials did not communicate with each other except with their own groups. Soraya's vision was praised by the guest. Though Austrian now, her concern for Afghanistan was known at the leadership level; some appreciated and others feared her.

At the end of over three hours of a delightful and friendly gathering, this important leader said, "We need you, madame, Why do you not join me?" he asked.

"I have heard this earlier. But it is too late now," she said.

"I know the background and am ready to reveal details of my proposal," he assured her.

"No, thank you. With a new team perhaps! Let us see what the future brings us," she concluded.

In Afghanistan, life and death are separated by the hair of a newborn baby. And Soraya knew it perfectly. The country faces insurmountable challenges currently. President Ghani antagonizes and divides more than uniting people. The country seems at the verge of a major catastrophe, and the 2019 presidential elections, if held, may be the trigger factor. In her retirement, Soraya still and strongly advocates for the formation of a dynamic transitional team to take charge of the country at this crucial moment with a few realistic, achievable, and time-bound objectives. Any ethnic-based conflict in Afghanistan would certainly have major regional or even international dimensions. Dubious policies and short-term gains would ruin humanity's long-term well-being. God knows how much she tried to open national and international deaf ears and blind eyes.

In March 2018, I met Soraya in the heights of Seefeld, the beautiful Austrian alpine town near Innsbruck where she has her Kandahar chalet. Actually, her family and I were stuck by the fall of heavy snow and had no option but to remain till the tiny mountain roads were cleaned the day after. We had coffee in the Schwarzer Adler and a long discussion about her efforts in the past thirty-six years to advocate for freedom, justice, equality, and fairness in Afghanistan. The beauty of mountains full of dry snow and the dancing flame of the fireplace added to the depth of the discussion, mainly on the plight of women since 2001.

Soraya candidly recognized that while international assistance had not reached its target in Afghanistan, freedom of expression and women's emancipation had seen some progress, but mainly in the capital city of Kabul. Journalists had been targeted by suicide bombing and killed in the exercise of their duties. Some media outlets were particularly hit. The pressure on media increased on a daily basis with different means, yet they courageously continued their noble tasks. She was particularly fond of those men and women who covered conflicts and investigated corruption to keep the population abreast of the situation. They comprehended the risk that their devotion implied but faced it

SORAYA: The Other Princess

with honor and dignity. She also praised a number of women who at the cost of their lives defended the interest of the people publicly or on the benches of the Parliament. Some are exemplary in their efforts to advocate for implementation of the law and fair treatment of all citizens. Their job was not easy as women can easily be victims of nonsense. There were very brave women who defied the impossible by joining the army to serve the country with utmost efficiency and dedication. Others excelled in sports, journalism, diplomacy, and even business. However, a deeper look demonstrates a completely different picture.

Women were the prime victims of corruption and nepotism, encouraged and developed by individuals in power since the liberation of Afghanistan from the Taliban regime. Not only did the notion of equal rights remain utopian, but reports that pensions of slain soldiers were robbed from families who did not have young male members were public, and the best jobs were given not to competent women of modest families but granted to those who had ties with authorities. The situation of children and girls in particular did not improve much since 2001, when Afghanistan fell under care of the international community. The number of street boys and girls as well as child laborers increased dramatically. They had to rescue their families on the verge of collapsing after losing breadwinners either in a suicide bombing or in the combat fields. While progenies of high government officials were exempted from all national services and sent to get the best education in foreign universities, common men and women were pushed to serve in the most remote areas of the country without even proper food and support.

Referring to the British or American posture that Afghan leadership wished to portray, people often asked if Crown Prince William, his brother Prince Harry, or Vice President Joe Biden's beloved son Beau could serve in the harshest battlefields in Afghanistan, Iraq, or elsewhere, what was then so special with the sons of Afghan leaders? Why could they not serve, even for one week, in Helmand,

Kunduz, Paktia, Nangarhar, or other war zones to fight the enemies? Did they not have an obligation toward this country, the resources of which were extracted by their parents and partially devoted to their well-being, education, and development abroad? Young widowers of soldiers did not wish to go to government offices due to the demoralizing ethics of senior and deciding officials. They preferred to ignore the meager pensions of their slain husbands. People felt duped by those who governed them. Suicide bombers could reach anyplace in the country and enter any highly guarded building such as army bases, military hospitals, national security edifices, and other sensitive locations to commit their atrocious acts and cause maximum casualties.

When describing current realities in Afghanistan, Soraya had tears in her eyes. She wept for those who honestly sacrificed their lives and lamented the carelessness and inefficiency of those who managed the country, foreigners or Afghans. In front of the fireplace on her green leather sofa, she had piles of paper. Since the public killing of Zarmeena in November 1999 by the Taliban in the Kabul Sports Stadium and countless other women and girls of the country, the situation had not improved. It even worsened since 2001 after the arrival of international troops and "democratic" government, considering efforts and means put in place. The more the Taliban and Islamic State gained strength and occupied territories, the more atrocities against women and girls increased. Soraya recited some of the cases that have been registered either by human rights entities or media as she would love to see justice rendered.

In November 2005, Nadia Anjuman, a twenty-five-year-old wonderful poet and writer who had challenged the Taliban to study in her hometown of Herat and had published a fascinating book, *Gul-e-Dudi,* The Dark Flower, was brutally murdered by her husband. She was full of life and wished to become a professor, in memory of the one who had taught her secretly when religious extremism ruled Afghanistan. September 2008 in Kandahar is sadly remembered, when Malalai Kakar, the first policewoman heading the crime department, was gunned down by the Taliban. But she paved the way for many to follow her footsteps. In April 2010, the Taliban assassinated the twenty-two-year-old, beautiful Hossai in Kandahar, simply because she refused to quit her job. In the summer of the same year, the Taliban husband of Bibi Aisha Mohammadzai cut her nose and ear with a sharp knife as she tried to flee a forced marriage. Hamida Barmaki, a prominent lawyer, academician, and human rights activist, her medical doctor husband, and their four very young children were brutally assassinated in January 2011 by the explosion of a bomb in a supermarket, claimed by Hekmatyar's group. She and her family are examples of hundreds of thousands such shattered families in the country.

Sahar Gul was only thirteen in 2011 when she was forced to marry someone she did not want. She was brutally tortured by her husband's family, who lived in Baghlan. In August 2012, the Taliban beheaded seventeen people, including two women, in Helmand. Their "crime" was to attend a family party. In the first six months of 2012, the country's independent human rights commission recorded fifty-two murders of girls and women by the Taliban, among whom as many as eleven lived in the Parwan Province. In July 2012, video of the killing of twenty-two-year-old Najiba, who according to her Taliban relatives committed adultery, shocked the whole world. She was shot several times at close range, exactly like Zarmeena three years earlier. In the same month of July 2012, fifteen-year-old Tamana was assassinated publicly in Parwan because she refused a forced marriage and wished to continue her education. Again in July 2012, Hanifa Safi, head of women's affairs in Laghman, was brutally murdered with a car bomb. Sushmita Banerjee, well-known author of *Kabuliwala's Bengali Wife* was murdered by the Taliban in Paktia. She was shot twenty-five times. Her "crime" was her book, transformed into a Bollywood movie.

The government continues to fail to protect its own female officers. The Taliban and their Islamic State associates murdered in July 2013 Islam Bibi, the most senior policewoman of the country in Helmand. A month later her friend and colleague, Nigara, faced the same fate. Later, in December of the same year, Sitara was the victim of her addicted husband, who mercilessly cut her nose and lips in Herat. In early 2015, Roza Gul's nose was cut by her husband in Faryab. Akhtara, Nouri, Latifa, Atefa Bibi, Nafisa, and hundreds or thousands more victims of acid attacks in different corners of Afghanistan awaited action on the part of the government. Their "crimes" consisted of promoting the plight of women in society, refusing forced marriage, or desiring to continue their education. The Taliban declared war against Afghan women in general, but educated ones in particular, through one of their officials who was released from Guantanamo. In July 2010, he declared to the *Wall Street Journal* that "*if you put a young adult man and woman in one room for some time, of course there will be some interactions, which is against Islam. This is like a virus here, and it will spread.*"

By piling up documents and recounting every case, Soraya looked more desperate for the future of women in Afghanistan. What was most unacceptable was that perpetrators were either the Taliban operating in government-controlled areas or sought refuge in areas under the control of enemies, remaining therefore at large forever. She repeatedly emphasized that the above were known cases and consisted of only the tip of a very gigantic iceberg as in reality women victims of violence, tortured, beaten, and murdered in Afghanistan under a regime that is heavily supported politically and financially by the international community may perhaps be thousands or even tens of thousands.

In front of blazes of fire and on the warm green leather sofa, she spoke at length about Rokhshana and Farkhunda Malikzada, sipping from time to time her cup of green tea. For her, the situation of these two unique women described what went on in the country.

Rokhshana, a nineteen-year-old young girl, went to school in Ghor. Like all women of her age, she fell in love with a boy, whom she often met on her way to school. She was fresh, full of energy and ideas for herself, her family, and her country. Few girls went to school in this remote central area of Afghanistan. Rokhshana knew that she would have a bright future, at least in her home province. But her dreams were short-lived when she learned that she had to marry another person much older than her. She protested and argued to no avail. In Afghanistan, the religious sacred principle of "*Ijaab*" and "*Qabool*," request and acceptance of both sides, had been ignored for obscure and archaic traditional dogmas, often leading to honor killings and domestic violence. Rokhshana knew that her family and the society were wrong as she did not consent with the marriage and asked her lover to take her to a place where they could marry each other in accordance with the religious and civil laws.

"Rokhshana, we live in a very remote area and need days of travel to reach a safer location. Our escape would be noticed," he said.

"Living the rest of my life with someone I did not want is worse than death," Rokhshana said. "With or without you, I will take the risk."

"I love you and am ready to accompany you. Only pray that God renders blind our enemies," he replied.

Hours after their fugue, a bus was stopped just before the provincial capital. Dark, long-haired men jumped in and looked at everyone. They had machine guns in hand and stopped where Rokhshana was seated. They asked her to unveil. She suddenly recognized her "husband" behind the men. She and her friend were dragged down and captured. The captors claimed to be the Taliban and asked for all men of the area to appear in a desert court, as they called it. The bus left, and the news spread with the speed of light. There was no doubt about the outcome of the Taliban justice; she faced death by stoning. What surprised Soraya was the inaction of the government

481

authorities. They had enough time to intervene but did not. Were they afraid of facing their enemies? Did they not believe in what the common people reported? Did they not consider precious the life of a common little woman with great aspirations? Indeed, she was not the daughter of a governor, minister, or president, for whom even foreign security forces would sacrifice their lives.

Later on that cold day at the end of October 2015, she was pushed into a hole like Golalai years earlier and stoned to death. It took hours as she did not want to die. The inhuman torture was beyond any belief. Rains of stones poured on her head, face, back, spine, eyes, and nose till she expired. The sadism of the event was to the extent that it was filmed and distributed to international media. Soraya was emotional when recounting the incident and watching on her computer screen Rokhshana crying for help. She had a deep breath of sorrow and underlined that little has changed for Afghan women. Golalai was stoned by the Taliban under their regime, but Rokhshana was killed under the eyes and nose of an internationally supported government. As usual, Soraya took a profound inhalation of her cigarette and shook her head repeatedly.

Months earlier, in March 2015, a twenty-seven-year-old theology university student, Farkhunda Malikzada, was tortured, burned, and killed in front of security officers and cameras in the heart of Kabul, just a few hundred meters from the Presidential Palace. She knew her religion and the charlatanism that women faced in shrines, where they were robbed of their money and dignity. In Afghan history, whenever religious imposters were unveiled by knowledgeable people and saw their interest jeopardized, accusations were the most efficient means of safeguarding their positions. Farkhunda faced the same scenario. The swindlers of religion accused her of burning the Holy Koran. An ignorant mob attacked her in the presence of police officers, dragged her into the street, stoned her, ran a pickup truck over her, threw her in the dry Kabul River, and burned her.

The calamity lasted over an hour. Why did officers not shoot in the air to disperse the mob or call for help? The assassins were all known as they were caught in action by numerous cameras of mobile phones. Soraya was furious about justice not being rendered. The culprits were certainly linked to regime nobility and therefore remained unpunished. As she often said about other cases of violence on women, the issue was not about Farkhunda's belief or action in the shrine. She may have insulted the imposters. But as a human being, she should have been protected and saved by security forces present on the scene. It looks like her assassins have even been released instead of receiving the heaviest punishments possible. Sharp criticism was also addressed by the population, particularly women activists, toward the "enlightened" First Lady and her inaction to effectively protect female victims of violence amid her much orchestrated claims and propaganda. Some even spoke of hundreds of millions of United States dollars wasted in the name of promotion of women's plight! Farkhunda's death and that of a thousand other women and girls will always remain as an unmovable and unbending thorn in the throat of the Afghan government till justice is rendered. She and Rokhshana represent millions of Afghan women who died and still perish silently away from the eyes of cameras or attention of their government. They deserve heaven on earth.

Soraya went on to deplore the situation of freedom of expression. In January 2016, terrorists targeted a minibus that carried journalists and media employees, killing seven and injuring dozens. In July 2016, a peaceful demonstration was marred by two suicide bombings that killed more than eighty individuals and injured nearly three hundred. In November 2017, an attack on a political gathering inside a building left fourteen people killed and scores injured. Government forces deliberately opened fire in November 2015 and more brutally in June 2017, killing and injuring demonstrators who expressed anxiety over rising insecurity in the country. She deplored that funds provided by the international community served to kill innocent people who expressed their opinion. On December 27, 2017, a suicide attack that hit a news agency and cultural center killed forty-one and injured more than a hundred. She underlined that the list was long and could not believe that the government deployed all forces for the security of corrupt, inefficient, and useless officials and politicians but could not ensure the safety and security of innocent citizens. In the year 2017, twenty-seven courageous and valorous journalists were brutally murdered. Even recently, on April 30, 2018, ten journalists were butchered at once.

Soraya's assessment of women's emancipation and freedom of expression was very gloomy. So what was the legacy of international intervention and assistance in Afghanistan since 2001? After each terrorist attack, statements such as "horrified by the cruelty of ... attack on ... and hope those behind this attack are quickly brought to justice" issued by all major foreign representations or their capitals exacerbate further the feelings of the population. This drama has lasted for years now, and such declarations have totally lost their significance. With tearful eyes, Soraya candidly asked me, "What did they do with this country, the land that Allama Iqbal considered the heart of Asia?"

I had no answer to her question except to blame those who accepted to rule Afghanistan after the arrival of massive international troops. They had international backing, security, money, power, recognition, and admiration but failed to respond even to the basic needs of their population. After the horrendous ravages of the Second World War, West European countries were rebuilt with only 12 billion United States dollars under the Marshall Plan. But in Afghanistan, it is rumored that 3 trillion United States dollars of international aid and public money has so far been spent. Afghan leaders should indeed be tagged as "first brains of inefficiency and mismanagement." Furthermore, they allowed terrorists to regain force, come back, and martyrize the entire population. This was Afghanistan today, for which they should be shameful forever and ever. Assuming leadership enshrines fulfilling responsibilities for the well-being of a population. For years and years, Soraya's statement of 1994 will resonate in my ears and mind. "This is not the Afghanistan for which we fought! From a proud people fighting the Soviet Union, the mightiest of invaders, we became the shameful individuals killing our own brothers and sisters."

Soraya's father had encouraged her to read and understand Allama Iqbal, who as a Punjabi valued Afghanistan. However, realization of his dreams proved most harmful to the same people he loved so much. She felt sorry for the great philosopher and often asked if he was alive, would he be proud of his Pakistan's stand and actions toward Afghanistan? She oftentimes reminded others of the famous poem attributed to the great philosopher Bedil Dehlavi (1642–1720), who glorified Persian literature in India, that *"Human beings were like waves. Their rest was their death. They lived because they undertook and moved."* Martin Luther King Jr. believed that *"If you cannot fly, then run! If you cannot run, then walk. If you cannot walk, then crawl. But, whatever you do, you have to keep moving forward."* With her children and grandson around, Soraya always shone, proposed ideas, and moved forward. But this time, her eyes often fixed on the fire. She seemed extremely worried.

The crystal vase called Afghanistan was at the verge of breaking into pieces again, with devastating human costs. The reports and allegations of vote rigging for the forthcoming elections were terrifying. Ethnic and religious divide has reached its most dangerous threshold. Leaders like Mahatma Gandhi and Nelson Mandela came to power with no money but great ideas. They died proudly with no wealth but billions of humankind weeping for their loss. They had no other material heritage except a few pants or suits. Their legacy was their service to the people and tracing the road to dignity, prosperity, and security of their nations. In Afghanistan, rulers reach glory with a meager income or a simple pair of local shirt and trousers but gain tens of millions of United States dollars and in some cases even more that they have left or will leave behind for their descendants.

Their legacy is a country destroyed and shattered, millions of innocents perished, injured, or rendered homeless, resources misused and distorted, and exorbitant amounts of drugs produced. And the shameful list continues.

Nelson Mandela, the greatest of all Africans, made it clear: "*It would be very egotistical of me to say how I would like to be remembered. I will leave that entirely to [my people] South Africans. I would just like a simple stone on which is written 'Mandela.'*" Photos of inefficient and corrupt leaders in all Afghan government offices must be replaced by Mahatma Gandhi's advice that "*leadership at one time meant muscles; but today it means getting along with people.*" This is the difference between real and fake or fabricated leaders. The "Genius of the East" or the "Second Brain of the World" must emerge naturally from the people, not in a fictitious manner.

Perusing the post-World War II history of humankind, it is evident that genocide, crimes against humanity, and war crimes have been given serious attention. Many special tribunals and courts have been constituted for flagrant violations of human rights and killings to ensure that at least international justice is rendered. Afghans hope that there will be soon one for their country. There is enough ground to do so. Statements and assumptions about who fathered, mothered, nurtured, and developed given criminal groups or terrorist networks are abundant and frightening. At the same time and reflecting on the examples of South Africa or Rwanda, where heinous apartheid and genocide were committed in the name of supremacy of one race aiming at domination and annihilation of the others, their new leaders had the wise approach of opting for national forgiveness and healing instead of revenge and more bloodshed.

Will it happen in Afghanistan one day? Will communists, mujahideen leaders, the Taliban, Mr. Karzai, Mr. Ghani, and others come to kneel and plead for forgiveness from the people for mischiefs committed? Will they know that the deepest, darkest, and hottest place in hell is reserved to those who cheat the trust of innocent men and women? Will they comprehend Mahatma Gandhi's wisdom that *"confession of errors [was] like a broom which [swept] away the dirt and [left] the surface brighter and clearer"*?

The peoples of Afghanistan too have a dream that one day they will live in a country free of corruption, nepotism, and discrimination; a land in which they will have equal rights and opportunities; a country in which they will not be segregated because of their gender, ethnicity, or religion; a powerful and self-reliant nation that will keep its enemies at a distance; a reputable state that will effectively contribute to strengthening peace, prosperity, and security of humankind; a united, egalitarian, fair, and competent state that will endeavor for the well-being of all its inhabitants, where skill, knowledge, dedication, and hard work are valued at all costs, and finally, where leaders put the interest of their populations at the center of their concerns and have the courage to act in accordance with the seriousness, dignity, and honesty that are expected from them, virtues that have been missing for long years in this wounded country!

We spoke extensively till lunchtime. She served a delightful *kitchiree quroot*, the special sort of Afghan risotto served with distilled yogurt and meatballs.

"You see, Afghanistan is a small piece of the bigger picture," she suddenly said. "Efforts to bring democracy have failed so far. Either it was misconceived or derailed. No matter the reasons. Hopes have been transformed into despair for many. The danger of regretting the 'old devils' is real. I think the world is going through a transformation, and Afghanistan is and will remain one of the battlegrounds of this new 'great game,'" she emphasized.

Her reasoning was clear and logical. Soraya believes that in this rapidly evolving world, universal rules and regulations, ensuring respect, equity, ethics, and diversity among human beings of all origins, nationalities, and geographic zones, are challenged by selfish interests and international realities. The collapse of the Soviet Union and the end of the cold war were to usher in a fresh era of peace and stability and a "new world order," guaranteeing a better future for humanity. Instead, the world encountered dangerous armed groups bent on violence and terror. The new millennium witnessed the rise of ethnic cleansing and sectarian conflicts, placing international conventions, norms, and standards at risk of being redundant. Moreover, the much-expected reduction of disparity between the poor and rich of the world became elusive and untenable. Development efforts failed to produce the expected results, increasing suspicion of the world's poor countries with respect to the rich and technologically advanced nations. Today, international forums, in general, are perceived as gatherings to defend and promote the particular interests of the well-endowed and powerful, rather than the concerns of the vast majority. This reality has contributed further to fueling international terrorism, endangering the existence of states and nations, as well as peace and security around the world.

The increasingly widening gap between rich and the needy and growing conflicts have resulted in massive migrations from the poor to the wealthy countries in Europe, Australia, and North America, often under the most arduous and life-risking circumstances. At the same time, the use of sophisticated weaponry such as drones, robots, and other inventions did not obey any international regulations, thus allowing users to interpret rules of engagement in their own interest and on their own terms. Armed conflicts, particularly in Asia, the Middle East, and Africa, were taking scores of lives daily, increasing suspicions with regard to the sincerity of the international community and the efficiency of world and regional organizations in resolving disputes and clashes. Peace and security and the future of humankind have never been so much at risk. As technology advanced, so too did the means of physical and mental advantages of children born in the technologically advanced societies. This would further widen the disparity between the rich and poor of the world's populations, rendering the disadvantaged subservient and even more vulnerable than witnessed today, laying the ground for even greater conflicts and struggles for survival in the near future.

Soraya referred to Albert Einstein, who once said, "*It has become appallingly obvious that our technology has exceeded our humanity.*" Lord Charles Snow, a famous British physical chemist, acknowledged too that technology was a "*queer thing.*" It brought "*great gifts with one hand*" and stabbed "*in the back with the other.*" In his famous work entitled *Two Cultures*, that is, science and the humanities, he stated that "*the breakdown of communication between the two cultures of modern society was a major hindrance to solving the world's problems.*" Numerous other scientists, philosophers, and thinkers, such as Noam Chomsky, have supported Lord Snow and expressed concern about the future of the globe and the well-being of humanity.

Unfortunately, the breakdown between the two cultures has significantly increased in recent decades. States encouraged creation of paramilitary and militia groups to fight for their interests, contravening international norms and conventions. The strategy of enforcing democracy in Iraq, Afghanistan, Egypt, Tunisia, Libya, and many other countries had rather been counterproductive due to rampant corruption, nepotism, and ethnic divide. In most cases, unlawfulness and even human slavery followed, to the exasperation of the population. This was perhaps why success in most hot spots in Africa, the Middle East and Asia proved very difficult, resulting in catastrophic human casualties. Politics became the art of lying and international justice deemed partial and unilateral. Internet hacking, data collection, and related matters were now national security threats, allowing mighty states to enforce measures of their own. The environment has seriously been tampered with, and conquest of space is considered a challenge rather than an opportunity for the majority of humankind. Too much power is in the hands of financiers and politicians.

Soraya believed that the World Economic Forum proved an excellent platform to exchange views and opinions among financial and political leaders of the world and to strategize for a better future. However, additional space was needed for scientists, engineers, and social science thinkers to gather and deliberate on the future of humanity. Soraya was endeavoring to see if a platform or forum could be established to debate and recommend on the uses of technology as a means to support economic development for all, thus building a constructive bridge between poor and rich nations. She believed it was worthwhile, contributing to world's peace and security. Her thoughts fascinated me. As usual, they were realistic and the vision true.

She was fond of saying, "Human beings have progressed due to courage in supporting new initiatives, hypotheses, and ideas. Where we would go then without them?"

We ended up our mountain discussion with a note of uncertainty about the future and a hope that movers and shakers from around the world would come forward to fight for a real change of the existing political and financial cultures such that, if not all, at least the overwhelming majority would be recipients of the collective efforts. Otherwise, we carve the path for our own destruction.

Epilogue

It is a far, far better thing that I do, than I have ever done; it is a far, far better rest that I go to than I have ever known.

—Charles Dickens,
A Tale of Two Cities

Soraya's life has been inspirational in many ways for young Afghan women and girls within and outside the country. She had a healthy, warm, and supportive family that provided her the liberty to grow up with her own qualities. Little was imposed on her. Her honesty, brilliant mind, solution orientation and quick thoughts, unbelievable charm and beauty, hardworking spirit, and an amazing courage distinguished her from the moment she could first express herself. Her father, confident and friend, adviser and mentor, played a key role in her fascinating life. He let her be who she wanted and assisted her to develop on her own terms. He laid out possible risks and opportunities at crucial moments, but ultimately she decided. For her, a healthy family was the basis on which the rest relied.

As a child, she moved forward. In the garden, she ran after butterflies or played with mud. In the kitchen with Abai, she learned the art of cooking. In the library she chattered with her dear father, and in primary school she challenged the tutor for what she felt was right. Vulnerable people were her friends. She defied oppressors and those who imposed their views either by the force of guns, social or political standing, or wealth. Nothing impressed her but knowledge, determination, and work ethics. She loved people who fought for innovative ideas that took human beings a step forward.

She is one of the few remarkable individuals who have their heart and mind associated. She never liked politics for the sake of politicking but only as a tool to improve the plight of citizens. Her structured and logical brain is a gift of God, as some friends and colleagues described it. She had the passion and endurance to search, work hard, and consult in order to comprehend the essence of an issue. The beauty of her soul was coupled with a physical splendor that oftentimes caused her trouble in Afghanistan. She mastered all household arts, cuisine, design, gardening, and receiving family members, friends, and colleagues. Educated, talented, sophisticated, knowledgeable, and stunningly attractive, she represented the aspirations of each girl and young woman in Afghanistan.

Her professional career for an Afghan woman of her time was exceptional. In her childhood, she was already taught the alphabet of diplomacy and politics by her great father and received in palaces. Later on, with her own international and national experience, she ascended to the atriums of power, assisting one of the brightest prime ministers of Afghanistan and witnessing agreements on controversial matters between states or debates and political bargains with parliamentarians. She was tutored by one of the renowned British modern philosophers and encountered many others in her life. She met John and Alicia Nash in May 2012, when they too attended with eleven other laureates of the Nobel Prize the Fifth Astana Economic Forum, exactly three years before their tragic deaths on the New Jersey Turnpike. They had lengthy discussions, particularly regarding what Soraya called the technological economy, its dimensions, repercussions, and bridge with the virtual existence of humankind. The conversation seemed like an exchange on a science fiction scenario. For many in Afghanistan who know Soraya, she too is a beautiful mind.

At any given age or circumstance, she was inspirational. Her interlocutors respected her above all for her clarity of thoughts and vision, her honesty of heart and spirit, and her uncompromising stand on the respect of rules and rights. She certainly rejected many tempting and lavish proposals of union that could offer her a palatial lifestyle. She always considered her modest apartment in New York, Kabul, or Vienna as a palace. And indeed, it has been so everywhere. Her mountain house of Kandahar is called *"Chalet Palais"* by her Austrian neighbors, due much to its sophistication and class.

She returned to Afghanistan to serve her motherland, the country that her father found back permanently only in his death. She devoted her time, energy, and meager economy to assist by all means the successive governments, but above all, her fellow countrymen and women. She was never shy and afraid of defending the right of the weakest against the mightiest. Certainly, her knowledge, subtle approach, courage, charm, and ability to transform a downbeat feeling into an affirmative thought were all helpful, but the real engine had always been her firm conviction that Afghanistan belonged to all her sons and daughters equally and unequivocally. Her most delightful souvenirs never included the palaces she had been in, but dwellings of very ordinary Afghans in deep Hazarajat, Maimana, Kandahar, Panjshir, Herat, Badakhshan, or her own Logar. Her father had forged her to be and remain just. When decision makers were cruel, then she sided with the people.

Her concerns for her country during the Daoud Khan period, engagement against the communist regimes, struggle for withdrawal of the Soviet Union, devotion to the cause of Afghan refugees and internally displaced persons, ardent advocacy to denounce oppressive regimes and breaches of human and cultural rights, and criticizing the Caesarean post-2001 governments in Afghanistan are inspirational for the young female generations in the country and those of Afghan origin abroad. Overwhelmingly, her view and vision proved right.

Had Charlie Wilson listened more attentively or advised some of his aides to dig deeper in what was brought to his attention, perhaps we would not have shameful terrorist training camps in Pakistan today. Her meticulous reasoning that putting out the blaze and playing with fire were two different political conceptions is a fundamental of new political science. While one may burn part of a forest, the other destroyed the entire house of humanity. Her openly expressed opinion that the world had jested too much with a serious issue such as terrorism, which would burn everything that belonged to any religion, *"civilization,"* or people for short-term political and economic gains here and there has been remarkable. The energy and time she devoted to alerting international opinion about looming tragedies in Afghanistan have been unlimited. She hit at all doors, open or closed, and did what few had done so far. She supported the fight for justice, equality, and fairness and protested against wrong decisions and insensitivities of superpowers. She never asked for *"compensation"*!

Soraya also highlighted limitations of the mujahideen chieftains based in Pakistan or Iran, urging the international community to look for and support leaders within the country who earnestly and honestly fought the invaders. She courageously advocated that Afghanistan needed substantive efforts on nation building, referring to ignorance by the former rulers of the rights of ethnic groups other than theirs as well as the ability and merits of those outside power circles to contribute to the well-being of their country too.

Her combat was silent, like that of millions of Afghan women. She deliberately chose to be in the backstage of politics and diplomacy. However and for many, it has always remained an enigma why she did not put her thoughts on paper and publish them. Her writing mind was clearly divided into two. With scientific and diplomatic texts, she was logical, profound, and substantiated. But she also drafted beautiful literature pieces. I urged her many times to draft one page a day and let me have them, but she never did. There certainly must have been compelling reasons.

Communist regimes may have been unaware of who she truly was and what contribution she could have made to Afghanistan. The mujahideen groups and the Taliban may have ignored her on the basis of ideological difference and religious obscurantism. But, nobody would comprehend the *"unconsciousness"* of the post-2001 so-called democratic governments about her ability to contribute to the well-being of her country women and men. She would have certainly opened too many closed and blind eyes to the real issues in the country, given priority to resolving simple problems faced by the common people, fought ferociously against corruption, publicly denounced without fear those who attempted to make personal gain from the public treasury, promoted highest work ethics among government dignitaries, and separated fake and real managers for the sake of efficiency. She would have assisted the occupiers of the Presidential Palace and foreign friends in developing a realistic and achievable vision not only for Afghanistan but for a peaceful and prosperous region.

From another perspective, it may not be a surprise that she did not attempt to join the post-2001 governments as there was a clear perception that leaders had never been seriously interested to make a difference for their people. Otherwise, Afghanistan would not be in its current miserable situation. While they seemed busy with political and financial dealings, the country was essentially run by unexperienced and unfamiliar people brought in based on ethnic and relationship grounds. They "offered" simplistic responsibilities to brilliant and talented sons and daughters of the country who could have made a difference by the force of their love for their motherland, intelligence, and dedication, keeping decision-making positions for their family members or inefficient and clueless political allies. Most valorous women of the country did not count. Their biggest reward was to be alive.

But for me, every Afghan woman, particularly those educated, embodies Soraya, a princess. And they must be supported for their continued fight to gain a respected and meaningful status in their shattered country. As Antoine de Saint-Exupéry said in his *The Little Prince*:

> *If you love a flower which happens to be on a star, it is sweet at night to gaze at the sky. All the stars are a riot of flowers.*

Final Words

As the book goes to print, there is much discussion about direct talks between the United States and the Taliban. Clearly, the Trump Administration's strategy to curb progress of the "religious students" and their Islamic State counterparts has not produced the expected results. The Afghan government appears to be sidelined from the "peace deal" negotiation.

Eager to leave Afghanistan at the earliest opportunity and put an end to its longest war, the United States may push the Afghan authorities into power-sharing with the Taliban or simply let the extremists take over. In both cases, it would be another major set-back and a let-down witnessed in the 1990s when the West turned its back, once the Soviet Union was defeated by the mujahideen. The destiny of Afghanistan was left in the hands of regional powers. The world then witnessed consequences of that decision with the dramatic rise of Islamic extremism and terrorist acts, the horrors of which struck at the heart of the world's financial center in New York and the Defense Department in Washington. A recurrence would have even more devastating effects.

In any political settlement that the United States government would contemplate, they ought to consider some non-negotiable fundamentals. All individuals or groups who have committed mass murder and human rights abuse should face justice. Moreover, Afghans must be spared the cruel fate of proxy wars witnessed by the unfortunate peoples of Syria and Yemen. The plight and protection of Afghan women who endured great hardships during the Taliban regime must remain at the center of all concerns. The hard-earned and still shaky democracy in Afghanistan should not be traded with. The young service women and men engaged in fighting extremism and terrorism in Afghanistan contribute directly to the safety of the

World. They deserve the support of the international community. The Taliban may have certainly gained territory, but it is doubtful that they enjoy the support of the population!

December 2018

List of Abbreviations and Names Used

Book Designation	Real Name	Description
Abbasid Caliphate	Abbasid Caliphate	The third Islamic caliphate (750–1517), most renowned for its unhindered support to sciences, astronomy, literature, and good governance. The period of 750–861 is called the golden era of Islam.
Afghanistan	Afghanistan	A landlocked, mountainous country situated in the heart of Asia and surrounded by Iran, Pakistan, Tajikistan, Uzbekistan, and Turkmenistan.
Ahmad, Fazel	Ahmad, Fazel	De facto deputy of Commander Ahmad Shah Massoud. His war nickname was Doctor Abdur Rahman. Minister of tourism and aviation under Hamid Karzai, he was assassinated in 2002.
Ahmad, Shah	Ahmad, Shah	From the Durani Pashtun tribe, founder and king of modern Afghanistan (1747–72). He undertook several bloody campaigns in India.
Amin, Hafizullah	Amin, Hafizullah	Devastatingly ruthless deputy of Khalq Communist Party, president of Afghanistan (September–December 1979), killed as a result of the Soviet invasion of the country.
Ana, Nazo	Ana, Nazo	Mother of King Mirwais Hotak, founder of Afghanistan, who lived toward the end of the seventeenth century. She is considered the first female Pashtun poet.

Ashraar	Ashraar	Counterrevolutionaries or troublemakers, terminology used by communist governments to identify mujahideen who fought against them.
As-Saffari, Ya'qub bin Laith	As-Saffari, Ya'qub bin Laith	Founder of the Saffarid dynasty, who opened the gates of Kabul to the Islamic faith.
Balkhi, Rabia	Balkhi, Rabia	Semilegendary personality who most probably lived in tenth century in Balkh of Afghanistan. She is believed to be the first Afghan woman poet.
Baloch	Baloch	People of Balochistan, an area situated in West Pakistan, the southwest of Afghanistan, and the southeast of Iran. The Baloch are divided among at least 130 tribes. Their aspiration of independence is suppressed by the powerful states in which they dwell.
Buddhas of Bamiyan	Buddhas of Bamiyan	Monumental statues of Buddha carved into the cliff of a mountain in Bamiyan, Central Afghanistan, and capital of Hazarajat between the fourth and fifth centuries of the common era. In addition to the two largest, Salsal (58 meters tall) and Shamama (38 meters tall), considered a World Cultural Heritage Site, there are countless small ones in the caves. Numerous Muslim rulers tried to destroy Salsal but failed. However, Amir Abdur Rahman Khan in 1890 started and Mullah Omar, the Taliban leader in 2001, finished the horrendous destruction of this jewel of humankind history.
Buzkashi	Buzkashi	A fascinating game between two horsemen teams who try to capture and carry the carcass of a dead calf while fighting for its possession at high galloping speed.

Charkhi Family	Charkhi Family	Three brothers—Ghulam Gilani, Ghulam Seddiq, and Ghulam Nabi—heroes of Afghan independence, murdered in 1930 by King Nader Shah, father of King Zaher Shah.
CIA	CIA	Central Intelligence Agency, United States spy agency.
Dostom, Rashid	Dostom, Rashid	Controversial general, politician, and current first vice president of Afghanistan, who often changed alliance and is accused of serious violations of human rights.
Durand Line	Durand Line	Over 2,400-kilometer border line agreed upon between Amir Abdur Rahman of Afghanistan and Sir Mortimer Durand of the British Empire in 1893. A significant portion of Afghan territory was handed over to the British for a defined period of time. However, after the creation of Pakistan in 1947, it transformed into a dispute between the two countries that is still unresolved.
Durani	Durani	One of the main Pashtun tribes, who ruled Afghanistan from 1747–1978 continuously through its Sadozai and Barakzai subtribes.
Durani, Aisha	Durani, Aisha	Wife of King Timor Shah Durani (1772–1793). She was a renowned Pashtu poet. She was among very few educated women in Arabic and Persian literature.
Gandomak Treaty	Gandomak Treaty	Treaty signed by King Yaqub Khan of Afghanistan and Sir Louis Cavagnari of the British Empire in 1879. Various frontier areas were ceded to the British by the king.

Ghani, Ashraf	Ghani, Ashraf	Current president of Afghanistan. He is from the Ahmadzai Ghilji Pashtun tribe and a United States-educated scholar.
Ghaznavi, Sultan Mahmoud	Ghaznavi, Sultan Mahmoud	The renowned sultan of the Ghaznavid Empire, who ruled from 1002 to 1030 over Khorasan (current Afghanistan as well as parts of Iran, Central Asia, and Punjab). He is believed to have initiated the expansion of Islam in India. One of his famous misdeeds was attack on and partial destruction of the Somanath temple in Gujarat. Ferdowsi wrote *Shahnama* (the *Book of the King*) to glorify his military conquests. He is perhaps the only ruler who used a navy to reach India.
Ghilji	Ghilji	One of the main Pashtun tribes, who founded the Pashtun dynasty through their Hotak subtribe. The current Afghan president, Ashraf Ghani, is a Ghilji Ahmadzai.
Greco-Bactrian Empire	Greco-Bactrian Empire	Corresponded to the easternmost part of the Hellinistic world from 250 to 125 before Christ, encompassing current Central Asia, Afghanistan, northern Iran, and Pakistan. In addition to Hellenism, Zoroastrianism, Buddhism, and Hinduism were practiced by the people.
Haq, Abdul	Haq, Abdul	A famous mujahideen commander in charge of the eastern parts of Afghanistan, who was mysteriously assassinated in 2001 at the age of forty-three.

Haqani, Jalaluddin	Haqani, Jalaluddin	An extremist mujahideen commander of south Afghanistan who received significant backing from the ISI; founder of the Haqani terrorist network.
Hazara	Hazara	One of the main ethnic groups living in Afghanistan. They are essentially of Shia Islam obedience and have been discriminated against in the course of history. King Abdur Rahman Khan was most ruthless with them. The current second vice president, Sarwar Danish, is a Hazara.
Hekmatyar, Golboddin	Hekmatyar, Goldboddin	Leader of radical Hezbe Islami, allegedly handpicked by the ISI to serve their purposes. He is accused of pouring acid on young female students, orchestrating suicide bombings, and killing innocent people.
Hotak, Mirwais	Hotak, Mirwais	Founder of the Pashtun dynasty in Afghanistan, who ruled (1709–15) in Herat. He is from the Ghilji tribe and declared independence from the Iranian Safavid Empire.
Iran	Iran	The Islamic Republic of Iran is to the west of Afghanistan.
ISI	ISI	Inter-Services Intelligence, the Pakistani military spy agency, who at the request of the CIA acted as chief orchestrator of the mujahideen struggle against the Soviet Union. ISI is accused of sponsoring terrorist training camps in Pakistan as well as subversive operations in Afghanistan, Kashmir, and even India, with devastating political, human, and material ramifications.

Jalalabad	Jalalabad	Capital of the Nangarhar province, bordering Pakistan in the eastern part of Afghanistan.
Kaarez	Kaarez	Network of underground water streams in Afghanistan.
Kabul	Kabul	Capital of Afghanistan.
Kalakani, Habibullah	Kalakani, Habibullah	King of Afghanistan for nine months in 1929, who was allegedly brought into power by the British to oust King Amanullah Khan. He was brutally killed by Nader Khan, father of King Zaher Shah.
Kamal, Meena Keshwar	Kamal, Meena Keshwar	Devoted Afghan female advocate for women's rights, who started her struggle through establishment of an organization and publication of a specialized magazine under the communist regime. She was cowardly murdered in 1987 in Quetta of Pakistan by extremists three months after her husband was slain.
Karachi	Karachi	Capital of Pakistan from 1947 to 1958.
Karzai, Hamid	Karzai, Hamid	Former president and chairman of transitional administration of Afghanistan (2002–2014). He is from the Durani Pashtun ethnic group.
KHAD	KHAD	State Intelligence Services, Afghan spy agency (1980–92), and brutal torture and killing machine of the communist regime under the guidance of Mohammad Najibullah.
Khalq	People	Pro-Soviet Afghan communist party, dominated by Pashtun ethnic-group politicians and military officers of the country.

Khan, Abdur Rahman	Khan, Abdur Rahman	King of Afghanistan (1880–1901), known as Iron Amir for his brutality; partially destroyed the Buddhas of Bamiyan. He is accused of killing and sending into exile about 60 percent of the people of Hazarajat in retaliation to their legitimate expression of unhappiness about their social, political, and economic plights.
Khan, Akbar	Khan, Akbar	Prince of Afghanistan and hero of the First Anglo-Afghan War in 1841. He is known for having killed William McNaughten in self-defense. He was allegedly poisoned in 1845 by his father at the instigation of the British Empire in order to recapture the throne.
Khan, Ali	Khan, Ali	Deputy prime minister and multiple times minister (foreign affairs, justice, court affairs, etc.) under King Zaher Shah and close friend of Soraya's father; remained as a good friend of the family.
Khan, Amanullah	Khan, Amanullah	King of Afghanistan (1919–29), husband of Queen Soraya; modern couple who were ousted by an allegedly British-guided revolt and exiled in Rome.
Khan, Daoud	Khan, Daoud	Ambitious prince, multiple times minister, prime minister, and president of Afghanistan (1973–78). He openly rivaled King Zaher Shah. His thirst for supreme power and alliance with the Soviet Union are alleged to be the source of the current situation in Afghanistan.

Khan, Hashem	Khan, Hashem	Eldest uncle of King Zaher Shah and Daoud Khan. He was de facto ruler of Afghanistan from 1933 to 1946. Astute and merciless, he was known as the Machiavelli of the country.
Khan, Dost Mohammad	Khan, Dost Mohammad	King of Afghanistan on two occasions (1826–39 and 1845–63); allegedly poisoned his son Akbar Khan at the request of the British Empire. He oscillated between the Russian and British Empires to maintain his position.
Khan, Malik	Khan, Malik	Minister of finance of Afghanistan; put in jail by Daoud Khan for differences of opinion; spent over twenty-five years in prison without any trial.
Khan, Naim	Khan, Naim	Prince, several times minister, and brother of Daoud Khan. A man of wisdom who at the end was ignored by his president brother. He was a friend of Soraya's father.
Khyber Pass	Khyber Pass	The eastern-border pass between Afghanistan and Pakistan, used often by the British Empire troops to enter and invade Afghanistan.
Kushan Empire	Kushan Empire	A syncretic empire between the first and fourth centuries, it encompassed nowadays Central Asia, Afghanistan, Iran, Pakistan, and north India. Hinduism, Zoroastrianism, and Buddhism were practiced.
Lataband	Lataband	A nearly 2,500-meter-high pass that links Kabul to Khyber Pass. It became famous as it was used by the British troops during the first Anglo-Afghan war, which ended with the defeat of the invaders.

Logar	Logar	A province in the south of Kabul. Invaders often used it as it was the shortest way to reach British India.
Ludin, Kabir	Ludin, Kabir	Soraya's distinguished father, who served as minister of public services and ambassador to the United Nations, United States, United Kingdom, and India. He passed away at the age of only fifty-four. The character of Mr. Suri in the book is inspired from his existence and great achievements.
Mahmoudi Family	Mahmoudi Family	Two brothers, Rahim and Hadi, who created the Maoist Communist movement of Afghanistan, Sholay Jawed—Eternal Flame.
Maiwand, Malala	Maiwand, Malalai	Legendary Afghan young poet and warrior, known as the Jeanne d'Arc of Afghanistan, who at the age of nineteen, defied the British Empire Army in the Battle of Maiwand that took place in July 1880. She was martyred, but her poems live forever in the hearts and minds of Afghans.
Maiwandwal, Hashem	Maiwandwal, Hashem	Minister and prime minister of Afghanistan under King Zaher Shah. He took over the Washington embassy from Soraya's father and was assassinated in 1973 when Daoud Khan became president.
Majrooh, Bahaouddin	Majrooh, Bahaouddin	Afghan prominent intellectual and dean of the Faculty of Literature in Kabul. He was director of the Afghan Information Center in Peshawar and cowardly and mysteriously murdered in 1988, probably by extremists.

Malikzada, Farkhunda	Malikzada, Farkhunda	A young twenty-seven-year-old theology student at the University of Kabul who was brutally tortured, burned, and murdered by a mob in March 2015.
Massoud, Ahmad Shah	Massoud, Ahmad Shah	Charismatic and undisputed mujahideen commander and minister of defense in post-communist era. He embodied the Afghan resistance and is considered a heroic person. KGB, KHAD, ISI, and extremist groups tried in vain to assassinate him. He was, however, victim of a fatal suicide bombing in 2001.
Maurya Empire	Maurya Empire	Founded by Chandragupta, it covered Afghanistan, Iran, India, and Bangladesh from 322 to 287 before Christ.
Mazari, Abdul Ali	Mazari, Abdul Ali	Charismatic leader of Shia mujahideen group Hezbe Wahdat. He defended the right of the Hazara people and was assassinated by the Taliban in 1995.
Moqamaat	Moqamaat	"Authorities," terminology given by mujahideen commanders to ISI officers who instructed them in and outside Afghanistan during the Soviet invasion.
Mujahideen	Mujahideen	Holy warriors, combatants who ousted the Soviet Union from Afghanistan and toppled the communist regime. President Reagan called them "freedom fighters."

Najibullah, Mohammad	Najibullah, Mohammad	Brutal head of the Afghan spy agency KHAD (1980–85) and president of Afghanistan (1987–92). Put in place by the Soviet Union, he was accused of orchestrating the imprisonment, torture, and killing of countless people. He was the last communist president of Afghanistan, hanged by the Taliban in 1992.
Nawroz	Nawroz	Solar new year's day and the beginning of spring, celebrated in Southwest and Central Asia as well as Caucasian countries, Black Sea Basin, and the Balkans. It corresponds to March 20 or 21. The occasion is celebrated massively by people.
New City	Shahre Naw	Modern area of Kabul city, where Soraya grew up and spent her years of living in Afghanistan. Most dignitaries of the country dwelled in New City.
Niazi, Ghulam Mohammad	Niazi, Ghulam Mohammad	Scholar, academician, and leader of the Muslim Brotherhood, assassinated in 1978 by the communist regime.
Pakistan	Pakistan	Situated in the east and south of Afghanistan and created in 1947 as a result of the partition of India.
Parcham	Flag	A pro-Soviet Afghan Communist party, dominated essentially by non-Pashtun politicians and military officers.
Pashtun	Pashtun	One of the major ethnic groups in Afghanistan, who ruled the country continuously from 1709 to 1929. There are also Pashtuns in Pakistan on the other side of the Durand Line.

Pashtunistan	Pashtunistan	Part of the Afghan territory ceded to the British in 1989 by Amir Abdur Rahman Khan for one hundred years under the scope of the Durand Line. It was never recovered. Now an integral part of Pakistan, Afghan rulers have always demanded its restitution.
PDPA	PDPA	People's Democratic Party of Afghanistan. Pro-Soviet Communist Party, composed of Khalq and Parcham and established under Soviet Union pressure.
Persian Empire	Persian Empire	A series of empires that began with Cyrus in the sixth century before Christ and lasted to the twentieth century common era.
Peshawar	Peshawar	Capital city of northwest frontier area of Pakistan.
Pule Charkhi	Pule Charkhi	Infamous prison located in eastern part of Kabul on the way to Jalalabad, constructed by Daoud Khan at the beginning of his presidency in 1973. Hundreds of thousands of people were detained and tortured in this prison, most of whom disappeared, in all likelihood victims of mass murder operations by the communist government's secret services.
Puzanov, Aleksander	Puzanov, Aleksander	Soviet minister to Afghanistan (1972–79) and the maker and shaker of his government's policy that led to the dethronement of King Zaher Shah by his cousin Daoud Khan, who in his term was assassinated to make way for a communist regime, finally leading to the invasion of the country by the Red Army.

Queen Gawhar Shad Begum	Queen Gawharshad Begum	The "joyful jewel" and Timurid queen (1405–1447) was the real engine of women's, cultural, and artistic emancipation. She was instrumental to move the capital of the Timurid Empire from Samarkand (currently in Uzbekistan) to Herat (currently in Afghanistan) and was cowardly murdered at an age beyond eighty.
Queen Soraya	Queen Soraya Tarzi	Queen of Afghanistan (1919–1929) and inspired by the Turkey of Kemal Atatürk, she advocated for women's emancipation as well as social and cultural reform in the country. She was exiled together with her husband, King Amanullah Khan, to Rome.
Rabbani, Burhanuddin	Rabbani, Burhanuddin	Leader of the Muslim Brotherhood and later of the mujahideen movement Jamiate Islami of Afghanistan, President of Afghanistan (1992–2001) and assassinated in 2011 by the Taliban through a suicide bombing in his own house.
Ratebzad, Anahita	Ratebzad, Anahita	The only female Parchami communist leader in Afghanistan. She was de facto deputy to Babrak Karmal (installed as president of Afghanistan by the Soviet Union when they invaded in 1979) and died in 2014 in Germany.
Salang Tunnel	Salang Tunnel	A tunnel through the Hindukosh massif, linking the north and the south of Afghanistan. The edifice was constructed by the Soviet Union in 1955.
Samanid Empire	Samanid Empire	Centered in Khorasan, it covered Central Asia, Iran, Afghanistan, and Pakistan between 819 and 999 common era. It can be considered the first non-Arab Muslim Empire.

Shafiq, Moussa	Shafiq, Moussa	Afghan foreign minister and prime minister (1972–73). A brilliant politician who was put under house arrest by Daoud Khan (1973) and assassinated in 1978 by the communist regime of Nour Mohammad Taraki.
Shah, Zaher	Shah, Zaher	King of Afghanistan (1933–73); astute individual who was ousted by his cousin and brother-in-law Daoud Khan and exiled to Rome. He returned to Kabul at the age of eighty-eight and passed away in 2007.
Shah, Nader	Shah, Nader	Brutal and merciless King of Afghanistan (1929–33) who murdered his predecessor, Habibullah Kalakani, and his lieutenants as well as many other influential individuals. He was assassinated by a student while visiting a school in Kabul.
Shan, Shuja	Shah, Shuja	Twice king of Afghanistan (1803–09 and 1839–42). He is known to be a shameful ruler at the service of British India and was killed by a popular revolt.
Shaheed, Naheed	Shaheed, Naheed	Young and remarkable eighteen-year-old student who defied Soviet occupation of Afghanistan and was brutally murdered in a demonstration in 1980 by communist Parchami "youth" guided by KHAD of Najibullah. She became the symbol of women's resistance in Afghanistan.
Sholay Jawed	Sholay Jawed	Maoist communist movement of Afghanistan, led by the Mahmoudi brothers. This movement disappeared following the pro-Soviet communist coup of 1978.

Sokhandan, Saidal	Sokhandan, Saidal	Prominent young emerging figure in Sholay Jawed, student at the Faculty of Sciences of Kabul University, who was allegedly killed by Hekmatyar in 1972.
Tabeyev, Fikryat Akhmedzhanovic	Tabeyev, Fikryat Akhmedzhanovic	Renowned Soviet Tatar politician who served as minister to Afghanistan from November 1979 to August 1986 in replacement of the famous Aleksander Puzanov.
Tajik	Tajik	One of the major ethnic groups in Afghanistan. They ruled Afghanistan in 1929 (Amir Habibullah Kalakani) and from 1992–2001 (President Burhanuddin Rabbani).
Taliban	Taliban	Religious students, a brutal and merciless extremist and terrorist group who ruled Afghanistan (1996–2001) and destroyed completely the tallest Buddha of Bamiyan. They receive financial assistance, training, and operational and military support from the Pakistani ISI and some Arab states.
Taraki, Nour Mohammad	Taraki, Nour Mohammad	Chairman of Khalq Communist Party, president of Afghanistan (1978–79), killed by his deputy, Hafizullah Amin.
Timurid Empire	Timurid Empire	Also called the Gurkani Empire, it covered current Central Asia, Caucasus, Turkey, Iraq, Iran, and Afghanistan between 1370 and 1507 common era.
Turkman	Turkman	One of the major ethnic groups in Afghanistan, known for their glorious history as well as wonderful carpets and great horses.

Umayyad Caliphate	Umayyad Caliphate	Second Islamic caliphate (661–750). Based essentially in Damascus, they ruled over the entire Islamic world, covering Asia and north Africa.
Uzbek	Uzbek	A major ethnic group in Afghanistan who are known for their rich history and famous buzkashi horses. Rashid Dostom, the current first vice president, is Uzbek.
Yusof, Mohammad	Yusof, Mohammad	Minister of mines and industry under Daoud Khan and prime minister of Afghanistan (1963–65). He was forced to resign and was appointed ambassador to the Soviet Union. Following Daoud Khan's coup in 1973, he left his post and went into exile to Germany.
Zaher, Ahmad	Zaher, Ahmad	Famous young singer, son of Prime Minister Mohammad Zaher, who was a colleague and friend of Soraya's father. He was brutally murdered by Hafizullah Amin in 1979.
Zedong, Mao	Zedong, Mao	Communist leader of the People's Republic of China (1943–76). His fourth wife, Jiang Qing, was notorious for her role in the devastating Cultural Revolution.

Important Quotes

Food for Thought for Any Ruler or Decision Maker,
But Especially Afghans

The Holy Koran

O you who believe! Enter wholeheartedly into rightness and follow not the footsteps of the Satan for he is to you avowed enemy. (2-208)

Let there be no compulsion in religion. Truth stands out clear from deceit. (2-256)

God does not forbid you from being good to those who have not fought you in the religion or driven you from your homes or from being just towards them. God loves those who are just. (60-8)

We have appointed a law and a practice for every one of you. Had God willed, He would have made you a single community, but He wanted to test you regarding what has come to you. So compete with each other in doing good. (5-48)

God does not love mischief. (2-205)

O mankind! Fear your Lord Who [initiated] your creation from a single soul, then from it created its mate, and from these two spread [the creation of] countless men and women. (4-1)

Women too have rights over men similar to the rights of men over women. (2-228)

The believers, men and women, are protectors of one another, they enjoin what is just and forbid what is evil. (9-71)

The same religion He has established for you as that which He enjoined on Noah … Abraham, Moses, and Jesus: Namely, that you should remain steadfast in religion, and make no divisions therein. (42-13)

O mankind! We created you from a single [pair] of a male and a female, and made you into nations and tribes, that you may know each other, not that you may despise each other. Verily the most honored of you in the sight of God is the most righteous of you. (49-13)

O you who believe! Stand out firmly for justice, as witnesses to God, even as against yourselves, or your parents, or your kin, and whether it be against rich or poor—for God can best protect both. Follow not the lusts of your hearts, lest you swerve, and if you distort or decline to do justice, verily God is well-acquainted with all that you do. (4-135)

O you who believe! Stand out firmly for God, as witnesses to fair dealing, and let not the hatred of others to you make you swerve to wrong and depart from justice. Be just, that is next to piety and fear God. (5-8)

God shows unto all that seek His goodly acceptance the paths leading to peace and, by His grace, brings them out of the depths of darkness into the light and guides them onto a straight way. (5-16)

Leading correct and straight is the way of God who has detailed the signs for those who receive admonition. For them [who lead right] there shall be an abode of peace with their Lord; and He shall be near unto them in result of what they have been doing. (6-127)

We believe in God and the revelation to us and to Abraham, Ishmael, Isaac, Jacob and the tribes, and that given to Moses and Jesus, and that given to all Prophets from their Lord. We make no distinction between any of them, and to Him we have surrendered. (2-136)

To every people, God appointed rites and ceremonies which they follow; let them not then dispute on the matter but do invite [them] to the Lord: for you are assuredly on the Right Way. (22-67)

Anyone who kills [an innocent] soul, it is as if he slew mankind entirely; and whoever saves one—it is as if he salvaged humanity. (5-32)

Nelson Mandela

As long as poverty, injustice and gross inequality persist in our world, none of us can truly rest!

There is no easy walk to freedom anywhere and many of us will have to pass through the valley of the shadow of death again and again before we reach the mountaintops of our desires.

The struggle is my life. I will continue fighting for freedom [and justice] until the end of my days.

I have cherished the ideal of a democratic and free society in which all persons live together in harmony and with equal opportunities [and rights]. It is an ideal which I hope to live for and to achieve. But if needs be, it is an ideal for which I am prepared to die.

Only free individuals can negotiate; prisoners cannot enter into contracts.

I cannot and will not give any undertaking at a time when I, and you, the people, are not free. Your freedom and mine cannot be separated.

I am not less life-loving than you are. But I cannot sell my birthright, nor am I prepared to sell the birthright of the people.

I greet you all in the name of peace, democracy and freedom for all. I stand here before you not as a prophet but as a humble servant of you, the people. Your tireless and heroic sacrifices have made it possible for me to be here today. I therefore place the remaining years of my life in your hands.

I have become more convinced than ever that the real makers of history are the ordinary men and women of our country; their participation in every decision about the future is the only guarantee of true democracy and freedom.

A critical, independent and investigative press is the lifeblood of any democracy. The press must be free from state interference. It must have the economic strength to stand up to the blandishments of government officials. It must have sufficient independence from vested interests to be bold and inquiring without fear or favor. It must enjoy the protection of the constitution, so that it can protect our rights as citizens.

The task at hand will not be easy, but you have mandated us to change [the country] from a land in which the majority lived with little hope, to one in which they can live and work with dignity, a sense of self-esteem and confidence in the future.

Death is something inevitable. When a man has done his duty to his people and his country, he can rest in peace.

Humankind's goodness is a flame that can be hidden but never extinguished.

It would be very egotistical of me to say how I would like to be remembered. I'd leave that entirely to South Africans. I would just like a simple stone on which is written "Mandela."

Real leaders must be ready to sacrifice all for the freedom of their people.

It always seems impossible until it's done.

What counts in life is not the mere fact that we have lived. It is what difference we have made to the lives of others that will determine the significance of the life we lead.

Those who conduct themselves with morality, integrity and consistency need not fear the forces of inhumanity and cruelty.

I wanted to be known as Mandela, a man with weaknesses, some of which are fundamental, and a man who is committed, but nevertheless, sometimes he fails to live up to expectations.

Mahatma Gandhi

Happiness is when what you think, what you say and what you do [for your people] are in harmony.

An eye for an eye only ends up making the whole world blind.

Live as if you were to die tomorrow; learn as if you were to live forever.

First they ignore you, then they laugh at you, then they fight you, then you win.

You must not lose faith in humanity. Humanity is an ocean; if a few drops of the ocean are dirty, the ocean does not become dirty.

Strength does not come from physical capacity. It comes from an indomitable will.

A man is but the product of his thoughts; what he thinks, he becomes.

The future depends on what you do today.

The difference between what we do and what we are capable of doing would suffice to solve most of the world's problems.

It's my conviction that nothing enduring can be built on violence.

I will not let anyone walk through my mind with their dirty feet.

Confession of errors is like a broom which sweeps away the dirt and leaves the surface brighter and clearer.

Let hundreds like me die, but the truth remain alive.

To give pleasure to a single heart by a single act is better than thousands of heads bowing in prayer.

Truth is one, paths are many.

Leadership at one time meant muscles; but today it means getting along with people.

Honest disagreement is often a good sign of progress.

Man becomes great exactly in the degree in which he works for the welfare of his fellow-men.

Earth provides enough to satisfy everyone's needs, but not everybody's greed.

The best way to find yourself is to lose yourself in the service of others.

Martin Luther King Jr.

Only in the end, we will remember not the words of our enemies, but the silence of our friends.

We must accept finite disappointment, but never lose infinite hope.

The function of education is to teach one to think intensively and to think critically. Intelligence plus character—that is the goal of true education.

Be a bush if you can't be a tree. If you can't be a highway, just be a trail. If you can't be a sun, be a star. For it isn't by size that you win or fail. Be the best of whatever you are.

The ultimate measure of a man is not where he stands in moments of comfort and convenience, but where he stands at times of challenge and controversy.

Human progress is neither automatic nor inevitable … Every step toward the goal of justice requires sacrifice, suffering, and struggle; the tireless exertions and passionate concern of dedicated individuals.

Nothing in all the world is more dangerous than sincere ignorance and conscientious stupidity.

Our lives begin to end the day we become silent about things that matter.

Injustice anywhere is a threat to justice everywhere.

The ultimate tragedy is not the oppression and cruelty by the bad people but the silence over that by the good people.

We must learn to live together as brothers or perish together as fools.

We may have all come on different ships, but we're in the same boat now.

Life's most persistent and urgent question is, "What are you doing for others?"

Our scientific power has outrun our spiritual power. We have guided missiles and misguided men.

Every man must decide whether he will walk in the light of creative altruism or in the darkness of destructive selfishness.

The hottest place in Hell is reserved for those who remain neutral in times of great moral conflict.

An individual has not started living until he can rise above the narrow confines of his individualistic concerns to the broader concerns of all humanity.

Law and order exist for the purpose of establishing justice and when they fail in this purpose they become the dangerously structured dams that block the flow of social progress.

A lie cannot live.

The quality, not the longevity, of one's life is what is important.

A right delayed is a right denied.

Oppressed people cannot remain oppressed forever. The yearning for freedom eventually manifests itself.

He who passively accepts evil is as much involved in it as he who helps to perpetrate it. He who accepts evil without protesting against it is really cooperating with it.

Whatever affects one directly, affects all indirectly. I can never be what I ought to be until you are what you ought to be. This is the interrelated structure of reality.

If physical death is the price that I must pay to free my white brothers and sisters from a permanent death of the spirit, then nothing can be more redemptive.

Printed and bound by PG in the USA